Sketch Me Naked

An Erotic Romance

Bonnie Louise Williams

http://www.bonnielouisewilliams.com

To Gene, with love.

Prologue

SHE AWOKE IN A STATE OF AROUSAL. *The dream more vivid, more real than before. Unable to bear the heat, she rose from bed and placed her bare feet on the hardwood floor. Mindless of the cold against her soles, she walked to the heavy oak desk and opened the side drawer picking up the sketchpad and graphite pencil.*

With fluid motions, she drew him as swiftly as her hand would allow lest she forget his body... his touch.

But she never forgot. It was always the same. In sleep or in daydreams—she remembered. He appeared to her on paper as she had left him in her dream. Quick strokes created his classically handsome form, angular and strong, as if they were etched from marble instead of the flesh and blood she yearned for. She drew his hands, beautiful and long-fingered, connected to powerful arms and a broad muscular chest brushed lightly with dark hair. His naked male physique was beautifully proportioned—only marred by a long, thick scar on his right thigh. His face—hidden in the shadows of the darkened room, taunting her with a brief glimmer of moonlight reflecting in his eyes.

Liquid heat poured through her body as her pencil rendered the hard planes of his abdomen trailing a fine line of hair to his navel and lower... He was fully erect and ready. Waiting for her.

She drew him as he was when she had left him. Reclined, raising himself on one elbow as he held out his hand reaching for her. Inviting her. Her body ached to touch him. She longed for the fulfillment of his lovemaking that could never be attained beyond her sleeping state. A delicious shudder rippled through her body as his image brought her untried senses to life. With the last few strokes of her pencil, she finished with his strong yet indistinct brows as a swath of dark wavy hair fell playfully across his forehead.

Sighing deeply, she closed the sketchpad and placed it carefully back in the drawer then went back to bed.

Sated, she drifted back to sleep wondering if her dream man truly existed. Would ever exist. Could any man, real or imagined, ever measure up to the two-dimensional image she carefully kept locked away in a drawer... and in her dreams?

Chapter One

SHE HAD THE KIND OF EYES A MAN could sink his life into—a sparkling shade like polished copper that seemed to radiate with an inner glow. Bright and expressive, possessing an invisible magnetic pull, a man could lose himself in their depths. That was assuming a man was worthy of losing himself in their depths.

Romano   DeMitri   didn't   consider   himself   that   kind   of   man.

He had a track record of empty relationships. Determined his entire life to overcome his father's notorious legacy as the founder of *Volupté*, a raunchy adult magazine, Rome either met and dated women who wanted a shot at a centerfold, or once they learned about the family business wanted nothing to do with him. He wanted to travel the world discovering ancient ruins while making a determined effort to avoid long-term relationships that might interfere with these plans. And marriage would do just that. Right now, even a brief affair would be a hindrance. Because, inevitably, women liked to cling, become possessive even when he'd make it clear the affair was sex, and only sex—women always seemed to say "okay" but had ulterior motives to convince him otherwise. It was damned inconvenient.

Christ, he was turning into his old man.

He sat at the bar of *The Lava Lounge,* while his jazz band took a well-deserved five. His half-brother, Tony, jerked him from his thoughts.

"Hey, Rome, did you check out the betty at table six? Man, I wouldn't mind having those thighs wrapped around my waist."

Like you did with my ex-girlfriend?

He may not have deserved a woman like his ex, but neither did his playboy of a brother. And that's what burned him the most.

Rome shifted his attention back to the fairy-goddess disguised as a seductress—at least that was what she looked like to him.

He'd briefly gave the mystery lady a once over when he first spotted her, then just as quickly dismissed her as just another bar flower. That was before she looked his way. He breathed in deeply, noting the way her eyes darted nervously about the lounge, surveying the room as if looking for something. Rome's gaze roamed freely from her sexy high-heeled sandals, all the way back up to the low-cut neckline of her dress.

Strange, he thought, she was seductive, yet totally ill at ease with it.

Annoyed with himself for staring, and more annoyed for the interruption, he said, "Take your boner somewhere else, slick. I'm not in the mood." Actually he was just pissed Tony had spotted her, too.

He should have been used to it by now. He'd been losing women to Tony all his life. Or was it him pushing them away?

"Hey, you don't have to get all attitudinal with me, Rome. I know you've been beating yourself up lately, but, *Jesus*, gimmie a break, will ya?" Tony let out an exaggerated sigh as he hopped from his barstool and sat next to their cousin, Echo. To get a more advantageous view of miss bright eyes, no doubt.

Damn him. Damn Tony for reminding him they were both too much like their father.

Rome ran his fingers through his hair. It wasn't his intention to let out all his pent up frustrations on his brother. Tony was just being Tony—following a long legacy of womanizing men.

Something Rome continued to fight within himself.

Tony could treat women like shit, yet they'd always come back for more. But what the hell did it matter anyway? Rome knew he was crappy at relationships, family or otherwise and he felt the sting of that fact now. And tonight in particular, the feeling was running deep in his bones. The lure to wallow in self-pity felt nearly as tempting as the copper-eyed fairy goddess.

"Another Evian, Rome?" the bartender asked.

"Yeah, sure, Spike," Rome muttered.

Spike was the co-owner of the lounge, and in typical bartender form wore loud shirts that matched his bright carrot-red hair that stood up in all direction like a porcupine, plus, he had a natural ear for anyone in need to talk.

But Rome wasn't in the mood to talk.

"Your bro's right. She *is* a betty," Spike said, as he shook up a martini. "But a little out of place here, don't you think?"

"I hadn't noticed," Rome lied, raising his voice to be heard over the throng of people squeezing in close to the bar and the loud voices of men and drunken conversations.

Rome scanned the lounge slowly with his sharp photographer's perspective, trying to keep his gaze on something other than her.

The Lava Lounge was small for L.A. standards with several round black-painted tables and twice as many matching chairs crammed close together for maximum capacity. The crowd was already packed in nearly reaching the max already.

At the center was a circular-shaped bar with a ceiling-high rock formation as the focal point tapered out like a Beverly Hills Jacuzzi fountain. Water trickled down into an unseen moat as steam hissed from various rock clefts—down the center a fiery orange-lighting effect—an obvious attempt at creating rolling lava. The monstrosity commandeered a lot of the floor space.

"She been in before?" Rome asked, failing to distract himself and continued watching her with fascinated interest as she discreetly adjusted the tight-fitting bra thingy she was wearing.

Sweet.

Her make-up was a bit heavy for such an angelic face, and she wore her long honey-gold hair in a mass of sexed-up curls, pulled back slightly, revealing an elegantly slender neck. A neck he wouldn't mind taking a bite or two out of. He was a sucker for stunning eyes and a slender neck.

"Nope. Not that I remember," Spike replied.

She *did* appear out of place. She fidgeted in her seat and sat ramrod straight on the lounge's lackluster, black wooden chair. He caught a breath-taking view of her black-lace panties when she tried to sit back and her black leather skirt hiked up.

A single tendril of hair fell across her face, straying from the comb holding it in place. *Oh, yeah.* She took his breath away.

Despite her engaging yet awkward manner, this bright-eyed lady had beautifully delicate wrists and small, elegant hands that shook slightly when she adjusted the straps at her ankles, giving Rome a delicious view of her firm breasts covered with the same lace as her matching, mouth-watering panties. He groaned as his dick twitched from the erotic peep show.

Ah shit, he was starting to sound like Tony. But how long had it been since a woman made his body stir with the simple hint of skin? He couldn't remember. After his ex, he'd sworn off women—but this one—she could blow that vow all to hell.

"But if I were you," Spike added, as he slid a bottle of beer to the guy seated next to Rome, "I'd get off my ass and stake a claim before your brother does."

Tony casually sat in one of the empty chair at her table. "Is it hot in here?" Tony asked in his practiced smooth tone. "Or is it just you, sweet thing?"

Rome groaned. He couldn't believe his brother still used that tired old line, but for some reason that escaped Rome. Women fell for Tony, even if he asked if he could wear their ass for a hat.

"What the..." Rome's attention diverted when the contents of her tiny purse spilled from the table and sprang across the black tiles of the floor like shattered glass. Lipstick, mirror, comb, and a mother-lode of condom-packets in a variety of pastel colors like tossed rose petals.

He smiled to himself as he stared down at the packets.

One bright pink-neon packet skidded across the floor and hit his booted foot. A tiny little invitation if he ever saw one. Rome picked it up and discretely slipped it into the back pocket of his black Levis, then, just as quickly pulling it back out. *What was he thinking*?

She bent down to recover her things, making the fabric of her skirt tighten around her hips. Oh, man—she had a nice round behind, too. As if an explosion had been set under his barstool, Rome jumped to his feet to help recover the telling items. His libido knew an opportunity when it saw one, even if his logical ambition refused to cooperate.

Unfortunately, his brother beat him to the punch. *Damn*. If Tony started in, she'd be a slam-dunk in his brother's proverbial hoop.

"Told ya," Spike snorted.

Tony collected women the way most men collected socks. Once used and washed, they were folded neatly in the drawer of his sexual mind and forgotten—until he needed them again.

No way in hell was Rome going to allow Tony to supplement his babe collection with this delightful creature. She needed protecting, not only from Tony's slick, practiced moves, but—after observing her purse contents—from herself.

She was way out of her league.

She needed someone to shield her from Tony's perfect seduction scorecard.

Rome intended to be that protector.

While several other men, including Tony, scattered to help the lady in distress, Rome walked to her table and crouched down with her as she shuffled to recover her things.

"Oh, geez Louise. I'm so embarrassed," she said when he retrieved her lipstick, mirror, tissue, and a torn sheet of paper with a printed map that looked like directions to the lounge. "Thank you so very much, I'm grateful to know gallant men still exist." She looked up at him, her long doe-brown lashes swept up and Rome couldn't help how mesmerized he was by the shimmering copper and gold of her irises.

Oh, she had a sweet voice, too. Again, Rome thought something about her didn't fit, and that made him want to know more about this mystery lady. As they both stood, he held her elbow to support her while she regained her footing. "Here. I believe this is yours," he said as he held out the bright pink foil pouch. He stared down at it before she took it and he laughed. "You know? This brings a whole new light to the old line 'I have a condom in my pocket with your name on it.'"

Rome flashed her one of those "DeMitri" smiles, which his mother used to say, "could make women melt like butter."

Who was he kidding? *His* melting smile was part of the past. "I'm sorry about my brother. He tends to come on to women like he's out to win the Grand Prix of best used pick-up lines."

"That's okay, I guess." She looked up at him. "What line would you have used?" Her brows arched with innocent curiosity.

"Something more like, 'Your eyes are so bright, you give the sun a reason to shine.'" He looked at her intently because he truly meant it.

Her face flushed and her eyes turned liquid. "That's so sweet," she whispered and her voice quivered a little. "I... would consider—I mean, would you like to have sex? With me?"

Rome opened his mouth to speak. Then closed it and took a deep breath. "I can't."

She covered her face with her hands. "I shouldn't be here," she said softly. "I'm really no good at this." She sniffled a little, as she shoved the foil packet back into her purse, teetering on the spikes of her heels.

"Hey, it's okay." Rome reached out to thumb away the embarrassed tear that fell down her cheek when...

"Oops." She bent back down after dropping her lipstick again.

Tony snagged it from the floor, then placed it in her palm with one hand as he caressed her wrist with the other.

Damn.

"Oh boy," she laughed nervously with a cute little sniffle. "Thank you." Her face was as red as a Los Angeles fire truck.

God, she was adorable. By the expression on Tony's face, he was ready to light her up. Rome was more than ready to hose his brother down with a generous dose of cold water. He felt his fists clench and unclench before he turned away to finish off his water at the bar.

"My pleasure." Tony offered. "I've never seen you in here before. You new in the area, baby girl?"

Rome knew that in Tony's mind that translated to 'I think you're sexy. Wanna fuck?' Rome ground his teeth. He struggled with his wanting to ignore the way her cute, nervous smile quivered at his brother's flirtations.

He wasn't himself tonight. But then, the only thing he and his ex shared was a traveling wanderlust and sex. Maybe he was more like his brother than he wanted to admit.

"Ah...well, not really. I mean, yes. I'm new around here."

"Well, then. Can I get you something from the bar?" Tony asked.

"Oh...um, just a club soda would be fine. And thank you." Bright-eyes smiled sweetly at his brother. If she only knew she had a tiger by the tail.

Was it getting hot in here?

Rome glared at Tony as he approached the bar. "What the hell do you think you're doing?" Rome asked. The music was getting loud and he nearly had to shout.

"Buying the lady a drink," Tony said incredulously. "You have a problem with that?"

"Yeah. I do."

"What?" Tony laughed. "You saw her first so she's your game?"

"Something like that."

"Forget it, Rome. You saw the spread of love-gloves bulging in her purse. She's here for one thing—and I'm the guy to deliver."

"Like hell you are. She's not what she seems, Tony."

"You know what, Rome. I'm tired of your bullshit. I'm sorry your mom is sick, and I'm sorry your lady left you."

Yeah, but did you have to sleep with her two seconds after she packed her bags? Rome thought.

"But you can't keep me from having a good time." Tony raised one blonde eyebrow. "And you're bringing me down, man." Tony motioned Spike over. "Give me a Miller, a club soda, and...," he smirked at Rome, "and a *Slo Comfortable Screw* for my bro here."

Rome caught Tony whispering to Spike. He leaned in close when he heard Tony say, "Heavy on the comfort, if you know what I mean."

What the hell was that supposed to mean?

"You got it, Ton'."

"What the hell did you just order me?" Rome asked.

"Relax, Rome. It's pineapple juice. It'll loosen you up so you won't make everyone around you so fuckin' miserable."

Rome took a whiff of the liquid when Spike set it on the bar, shrugged, then took a sip. "Not bad." Tony turned to leave, and Rome had him by the wrist. "Just stay away from bright-eyes. Okay?"

Tony laughed. "Not on your life, bro. Finders keepers."

Rome growled as Tony sauntered back to her table, styling his Armani jacket and Gucci shoes.

Shit. Rome loved his brother. But did he constantly have to drive him insane? They were so different when it came to women, but ultimately, the result was the same.

"Your brother's right." Echo sat next to him with a smirk. "You do need to loosen up. Your guitar riffs suck lemons tonight, man."

"Yeah? Well, your singing's not so hot either, Pavarotti."

Echo punched his fist into Rome's shoulder.

"Ow," he said, rubbing his arm. Rome knew the punch was just to get his attention. His cousin, Echo— whose real name was Brandon though he refused to acknowledge it— was half Vietnamese. But he was just as big and tall as Tony and himself, and was a *Jeet Kune Do* Master. Echo could put Rome out in a heartbeat if he chose to.

"I hear you landed the début CD cover photo job for that luscious new pop singer," Echo commented. "Need any help with the lighting?" he asked as he wriggled his dark brows.

"No. I have employees for that, *Brandon*."

Echo looked like he was about to give him a good one. "Are you sure, cuz? I've been told I could light up a room," he winked.

Ah, man. Now, Tony was rubbing off on his unassertive cousin. "I'm sure." Echo was always so reserved, Rome had to laugh. "But I've got it covered, thanks."

"Too bad. She's *hot*."

"Pipe down, Casanova. Besides, I'm canceling the photo job."

"Are you nuts? Why?"

"Dad's will," he said wryly. "Tony and I are meeting Dad's lawyer tomorrow." He shrugged with indifference. "Shit knows what will come of it. Dad was such a manipulative son-of-a-bitch while he lived. I can't imagine what he had in mind for us after death."

"Geez, man. I'm sorry." Rome knew he truly meant it. "Why not just reschedule?"

Reschedule. Hell, Rome felt as if he'd been rescheduling his whole life for his family—dysfunctional as it was—and now his mom... "There's just too much shit going on right now." He sipped at his drink.

"No wonder," Echo snorted, "You've got three studios. That's pretty damn good."

"Yeah. I guess." God, all he wanted to do was get his photo studios running on their own with capable, talented people to manage them, so he'd be free to pursue his true passion—ancient ruins.

Central America was his first stop. He wanted to photograph and research the lost culture of the Mayans and the stone ruins of their remaining temples. Just the thought of losing himself in another century seemed be more blissful than sex with a beautiful woman.

His eyes shifted back to Miss Bright-eyes. *Well, almost.*

"C'mon. Let's get off our asses and jam, guys," he said to the rest of his band as he finished off the pineapple juice. Rome hated to admit that his brother was right. He did feel pleasantly relaxed. He'd have to order up another before the night was over.

"Give me another, Spike." Rome placed his empty glass on the bar. "And heavy on the comfort," he added, "whatever the hell it is."

Was it hot in here?

"Who's the new chick with Tony?" the band's bass player asked, as he slid onto a stool next to him. "Not bad, but not really his type."

"Anyone with tits is Ton's type," their drummer added. "Another for the road, Spike, when you get the chance."

Rome tensed. Bright-eyes flinched as Tony flung a nonchalant arm across her chair. The lounge was unusually busy tonight. There were dozens of other women his brother could be hitting on. *Why her? And why was she here?* Or better yet, why did he care? There was just *something* about her. She exhibited such innocence under the façade, compared to the usual female patrons of the lounge—or even most females he'd known. *Especially those big twinkling eyes.*

She looked up, caught him watching her, and smiled. A cute timid smile that made him groaning with male pleasure.

And she had a zillion condoms in her purse. He smiled back.

Just then, the band's bass player climbed onto the two-foot tall black block, six-by-ten foot platform, loosely describe as a band stage. "Hey, we gonna play music or twiddle our dicks all night?"

*****

Echo was right. Rome's guitar playing sucked tonight. He blamed it on his brother, but in truth, he had too much weighing on his mind. And bright-eyes was still flirting, somewhat awkwardly with Tony, as if it was something she wasn't accustomed to doing, something he assumed came natural to women—at least when they were in his brother's presence.

Her cheeks darkened at every practiced compliment his brother offered.

The crowd began to thin out around one o'clock. After the band's final tune, Rome polished his Taylor, though never taking his eyes off her, then placed it carefully in its case and ordered up another "pineapple" juice.

Spike gave him an odd look when he said, "Ya sure about that, bud?"

"Just put it on my smartass-brother's tab," Rome said before he took it, and gulped it down. It went down smooth on his parched throat. Rome typically drank bottled water when he played to keep from becoming dehydrated, but one night of "juice" wouldn't hurt.

"Hey, check out the Tonster," Echo laughed. "He's going in for the kill."

Just then he heard a woman yelp. He turned and found his brother hovering over her, lips puckered for the ready, but she held up a shaky hand with shock and uncertainty in her eyes.

Rome growled for the second time in one night, moving toward her table as a strong urge of protectiveness settled in his gut.

"Ow, shit!" he sucked on his teeth and rammed his big toe into a chair leg while trying to make it to bright eyes before Tony made more serious moves—like hauling her butt into his shiny red BMW. But she removed herself from Tony's tiger paws before Rome could reach her table.

Steam from the glowing-red faux volcano in the center of the circular bar clung up and around her and the surrounding crowd of people as she escaped from Tony, and hobbled on her spiked heels, leaving a whiff of her sweet perfume when she passed him.

He followed her, but lost her as she walked toward the restrooms.

"Damn." What the hell did he plan on doing if he reached her anyway? He was suddenly hit with the realization that he wanted to wrap her in his coat to keep her from the prying eyes of the riff-raff of the lounge. *And Tony's love'em—leave 'em attitude.*

There was a line to the ladies room, and he didn't see her, but where could she have gone? He glanced around the lounge, turned, and started for the main floor.

Wham!

Something smacked into him. "What the hell?" he said, falling back, landing hard on his ass. Rome saw white spots in front of his eyes, and felt the slight weight and warm heat of a soft body land on his crotch. Her spiked heel was a little too close for comfort.

"*Oh, God!* Sorr..."

"Lady, don't move an inch or you might injure my future children." He was afraid to breath for fear of being castrated by *Fredrick's of Hollywood's* finest faux leather.

She tried to roll off, but her hair got tangled under his heavy weight. He thought he heard her mumble something about "a stupid idea" but he couldn't be sure. His ears were buzzing. Rome wasn't sure if it was because he'd hit his head, or because her face was so close to his package.

Her lips quivered as her feet kept slipping out from under her. She fell one last time before Echo pulled her up.

As Echo jerked her up from Rome's lovelorn body and his suffering, unrequited lust muscle, a few strands of glistening-gold blonde hair were left under his elbow as she was torn from his lap.

As his cousin stabilized the misplaced beauty, Rome's eyes crossed and refocused. He was feeling a little drunk in a lust-love haze at her feet.

"Dude," Echo laughed. "Are you okay? How many fingers am I holding up?"

"Funny, cuz. Very funny." He rubbed the back of his head.

"Oh, geez—are you okay?" she asked.

When he blinked up, his eyes had a spectacular, cocker spaniel's view of her thong-clad blonde curls beneath her skirt. A hint of pink lips peeking out, tempting him through the sheer black lace. Rome felt his mouth water with a strong urge to place a hot, wet kiss between her legs.

"Someone wake me. I think I'm having a wet dream," he blurted out loud.

"No, dumbass," Tony laughed as he hovered over him, "You just hit your head and you're delirious. Help me get this idiot up," he said to Echo as they each grasped Rome by the armpits to hoist him upright.

"Why'z the room spinnin'?" Rome slurred as he stood on shaky legs.

Bright-eyes placed her warm hand on his arm. "I'm so sorry. I'm not usually this clumsy."

"My pleasure...beautiful," he said as he went to touch her cheek. He missed. Then he realized what he'd just said. *Shit, he was a dumbass.*

She giggled when she looked up at him through warm-brown lashes. "You're cute," she said with the prettiest pink blush to her cheeks.

Nothing about her mannerisms seemed to fit the outer image. He smiled at her and turned to Echo. "She thinks I'm cute."

"Whoa—" Echo fanned his hand at Rome's breath. "No more jammin' for you tonight. Rome, you need to cut back on the Southern Comfort. You can't hold your liquor, man."

"What—?" he snarled at Tony. "What the *fuck* was in those drinks?" Rome rarely even drank tap water, let alone booze. He should have known that pineapple juice tasted funny. He should have known better than to trust Tony.

"You were being a pain in the ass," Tony shrugged. "I thought it'd lighten you up."

*****

This was definitely not the way she'd envisioned starting her life over.

Dana Baker stared incredulously between the two brothers. *Is this the way men behaved all the time?* Or was it just sibling rivalry? She never had any siblings. Not even cousins, so she had nothing to base it on. But she was intrigued by this attractive, no—this stunning man who, even though he was obviously drunk, still found a way to protect single women from his playboy brother.

Figures.

Since her grandma's passing, Dana wanted—needed to know what it felt like to live a little on the wild side. If she could actually find it.

Have sex with a stranger. Now that was wild. Wasn't it?

She wanted to spread her proverbial wings, finally be free to just let go and be selfish for once in her life. Maybe ride a motorcycle, run naked in Griffith Park... well maybe in a bikini—a thong bikini.

Instead, she was here, witnessing a family squabble—with her as the subject.

I'll never have a sex life at this rate.

She'd chickened out when the nicely dressed, smooth moving attractive man with the ponytail whispered what he'd like to do with her—to her—something she'd never even say out loud, much less do. But now, with her tenuous bravado back in place, she was darn mad that this same man would treat a family member so poorly.

"That wasn't a very nice thing to do to your brother," she said to the playboy flirt. Dana knew her tone was patronizing, but the guy deserved it. Especially after that ridiculous suggestion he made, followed by "Wanna go to my place and blankety-blank all night?"

She felt several male eyes staring her way. "What if he injures himself while driving home, not knowing you've spiked his drink?" She had to step around Mister Nice Guy's very nice legs—still flat on the floor—to raise her chest high enough to make her point to the guy with the sexy moves and nice clothes. "And...and from what I can tell, he trusted you, his brother to— *honor* his preference of non-alcoholics beverages." She stuck her chin out for added emphasis. There, that'd show 'em. Patronizing tone and all.

"Oh, he didn't drive," said the tall attractive singer. "Me and the guys gave him a lift."

"Oh." Someone bumped soundly into her and caused her the misfortune of falling firmly right back into the cute guy's lap. Rumples of male laughter founded.

Dana saw two guys exchange a high-five as they left her alone with Mister nice guy—still supine on the beer-stained linoleum. She wrinkled her nose at the smell of stale booze wafting from the dirty floor.

Eww.

But now, at eye-level with the very nice, very cute, drunk guy, she wasn't thinking about the smelly floor. Dana placed a hand on his shoulder and offered him an apologetic smile. Whoa—he was way more than cute. And a heck of a lot more attractive than she thought. Looking directly into his eyes, she felt a hum of vibration run down her legs and all the way down to her newly-painted toe nails.

Yikes. She'd never remembered feeling like this before. It was...nice. But, he wasn't interested.

"Thanks for protecting me, bright-eyes," he said in a low husky tone. His breath felt warm against her face and thought he might actually kiss her. But his smile faded.

Dana felt her face and neck turn hot. She wasn't used to blatant sexual innuendos. Her surprised expression must have given her away because he chuckled as he grasped her around the waist and tugged them both up from the floor. He held her by the waist, just holding her there as if to steady himself, her body pressed to his from chest to knees.

Double yikes.

She cleared her throat. "Please, let me give you a lift home. It's the least I can offer after..." she waved her hand indicating the falling incident, a little too embarrassed to speak it out loud. *A remnant from her old self*, she thought.

"I'll let you take me home, beautiful—but be gentle."

So, she *was* going home with him. Correction—she was simply giving him a ride—because he'd made it very clear he didn't want her. She's lost her chance to do what she'd set out to do tonight? Sex for the sake of sex? *Wild, indeed.* No one would believe Dana "dull" Baker could do something this... slutty anyway. Yuck—such an ugly word. *Impulsive.* That sounded better, but no less accurate. She needed to gain the courage to start this new direction in her life. Her new wild detour. No more self-doubt.

She heard his brother gruff as she and Mister cutie walked out the blackened glass doors of the lounge.

"Hey, man. Looks like you've been bested, Tony," she heard someone say.

"Yeah, whatever. But I'll make a bet big brother will be out cold before the hour is up."

Dana exhaled a deep breath as the noise from the lounge faded away from the parking lot—a parking lot she was leaving—with a guy. A guy she didn't know. A guy—with his arm at her waist.

Don't be a ninny. It's just a ride home.

She watched in female admiration, as her new passenger folded his long masculine legs up like an accordion to fit into her little blue Toyota.

Drunk, or not, this was a walking female fantasy come true.

She had exactly zero practice with this seduction stuff.

No, no, no. She would, would, would *not* let her old self—her *old* insecurities get in her way. No self-doubts. Not tonight.

Her blood pounded when she glanced at the man half asleep in her car. He oozed testosterone and it made her excited and, well, uncomfortable at the newness. Her face grew hot and her breath quickened when she stole a glance at him and found his eyes open looking at her intently. His compelling eyes—that's what it was, his eyes—dark. They were riveting and she found something else...something she couldn't quite place her finger on... Watching made driving a challenge. So she quickly looked away and concentrated on the road.

Though drowsy, his vitality still captivated her, his nearness overwhelming. He rolled down the window, letting the cool L.A. night breeze wash over them both. The chill made her nipples pinch into full alert and her black lace-up silk blouse concealed nothing. If she looked down she knew they'd be very hard to miss should her sexy-as-heck passenger decide to look.

Dana tittered between wanting to be his mattress for the night and offering herself as his love-slave. The pit of her tummy churned again and again. It'd been tied up in knots all night. Frankly, she was grateful to leave the lounge. She didn't think she could go through with it anyway. Her nervous stomach was a problem as it fluttered uncomfortably.

"Pull over here," he directed.

She did as he said and helped him out of the car and to the elevator.

"Come on up. I'll make us some coffee," he said as he favored his right leg, pulling his keys from his front pants pocket.

"Okay. Sure." Dana sighed inward.

Coffee. Men always offering her tea, cookies, coffee... never wine, or coolers, or dinner...or sex. She was not a sexual animal. Maybe her body lacked the ability to make pheromones... She was definitely going to have to make a move. Her stomach knotted, and her throat tightened.

Don't be sick. For heaven's sake don't be sick.

Her self-respect depended on it. She needed to know once and for all she was a true, living, breathing female, with breasts and a vagina. She needed to prove to herself, after all the years of celibacy and caring for her grandma, she was capable of having a normal woman's needs and desires. She had to stop dwelling on the past. And the pain. *No!* That was too long ago. She wouldn't allow it another thought. Ancient history. She fought to never think of that one time ever again.

She caught him by the forearm before he staggered to the kitchen, and threw herself in his arms planting an unpracticed kiss firmly on his mouth. She felt him stiffen, then held her breath for two seconds, or was it ten?, she felt his mouth soften against hers as he captured her face in his hands, holding her there as his tongue tried to find hers—hiding behind her throat somewhere.

He moaned deep in his throat and Dana took it as a good sign.

"Take me to your bedroom, please. Now," she pleaded, trying to sound seductive, but certain she missed the mark. She feared she sounded more like a croaking frog, and not the desperate woman hidden deep inside a ridiculous slit-skirt and high heels.

"You sure about this, sweetheart?" he asked as he placed his forehead to hers, running his large hands lightly up and down her arms.

"I know you said no before, but I need you to do this for me." She pulled him closer, just in case he tried to break the embrace. This was her only chance and she wasn't about to blow it now.

"But——" he groaned.

She pressed her mouth tighter to his. "No. Don't talk." If he did, she might chicken out.

Somehow they managed to find the bed. Dana felt her thighs hit the edge of the mattress and they both fell into the mass of soft pillows at her back, while his body felt hard against hers. The pillows flew from the bed to the floor in a heap with him groping at her bodice and her awkwardly reaching for his fly.

Dana groped awkwardly at his zipper, pulled it down and tugged at his briefs to grasp his semi-erect penis. Okay, so she was not such a hot seductress, but what was a desperate woman to do? She did hear him suck in his breath, so she must have done *something* right.

"Take off your panties, sweetheart. I can't do this with 'em on."

Do it? Panties? Oh, God. Was she really going through with this?

Darn right she was.

She tugged them off.

He formed his body to hers, quickly sliding one large finger up inside her. She gasped from the intrusion.

"Mmm, you're so tight and wet," he whispered as he nibbled at her right ear.

Relax. Just relax.

She still had his penis between her fingers and she felt the amazing pulse of it as he grew more excited.

I can do this. I want this.

Her jeweled earring caught in the fabric of his bedcover. She tried to wedge it free but he captured both her hands with his and raised them above her head and kissed her again deeply. This time she didn't hesitate. Her tongue danced with his.

Dana felt a slight prodding against her entrance, lifted her hips to his, ready, willing. She felt the head of his penis slide in, when a rush of panic filled her—the condoms!

"Wait! I have to..."

Dana felt his full weight lay heavy against her chest as the distinct sound of deep breathing reached her ears.

He was snoring.

Mister Nice Guy had just fallen asleep. On top of her.

Chapter Two

"YOU WANT ME TO DO WHAT?" Rome stared at his father's attorney not quite believing his own ears.

"One of you must be married within six weeks."

Had the man lost his mind? Rome glanced at his younger brother, Tony, sitting at his right and picking lint off his Armani jacket. Although Tony was the younger of the two, he already held the high-ranking position of CEO to his father's company—*Volupté*, an upscale adult magazine.

Rome glanced out the window that made up the entire back wall of this crusty man's office. From this fourth floor vantage point, he had a perfect view of the smog-filled skies of Los Angeles. He inhaled deeply, breathing in the distinct odor of stale cologne and cold coffee. Frowning, he leaned toward the worn mahogany desk, separating him from this insanity.

"And if we don't, Mr. Finkleman?"

"If you don't..." The attorney briefly thumbed through Alberto DeMitri's last will and testament, then looked up slowly at each of the two brothers. "...You'll forfeit all your inheritance left to you by your father..."

A humorless half-smile appeared on Rome's lips as he interrupted the attorney, "I don't need my old man's money."

"You'd also lose your controlling shares in the business, all his property, and the remaining liquidity left after all taxes and debts have been settled."

Tony let out a sharp whistle. "Man, that's the breaks."

Rome gave him a sideways glare knowing his little brother assumed Rome would step right in and do his father's bidding. *Like hell.*

Rome's trip to the Mayan archeological tour was in two months. He refused to let his father screw with his plans.

Finkleman held up a brittle hand before Rome could respond. "Before you make your decision final, you should know that if either of you choose to decline *or* fail to marry within six weeks, you, Rome, receive nothing..."

Rome snorted.

"...and Antony, you will be forced to resign as CEO of the company."

Tony shot up from his seat. "Hey! Now wait just a damn minute." The man finally had his attention.

"Let me get this straight," Rome continued, "if we choose to forfeit my father's money *or* fail to marry some woman off the street..."

"Actually, not just any woman." Finkleman scratched his balding head and took a deep breath. "One of you must marry a woman from the old Baker family from Boston."

"Fuck!" Tony sank down hard into his seat like he'd been kicked in the solar plexus.

"Whatever." Rome hid his smirk. "So, decline our inheritance *or* marry some wilting lily from Beantown?"

"Actually, your brother can remain on the payroll as head photographer, if he chooses to, and still receive a modest annual salary."

"Why?" Tony asked. "What the hell's the point?"

Rome saw the blood drain from his brother's face and thought, *Because our father was a son-of-a-bitch with a twisted sense of humor.* But his brother idolized their womanizing father, so he'd keep his disparaging thoughts to himself.

"Good question," he said, not that Rome cared one way or another. He never allowed his father to rule his life when he was alive. Rome had no intention of letting him after death. "What connection does my father have to this *Baker* family? I don't remember him ever mentioning the name before. He owe them money, or something?" He shook his head slightly and thought, *No—Volupté* Magazine made his father a wealthy man. But Rome couldn't think of anything other than money to motivate dear ol' Dad into doing something this asinine.

He looked over at his brother. Tony had suddenly turned catatonic. He'd never seen him so completely speechless. If the situation weren't so serious it would've been laughable.

Finkleman opened a side drawer in his desk and pulled out a neatly wrapped package the size of a shoebox. "This should help explain everything."

Rome hesitated as Finkleman held out the box that supposedly explained his father's dementia. When he didn't take it, the man set it down on the coffee-stained desktop.

"Would you like to open it?" he asked.

"Eventually," Rome said flatly.

Tony stared at the neatly wrapped box as if it contained a venomous snake.

Rome leaded back in his chair and folded his arms.

Finkleman peeled off a white envelope attached to the box and opened it. "I'd been helping your father track down the women from the Baker family," he unfolded a sheet of paper then handed it to Rome. "The only two unmarried females we found are listed there on the sheet."

That didn't answer his question, but innate curiosity made Rome take the paper. He glanced at it, hoping to see photographs of Gwyneth Paltrow look-alikes, but the only information were brief bios. One lived in Boston, the other in Los Angeles.

"Found the woman in Boston, but damned if I can't find the woman from Los Angeles," Finkleman told them. "I do have one lead. Discovered a piece of property she owns. Part of a strip mall down Greenrich Street. An old part of Los Angeles—a classy shopping area several blocks North of Melrose. The business addresses are also on that sheet."

Rome rubbed at his roughened chin and over his mouth in irritation, closing his eyes briefly. "How long do we have to decide?"

"Before you walk out of my office."

"Today?"

Finkleman nodded.

"Well, which one?" Tony's voice hiked up a few octaves. "Which one of us has to—?"

Rome rubbed his closed eyes and twelve-hour beard stubble. "Tony, sit down, man you're giving me a goddamn headache," he muttered as he stood up to pace the small expanse of the dank old office. He shoved his hands deep into his pockets. He needed time to think.

Fisting his hands in his black jeans, Rome felt the change from his morning coffee in his left pants pocket and pulled out a quarter.

"We'll flip a coin."

"You gotta be shittin' me?" Tony turned to the attorney. "Can he do that?"

The older man looked at Rome. "It's your choice."

"Can you be our legal witness?"

Finkleman nodded in agreement.

"In fact," Rome handed him the coin. "To make this impartial, sir, you should be the flipper."

The old man actually laughed. "Can't wait to tell my poker buddies." He took the quarter and flipped it expertly up near the ceiling. While it spun in mid-air, Tony called heads, Rome called tails, before a smiling Finkleman caught it.

"Heads."

"Whoo hoo," Tony threw his fist in the air. "You're gettin' married bro."

*****

Dana didn't dream last night. But then she didn't sleep either. Hadn't really since she failed at her lousy attempt to "get laid" two weeks ago. It didn't help that there were picketers on her sidewalk all-night, plus someone next door with a hammer, or a chainsaw, or something, pounding against the adjoining walls, keeping her up all night.

Mug of coffee in one hand and her sketchpad in the other, she rolled her shoulders and stretching her aching neck as she forced herself to walk downstairs to her soon-to-be-opened art shop.

She hoped the loud-mouth ladies camped outside would settle their union dispute, or whatever it was, so she could get some rest.

An antique table her grandmother gave her years ago was scheduled to be delivered from storage this week. It wouldn't fit upstairs in her apartment, but she had the perfect place for it here in her shop. Her fingers and toes tingling with excitement—she couldn't wait for its delivery.

Now all she had to do was stock her shelves and hire help.

Agh!

Dana set her mug down on the box labeled acrylic paint-crimson and gazed down at her sketch. She traced her finger along the lines of her drawing, wishing *his* face would one day become clear to her. As clear as the sculpted lines of his chest, his strong lean legs, the scar on his thigh—his sex...

Her cell phone hummed. Dana set her mug down on the newly tiled floor and answered. "Hello?"

"Hey, angel. How's the art framing business?"

"Leo. I'm not speaking to you. Remember?"

"That was two weeks ago. I was sure you'd have forgiven me by now."

Leo was Dana's closest friend and her co-worker at the Huntington Library before she resigned to open her new shop.

"Well, maybe. But I'm still ticked that you forced me to hang out at that jazz bar— and in that skirt. It made me looked like a floozy, or something worse that I can't even think of. What if I'd been robbed or attacked?"

"Honey, you were a gorgeous knock-out, that night. And you weren't attacked. I waited in the parking lot with Roger 'til we knew you were okay."

"Yeah, well, I did knock some guy on his head." She grimaced, remembering the chain of events after. "And I looked like a female impersonator, or something."

"Honey, Roger is a female impersonator. You, however, *are* very female. You can't fake what you already are."

"I *was* a fake. I was trying to be something I'm not."

"This is about *him* again, isn't it?" Leo asked gently.

"Who?"

"Honey, this is me, Leo. You never could keep secrets from me."

Silently, Dana glanced at her sketchpad.

"You're having dreams about him again. Aren't you?"

She just sighed heavily.

"Fine. Don't tell me. But I'm here if you need an ear to chew on."

"Thanks, Leo. So, how's Roger these days?"

"Oh, the *Queen Mary's* having these late night drag-queen parties. They are to *die* for. Roger's a cocktail waitress. Oh— a Japanese tour group just got here, hon. Gotta go."

Dana laughed. Rarely did she ever get a chance to say good-bye back. She stood from the large box labeled "acrylic paint tubes—cerulean blue" that temporarily served as a chair, spreading her arms wide and twirled on her heels with a giggle bubbling up from the pleasure of sweet independence and pride. From the seafoam green walls to the freshly laid faux-marble floor tiles, this was her shop. Her dream. *The Enchanted Frame & Art Shop*. The name had a pleasant ring to it. And it was all hers.

"Hello?"

"Geez, Louise!" Dana was jolted from her thoughts when a tall, thin elderly woman with curly gray hair and a green apron entered her front door.

"Is anyone here? Oh, hello. There you are. I'm Helen Hilson. I own the bakery next door." The woman offered her hand and smiled brightly at her.

"Hi. I'm Dana." She noticed the woman smelled of baked bread.

"Yes, I know. I know about everyone here," she said. "Had to come by and meet our new landlady," she said as she looked around the shop. "My, but this does look wonderful! You fixed it up nice."

"Thank you."

"Oh! These are for you..." She handed Dana a paper plate full of cookies. "Those are my specialty. I call them Sugar Bliss. Your grandma had a delightful dress shop here once. It was a shame she had to let it go unused for so long. But she kept her rents fair. So sorry to hear about her passing. "

"You knew my grandma?"

"Yes, dear. *Silk n' Treasures* I believe was the name of her shop. Delightful..."

Dana marveled at how the woman could talk without taking in a breath.

"...the salon...such a shame...hated to see them go... then the man next door..."

Dana bit into a cookie and gagged. "I'm sorry," she croaked. "What were you saying about the man next door?"

"Oh, sorry, dear. These cookies must be from the batch I mistook salt for sugar. I thought I tossed those. Here, give them back." The woman smiled apologetically. "I'll bring you a fresh plate of chocolate chip instead."

"No really, it's okay." Dana *did* love chocolate chip cookies. "What about the man next door?" she repeated as she grabbed her coffee then took a big swallow.

"Why, he bought out the salon, dear. Sublet the place from Rose and Felicia. Funny thing is I had no idea they were planning to retire. One day, that photographer up and bought 'em out. Started movin' in the next day."

"Really? When?"

"Oh, maybe ten days ago, I guess. That's when all the protestors started showing up. The ladies of "Family Values for a Better L.A." He's a *DeMitri*, you know." Her voice dropped to a whisper as if others were within earshot. "His family founded that filthy girly magazine. Some unpronounceable French name... Voile, Vula or some such."

"*Volupté*?"

"Yes, I believe that's it. Filthy stuff. When the owner died, the women were forced to protest in front of his son's portrait studios. L.A. would be a much nicer place to live if they just moved all their filth back to Alta Dena where they belong."

Dana noted the woman never took a single breath.

"Can you believe it? The oldest son owns several *family* portrait studios." The older woman made a subtle little snort.

"No, I didn't know." Dana wasn't sure how she felt about this news. But Helen seemed to take great exception to it.

"Hurtin' my business too. Terrible. Having our nice little shopping area to be sullied by his ilk." The old woman wrinkled her nose up. "Portrait studio, indeed. More like boudoir studio. Oh, my! Look at the time. I need to open up. It was nice talkin' to you, dear." She was still chatting away when she waved goodbye.

Dana let out a sigh and wiped her mouth of salty cookie as she heard the screams of "Save Our Neighborhood" drift through her door as Mrs. Hilson left.

Silently, she calculated the remaining days left before the announcement of her grand opening. Hopefully with the ad in the local paper, she'd have a framer and a salesperson before then.

"Pardon me, beautiful." Dana heard a low masculine voice coming from her back door.

She turned to find a tall man, well over six feet, with a powerful set of shoulders and long sturdy legs filling her doorframe. He wore dark glasses, a dark polo shirt and black pleated Levis. On his head a hideous green fisherman's cap covering dark silky hair that fanned out around a strong neck and determined forehead.

"Yes?"

He waved her over.

Dana was acutely aware of his massive size and her pulse kicked up a beat. She backed away, taking several steps looking for a weapon. "Do I know you?"

"Oh, sorry," he said in a soothing, apologetic tone. He removed his sunglasses revealing intense dark-chocolate brown eyes that flickered with mischief as he looked at her.

She froze, his compelling eyes riveted her to the spot. There was something about him...She *knew* those eyes.

"Hi, I'm your neighbor, Rome." He laughed uncomfortably, "Umm, I'm having a little trouble getting to my car. Can I use your front door? There seems to be an angry crowd at my side of the building."

As his lips moved she noticed they were firm and sensual. Kissable actually, and was shocked when visions of sucking lightly on his bottom lip entered her mind.

Oh, God! No. Please, not him. Her breath shallowed as she fiddled with the small pearl buttons of her cotton blouse.

A bit breathless and feeling a little silly for staring, she said, "Oh, sure. Come on in."

Please, don't recognize me.

She saw he had a nonchalant grace as he moved that held an attractive self-confidence along with a restless energy about his movements. It instantly drew her.

But it was those dark compelling eyes... They held a sensual spark, a kind of worldly glimmer that caught her attention in the lounge that night. Just as they did now.

Dana thought whimsically, that even if he'd seen the corners of the earth, it wouldn't tame that thirst for adventure she now saw in his eyes. So different from that night. For a hopeful moment, Dana thought perhaps he was a different guy.

He seemed so unlike herself, she thought. Dana was comfortable at home around a cluttered apartment with lots of furniture to paint. Comfortable, safe, and well...dull. Something she was turning around in her life—slowly.

The almost-sex thing notwithstanding.

But still, there was something about him—something... something other than that awful night—reminder of how terribly inadequate she was—something important, familiar, as if his eyes held a secret passion, a hidden memory shared, then forgotten.

"Thanks. Wow. You've really transformed this place," he said as they walked toward the front.

He put his glasses back on as he looked out the window, scanning the distance between his car and the women on the sidewalk.

She was ashamed to find herself admiring his behind, realizing how nice his jeans fit around a perfect example of the male butt. And she wanted to groan aloud.

"Shit, how the hell did they find me?" he muttered.

"Sorry?"

He glanced at her, "Oh, nothing. It's just that I've been dealing with protestors all my life." He shrugged. "And I thought I could avoid it when I moved here."

She noticed the aggravation in his voice yet he smiled at her. He had a nice sexy smile. She had an urge to stand on her toes and kiss him—*like that night.*

I'm an idiot. I never learn.

He grabbed her by the hand he said, "Walk with me to the car?"

"Uh, all right," she muttered, as he led her outside. "Why do they bother you?"

"Something about the sins of the father passing to his sons and all that bullsh...ah...malarkey."

"Oh."

"Frigin' nuisance," he said as they were instantly spotted by the pack of picket-toting, Bingo playing, aging amazons.

"Hey. It's him. It's DeMitri." And then, "Get him!"

He captured her by the shoulders, tugging her to the opposite side of the building. "I'm sorry," he said before he swiftly pinned her between his hard body and the brick wall of the building. "Just act natural."

"Wha...," She didn't have time to react before he firmly placed his mouth against hers. "Mm..." she inhaled sharply at the contact, taking in the contrast of his hard body and his soft lips.

"Shh. Their running passed us. Open your mouth."

Despite her initial shock, she complied.

Oh Lord, his mouth felt warm and coaxing against her own as an unwanted thrill trickled down her belly. After years of erotic dreams as her only sex life, years without a simple sensual touch of a man, this confusing, forceful, and oh, so arousingly sexy kiss left her knees weak and her heart hammering. *It wasn't like this before.* In her dreams—nor that night.

He shifted his head, deepening the kiss, as the stragglers of angry shouts passed them by, overlooking the couple in a passionate embrace, and she found herself going with it, melting into him—and with more hunger then she even knew existed in her nearly-sexless life. As his tongue thrust deeper into the recesses of her mouth, demanding more from her, heat seeped between her legs, and she suddenly had an urge to wrap her legs around this stranger's waist and rub herself against him right where it would do the most good.

"Yes," she thought. Or had she said it out loud before—?

"Where'd that DeMitri trash go?"

Confused anger pulsed through her initial shock as she pushed hard against him. "You're *DeMitri*?"

"Get your hands off her," she heard Helen screech as she ran out of her bakery with a cookie sheet swinging. "You lowlife, no-good son-of–a-whoreson..."

"C'mon," he yelled as he released his hold on her and pulled her back inside her shop before Helen could bop him a good one on the head with it.

"I thought you said your name was Rome," she said, tugging at his strong grip.

"It is," he whispered as he ducked behind a stack of boxes labeled sable-hair brushes, towing her behind him. "It's Romano DeMitri—nice to kiss you—I mean, meet you." He smiled at her.

Dana harrumphed, tugging at the hand still holding her own. Her lips still tingled from the heat of his mouth. Before she gave in to the impulse to lick them, she wiped at her lips with her free hand. "I can't believe you did that."

"What? Kiss you?"

She glanced at his eyes through the dark shades and nodded. That mischievous twinkle return. Recognition? Lord, she hoped not. He was probably used to kissing women—lots of them.

"I was just trying to..."

"Look Inconspicuous?" she accused.

He grinned. "Exactly." His eyes dropped to gaze down at her mouth when he asked, "What to try again?"

He was teasing, wasn't he? Dana made an unladylike sound when a bone-jarring crash sounded. An object and several splinters of glass flew over them.

"My window," Dana cried as a gasp of disbelief washed over her. With one sharp tug, she released herself from his grasp to assess the damage.

Pieces of her beautiful design and jagged glass shards lay in a shiny heap at her feet. She turned back to him, refusing to give in to angry tears. "This is *your* fault! If you hadn't shown up..." her throat tightened in a haze of red-hot fury, "...you and that...that stupid, disgusting... *magazine*."

"It's not *my* magazine," he said dryly, "It was my father's."

"Well, maybe they think the fruit doesn't fall far from the tree after all."

"You didn't seem to mind a few minutes ago." With a deceptively hurtful expression, he turned away, searching for something.

"Yeah, well you're a lousy lover," she cried. Shocked by her own hurtful outburst, she slapped her hand to her mouth, immediately wanting to take it back.

He opened his mouth to say something, then frowned and turned on his heel as if looking for something.

"What are you doing?" Her voice caught, ashamed about demeaning his sexual prowess.

"Looking for a phone. I'm calling the police. Then I'm calling that Baker woman and see if she's got a number for a glass company."

"What baker woman? Helen Hilson?"

"No. The woman that owns this building...what's her name...Dana Baker. Ahh, here it is."

She stared up at him.

"What?"

"*I'm* Dana Baker."

The phone slipped from Rome's finders and hit the hard floor with a thud.

Chapter Three

"WELL?"

Rome looked up from his computer screen and saw his brother swagger through his studio door looking typically refined in a tailored black wool suit and an equally expensive-looking pair of loafers. "Well, what?"

"When's the wedding date?"

"Gimme a break, Tony. I've been up all night."

"Doing what? It better be because you were picking out China patterns or I'll..."

"You'll what? Marry her yourself?"

"Bite your tongue. And for the record—the coin toss was your idea."

"Look, I don't need you hanging over me, Tony. I'm still trying to remove all those sinks and salon chairs from my work area. Plus, I need to have my itinerary worked out this week if I plan to make the next scheduled archaeological tour. And my right log aches like the hell. So lay off, okay?"

"Shit, Rome. My future's hanging by a thread...and you're researching some dead culture's architecture?"

His jaw tightened as he rubbed at the back of his neck. Tony was right, of course. Rome should've been planning his next move with Dana, but he was certain he'd bungled things—badly.

Her window.

Damn it, it wasn't his fault.

And that kiss. Lord, she had a sweet mouth. Despite her plain, outward appearance, he felt a brief spark of something... under that demure exterior. An unpretentiousness he found refreshing. He'd be willing to bet there was a fire kindling underneath. Plus, there was something else. A familiarity he couldn't place.

Rome usually had an excellent memory when it came to remembering faces. He supposed that came with being a photographer all these years.

It was her bright sparkling eyes..., he thought. Her bright eyes?

Bright eyes.

Holy Christ.

Rome felt his stomach drop to the floor.

The night at the lounge. The night he couldn't remember how he got home. Then he found it. That one earring caught in a loose thread of that god-awful purple quilt his mother gave him for Christmas last year. But that was his only hint that a woman had taken him home. Was the earring Dana's? He couldn't remember if she wore any that night.

Pink cheeked and snug light-blue pants—this Baker female was not at all what he'd expected. Rome saw a glimpse of anger quickly replaced the shock from his impromptu kiss. His "wilting lily" appeared to be more like an ethereal fairy.

Honey-blonde hair falling in disarray just passed her shoulders, womanly hips. He felt his cock harden at the thought of her sensually soft lips—and other places he'd like to have those lips... *Don't go there pal.*

She wasn't beautiful, he thought, but Dana Baker had an unearthly grace he found sort of appealing... and well... sexy. *Shit*, he'd nearly given her a concussion, throwing her against the wall as he did, and here he was, thinking about a blowjob—

"Helloooo. Earth to Rome?" Tony snapped his finger in Rome's face jolting him from his erotic thoughts.

Rome furrowed his brows at his obnoxious sibling.

"*Jesus!* If it was me..."

"If it was you—what? You'd be between her legs already?"

"I don't know," Tony said. "Is she hot?"

"I shouldn't need to remind you, Tony, but Dana isn't a sexual conquest. My life is just as much at stake as yours. For chrissake, you're a selfish bastard."

Rome laid his tired head in his hands and rubbed at his throbbing eyes and cheekbones. He'd stayed up all night because he couldn't sleep. Dana's soft hazel, unmade-up eyes brimming with unshed tears over her beautiful window, in shatters at her feet, kept swimming around in his head. Okay, so she was more than just sexy and appealing. *But those eyes... it was her eyes.*

"I'm selfi..." Tony yelled then lowered his voice to a cool sneer. "Who's the one who stole Cammie Davis from me when we were in high school, huh? You knew I was in love with her... and who's the one who took the heat from Dad when you decided to take a hike instead of staying in the family business. It broke Dad's heart, you know, when you snubbed the magazine and broke out on your own. So don't give me this crap about who's the selfish bastard in this scenario."

Rome was too tired to point out that it was their father who was the bastard in this scenario. And he wasn't about to talk about Tony sleeping with his ex.

No, he wouldn't bring it up because he was suddenly facing his own demons of guilt. He needed Dana Baker. But he also *wanted* her. His own selfish pride kept him from simply asking for her to agree in a possible contract agreement of marriage by offering some kind of incentive for becoming his wife.

No. He couldn't.

Rome wanted Dana to want *him* as a man, and that alone kept him from striking out at his brother.

"Look, Rome," Tony's voice lightened, "I'm sorry to bring up ancient history, man. And it's obvious you need my help in this. Let's say we leave the past to the past, okay?"

Rome lifted his aching head from his hands and looked up at his brother. Tony's eyes, so much like his own, so much like their father's. The only hint the two brothers didn't share the same mother was Tony's dark blonde hair—a striking contrast to Rome's own chocolate brown.

In his brother's face, he saw the same weary expression that stared back in his own mirror for the past several weeks. At that moment, Rome thought the past should be buried along with his father and the animosity he carried for his brother.

"Maybe you're right, bro. She isn't... She's just..."

"Oh, I see what's going on here. You like her and you're scared to death." Tony smiled.

"No, really," he lied, "Tony, she's kind of... skittish..." But he admired her spunk.

"Well then it's fortunate for you that I stopped by. *The looove doctor is here...*" he said spreading his arms wide.

"Gimme a break, Tony." Rome dropped his head back in his palms and groaned. "Not another tactless story about your sexual escapades."

"I'm not talking sex here. What I'm talking about—even the Elephant Man could score with."

"All right. I'm listening."

"Young, old. Beautiful, homely—all women respond to sincerity, to men who listen to 'em. Find out what her dreams are. What her hopes are for the future. And get someone to go behind enemy lines so-to-speak. Find out what her likes and dislikes are. What's her favorite food? Her favorite color, favorite flower? Her desires...her magic buttons..."

"I thought you said this doesn't involve sex."

"Well, eventually it will. Assuming you want it to. You do want it to?"

"Oh, yeah." Damn. Rome realized too late what he'd revealed with that statement.

"You can't go wrong, then."

"So what you're saying is I need someone to spy on Dana?"

"Just to find out what makes her tick."

The idea had merit, but Rome hated deceptiveness, and he was feeling a little desperate. He'd finally gotten ballsy and approached her, but all he'd managed to do was throw her against a wall and get her window smashed in. Shit.

At least the protestors left when the police arrived.

Rome also made arrangements with an old buddy in the glass business for an emergency trip to replace her broken window.

"I'll give it some thought."

"Do I need to bring up Cammie Davis again, bro?" Tony asked.

"Let me enlighten you, little brother, about Cammie Davis. I was a horny sixteen-year-old virgin when Cammie came on to me. She came on to a lot of guys, Tony. Not just me. Okay? I said I'd give it some thought and I will. Besides, what makes you such an expert?"

Tony crooked his lips into a smirk and stared at him. "You know the difference between you and me, Rome? You like women."

Rome quirked his eyebrow.

"I, however, love women."

*****

"*I need you.*"

Rome turned in the direction of the sweet voice coming from his studio back door and smiled.

Dana's earthy appearance in a white cotton shirt and light blue pants were a sharp contrast to his starchy black and white studio.

With her burnished blonde hair tumbling carelessly from her ponytail, Dana was cute even when disheveled and wildly panting.

His grin widened, "Hey, slow down, sweetheart. What's the rush?"

Her haste brightened her eyes as she approached. Her chest rose and fell with every breath, tightening her appealingly firm breasts against the fabric of her button-down shirt. He nearly dropped his Bronica camera from its tripod as his blood pressure escalated.

Although his enchanting neighbor appeared in distress, he couldn't help but remember how soft her lips were, or the first time he saw her. She was decorating that very same shop window. Or was it that night at the lounge? His mouth began to water.

He felt a twinge of guilt for her beautiful window... *Damn*, he never meant to cause her trouble. But he couldn't—*would not* feel even a flash of guilt for the bogus kiss. It felt too good. *Ah*, but that first time—strike that—the second time he saw her... the afternoon sun was gleaming against her hair and through her light-blue dress, silhouetting the lush curves of her feminine body.

Smiling to himself, he remembered how his jaw dropped to the ground when she'd told him who she was—Dana Baker—*the woman he was going to marry*. His brain cells nearly collided when he'd realized the two women where one-and-the-same.

"Please, *hurry*," she yelled, as she ran toward the door. Her soft hazel eyes, burned brightly with steadfast determination. Rome guessed asking others for help went against her nature.

Lord, she was just as cute going as she was coming.

Her beautifully slender neck, slim waist and agilely rounded hips left his camera aching to capture her essence. He felt a powerful awareness of her and wondered if she like soft tender kisses? Or did she like it hard, wet and hungry?

He wished to hell he could remember that night with full clarity. Actually, all he *could* remember was the earring left stuck in his bedspread and a full-blown hangover the next morning.

A surprising flash of passion, buried beneath her serene appearance, emerged for a mere instant before she looked away and ran out the door.

"Hey! Are you coming?"

Jarred from his thoughts, she grabbed him by the hand, she dragged him along. He ignored the warmth of her hand as he obediently followed to a grubby looking white delivery truck parked at her shop's back door, the truck's engine still running.

"Wait a minute, sweetheart." He pulled back on her hand to stop her. "What exactly is the problem?"

"I don't have..." she panted, "The delivery...the driver won't wait..."

He still held her by the hand, enjoying the feel of her.

"I can't unload it myself and this... *idiot* won't help me!" She motioned her hand toward a man leisurely smoking a cigarette in the cab of the vehicle.

"I'm desperate. I can't wait another day for this shipment. Please, before he leaves."

"No problem. I'll handle it." *Whatever it was.*

But how did a guy prove his manly prowess and expertise to a woman after the inept fuck-up he'd been that night? *One thing at a time.* Reluctantly releasing her hand, Rome casually strolled to the open window of the truck. "The lady needs help here."

The driver glared at Rome. "If the broad can't unload this stuff it's not my problem."

Rome jumped through the open window of the truck, turning off the ignition and taking the keys in one swift movement.

"Hey..."

"Look bud, if you want your keys back you'll get your sorry ass out of that truck and help. Do we have an understanding?"

Rome turned and winked at her.

She bit her lower lip as she gave him a small, trusting smile.

Oh, yeah. He'd have his second chance.

*****

Dana was still steaming over that stupid kiss. Did he really think that stunt would work like it did in the movies?

But what a kiss... she thought, recalling the smoldering passion that thrilled and aroused her more than any— No. No. *No.* She refused to think about that. The man was probably a playboy given his family's reputation.

Even for L.A., porno held a certain politically incorrectness despite its booming industry.

She had tried and failed to deny that spark of something between them. It felt like... recognition. But that was impossible. It must have been her initial strong attraction to him that night in the lounge. But she'd felt it then, hadn't she? Why else would she have gone so willingly to his condo?

Dana couldn't remember ever having such a strong, jolting burst of arousal over a man. But it hadn't mattered. Sex wasn't something she was good at—nor very lucky with.

She was pretty sure if those wacky protesting ladies hadn't interrupted them she'd have begged him to make love to her right there—in the day light—in public—up against the wall. Would it have been any different, she wondered.

Geez, Louise. She wasn't acting like herself. She wasn't the type to tongue-twist with a stranger. But she did have sex with him—sort of.

But she wanted to be.

Especially now. Now, she was the new Dana. Not the poor old Dana.

She felt the sweat trickle between her breasts as she watch the men carry her grandmother's gilded table down the ramp and into the backroom of her shop.

After Rome paid the idiot driver fifty bucks, the man finally agreed to get out of the truck. It was probably the jerk's intent all along but Dana didn't care as long as her beautiful table made it down safely.

Rome had shrugged out of his black denim shirt, now naked from the waist up. Dana felt her throat go dry as she watched his well-defined body move with an artless grace as his arms flexed and chest bulged from the strain of carrying her table out of the truck.

The driver cursed and swore, drawing her out of her daze, while calling his mother a bad name as beads of perspiration rolled down his forehead. She smiled to herself as she watched the jerk struggle.

Then her eyes drifted back to her neighbor. At his rear-end actually. Did she remember his rear end, or did she never get a chance to see it? He stopped and looked over his shoulder at her.

Caught. Her face heated as he raised his eyebrows at her.

"Well?"

Well? Well what? You look sexy in black? Nice butt? Then her brain began to work again.

"Oh gosh! I'm so sorry." Dana rushed to open her back door and felt her cheeks flush miserably. She hated herself for such ill-mannered thoughts. But there was something about this relative stranger that made her feel uneasy. She'd remembered him, and she felt a twinge of disappointment he hadn't remembered her. Intellectually, she knew the man was drunk that night. And he did pass out on her. But still... was she that forgettable? The thought stung though logically, Dana knew it was better this way.

"Where do you want this?" Rome asked.

"Please, just set it at the wall to the left."

"Sure, Dana."

His remark resonated through her body. It made her feel special even though her logical brain tried to tell her he was just saying her name. But the *way* he'd said it sounded like an endearment.

Twenty minutes and several tiny heart attacks later, her stock was stacked neatly in the storeroom and her beloved table strategically placed for customer usage. After twelve useless interviews, Dana wasn't any closer to a full staff than she was this morning. At least, thanks to her neighbor, her window was fixed. There was still so much to do.

She ran her hand along the tabletop and longingly thought of her grandma.

"It's beautiful," she heard him say behind her.

"Yes. Yes, it is." She turned to face him. "Is he gone?"

"Yeah. Hopefully for good. I wouldn't recommend using his company's services again."

"Believe me, I won't, I just couldn't afford anyone else."

"You must have blown your budget on this beauty, though."

"The table? Oh. No, actually it belonged to my grandmother. She gave it to me years ago, but it's been in storage. Now that I'm on my own I wanted to bring it out where I can see it. It makes me feel closer to her somehow. Anyway, it won't fit upstairs in my apartment, so I decided to take it out of storage and put in my new shop."

She knew she was rambling and raised her eyes to find him watching her, searching her face as if reaching for her thoughts. Dana was suddenly faced with old fears and anxieties when around men—especially half-naked men. He'd thrown his shirt over his bare shoulder, not bothering to put it back on. She raised her eyes to find him watching her, searching her face as if reaching for her thoughts. His unfathomable dark eyes flickered with an intensity that entranced her. Intelligent and magnetic.

"On your own?" he asked as he raised his hand up to her face.

She flinched slightly.

"Careful, I'm not going to attack. You just have a dark smudge on your cheek."

"Sorry. I'm still a little wound up." The gentle massage of his thumb against her face sent currents of electricity all the way down her legs. Her eyelids felt heavy as she studied his face. His strong features and inherent strength held a certain sensuality that drew her in, just as he had that night in the lounge. His touch now felt so incredible that a sense of urgency to have him kiss her again—it was overwhelming. These feelings were so unlike her. What was it about him?

"No problem. You said you're on your own. Divorced?"

"Oh, no. Never married. My grandmother, she died six months ago and left this building to me. This section used to be her shop. But it's been vacant for quite some time. She suffered from arthritis and when it got too painful for her, she had to close her shop."

"Ah. Well, that explains the dirt then. I'm sorry you lost her."

"Thanks. She'd been ill for a long time. The arthritis left her nearly bed-ridden at the end." Dana sighed. "I'm just now getting use to having time of my own. I've never lived alone before. It's lonely sometimes, but kind of liberating too." Dana bit her lip, "Sorry, I'm rambling..."

"No. I don't mind. Really," he said.

"Umm... can I get you something to drink?" she said, fighting for something else to say. "It's the least I can do..."

"No, thanks." He grinned at her.

Oh boy. "So, is it true then? About your father, I mean?"

His smiled faded. "What about my father?"

"That he founded *Volupté* Magazine."

She noticed his jaw tighten as he looked away. "Yes," he replied, the sudden coolness in his voice evident. "Does that bother you?" There was a spark of pleading in his eyes when he looked back to her face.

"Yes. No. It's just...well I felt terrible after I insulted you yesterday. It was uncalled for."

"Hey, it's okay. I'm used to disdain and insults because of my father. I've been dealing with it...and trying to avoid it all my life." He shrugged. "I used to travel a lot, just to get away."

"You don't get along?"

"You could say that. He died."

Now she really felt like dirt. "Oh, no. I'm truly sorry."

"It's okay. And you're right. We weren't on the best of terms."

She heard someone walk up behind her. "Umm, excuse me. I hate to interrupt but I'm here about the job." It was the young lyrical voice of a woman.

Dana turned to see a girl about Dana's age and height with short cropped black hair, a streak of blonde cupping the right side of her face, dressed all in purple with a pierced bottom lip. *Oh, great. Not another one.*

"Hello. I'll be right with you," Dana replied.

She turned back to Rome with an apologetic expression.

He smiled and kissed her on the forehead before he left the way he came.

"Wow! Who was *that*?" the girl asked.

"My neighbor," Dana said annoyed with herself for the twinge of jealousy in her voice.

"Oh, I didn't mean anything by it. He just looks familiar."

"Listen, aah, what was your name?"

"Cynthia Martin."

"Cynthia. I've just about interviewed every unemployed person in this town under the age of thirty. Tell me why I should hire you?"

To her surprise, the girl smiled at her. "Because, I'm studying decorating at the community college. I also learned how to frame my own watercolors when I was in high school... and you need help," she said it with such confidence Dana couldn't help but like her. She had guts. And Dana was tired.

"Can you run a cash register?"

"I worked at the grocery store last summer, and I work nights at *The Monkey Shop*."

"Do you know someone who's a qualified framer looking for a full time job?"

"I might."

"Good. You're hired, starting right now."

*****

By the end of the day, Dana and Cynthia had the walls fully decorated, complete with beautifully matted frame samples for customers to choose from.

The carpenter finally showed up and completed all the shelving units. And Dana had an interview with Cynthia's brother's friend who happened to be tired of working at the craft store downtown at minimum wage. Despite her unusual appearance, Dana's new employee was an angel in disguise. She'd managed to arrange ordinary painting supplies, brushes, and colored pencils on the shelves in such a way that would appeal to any novice or expert painter. Each aisle portrayed a theme of crimsons, cerulean blues, and chartreuse greens while another aisle was a striking contrast of blacks and whites.

"Hey, Cynthia—great job today. Go home. Rest up. We'll start again tomorrow morning—eight o'clock."

"Okay. Sure. Hey, thanks for giving me a chance."

Several minutes after Dana heard Cynthia's car roll out of the parking lot, she heard someone tapping at her back door.

"Hey, beautiful."

"Hi." Dana felt her face flush at the sight of Rome filling the doorframe to her stock room. She felt herself return his wide, open smile. His compliment felt so genuinely given, she wanted to believe he truly meant it.

"I wanted to give this to you." He handed her a basket overflowing with pink bouvardia.

"It's gorgeous. Thank you."

"It's sort of a housewarming gift, for your shop."

She inhaled its light, fragrant scent. "They smell wonderful, too."

"Listen, Dana. We didn't really start off right..."

"That's an understatement."

"Yeah," he said looking slightly embarrassed, "Will you let me make it up to you? Take you to dinner, maybe?"

"I don't know..."

"Friday night? How about it?"

"Huh...I'm aaa..." Dana swallowed hard, trying to manage an audible response. *Think, think, refuse... find an excuse...* She wasn't about to go through another humiliating evening with him again. When one didn't come she simply smiled back and nodded. Then he widened his grin and her heart thudded against her chest.

Yes, yes! No—he's just being nice, she thought.

"I felt like such an ass the other day, and I couldn't get you out of my mind after that kiss. And when I looked at your face...your window... Well, I just needed to... *Jesus*, 'apologize' is such a lame word. It should never have happened. I'm sorry." He laughed uncomfortably as he rubbed at the back of his neck. "But I'd like the chance to redeem myself."

"Oh." Well, she could understand his discomfort. But it stung a little knowing he regretted the kiss, no matter how inappropriate it was.

"And I'd like to do it again."

"Now? Really?" She felt a spark of shock and delight at the idea that he *really* wanted to kiss her. Then her eyes took in the sight of his full and generous mouth and her throat tightened.

"Eager?" he teased as he lowered his head slightly and studied her face for a moment. Her smile faded as a familiar sense of inadequacy swept over her like a bucket of ice cubes. But then he looked at her with such an expression of promise and reassurance that she felt a little giddy and lightheaded.

"Humm." Teasing he said, "No, I think I'll wait..." His lips a breath away, he whispered, "...'til you're ready. And...you're not ready."

If she just lifted up on her toes the tiniest bit, she could close the space between them. All thought drained out of her head as heat pooled between her legs.

Oh, yes. I'm ready. Now!

Geez, Louise, where were these new thoughts come from?

Then he backed away with that impossibly sexy grin again.

Dana tried to look everywhere but at him. The spot on the wall with missed paint. The new tiles at her feet. His feet. Big sexy feet clad in black nubuck-leather boots. Sexy feet? She glanced at him and he quirked his eyebrow at her.

He took her hand, kissed her palm lightly before he released it, leaving Dana a little off balance.

"Until Friday, then," he said. Then turned and walked out the back door.

Friday.

Dana fought to control her conflicting emotions. Excitement, desire and... panic... *Oh, Lord!* What was someone like her supposed to do with all that man? Was he really attracted to her or was he just being polite?

And what was she going to wear?

One thing for sure, she wasn't about to ask for Leo's help again.

Her normally sensible brain was temporarily malfunctioning. Not that it surprised her. After all, she was about to open her dream shop, and a man who made her knees quiver just asked her to dinner. Not only that, but he'd melted her brain with that silly, phony, *hot* kiss.

Maybe it was a good thing he didn't remember her.

But, darn it, she wanted him to remember.

"I gotta sit down..." But there weren't any chairs to sit on yet, so she sighed and plopped her butt down on the floor.

Chapter Four

"YOU HAVE A PLAN, I ASSUME?" Patricia Wilson peered over her Dior glasses at her nephew. She could always count on his loyalty, despite his smugness when it came to business.

"No."

"Well, what *have* you done?"

"Nothing yet." His voice was quiet yet held an undertone of cold annoyance.

"We need evidence and we need it soon." She spaced her words slowly as if speaking to a five year old. "I need back what that Greta Baker bitch stole from me."

"I'll get it." The long deep look they exchanged infuriated her.

"It's up to you to nail that granddaughter of hers. But I need proof. Video camera, photos, I don't care what it takes. And I don't want to involve your sisters. The less they know the better."

"Fine," he said flatly. There was a subtle yet familiar challenge in his tone.

"Fine," she repeated. "Just remember who raised you after your mother died."

"No problem, Aunt Patty, I *am* grateful."

Patricia gave him a thin smile. She had an affection for all her sister's kids. But Lord, how she detested it when any of them called her Patty, like a common cretin raised in some rural cow pasture like Chino Hills. More often, she remembered the resentment, her ruined chances for a full life. Now, here she was getting old and on the brink of ruin because her bitch-of-a deceased client got a healthy dose of conscious before she died.

Patricia thought of her nieces with envy that hung on the fringes of hatred and resentment—young and beautiful. And she'd use their beauty to her advantage if she had to. Thankfully, they held a strong sense of loyalty to her though she couldn't relate to the sentiment.

"Any of the DeMitri boys will do." *Lord, knows there's plenty of them.* Alberto DeMitri was a randy bastard. No telling how many brats he'd left behind the last thirty years.

"She's a bit insipid. What if she doesn't fall for the bait?" he asked with smug detachment.

"Just get me my proof!" She took a deep breath. She hated loosing control. "Get the fucking evidence. And get my property back."

He took a peppermint from the lead crystal jar on her desk and popped it into his mouth, seeming pleased with himself. Patricia held back her annoyance. He always took pleasure in breaking through her practiced composure. Tragedy had etched that composure into a refined dignity. Without her youth, dignity was all she had left.

Her nephew stood from his seat and left without another word. She pursed her once-full lips, feeling restless and irritable when she found that her hands were shaking.

She couldn't fail this time.

Everything she had, her pride, her business, maybe even her life, everything she'd gained depended on it.

*****

In a familiar dream-like state she imagines her lover coming to her—paper and pencil held ready. The lines from her pencil shaping the couple—her and him—together for the first time. Her own face, clear as a mirror image, yet only a hint of his strong jaw and confident chin revealed. His eyes and the ridge of his cheekbones vague and hidden behind the veil of her sleep-filled haze. She drew herself naked, supine and pinned beneath him. Their bodies locked together. Hers arched instinctively against his. With skillful hands he brings her hips hard against his own...

Dana awoke and found herself standing silent in the middle of her bedroom. A familiar flutter returned in her belly. She tried to reconcile the man in her dreams to the man who'd left her breathless with a fake kiss and an irresistible smile.

The images of both dream and reality illogically melded together in her mind—remembering the way Rome's buttocks flexed beneath his black jeans and the way his perfectly proportioned shoulders strained against the fabric of his shirt. How the sweat trickled down his naked chest. His presence stoked a gently growing fire within her and she fought the overwhelming need to go to him and beg him to make love to her—to fan the flame hard and fast before extinguishing the heat from her body with his touch.

Dana knew she wasn't pretty. She knew she didn't possess the femme fatale appeal or the experience to entice a man's interest. Especially a man as beautiful as Rome DeMitri, and it made her want to cry in frustration as a flash of longing and loneliness swept through her. Her heart pounded with uncertainty as she realized she wanted him to find her just as desirable as she found him.

She set her pad and pencil on the nightstand then climbed back into bed. Gratefully, she fell instantly into a dreamless sleep.

*****

Rome missed his condo downtown. He didn't mind the lacy shower curtains or even the flower-decals on the kitchen cabinets. The former residents had a flare for the nostalgic look. He was just more comfortable in his own skin when things were under control. He felt like a broken spoke in a wheel since the reading of his father's will.

He still had six sinks and just as many dismembered salon chairs piled up in the back room. He'd kept the simple black and white motif from the previous owners and the holes from the old sink drains were now patched up and ready for painting. Rome kept the salon mirrors in place. It gave his studio the illusion that it was larger than it really was, and he liked simple illusion. It's what he did best. Photography was a simple illusion—making the unattractive stunning with just the right lighting. Making dysfunctional families looking blissfully happy.

Simple illusion.

He'd paid a great deal to buy out the lady salon owners and although a challenge, managed to assemble a new studio in a matter of weeks.

The moment he met Dana, Rome never regretted his impromptu place of business. Her sweetness felt like a balm to the bitter resentment he still felt toward his father.

Geez, Tony would have a field day with that one if he knew.

"Get a grip, man." He shuffled his aching muscles to his desk and set his insomnia-sized mug of coffee down. He turned to stretch his muscles when he saw it.

Shoved under the front entrance was a light cream colored envelope.

"What the..." Rome picked it up and read his first name on the front in perfectly curved handwriting.

"This can't be good." He tore it open and read:

Rome,

I am sorry, but something has come up and I am unable to attend our dinner date this evening. However, I am still indebted to you and wish to pay you in full. Enclosed you will find a reimbursement check for fifty dollars. I cannot thank you enough for your help.

Sincerely,

Dana Baker

Rome's nostrils flared in frustration as he mutilated the note in his tightened fist. "Ah, shit." He'd spooked her. He recognized immediately Dana's innocence by her raw and untried reaction to his kiss.

Damn his impulsiveness and his infamous father—and the damned magazine. She'd said it didn't bother her, but after a time, she must have decided being with him—being seen with him, she'd be discredited by association.

He'd have to convince her that Rome DeMitri was not his father. Far from it. But how could he prove it to her when he wasn't convinced of it himself.

His own sparse love life was like an endless highway of road-kill on the Pacific Coast Highway. He'd wanted to keep it that way...until now. Perhaps he'd fought his father's reputation and womanizing tendencies all his life for nothing.

"I'll prove it to her," he said out loud. He had to. Dana Baker was safe with this DeMitri—personally and professionally. He wanted to protect her and show her that she didn't have to be alone or lonely. He'd do it. He had to. His brother was depending on him. Rome wouldn't—couldn't let him down.

*****

"Oh my God, Dana...you gotta come see this!"

Dana looked up from her mat cutter and saw Cynthia's excited face gawk out the front window. Her new employee seemed to favor a monotone attire. Today she wore all dark red. Dark red hair-band, tight blouse and a broomstick skirt along with matching boots with thick soles. "What now? Another female impersonator?" Dana laughed.

"No! Hurry..."

Dana moved beside Cynthia and looked out. "What is *that*? Is it a truck?"

"No, no... it's a limo. Isn't it bizarre?"

Dana looked again. The front looked like an ordinary large white SUV vehicle. But this one had eight windows—on both sides. It was truly a monster. "Geez, Louise, it's grotesque. I think they could fit an army platoon in there."

"Oh, wait. Someone's getting out."

Cynthia's excitement surprised Dana. Living in L.A. people got used to the conspicuous and the eccentrics that appeared daily on the streets.

A pretty young blonde woman with a low-cut blue stretch dress and a cleavage to match gracefully stepped out of the limo.

"Is she a celebrity?" Cynthia asked, "Oh, look—there's another one..." Another beautiful blonde babe dressed in a tight, bright magenta dress climbed out. "They're identical! Do you think they're those Barbie twins? Oh, hang on...who's that guy with them? Mmm, he's gorgeous."

Dana immediately recognized him. Rome's disrespectful playboy brother. Only she wasn't about to admit as much to her employee.

He stepped out holding a gym bag and walked into Rome's place. But not before yet another beauty followed behind him, wearing a pale lavender dress of the same oxygen-stealing tightness as her two clones.

"Three?" Cynthia asked as they both watched each one give the guy a generous kiss on the cheek before they climbed back into the vehicle and left. "Gee, I've heard of *ménage a trois* but *ménage a quatre*?"

"Eww, I don't even want to go there."

Several minutes later, Rome walked out with him.

Dana watched them through the newly replaced window and felt a pang of guilt—remembering the obtuse note she left under his door. She felt like a coward.

"Looks like your neighbor hurt himself."

"What?" she asked with a more concern then she should. "Humm, must have pulled a muscle last night," she muttered as she watched Rome favoring his right leg as he walked. "It's no wonder with all that banging and shuffling he made last night."

Both men were about the same height and build. The only obvious difference between the two was the other man's hair was blonde and slightly longer. Both carrying gym bags, they walked to Rome's old-model silver Jaguar. "They must be related. Cousins, maybe?"

"Cynthia?" Dana asked as she looked back at her employee's drooling admiration for the two men. She snapped her fingers in front of Cynthia's face before. "Earth to Cynthia. The ship has landed." Cynthia jerked to attention and they both started laughing at the spectacle they made.

"It's probably his brother...heeey," she said snapping her fingers. "Now I know why he looked so familiar. He's the son of that guy...you know, the one that owned that magazine. You know that magazine with all the revealing celebrity bios and the photos of airbrush-perfect naked babes. Anyway, I read somewhere, L.A. Times or Cosmo or something, that his brother took over his father's magazine after the guy died."

"Yeah." Dana said flatly, "I've heard of it." She also remembered Rome's discomfort discussing the subject.

"Have you ever read one?" Cynthia asked.

"No!"

"Oooh. Let's get one. See if there's a photo of the cute owner inside." She ran out the door.

"Cynthia! Where are you going?"

"I'm gonna run to Chuck's News Stand down the street. I'll bring back coffee."

*****

"Ooo, yeah. Umm, right there, right there... Oww! Watch it with the thigh, woman." Rome felt a hard smack on his backside. *"Hey!"* He was helpless when it came to Madeline doing her thing with his aching muscles.

"You keep talkin' to me like that, Romano DeMitri, and I'm gonna do more damage. Now, lay still."

Madeline was a very large black woman in her fifties whose breasts where as large as melons and her hands were like vice-grips. But she was the best masseuse this side of L.A. County. Rome had been seeing her for years for his aches and pains.

"I keep tellin' ya to take it easy on this leg and nearly every month you end up on my table."

"That's because you have the sexiest hands and a sweet deposition," he teased.

"Uh huh. And pigs fly, too."

"You tell him, honey." Tony poked his head in the massage room.

"Don't give me that 'honey' business. You're next on my list."

"Madeline, you're breaking my heart."

"Right. I've ten more minutes with your brother. Now, get out."

"But Rome won't mind if I sit in—do you, Rome?"

"You may as well let him, Madeline, or he'll pout the rest of the day."

Madeline harrumphed while Tony made himself comfortable in the only chair in the room.

"You know, Tony, it's your fault I'm laying here. If you'd shown up like you said you would and help me remove those damn salon chairs, my damn leg wouldn't be aching."

"Whine all you like. You should have hired help."

"I would have if you'd said you weren't going to show up."

"If you two boys don't stop belly-achin' in here I'll throw you both out on your ears."

"Sorry." They both said in unison like misbehaving children.

"You bringing the Perry girls with you tonight, Ton?"

"Oh, they'll be there. But no—I'm bringing Kimberly." Tony smiled wide.

"My Kimberly?" Rome asked.

"What do you mean *your* Kimberly? She's your assistant not your lover."

"I mean it, you two," Madeline said as she ground her palm into Rome's shoulder.

He breathed a sigh of relief when Tony fell silent for a moment. He knew it wouldn't last. Rome saw the wheels turning in his brother's over-active brain.

Three...two...one...

"So Rome, what was in the box old Finkle-*berry* gave you?"

Rome shrugged.

"You haven't opened it?" Tony's eyes widened and stared at as if Rome had suddenly sprouted antlers.

"I don't see any point. We'd still be in the same boat."

"Oh, man—give it to me then."

"Fine."

"So. What are you wearing Saturday night?"

Rome lifted his head from the table and gave his brother an odd look before Madeline pushed it right back down. "Since when do you care what I'm wearing?" Rome asked.

"Since what you wear might turn on a certain lady shop owner whose libido I'm relying on to save both our asses."

Rome clenched his jaw as Madeline worked his trapezius muscle and thought about the note left under his door this morning. Not to mention he hadn't ask Dana to the lounge for Saturday night. "Well, since you're such an expert on women's libidos—why don't you tell me what I'm wearing?"

Tony opened his mouth to reply when Madeline said, "Why don't you ask a woman what turns her on? Huh—I'll tell you. All black. Black is sexy. Mysterious. Women can't help themselves when a man is dressed to the hilt in black. Black pants, black boots, and a black turtle neck sweater. And don't bother shavin',' a little bread makes a man look dangerous and danger to a woman means adventure. And what woman doesn't want adventure?" She stopped to take a breath and dug into Rome's back one last time. "And don't comb your hair too perfect neither. Let some hang down in your face. I guarantee she won't know what hit her."

Rome let out a groan when Madeline hit home on his burning adductor muscle.

Then she swatted Rome hard on the butt.

"*Done!* Neeeext."

*****

Dana looked up and saw a slim young man with a mop of brown curls knocking at the shop door. He wore sloppy jeans and a black T-shirt shuffling from one foot to the other with his hands jammed in his pockets while he waited.

"Hi. Can I help you?" Dana asked as she opened the door.

"Hi. Yeah, umm I'm Rick. Cynthia told you about me?" He phrased it as a question and it made Dana smile.

"Oh. Yeah. Come in. You're here about the framer position."

"Uh huh."

After several minutes of the basic question and answer routine, Dana asked Rick to frame a small poster to demonstrate his skills. Forty-five minutes later, Dana learned that despite Rick's lack of verbal skills, he was, in fact, an excellent framer. Because he'd spend more time in the back room rather than helping customers, she didn't think it would be a problem.

"Rick, this is wonderful. I really like your unusual style with the gold frame liner and the triple matting."

"Umm, thanks. Sooo, do I get the job?"

"Yes. You've got the job. When can you start?"

"Well, I really should give the craft store a week's notice."

"That's fair. Let's say one week from today. First thing in the morning." She smiled at him trying to ease his nervousness.

"Okay." He smiled shyly back. "Thanks."

After negotiating his pay rate and working hours, Rick left just as Cynthia came in balancing two coffee cups, three magazines and a bag full of pastries in her arms.

"Oh, hi Rick. Did you dazzle Dana with your framing talents?"

"Hi, Cyn." He held the door open for her and looked at his feet before looking back at her. "Yeah, I've got the job."

"Excellent. Well, see ya then."

"Yeah, okay. Bye."

"He seems really shy," Dana said softly.

"Yeah, but in a cute sorta way." Cynthia unloaded the bags onto the counter. "Sorry it took me so long. Chuck didn't have it so I had to walk down to the liquor store to get it. Oh, here's your coffee."

"Thanks. What's in the bag?"

"Mrs. Hilson's finest."

Dana cringed remembering her last experience of Helen Hilson's finest. "Not her Sugar Bliss cookies?"

"No. Even better. Her chocolate-filled bagels."

Well, that was the magic word. Chocolate seemed odd in a bagel, but Dana didn't question it. She'd eat chocolate even if it were spread on a steak like meat sauce. "Gimme." She took a quick bite. "Oh, you're right. These are heaven." After a few bites she asked

"Cynthia, can I ask your advice on something."

"Oh, sure."

"Well, I...Oh, no. Never mind. It's stupid really."

"Go ahead—ask away."

Dana sipped at her coffee. "Maybe later. What else did you get?" She wanted some dating advice or even someone to back her up for canceling her date with Rome. *God, I'm such a chicken.*

Cynthia gave her a smirky grin, "Oh, a couple of Rag Mags aaand...hot off the presses—the latest issue of *Volupté."*

"I can't believe you actually bought it."

"Why not? It's a free country."

"Yeah, but..."

"You know, Dana—you need to loosen up a little. Don't be so terrified of what other people are going to think."

"I'm sure you're right. But I lived with my very conservative grandma. She'd never approve of such a thing. Twenty-five years of training is hard to break."

"Well let's break it...starting now." Cynthia said as she opened to page one of *Volupté.*

"I really should finish these mat samples."

"Yeah...I know...and I need to finish pricing the photo frames." Cynthia said lightly. "Come on, let's check it out."

"Well..." Dana began as she looked over Cynthia's shoulder, admitting to herself she was a little curious. She read some of the article titles: *A Complete Guide to the Female Erogenous Zones—Guaranteed to Make Her Cum. The Other Women—A Man's Guide to Balancing Multiple Partners Without Getting Caught. Top Ten Stroke-Videos of the Month. Her On Top-How to Release Your Shy Lady's Inhibitions.* "This just looks like the male version of Cosmo."

"I wish." Cynthia retorted. "You don't see too many totally naked hunks in Cosmo," she said as she flipped to the middle where a beautifully exotic dark-haired woman was pictured, naked and sensually accentuating her large breasts as her hands reached between her thighs, suggestively pleasuring herself.

"Mmm, if I was that gorgeous, I'd play with myself too."

"Cynthia!" Dana exclaimed—embarrassed by her employee's frankness.

"What? Here, let's go to the back and see if there's a picture of our mystery man. Aaa, here we go...Notes from the editor, blah, blah, blah, thanks to our photographers. Hey, they have female photographers on staff."

"Really?"

"Yeah, but no pictures. Bummer. Oh, well," she said as she thumbed through the rest of it. "Okay, let's see what else they've got in here. *Fun Favs and New Ways to the Yoga-Challenged Kamasutra Fans*, The Sensual Sidewinder, been there," she continued, "The Love Triangle, Sexy Scissors, Lap Mambo, done that—Ooo, here's one I've never tried..."

"Those can't be real Kamasutra names," Dana said.

Cynthia raised her eyebrow at that. "Here, take a look."

She faced the page to Dana, "I don't think I want to see..." she felt her face burn as she covered her eyes with her hands.

Cynthia shrugged then continued to read, "The Slow Back-slide. 'Have your partner lie on her stomach, her legs straight and slightly apart while you sit right behind her buttocks with your legs in front leaning back with hands braced on either side for support so you can join your penis with her vagina. Then rock back and forth for a smooth, slow ride.' What?"

"Is that actually possible? Let me see. Do they have an illustration?" Dana asked. Her curiosity beat out over embarrassment.

"I thought you weren't interested."

"I'm asking for purely...academic reasons."

"Right. Here. See for yourself. Agh, in fact just keep it. It might make me horny, which would be bad since I broke up with my boyfriend last month."

"Oh, I'm sorry. What happened? Never mind, it's none of my business."

"No, it's okay. I started taking the pill so we wouldn't have to use condoms, but then I found out he was cheating on me. At first I was just pissed. But then I got nervous—you know safe sex and all that...so I broke it off."

No. Dana didn't know. Not really. She took the magazine from her and felt the familiar twinge of meagerness again. The one that always crept up whenever she was faced with someone of her own age who'd actually experienced life while she had to stay home to care for her grandma. She couldn't completely blame her grandma, although some of her sheltering may have contributed to Dana's fear of trying new things. But she loved her grandma and after awhile, Dana became comfortable in her safe and predictable lifestyle. She had no idea how to move out of the self-made comfort zone she was living in.

But darn it—she should be able to have some fun too.

"Umm, can I keep this?" Dana asked, suddenly feeling a little empowered at the thought of taking something so provocative into her apartment.

"Sure," Cynthia laughed, "Knock yourself out. Just make sure you have plenty of batteries on hand."

Dana frowned. *What was that supposed to mean?* She wasn't going to ask—

because she probably wasn't ready to hear it...yet.

Chapter Five

"I KNOW SHE'S HERE. HER CAR IS PARKED out back."

Oh no. She heard the familiar, deeply sensual voice down stairs.

"Well, she's not. She just took a walk to the store."

Thank you, Cynthia.

Dana managed to sneak out the back door and make a mad dash down the street. After moving several blocks at a power-walking pace, she ducked into a trendy cigar shop equipped with a life-sized wooden Indian and an odor of nicotine that could kill a skunk before she caught sight of him. It was childish to hide, but she wasn't ready to face him. Not after she left him that ridiculous note.

In a desperate attempt to look inconspicuous, she grabbed a box... of anything from a shelf and Dana peered side to side like a common shoplifter before she glanced down at what she had in her hand.

"Buying a gift for someone?"

Dana gasped and found Rome towering over her. "Actually, I was thinking about taking up smoking."

"Humm, unwise. I hear it's bad for your health."

"Really?"

"Sir? Ma'am? May I help you with your selection?" A sales guy with a round belly and perfect posture approached them. He wore a white cotton leisure shirt and black pants. His short black hair looked like it was slicked back with a hand full of animal lard.

"No. The lady's just looking."

Dana skid past the pretentious Indian and out the door before Rome had a chance to invade her senses—again. She disappeared quickly into the sidewalk crowd before she sidestepped into another shop she'd never heard of.

"Welcome to The Monkey Shop. Can I interest you in a belly-button piercing," she heard someone say.

"Umm, no thanks," she said as she peeked out the display window. Good. He wasn't trailing her.

"How 'bout a nipple piercing. Get one done—the other is half price. Ten percent off nipple and belly-button rings."

"Huh?" Stunned, Dana turned to the kid behind the counter. He had spiky blonde hair, manicured eyebrows, and a sleeveless shirt revealing tattoo art that traveled up to his shoulder and down to his wrists. He couldn't have been more than twenty.

What kind of shop was this?

"Really? What if I want the whole enchilada?" Surprising herself at the bold question. Blend. Try to blend in.

"We can negotiate a price. We also have some new tattoo designs if you're interested."

"Not today, thanks. I'll just browse through your..." What else do they have in here? "...your ladies lingerie," she finally decided as she spotted Rome walking in her direction.

The guy shrugged and went back behind the counter to price some new bowling shirts with a very curvy female devil on the back.

The shop had several patrons of various ages and genders looking and buying. It amazed Dana how Los Angeles streets were always busy in the middle of a weekday.

She sifted through an assortment of black leathery things that looked like... bras? "Oh my." In the center where the supportive cup should be was...nothing. She quickly put it back. Just keep moving. Don't look conspicuous, she thought while she skimmed through an assortment of panties. Some were actually kind of cute with fluffy feather lining and silk ribbon for ties. She picked one up and realized they had no crotch. "Oh, well what's the point? They obviously can't be practical for... what the...edible panties? Why would anyone buy edible panties?" she whispered, "In case you're trapped in the desert with no food?"

"Do you think they carry those in root beer flavor? I don't care for strawberry."

She gasped then froze. Rome was so close behind her she could smell the intoxicating scent of his cologne.

"Umm, sorry." She cleared her throat. "Just ssstrawberry." She put it back before squaring her shoulders to face him. "Rome, why are you following me?"

"Why are you running away from me?"

"I'm not. I'm...shopping."

His left eyebrow rose as he held out his hand. "Here. You dropped your wallet back there."

"Oh. Uhh, thanks." Suddenly she felt one inch tall.

"I hope I didn't scare you?"

"No. Of course not."

"You broke our date."

He sounded more amused then hurt.

"Yeah. I..." what could she tell him? "Sorry, I'm...just not attracted to you," she teased, shrugging her shoulder.

"Uh huh." He made a small step toward her. She took one back.

Her gave her an amused smile and took another step. She took another back. An uncomfortable giggle escaped her throat. She could play this game.

Suddenly her back was against a rack of silver-studded teddies and spandex thongs. Oops. Nerves mixed with humor and insensible mischief had her blood pumping wildly through her body as the cool steel of the rack touched the backs of her arms.

"So, you find me unattractive, huh?" His features hardened in mock anger but the underlying sensuality of his voice captivated her. His gaze was as hard as his body as it molded against hers. Her heart pounded against her ribcage as her breath caught in her throat.

"Grotesque..." She had nowhere to go but suddenly felt decadent with her back against the naughty nighties and a sinfully sexy man sending her an unspoken challenge. "Hunchback of Notre Dame ugly," she added.

"I'll be willing to bet I can make you forget my appalling distasteful appearance with my charm and quick wit," he whispered, his lips a hairs breath away from hers as he grasped her wrists and held them against the display rack.

"Rome...please," she laughed nervously, a little fearful of the twinkle in his eyes. "I never bet my hard earned money against a lost cause."

"Nether do I," he said as his mouth covered hers with a hungry urgency. This wasn't the quick kiss like before. This one was a hard, punishing kiss that demanded a response. His moist, firm mouth forcing her lips open with a quick thrust of his tongue. Mindless of on-lookers, Dana succumbed to the forceful domination of his lips. His tongue. She felt a purr roll down her throat, surprised at her own eager response.

"You want this, don't you Dana?" Rome whispered in a mock severity with a trace of mirth in his voice, "Despite my hideousness." He looked at her with a hurt expression as he batted his eyes lashes, teasing her again. "Oh, please say yes," he pouted.

"Yes. Oh, yes...you're... repulsive." Dana felt the familiar tension in her stomach ease and wrapped her arms around his neck, pulling him back down as she returned his kiss with savage intensity, rousing his passion along with her own. She felt his erection press against the fly of his jeans as it pulsed against her belly and felt a panic swell in her chest. She squelched it down as the smell of leather mingled with the musky scent of Rome's skin tickled her nose. For once she wanted to fight her instinct to run.

Rome lifted his head and gave her a sly smile that sent her pulse racing double-time. "Good."

She heard a few hoots and whistles from behind her, but felt too light-headed to care.

"'til seven tonight, then?"

She growled at him when he straightened and turned to leave. She followed him out the door.

"Rome, wait!" He may have simply meant to tease her senseless, but apprehension returned to her like a slap in the face. She really couldn't sit in a restaurant all night wondering what Rome really thought of her normal, boring self. Her anxiety level was too high.

He stopped and arched one brow as he looked at her.

"I really can't go out with you tonight."

"Is there someone else?"

"No, nothing like that. It's just...it's me. Okay?"

He ran a hand over his face. "All right then." His features softened and he reached up and ran his thumb across her bottom lip. "Would you at least consider stopping by The Lava Lounge Saturday night?"

She bit her lip, remembering the one and only night she'd patronized the place.

"My cousin and I and a couple other guys get together a few times a month and jam."

She nodded. "Guitar, right?"

"Yep." He gave her a brilliant smile. "Blues mostly. I'd really like it if you'd stop by."

"Oh. Okay. I'll think about it."

"Great." He kissed her lightly and walked away. Still favoring his right leg, he left her standing there in the doorway with ten tattooed yahoo on-lookers and the guy who wanted to pierce her nipples.

"Eww.." She shook off her willies.

But her mouth was still burning from Rome's lips.

*****

"...Yeah, baby. Oh, yeah. Who's your daddy? Who is your daddy, mama? Come on. Come on. Oh, yes—do it! Mmmm..."

"What the hell?" Rome walked into his apartment and heard his brother yelling out in an orgasmic frenzy. "Tony, what the hell are you doing in my apartment?"

"Oh, hey, Rome." Tony looked up from the TV rather embarrassed, before he hit the mute button on the remote.

"What are you watching?"

"Nothin'."

Rome glanced at the TV screen and shook his head when he realized Tony was watching a fitness program. "You came all the way over to my place to watch Kathy Jones' boobs bounce? I'd think you'd get your fill at the office."

Tony turned off the set.

"Yes. No. I mean... your assistant, Kimberly, called me when you did your disappearing act. Apparently you had a heavy schedule of clients and left her in a bind."

He ran a hand through his hair and scratched his head uncomfortably. "Yeah, I did."

"Ya know—this isn't like you, Rome," Tony laughed. "I thought I was the irresponsible one. Anyway, she had to go to class, so I came by to help out."

"What about your schedule?"

"Didn't have one. Unless you count the breakfast meeting I had with the Perry triplets. Hoo, what a rush. Wasn't sure which set to lay my eye balls on."

"Oh, please."

"So, how's it going with Miss Art Shop?"

Rome fell silent as he looked woefully at his brother.

"Shit, don't tell me."

Rome nodded as he rubbed at his temples and closed his eyes. "She cancelled our date."

"Geez, Rome. I never knew you were so lousy with the ladies."

"Hey, I'm not...usually." Just the one that counts.

"Did you take her the plant like I suggested?"

"Yeah, I did. She seemed to go for it, too. I don't get it. The only thing I figured is she's running scared because she found out about Dad."

"Would you lay off that crap already? I've been hearing that shit from you for years. Look, man, if a woman wants you—I mean really wants you, it won't matter if your father is the Marquis de Sade. She'll be so hot for you she won't be able to help herself."

Rome frowned.

"Trust me on this."

"Tony, I don't think she's had much experience with men." Deep down, Rome hoped she hadn't.

"All the better, then. She doesn't know the low-down."

Rome snorted. "I've never heard anything so ridiculous..."

"Laugh if you want, but my methods are fail-proof."

"This isn't a game. This is a woman's heart and mind we're talking about."

"Look—what I know comes from experience, okay?"

Rome was still skeptical. "She's not your 'Miss July', easily pursued by smooth talkin—let's romp in the back of a limo kind of woman. I think this situation is beyond even your experience, bro."

Tony smiled. "So when do I get to meet her?"

Rome sighed. "Saturday. I've invited her to the lounge. Assuming you show up."

"Oh, I'll be there. I'm dying to meet the woman who's got my brother in a quandary."

*****

Dana suppressed a sigh and went back to her mat cutting designs, wishing she hadn't eaten that third chocolate chip cookie. She wanted to make some special mat designs that customers could choose from besides the boring rectangular windows to go around a picture. Anything to keep from dwelling on Rome and his limping leg and the way it fit so perfectly in his jeans as it flexed against the fabric.

"Stop it!"

Dana distracted herself by gazing out the front window watching Mrs. Hilson chase a cat out of her bakery. Dana laughed when she saw the cat get away with a glazed donut twist, happily trotting from the scene of the crime.

She sighed, still toying with the idea of going to *The Lava Lounge* tonight. *Geez, Louise.* She wasn't sure she could show her face in that dive ever again. But it was fool-hearty to even toy with the idea of going again. It would be like trying to be someone else—someone trying to fit in—someone she wasn't. Dana didn't know how to be that person. That one night she tried should have been enough to prove it to herself she wasn't cut out for slutdom. Unless...

She looked at Cynthia now taking another bite of cookie. "You know, Mrs. Hilson might be one slice short of a full loaf, but she sure makes damn good chocolate chip cookies." She took another bite.

"Cynthia?"

"Huh?"

"Remember I said I had a question to ask you?"

"Yeah. Go ahead—shoot."

"Well, let's just say—hypothetically, of course..."

"Of course." Cynthia laughed.

"Let's say someone you liked, maybe even...admired but didn't want to give them the wrong impression...and this person invited you somewhere—not as a date but just to...oh, I don't know...hang out, I guess, in a club type environment. How would you approach this situation?"

"Let me guess. Some hunky stud is interested in you and you're scared to death if you show up at this, whatever it is, he'll get the wrong idea and think you want to do the horizontal boogie."

Dana cheeks suddenly felt hot.

"Aha, I knew it!" she yelled as she shot her fist in the air. "This calls for a major wardrobe change."

"Cynthia, I don't have the money for that." But she had a point.

"I'm not talking purchase here. I'm talking trade. We're about the same height. You're a bit more curvy then me, but I think I can work with that. Add a little mascara, a bit of luscious lip-gloss... agh, and *take your hair out of that clip*. We'll add a little mousse and sex it up and mister hunky stud won't know what hit him."

"I don't want to 'hit him'."

"Don't worry. C'mon. Let's get started."

Chapter Six

OH, BOY.

This was stupid—really, *really* stupid to come here again, Dana thought walking into *The Lava Lounge*. Again. What was she thinking? Plus, she couldn't believe she actually let Cynthia dress her. She looked like she was ready for the Amazon jungle. *And this leather...agh.* This was worse than Leo's drag queen attire. The pants kept riding up in places they shouldn't and the ridiculous blouse constantly fell off her shoulders.

A nice navy pantsuit would've been just fine.

But all thoughts, all her anxieties faded when she walked in and found *him* staring at her. Not like before. Not that hard edge she remembered on their one very forgettable night together. This time is was more predatory—watching her like a sleek black panther in his black jeans and long-sleeved black T-shirt, just waiting to strike. The problem was she didn't think she'd mind if he did, and that troubled her immensely. It left her feeling vulnerable—well, more than normal.

Luckily, the crowd was moderate, otherwise she'd be elbowing people, and sharing table space.

It was dark inside and the aroma of beer on tap hung in the air and smelled of a fraternity house—not that she's ever been in a fraternity house. Gratefully, smoking wasn't allowed in the lounge, otherwise she'd be paying Cynthia for an expensive dry cleaning job.

Across the room, flirting with a pretty Asian woman was Rome's potty-mouth brother. He stood near the bandstand platform, searching the room and caught her staring. He smirked, then whispered something to his date then walked to the bar. The blonde triplets were there too, each hanging on a different attractive man, swaying to the music while the band took a break.

"Dana, you came." Rome's silky-rich voice made her all melty inside, like the chocolate filling from her morning bagel. She wanted to moan, but instead found herself returning his infectious smile.

*****

Finally, she came.

Nearly midnight, his band was on a break and Rome gulped down his third glass of ice water. That's when he saw her—and nearly dropped his glass.

God, she so looked radiant.

Dana stood there, looking at him, watching with him approach with those otherworldly eyes—beautiful eyes that mesmerized as Rome crossed the lounge to her.

"Hi," he said, smiling, feeling like and idiot for lack of words. "I'm glad you made it." Down right Giddy, actually. How did she do this to him? He couldn't remember the last time he felt this stupefied over a woman.

"I almost didn't," she said, shyly looking down at her shoes with the sweetest pink in her cheeks. "This isn't my scene, really."

He laughed and took her hand. "You look...great."

Her blush deepened.

Man, oh, man—how cute she was.

"Thanks. You look nice, too," she said, then sucked in her bottom lip.

Double cute.

"Come on. I'd like you to meet the guys."

Gone was the demurely dressed shop owner. In her place was a subtle seductress—sultry yet earthy. Her hair was down, long and flowing in delicate blonde strands across her shoulders and back. She was wearing a silky, tiger print, peasant-like blouse that fell softly off one shoulder and tied at the front. *Just right for a man's fingers to untie*, he thought.

Damn. His felt his cock stir at the thought and cursed himself as he continued watching her. Observing her. The way her legs looked perfect in the tight tan-leather pants. They emphasized the curve of her hips and luscious bottom. Her long beaded earrings accentuated her soft, sexy neck as he imagined kissing it up to her delicate earlobe and back down, then in between that loose tie at her cleavage...

Aah, Hell. Rome wanted to kick his own ass for that one lousy night they had together. Christ, he'd have thought he was a lousy lay if he were in her shoes—and he could only remember the good parts.

He needed another chance.

He wanted another chance. More than one chance.

Rome's eyes explored at their leisure before she caught him red-handed—staring at her like a horny teenager. All she had to do was walk into the room and breathe. She made him forget himself.

His father was the contributing factor for his lack of long-term relationships. His longest relationship was with a girl in college, which didn't really count, since their relationship was based purely on lust.

He'd made an art form out of "not to get involved." Oh, he'd had plenty of women willing to steam up his sexy life, but Rome had an innate fear of intimacy refusing to go through one failed marriage after another, like dear ol' Dad.

But as this strange surge of affection for Dana bombarded his brain, a familiar flicker of apprehension clenched at his gut. He wanted to protect her, even if her desperate need for independence made her withdraw from his protection. Even if it went against his own self-preservation. But his conscience continued to needle him. It wasn't entirely his feelings of male possessiveness—he had a family obligation to fulfill.

Dana fiddled with the bow at her cleavage, watching him warily through long auburn lashes.

A warning voice in his head, sounding oddly like his father's, aroused old fears and uncertainties he'd felt since childhood. Reservations formed from years of distrust that chilled his heart, remembering with vivid recollection the sparkle in his mother's eyes extinguished from his father's repeated affairs and broken promises. Years later, he watched that same sparkle of affection dim in his step-mom's eyes.

These old feelings at odds with his need for Dana. To hold her close and wake up in the morning with those sparkling eyes looking up at him—not to mention those luscious curves. He inhaled the light fragrance of her hair and his heart softened. Rome never had to fight these strange and confounding emotions before. Unfortunately, they paled in comparison to the years of emotional abandonment, and the aftermath of his father's weakness for the opposite sex.

Rome swore he'd never give in to disloyalty because his dick was thinking instead of his head, breaking his obligation to family—or the women who loved him, a love his dad so obviously didn't deserve. Deceiving the ones his father should have been protecting instead of hurting.

Was he fighting his inherited nature, fighting against fate? Was he inevitably destined to repeat history as his father had? Leaving behind tears and half-kept promises?

Rome turned to look at her again and wished like hell he wasn't his father's son. He'd marry her one way or another and he'd prefer to progress the old-fashioned way— attraction followed by desire and whatever else people normally did before they got hitched—

his father's example notwithstanding.

But time was against him. Rome had a few short weeks to woo her with the DeMitri charm. He'd have to go for instant and careful seduction. The thought cheered him into a wicked grin that had nothing to do with the straining bulge at his pants zipper.

Well, maybe a little.

He released her warm hand as he placed his own at the small of her back, guiding her to the bar. He gazed at her face while she searched the room before her eyes met his again. For a heartbeat, their eyes locked for a long sensuous moment—he offered a quick, lazy smile. She smiled back and his heart kicked up a beat—as did his jeans.

Down boy.

*****

Dana felt awkward walking, her feet slipped and sloshed in the tan boots Cynthia lent her. They were a size and a half too big, but Cynthia insisted they'd set off the outfit perfectly. *Yeah. Perfect.* As long as she was sitting down or standing on her head. But not for trailing behind a hunk whose pace was twice her own.

Dana smiled self-consciously as Rome introduced her to his friend and band members. The hissing steam behind the bar trailed around their heads like a bog—an eerie glow hovering above the bar—swirling like smoke signals.

"...and this is Brandon, my cousin and our lead singer."

"Hi, Dana. Just call me Echo."

"Why Echo?"

"Because everyone else does." His warm smile so much like his cousin's, Dana nearly gasped.

Rome introduced his bass player with the brilliant smile and their drummer who efficiently twirled a drumstick in his left hand while shaking her right.

"So you're Dana," a husky voice said from behind her.

She turned and found herself looking up at mister playboy himself—Cynthia's mystery man, who was no mystery to Dana.

"Ah, yes. Hello again."

He took her hand and kissed it like an English gentleman. She heard Rome clear his throat.

"Dana," Rome continued, "I believe you've already met my brother, Antony."

"We were never formally introduce, were we, cupcake? And call me Tony."

He winked and Dana felt her cheeks warm.

She saw Rome jab his brother in the ribs and glared nose-to-nose with him.

"What?" Tony asked.

Rome turned away and addressed his band mates.

"Okay guys, break's over. Let's get started."

She laughed as they all moaned and groaned about finishing their beers and hopped off their respective bar stools.

"Oh, Rome?" Dana asked.

"Yes?"

"Umm, what's your band's name?"

He kissed her lightly on the mouth then said, "Checkered Blues."

She smiled. "I like that."

Dana watched Rome step onto the elevated platform, his limp noticeably better tonight.

She found an empty chair and table near the back wall.

As the guys reassembled, Dana realized Brandon, or rather Echo, though dark skinned with long black hair, his build was nearly identical to his handsome cousin.

As the band finished their third piece and started their fourth, Dana tried like heck to keep her gaze from slipping back to Rome's handsome face and gorgeous dark eyes. Tough to do since he was systematically seducing her with those eyes, and her anxiety level hiked up a notch.

Trying to concentrate on the music instead of her ultra-sexy neighbor, Dana finished her club soda and pulled discretely at the seat of her pants. *Agh!* They were starting to itch. Then closed her eyes to relax her nerves while she listened.

She typically didn't like jazz. She preferred classical music. But the sound had a nice beat, repeating in a smooth four-by-four rhythm typical to traditional blues. But this song had a unique blend of melancholy sounds and a lyrical melody as the guitar strings vibrated and pulsed into her body. Rome's fingers bent and strummed the cords into an emotionally stirring vibrato. It felt as though each stroke of his fingers against the strings of his guitar was a stroke against her body as he strummed her to a new heightened awareness.

She felt a sigh, or was it a moan? slip from her lips, and when she opened her eyes.

Rome was watching her. Not with his usual knowing smirk, but an intense, heated expression that even her inexperience could understand.

Rome wanted her. It was exhilarating, which was odd considering her humiliation the night they made love. No—they hadn't made love. They attempted to have sex.

She laughed to herself. Wasn't the man supposed to fall asleep *after* they had sex? Somehow, Dana didn't care about what happened before. Rome wanted her now. Everyone deserved a second chance—didn't they?

The crowded around her table got larger and louder and the tables were filling up until Dana's table was the only one with an empty chair.

"Hi, do you mind if I sit here?"

It was one of the pretty blonde triplets.

"Umm, sure."

"Thanks. This place gets pretty crazy around midnight. It's tough finding a seat," she said. "I'm Victoria Perry, by the way. My sisters and I..." she pointed toward two identical beauties at the bar, "...Elizabeth and Grace, we come here all the time."

"Nice to meet you, I'm Dana Baker." She suddenly felt bland and inadequate in comparison to her new tablemate. "So, you come here a lot?"

"Oh yeah! Those DeMitri boys...whhooh!"

Dana stared blankly as Victoria fanned herself.

"What about them?" she asked, frowning into her club soda.

"Oh, ya know...gorgeous, charming, great in the sack..." She sounded breathless.

"Really?"

"Uh, well—I've heard." Victoria shrugged. "In fact, I've heard those guys, including their yummy cousin, has slept with every single woman in Los Angeles County under the age of forty." She giggled. "They may have to branch out into Orange County." She laughed again, then stood and said, "Oh, look. There's Tony. See you later, Dana."

Dana felt the blood drain from her face, feeling like a naïve fool. If Rome wanted her for just another notch on his proverbial bedpost, he'd have to find some other ditz to warm his sheets. But she was one—so maybe she deserved at least *half* a notch in his bedpost.

"Hey, honey, you're new here. Can I buy you a beer?"

Dana looked up at the half drunk middle-aged man in a wrinkled dress shirt and an ugly loosened tie staring down at her. Actually, he was looking down her blouse. She suddenly felt dirty and alone. "No! Umm, I'm here with friend."

Geez, Louise, she should make a run for the door.

*****

It wasn't just her looks, Rome thought, watching Dana from the stage, it was her graciousness and sweet persona. Endearing herself to him as she awkwardly tried to fit into to her unfamiliar surroundings. It was refreshing to be with a woman who was so unassuming.

Unpretentious. That had to be the word to describe Dana. He counted himself lucky—because it had to be pure luck that made her walk into the lounge that. Lord, how he'd wanted her that night... and how he wanted now.

Rome was grateful his guitar blocked the audience's view of his crotch as it pulsed against the vibrating wood of his instrument.

The song ended. And not a second too soon.

The same drunken jerk-off who slobbered all over women regularly in the lounge, started hitting on Dana. The asshole was leering down her blouse while trying to grab for her ass.

"Goddamn it." Rome handed his guitar to Echo before he jumped over two chairs and sprinted for the jerk.

"Hey, man. Where ya going?" He heard Echo yell, but Rome was already pounding his fists into the jerk-off's face.

The guy squealed like a roped pig as Rome kicked him in the groin.

"Aww, what I do, man? The bitch your wife or somethin'?"

That earned the bastard another punch in the eye socket.

"Ahh," was all he said as he fell to the floor holding his face with one hand and his balls in the other.

"Now get up and take your sorry ass out of here."

Rome shook off his throbbing knuckles as the man staggered out the door. "You okay?" he asked Dana.

She nodded, open-mouth as she looked up at him, then before he could say my bed or yours? Dana leaped from her chair and started toward the door.

Rome went after her.

His aching right leg hindering his strides, but he found her in the parking lot.

"Dana. Wait!"

He caught up just in time for her to slam her car door shut. He grabbed for it before it munched his fingers.

Dana wouldn't look at him as he held the door open.

"I'm not stepping foot in there again."

"You're running away," he said. "Don't let that drunken fool ruin your evening."

"I'm going home."

"Then I'm going with you?"

"Um...I don't..."

"I just want to make sure you get home safely. Okay?"

She looked skeptical.

"You'd be doing me a favor." He gestured toward the lounge. "I came with the guys tonight." He sigh then said, "I'm a little tired, and they'll probably hang out 'til the beer's gone. What do you say?"

"Okay. Sure."

"Great," he said as he ran to the other side, opened the door and slid into the seat.

He could hear several guys belching like croaking toads and debating the bra size of Pamela Anderson before he shut the car door. His long legs barely fit inside her little blue Honda. He felt a twinge in his leg and had to tug in his right thigh with his hands, groaning more out of habit than actual pain.

"You okay?" she asked.

"Yeah. Just an old problem that comes back to haunt me once in a while."

Dana nodded and silently drove out of the parking lot. She remained quiet for most of the drive.

"How'd you like the band? Great group of guys, huh?"

"Yes. They're all very talented."

"Sorry about my brother, though. He tends to come off a little heavy-handed when it comes to pretty women."

"He wasn't that bad," she frowned slightly. "I can't say the same for that other man... Is your hand okay?"

He flexed his fists. "Yeah, it's fine."

Dana shook her head as they drove passed the escalator domes of The Beverly Center. "I don't understand all the fuss. I'm not well endowed like Victoria and her sisters. I'm not even that pretty. Plain, short, bland, boring. But not pretty."

Rome felt his neck heat up and his nose flare.

"And you—," she gave him a sharp look before her eyes were back on the road. He knew what was coming. "You never even looked at me that night until Tony spiked your—"

"Stop it right now." His spaced his words long and evenly. He could tell his anger surprised her. Rome hadn't meant for it to come out so harshly. She'd just pissed him off. "Don't put yourself down, Dana," he said, clenching and unclenching his fists again and turned to look at her. "That night was a mistake, entirely my fault. I was too chicken-shit to even approach you until..." He pointed his finger at her then caught himself and made a fist. He sighed, then lightly grazed a finger along her jawbone and said, "It should have never happened. You deserve better then that. Shit, I can't even remember half of what happen or...didn't happen." He pulled back his hand and raked it through his hair. "And I wish I could take it back. You're a sweet, compassionate, and desirable woman—"

"No, you don't have to say that. I mean, you still can't possibly be interested in me." Dana shrugged her shoulder. "Plus, I'm not one to take a quick romp in the sheets—recent history notwithstanding," she muttered the last part. "And I'm not—"

Rome ran a hand hard over his face, before blind fury took over. "Pull over."

"What?"

"I said—*pull over!*"

As soon as she had the car in park he unbuckled her seatbelt and pulled her to him until her face was level with his. He saw fear flicker in her eyes but he didn't care.

"Listen. The first time I saw you I thought you were an angel or an apparition, appearing before my eyes that night."

He noticed her face relax slightly.

"And tonight. My God—"

"I know. It's this stupid outfit," she whispered. He still hadn't let go.

"You look sexy as hell in *this* outfit. And what you do to me—"

He watched as her pupils dilated as the cute blush came back to her cheeks. There was no denying it—she wanted him too.

"In case there's any doubt in your mind—"

"Rome...mmm—"

His mouth fell hard against hers with an urgency he could no longer control. He wanted to finesse and coax her. But his body flared with an intense heat mixed with anger that nearly choked him. He took her sweet mouth hard and deep, forcing her to endure his punishing, convincing kisses as he roused her passions, his own growing stronger. He groaned when she responded with an intensity that equaled his own.

"Dana..." he panted against her neck as he held her shaking body. He grasped her hand in his. "Oh, sweetheart, what you do to me," he said as he pulled her palm to the painful erection pulsing at the fly of his jeans. "I've been like this all night."

"Really?" Her voice quivered, but she didn't pull back.

He didn't care if his behavior shocked her. She *was* desirable. He wanted to drive that fact straight home.

"Mmm... really." He moaned as her innocently curious hand cupped him gently. Exploring. "But if you don't stop that, I'll have to take you right here in the car."

"Oh!" Dana pulled back her hand. "Sorry," she said as she looking down at the effect she had on him.

"It's okay. Nothing a cold shower can't handle." He chuckled at her wide-eyed response. "Now take us home before I make an even bigger fool of myself."

"Okay." Her laugh was a little jittery, but a big improvement from her self-deprecating nonsense.

He touched the corners of her mouth where a smile appeared. "That's much better."

She pulled back on to Third Street.

"You won't tell me you're undesirable again. Agreed?"

She nodded. "Agreed."

"I'd really like to take you to dinner. You backed out the last time."

"I know, but—" She sighed, concentrating on the road. "All right, Rome but—"

"Great! How about tomorrow evening?"

She looked at him briefly and smiled. "That sounds really nice. But not tomorrow." She made a turn onto Greenrich. "Evening after next?"

"You drive a hard bargain, sweetheart." He smiled, then held her hand for the rest of the way home. He told himself it was to reassure Dana, but he simply liked the feel of her skin against his own.

"Here we are," she said. "Do you mind if I park around back?"

"Uh, no. Wherever. Thanks for the lift."

"Sure. Hey, what was all that banging noise I heard at your place last night?" she asked.

"Come in and see for yourself."

She bit her bottom lip as she looked up at him. "I don't...it's kind of late."

"Come on. It'll just take a minute. Besides, it's easier to just show you. I promise not to take my hands out of my pockets...much."

She pursed her lips. "All right."

Yes. Rome hoped it would take much, much longer than a minute.

Chapter Seven

"MY GOSH, ROME, WHAT HAVE you done?" Dana slipped through his studio back door. She could see the changes just from the streetlights filtering through the windows.

"Come in and have a look." He took her hand and led her into the reception area. The studio filled with soft white light when he flicked on the light switch.

"Oh, it's wonderful."

"I'm glad you like it. It's cost me a few aches and pains around the edges."

Dana noticed he unconsciously rubbed at his leg as he spoke.

She let go of his hand to look around. The walls were still in their original bright white with black floor and ceiling moldings, but Rome added enlargements of striking black and white photos that softened the contrasts of the walls. Boldly painted on the dividing wall between the studio and the reception area was Rome's studio name: *Memories by Romano— Photo Studio*. The logo had a light box above, and viewable from outside even at night, negating the need for a marquee outside.

A massive oak desk painted in soft charcoal held a computer monitor and several catalogs while chairs with matching charcoal fabric lined the front and side of the walls.

"These are spectacular. Are they yours?"

"Yep. Most of them I took when I was still in college."

"This picture here—it looks like a pyramid. But not Egyptian?"

"No. That was taken in Central America. It's a Mayan pyramid. I was on a field study with my classmates at the time."

"What is this? It looks like a sculpture."

"It's thought to be a depiction of the Mayans' sacred bird, the Quetzal."

"I guess I never paid much attention in my art history class," Dana laughed. "I don't remember any Mayan history."

He kissed her then. A soft warm brush against her mouth as he continued to speak. "The physics of the step-like pyramid creates an echo-like sound from a simple handclap and causes a vibration or an echo that sounds just like a Quetzal bird." He left her lips as he nibbled down her neck, sending a swirl of heat all the way down her legs. "The locals say..." he continued up her neck and to her earlobe, "...that the pyramid speaks in the echo-voice of the Quetzal."

"Really? Was your cousin on this trip by any chance?" She smiled lazily and looked into her eyes.

His mouth moved from her neck and down to her exposed shoulder. "No, actually Echo and his family went there years before." His lips left her shoulder tingling when he stopped to look at the photo. Blindly taking her hand and kissing her knuckles. "His mom said Echo was so mesmerized by the sounds that he tried to emulate it." He shrugged, "We've been calling him Echo ever since." Rome rubbed her palm against his roughened cheek. "I'm taking an archeological tour to Central America... uh... soon."

Fascinated, she wanted to ask him more, but he kissed and licked at the inside of her palm and she forgot all her questions.

He let go of her hand and gave her a cocky grin. "I'm parched. You want something to drink?"

"Ice water?"

"You got it."

Dana took a deep breath to collect her turbulent thoughts. Rome upset her balance on so many levels. Her feelings for him were intensifying—his touch, his presence, everything about him threatened her peace of mind and created a storm of unfamiliar emotions she couldn't tame.

Hoping to distract herself, she looked around to discover something of this man that could curl her toes with a heated glance. She passed more black and white photos to where several portrait enlargements were hanging. Some were of families as big as twelve, others of hopeful couples, another was a beautiful women, glowingly pregnant. All happy people, she thought. Happy families.

Perhaps he took pictures of families to make up for the lack of one in his own life.

Dana tried to ignore the sudden ache in her chest, and moved on to another picture far different than any of the others.

This one was a soft-focused color photo of a little Hispanic girl, probably seven or eight years old, with a delicate oval face, dark features and a pouty rose-kissed mouth shyly turned up at the corners. Two dark braids hung gracefully over the girl's small shoulders as she cradled a squalling gray kitten against her cheek.

Staring into the little girl's beautiful wide eyes, Dana wondered if her faraway look was the same expression found on Dana's own face as a child, dreaming of faraway fairylands.

She couldn't suppress her admiration for Rome's work. There was a deeper significance to these images than just the visual display on the walls, revealing more about the photographer that inspired them, than the people themselves. Dana felt as a warm glow spread threw her as she fell a tiny bit in love with the man who could inspire these captured moments in time.

He wasn't simply taking beautiful photographs. Rome's passion was in finding beauty where others overlooked it.

"Her name is Lupe." Rome held out a glass of water to her. "She lives in Mexico City with her family."

"She beautiful, Rome."

"I thought so." He placed a guiding hand at the back. "Now, come back here with me. This should answer your earlier question."

She followed him to the back and saw discarded chairs and sinks wedged in a corner.

"I had a bitch of a time taking these things down."

"Oh, from the old salon?"

"Uh huh."

"Now I know what all that noise was that kept me up the past few nights. You removed all these things yourself?"

Rome raked a hand through his hair and rubbed at the back of his neck.

"Yeah." He sighed. "Sorry about the noise. Couldn't do it during business hours."

She nodded. "What're you going do with them?"

"Haven't decided yet. There's a beauty school down the street. Thought I'd donate them, you know, take a tax write-off or something."

"Do me a favor? Before you do that, let me know first. I might think of a use for them."

Rome raised his brows.

She shrugged. "I like to paint furniture n' things."

"Okay, sure," he said, grinning at her.

Oh, boy. That devastating smile was back.

Rome fell back into one of the chairs and it wobbled from its foundation since it wasn't securely bolted to the floor. He purposely tripped her when she turned away.

"Aaah, Rome! What are you doing?" she yelped as she fell hard onto his lap. He groaned when she fell hard onto his sore leg.

"Oow," he said through his teeth.

"Sorry. You okay?"

"I'm... fine," she heard pain in his voice.

"Well, serves you righ—"

He didn't let her finish as his mouth covered hers hungrily. His large hands held her face gently as his tongue explored the recesses of her mouth.

Dana put her arms around his neck, giving herself freely as his tongue continued to search for hers. She answered his plea, tentatively. Gently touching, creating a search of her own. He moaned as her tongue boldly dove for his, leaving her with an exhilarating sense of sensual power.

"Dana," he whispered as he raised his lips from hers, gazing into her eyes.

Her breathing labored as she pulled him back down, recapturing his lips to her own. His hands fell from her face and down to her ribs and back, pulling her closer to him. Holding her before reaching up to caress the hollow base of her throat. The heat of his fingers against her skin had her body vibrating with an unfamiliar need.

His lips left hers again, trailing light kisses down her neck and shoulder. The light fabric of her blouse fell away when he quickly untied the front, revealing the lace of her strapless bra. The skin on her chest and shoulders felt exposed as a chill from the cool salon air reach her.

She gasped as he lightly traced one nipple through the thin lace with his finger. His lips left feather-light kisses down her throat and chest trailing down to the soft skin of her breasts just above the lace bra. A strong sense of urgency drove her as she felt an eager affection, not sexual, coming from him as he lovingly caressed her.

His tongue traced the fabric, up and around until it came across to the other side, searing a path of heat and desire.

He lifted his head, looked into her desire-filled eyes. Every gaze, every caress had her heart turning over in a heated response mixed with newly discovered admiration.

He watched her, photographing her with his eyes and Dana wondered what he saw when he looked at her. He brought his lips to hers, a caress more than a kiss as his hand swooped down under the cup of her bra and captured one nipple between his fingers.

"Aah." An uncontrolled cry escaped from her throat as his fingers continued their magic. Rolling back and forth, sending electrical currents down between her thighs. He bent his head, his lips replaced his fingers, suckling, lightly grazing with his teeth.

The sharp sensation had Dana holding his head hard against her chest, afraid the feeling might disappear. She felt a sigh of relief and regret when his mouth left one breast then quickly worked at the other. Cupping it with his hand, raising it up to savor it with his mouth. Had it been with any other man, she'd have demanded a halt to the intrusion. With Rome, she felt safe. Protected. Cherished.

His hand skimmed down her belly to cup gently against the heat between her thighs. The leather was no barrier to the scorching caress of his hand.

His mouth left her breast as he looked back into her eyes as his fingers unfastened the button and zipper of her pants. She was panting with fear and anticipation as his hand slid down into her panties, then between the slick folds of sensitive skin.

"Oh, God..." she screamed as her head fell back. Rome sunk one finger into her wet heat, then pulled back using her own wetness to stimulate her sensitive clitoris that pulsed against his hand.

"Yes, sweetheart. Go ahead..."

"Rome...I never...," she was gasping for air as he fondled and teased. His fingers were searching and stroking, exploring her soft flesh—leaving her senseless.

"Tell me. Tell me you want me to touch you."

"Yes. Oh, yes."

Her breath caught in her throat as he inserted two fingers into her, stretching her tight entrance wide while his thumb rubbed deliciously at the swollen nub of flesh. Shocked and delighted by her body's response, squirming beneath his hand as she rose to a level of ecstasy that cried for release.

His fingers stroked and probed sending jolts of pleasure through her. The pleasure was pure and explosive. "Rome!"

"Yes, Dana...come for me, honey. That's it. God, you're so beautiful."

She sucked in her lips, holding back the scream that wanted to let loose from her mouth.

She heard his tormented groan, fully aware of his erection bucking against her bottom. But she was suddenly powerless as the involuntary tremors of her orgasm began. Her breath came in long, surrendering moans as she rode wave after wave of sensation.

Rome's hand stopped its torturing caress and he withdrew his fingers from within her body, holding her while the shaking tremors stopped. He kissed her forehead, then her nose, Silently telling her it was all right. Dana felt him ease her bra back into place and her shirt back onto her shoulders as she caught her breath.

"That was the... most amazing thing to see." Rome's hoarse voice brought her back to the present and out of the sex-filled haze of release.

"Oh, God... what have I... what did you do to me?" Shocked by her own behavior, Dana leaped from Rome's lap and quickly re-fastened her pants. "I...umm... I have to go... I shouldn't have... I have to go."

"Dana? Dana, stop!" he called out as she ran through the back door.

She heard the yearning in his voice but was too mortified by what she'd allowed him to do. She couldn't stop the impulse to run back to the safety of her apartment.

She heard him following her. "Dana..."

Grateful her keys were in her pocket, she got to her door in time to close it before he caught up with her.

He banged frantically on her apartment door. "Dana, honey. Would you please stop running away? Please, Dana. Come out."

"Go away Rome, please."

"I'm not leaving things like this," he yelled through the door.

"Please go, Rome."

"Goddamn it, Dana..."

"Go... Don't do this, Rome."

"All right, I'll go. But this isn't the last of it."

She heard the door to his apartment open and close before she breathed a sigh of relief.

Until she realized she'd left her purse in his studio.

*****

Defeated—again.

Rome leaned his forehead against Dana's apartment door for several minutes before leaving to his own lonely apartment. *Two step forward, three steps back. Damn it!*

Why was she so frightened of her own desires and his desire for her?

He knew she wanted him. He could tell by the way her cheeks flushed and her eyes softened when he was with her.

Her reaction tonight was proof of what he'd expected. Deep down, Dana hid a passion underneath that thick layer of introverted timidity and reservation. And he was desperate to break through her wall of repression.

She thought she wasn't pretty.

He'd have to agree with that. To him, she was radiantly beautiful. Rome wasn't lying when he told her so at the moment of her release.

Rome saw an inner strength in Dana that most men wouldn't bother to find, let alone appreciate.

Courageousness under a demure veil of hesitation and shyness.

Rome accepted his momentary setback and returned to his studio to turn off the lights. That's when he noticed she'd left her purse on the front desk.

Rome wanted to weed through the contents and find some fragment, some piece to the puzzle of Dana Baker the woman. But honor was something his step-mom, Barbara, taught him as a child. And it would be dishonorable, even if it were for her own good as well as his, to break into her privacy.

At least now he had a viable reason to see her in the morning.

Rome shut off the lights to the studio and went upstairs.

Too restless to sleep, he went to the coat closet and took out the package Finkleman had given to him from his father.

It would at least get Tony off his back if he opened it.

He turned on his CD player to some B.B. King and sat on sofa. As he opened the box, Rome expected to find some sappy letter from his father apologizing for his sins. Instead, he found a red leather-bound book and a tiny gold box wrapped in pink lace with an old piece of red ribbon tied around it. The book looked like an old-fashioned diary with strip of burgundy colored ribbon marking a page near the end.

He carefully untied the ribbon and opened the cover. Out fell a very old newspaper article folded several times and a note folded in half with Rome's name at the top.

He unfolded the note and snorted. It was written on *Volupté* letterhead with a brief note from his father. *Typical*, he thought,

Dear Romano,

If you are reading this note then I am most likely dead.

Rome laughed at his father's odd brand of humor.

By now you are wondering what the hell your old man is up to. Well, I hope you'll take the time to consider the journal you have in your hands. It has been a curse to the men in our family for years. It may not be the kind of curse one thinks of with spells and potions and whatnot, nevertheless, it is a curse. I, as well as my father and grandfather, are proof of that.

From the last date of that journal, not a single DeMitri male has maintained a happy, successful marriage to date.

I received the journal the year my father died. The same year I married your mother.

I, of course, thought it was all bullshit. But after two failed marriages of my own, I began to realize how wrong I was.

Read the journal, Romano. Your happiness, the happiness of

your brother, and your future sons may depend on it.   *Dad*

"Shit. Leave it to Dad to blame a curse for his failed marriages." With nothing but time on his hands, Rome unfolded the article.

It was dated June 12, 1892: *Young Woman's Body Found Floating in Boston Harbor, Murder Investigation on Hold.*

Rome quickly read through the article. The woman was approximately twenty years of age, three months pregnant, with no sign of struggle—suggesting she knew or trusted her attacker. The suspect, her former lover, was released the same day he was arrested due to lack of evidence. Apparently, the man was attending his own wedding when the death took place.

"What the hell does this have to do with anything?" Had his father lost it? His family hadn't lived in Boston for generations.

Rome turned to the first page:

The Journal of Sarah Baker.

Baker? Rome thought. *Probably just a coincidence.*

The first entry was dated July 8, 1891:

I met a wonderful man at the summer festival today. He is the handsomest, kindest gentleman I have ever had the pleasure of meeting. He told me stories about his childhood in Italy. I told him I had never been anywhere but New England. Being a gentleman, he promised he would take me one day. I asked Father for the money to buy this journal just so that I might write down all the wonderful and exciting things we shared so I will never forget him, for I may not have a chance to see him again.

His name is Romano Antony DeMitri...

"What the...?"

Rome stopped reading and went for the phone to call his mother in Paris.

He needed answers—now.

Chapter Eight

...HIS VOICE—ROUGH, AND COAXING as he places the pillow beneath her belly and hips, feeling wicked and wanton on her hands and knees—her intimate secrets suddenly exposed for only him to see. Glancing over her shoulder, watching him as he trails hot, wet kisses along her spine. Licking his way down—teasing. Not reaching where she wants him most. His penis thick and swollen—ready for entrance as he kneels behind her. Fear and desire keeping her eyes locked to his, trusting him implicitly to give them both brief yet exquisite pleasure. He mounts her from behind... her mouth open, a moan escapes as his penetration enslaves her body... "Rome!" *She screams.* "Yes, please I need you inside me... Now..."

Dana's dream ended the moment she heard her own voice scream his name.

"Rome," she whispered into the darkened room. His face didn't appear to her in the dream. Merely the feel of his hands on her tonight left lingering sensations, an impression, unconsciously inspiring the erotic images in her subconscious.

Tormented with renewed arousal, Dana did what she'd always done. She sketched her dream man in his entire erotic splendor.

Had she found a face to match the perfect male form?

Dana smiled as she flirted with the idea of Rome's body matching her dream lover's.

She was fully awake when the sketch was complete. Her body still humming with need as Rome's touch still lingered in her mind.

*****

"It's about time you called me."

"Hello to you, too," Rome sighed. "How are you feeling, Claire?"

"Oh, stop with the 'Claire' business. Why don't you ever call me 'Mom'?"

"Because you hate it when I call you 'Mom'. You said it makes you feel old and wrinkled." This was an old issue with his mother.

"Well, now I am old. And why did I have to hear from your brother, Tony, that you're getting married, Rome? Really."

"Tony called you? When?"

"Oh, I don't know, maybe three weeks ago?" She sounded exasperated. "What does it matter...a mother should hear something that like from her own son. So, when's the wedding, darling? I can't wait to meet her. I'll be there in L.A. for some tests. The doctors or hopeful and believe my cancer was caught in time before it spread. Plus, Philippe and I have been planning on a visit anyway. Maybe I can even get Julian to tag along this time. It's been a long time since you've seen your brother. He was in the middle of exams when Philippe and I where at your father's funeral."

Rome rubbed at the back of his neck while his mother did the usual chattering she always did when he called. But since the news of her sudden illness, her chatter had increased. Rome knew ovarian cancer had a high mortality rate. It frightened him. He could only imagine what she was feeling. "Mom, I think Tony jumped the gun. Plus, he had no business calling you about it."

"Then you're not getting married?"

"Well, yes...but she doesn't know it, yet...exactly," he said somewhat embarrassed verbalizing it.

"What are you going to do? Drag her to the altar?" she laughed. "Baby, you shouldn't even have to ask her. All this girl needs to do is look at my beautiful boy to fall in love. And if she doesn't, then she's not worth your time."

Rome leaned his elbows on his knees and cradled his forehead in his hand. "Look, Mom, the reason I'm calling is I have a favor. Well, not really a favor. A question."

"I'm listening."

"Did Dad ever talk about his grandfather when you were married?"

"Well, sure. Alberto used to talk about a lot of things when we were first married. Why?"

"Did he ever mention anything about a journal that his father or maybe his grandfather gave him?" Rome asked, "Or was there anything that seemed unusual at first when you two were married?"

"No. Not that I know of. But it was a long time ago, Rome."

"Yeah, I know. I just thought he might have said something."

"I remember we had to wait until his father died to get married."

"Really? Why's that?" He groaned for asking, knowing his mother was on another tangent.

"I never got a straight answer from your father. I was young and stupid. In love. I would have waited forever. But his father was very ill at the time. We didn't have to wait for long." Rome heard her whispering on the other end.

"Mom, did he..."

"It's Rome, dear...okay I'll tell him. Philippe says *bonjour*. He's got another showing in two weeks. He's been working around the clock to get some his sculptures finished. He's been working with this wonderful mixture of clay and conc..."

"*Mom?*" He had to stop her before she ran his phone bill through the ceiling. "What about his great grandfather? Did he ever mention him?"

"Of course, honey. We named you after him. I don't remember why, other than I loved the name," she laughed. "His great grandfather apparently went a little crazy before he died. Sort of an embarrassment to the family, I guess."

"Did Dad ever mention the Baker family or a woman named Sarah Baker, by any chance?"

"Hmm, no I can't say that he did. But his father did say something rather odd to me one day when we were at a family picnic."

"What was that?"

"He said I wasn't *the one*."

"The one what?"

"Well, that's what I asked. I thought the old man had been drinking too much of his *special punch,* if you know what I mean. But when I told your father about it later, he was really upset."

"So when you asked his father why you weren't the one? Did he say why?"

"He said your father was destined to marry someone named Greta Baker and some nonsense about a family curse. Like I said, I just figured he was drunk. Why all the questions, hon?"

"Huh, oh no reason really. Just his name came up in conversation the other day."

"So, are you getting married or not?"

Rome laughed to himself. "Yeah, I guess I am. I just have to convince the lady that I'm *the one*."

He heard her laugh on the other end. "You go get her, tiger. Call me soon, okay?"

"Yeah, okay. Bye Mom."

He set the phone back down then laid his hand over the old dilapidated news article. So, his great-great grandfather went nutso. Rome wondered if guilt drove him there. Or even worse, if the woman he loved killed herself and his unborn child because of him.

Perhaps the answers were right here in his hand. He opened the journal back up and turned to page three.

> *My new gentleman friend came to call today and I learned the most wonderful news. He is the son of Father's dearest friend. Father allowed us to walk the gardens together...alone. He held my hand when no one was watching.*

"Agh..." This was like reading his auntie's diary. Rome skipped several pages.

> *...snuck into my room last night. He came to me, kissed me and caressed me, touched my breasts, my thighs. His fingers did naughty and wonderful things to my entire body. He said we were making love, and I truly believe we were—because I am in love with my beautiful lover, my Romano...*

Rome skipped several more pages, noticing the writing style changed as the months passed—from a child-like cursive to a swooping style of a lady's and then finally to a frantic and desperate jagged writing.

He found the last page—where the ribbon had marked. He read it. Then read it again.

"Could it be possible?"

Rome ran downstairs to his studio where Dana had left her purse. Propriety forgotten, he retrieved her wallet and took out her drivers license and read her full name: DANA *SARAH* BAKER.

So, Dana's Great-great Aunt had an affair with his Great-great grandfather. And his grandpa thought a union between his dad and Dana's grandmother would break the curse? Their ages were about right. His father was much older than Claire. But a curse?

With sudden clarity, Rome knew what he had to do. He may not be able to offer her his love, but he held a deep affection for her—his fairy-like beauty. Rome had an indefinable feeling of rightness about his decision. Curse or no curse, Dana would be his. Heart, body, and soul. The trick would be to convince Dana.

But right now, after all those glasses of water at the lounge—he seriously needed to pee.

*****

It was four in the morning when Rome gave up on sleep. The few times he did fall into a peaceful slumber, he'd had erotic dreams of Dana's creamy-smooth legs wrapped around his naked waist... then he'd wake up with an intense hard-on and couldn't fall back to sleep. His father must be grinning his ass off in Purgatory.

But he'd be seeing her tonight...

He had a full schedule of clients today. Some family photo shoots and several photo proof viewings. But he was certain he'd be seeing erotic images of Dana in the most ordinary things— coffee stains on the counter, patterns in the carpet, cracks in the ceiling tiles. He could still remember the light fragrance of her hair, the honey-sweet taste of her lips and the musky scent of her sex. A simple dinner date, that was his intension, but he'd have to keep his hands in his pants pockets all night if he wanted to follow through with his plans honorably.

Yeah right.

He really needed to pull back the reins of his desire. After last night, he expected Dana to be jumpy and apprehensive around him for a while. Rome needed her to feel safe with him. Trust him.

Rome took a long hot shower to ease the ache of wanting.

It wasn't working. *Should've made it a very cold shower, idiot.*

"Damn." Needing to take the edge off this intense need, Rome stroked himself with his fist, easing his throbbing penis in quick jerking motions. He placed his palm firmly against the tiled shower, leaning hard into the hot stream as it pulsed against his naked skin, imagining Dana there—with him. Her warm and inviting body thrown back against the cold white tiles of his bath, welcoming him, pleasuring him, taking him in deep as he looks into her eyes as she accepts and demands every inch of him as he drives into her sweet body again and again. Her face buried against his throat. Her legs locked around his waist.

With a groan of unsatisfied relief, he turned off the faucet and stepped out of the shower.

He'd been too long without woman.

But now, more certain then ever, only one woman would ease the need in his heart as well as his body.

He needed Dana.

Rome threw on a robe and a pair of sweats, then left the steam-filled bathroom to make coffee.

With his mug in hand, Rome thought about going down to his studio to work when he heard the timid knock at his apartment door.

*****

"I'm really, very sorry about running out on you last night." Dana shuffled her feet as she stood in the doorway to Rome's apartment. It was still early in the morning. The sun was peeking out over the horizon, but she just couldn't sleep. "It was immature of me...it's just..."

"It's okay, Dana. Come on in." Rome held his palm to his mouth for an exaggerated yawn.

"No. It's not okay," she said as walked past him and paced his living room floor. She was still in her drawstring pants and nightshirt, but she didn't care. She needed to get this out. Rome closed the door then leaned against it and crossed his arms. Geez Louise, the man was gorgeous even in his rumpled terry cloth robe and black sweat pants. She worried at her bottom lip before she could continue.

"It's just that...that was my fir...well, I've never, ummm..."

"Had an orgasm before?" he offered. His voice still rough and sexy from sleep.

She looked at him. Stunned. Then nodded. "Yeah."

Rome gave her a warm smile as he uncrossed his arms, then pulled her to him and held her there. His arms encircled her, one hand at the small of her back the other cupped her head as his fingers laced through her bedraggled hair. He was trying to comfort her, she knew. But it wasn't comforting. Sensual. Stimulating. Arousing. But not comforting.

"I understand, sweetheart," he whispered into her hair, "Thank you."

"For what?" she asked as she buried her face into the corded muscles of his chest. She inhaled his warm masculine scent and suddenly wanted him to do all those gloriously erotic things all over again.

"For letting me be the first to see your face the moment of your first climax."

"Oh." She knew her face was flushing. It seemed to do that a lot around Rome. "Well, I've had sex before, Rome."

He released her then, holding her at arms length staring at her. His dark eyes sharpened as he said, "Maybe. But he was obviously a fool."

He placed his index finger gently to her lips before she could ask. Dana looked up at him with surprise as an unexpected warmth poured through her. The tenderness in his response, the gentle look in his eyes, his understanding nearly undid her.

"He was a fool...because he took something from a beautiful and passionate woman without giving in return." He lifted his finger from her lips and traced her face, her nose, eyelids. As if discovering Dana, herself, for the first time, too. "And because with the giving there is so much more—the fulfillment is that much more...rewarding."

Her head fell back limp as her eyes closed—melting as Rome ran his lips lightly over her lashes then gently kissed each eyelid. "I don't think I'm passionate at all," she said, hardly recognizing her own her voice as she spoke in a soft tremulous whisper.

He chuckled then, watching her with such eagerness in his eyes. "You're right. A passionate woman wouldn't pound a guy's door down at the crack of dawn in her jammies with such a seductive look about her face, now would she?"

He laughed again at her wide-eyed reaction to his assessment then calmly placed an affectionate hand against her cheek.

"I want you, Dana. I need you to know that. But I won't rush you."

"Okaaa..." Her voice broke as her body shook. "Okay."

"All right. Now go back to your place right now before I change my mind and rip these cute drawers off and have my way with you."

"Yes...I'm leaving, I'm leaving!" She laughed and started toward the door. Then remembered she'd come here for something. What was it?

He made a step toward her. Then another. "Those drawers are coming off..."

She scrambled out before he could catch her.

*****

Dana was nearly finished putting Velcro on the backs of each frame-corner sample when a postal carrier arrived with an express-mail package for her.

"Are you Dana Baker?"

"Yes."

"Ma'am, I'm sorry about the mix-up."

"Huh?"

"Well, this package was scheduled as an over-night delivery but the post date is from several weeks ago. Apparently it was misdirected to your old address."

"Oh, that's okay. I wasn't expecting anything," Dana said as she signed for the package.

"Have a good evening, ma'am."

"Thanks."

"Since when does the postman deliver at seven o'clock at night?" Cynthia asked.

"Since they screwed up, I guess." Dana stared at the return address and frowned.

"Bad news?"

Dana looked again at the sender:

Greta Baker

C/O The Law Offices of Richard T. Wilson

Represented by Attorney Patricia L. Wilson, esq.

"No. Well, I don't know. It's from my grandma."

Chapter Nine

THE MINUTE CYNTHIA WAS OUT the door, Dana locked the shop doors and sprinted up the stairs to her apartment.

Why would Patricia send her a package from her grandmother now? Why not six months ago?

Ignoring hunger, thirst, and a full bladder, Dana sat on her bed and set the package aside. The wounds of bereavement were almost endurable now. But what was in that package might tear it open again. She couldn't face it yet.

Holding off a bit longer, she went to the kitchen to make tea, taking her treasured drawings with her and placed them on the dining table. Dana glanced at the image of her perfect lover, admiring the powerfully lean yet muscled body, the confident set of shoulders— the taut, silky skin of his erection and the dark curls of coarse hair that encircled it. She stared at the image longingly.

What did she really know about men? "Absolutely nothing."

She wasn't used to thinking of her sexuality in terms of reality. Her one and only experience with sex, except that night with Rome, was a teen-age disaster. She'd been a curious virgin then, but when it was all over...

While the painful images resurfaced, she took out a mug and a bag of chamomile tea from the cupboard then filled the mug with water from the tap. Dana thought about that awful night as she placed her mug into the microwave. A memory she preferred to keep locked away, never wanted anyone to know of her humiliation. Apparently, her date didn't feel the same way. He'd published their private act in the underground school newspaper— claiming she was "frigid and a lousy lay."

The boy's erection had been too large for her body to except. Either from pure ignorance or selfish lust, he forcibly entered her, tearing tissue and knocking hard at her cervix even as she screamed for him to stop. I was so painful she bled into the auto upholstery, upsetting him even more because it was his dad's car.

Horrified by the brutality, the pain, and the betrayal, Dana stayed in bed for two weeks unable to move or eat, explaining to her grandma she simply had the flu. After that horrible night, Dana wasn't curious about sex anymore. In fact, she'd stayed away from dating completely.

She turned a page of her sketchpad to her newest drawing, surprised at her own vivid image in this one.

In all the years she'd had the dreams—created the sketches—this was the first with her own image.

The microwave beeped and she took out her mug and plopped the tea bag into the steaming water.

She sighed as she sat at the table and gave the sketch one last look before forcing herself from the table.

She had to face whatever was in the package. Whatever memories, whatever sorrows it might rekindle.

"May as well get this over with."

Dana ripped open the package and found a small velvet pouch along with an envelope with her name on the front in her grandmother's familiar boldly scripted handwriting. The pouch seemed less ominous, so she started with that. Carefully pulling apart the gold silken thread, she opened the top and peeked inside.

She turned the pouch upside down and let the chain fall into her palm. It was an old-fashioned charm bracelet with a delicately designed chain. Dana held it up, closely examining its delicate beauty. The clasp was an elegant hand in the shape of a circle with the pinky held up as the release from the hook. The chain had spaces for twelve charms. Eleven were occupied, the last left empty.

"Well, this is lovely."

The chain was made of gold and sparkled as she played with it again the light from the bedroom window, but the charms shaped in various figures had semi-precious stones imbedded within. One was of a fully bloomed rose, another of a teacup, and one a miniature of an engagement ring. Each of the others, quaint little trinkets a girl of twelve might cherish, with the exception of one. It was an abstract, almost crude, yet recognizable image of a naked couple embracing. Reclined, the man and woman were in an obvious state of sexual bliss. A diamond attached at the joining of their bodies.

"Oh, my..." she said, feeling slightly appalled.

This wasn't the bauble of a young girl. It was an extremely poor exhibit of artistic talent, but its crudeness seemed to make the charm all the more scandalous. It wasn't the subject matter so much as the inept representation shown in the piece that repelled her.

Dana found it hard to believe her grandmother would own, much less wear, the last charm on her wrist.

Quickly placing the bracelet back in its pouch, Dana took a cleansing breath and opened the envelope. As she suspected, it was a letter from her grandma.

To my darling grandchild,

By now you are probably in your new home and on your way to becoming a business owner. I know it's what you've always dreamed of when you weren't caring for your feeble old granny. Now, don't get your hackles up, Darling. I know what a burden I was. You gave up many years of your youth for me. I hope what I have left for you can make up for it.

Please forgive Patricia for not giving this letter to you sooner. I gave her instructions to wait until you had time to settle into your new life. And I hope it's everything you'd hoped for.

By now you're also wondering about the mysterious charm bracelet. The story behind it is a piece of your ancestry that has been hushed for generations—only revealed to the one in possession of the bracelet.

My Great Aunt Sarah Baker had a love affair with a man named Romano Antony DeMitri...

Romano Antony...? Dana head spun. Could it be?

...Or so the story goes. He gave her the bracelet you have now. According to my mother, each charm represented a time they spent together in secret. Apparently, his family didn't approve of Sarah. His father had chosen a wealthy widower's daughter for his son and didn't want him dallying with a woman who couldn't raise his station in life. But soon, Sarah became pregnant with Romano's child. Being a naive romantic, she falsely believed he would choose her over money and family obligation, and told him of the child. The next morning, Sarah's body was found floating on the shore of the Boston Harbor.

My great grandfather, Avery Baker, and Marcello DeMitri, Romano's father, had been business partners and great friends for years. After the unfortunate death of Sarah and the news of her condition, a monumental scandal broke out. Her lover, Romano, was arrested for murder, and as you can imagine, the two families were at each other's throats ever since. Business sabotage, affairs, vicious rumors—the DeMitris accused our family for all of it. But Avery didn't take any of it lightly. He rightfully sued Marcello and his family for rape and wrongful death of his beloved daughter. Copyright infringements. Horse maiming. All, I'm sure, they were guilty of. I understand the family has since led a life a wealth and power from an assortment of questionable businesses and resources. (No doubt from sex, gambling and drugs.)

The DeMitri name may sound familiar to you since this man's legacy is now in the hands of this infamous family whose life of degradation leaves a stain on our own. And because of this I, as my mother did before me, must forbid you from establishing any ties with this family.

"Oh...no..." Dana lifted her hand to her mouth.

This may sound like strong language to you dearest, for I'm sure you've never once had contact with the lot of them, but I must insist. I've left instructions with Patricia that if you are ever seen associating with a member of that family everything from my estate will be stripped away and left in the hands of The Wilson's Attorneys Office to do with as they choose. But have faith, Dearest. I know you're a sensible woman and can understand my reasons for even mentioning such a thing. You've always had more sense then the rest of us Bakers.

Live well my Darling.
With all my love and wishes,
Grandma Baker

Dana's felt her throat twist as silent tears of confusion and anger hovered at her lashes. But she refused to let them fall.

Wadding the letter into a ball, Dana threw it hard against her closet door.

In what might have been a loving good-bye letter, her grandmother chose, instead, to leave her with an ultimatum. An odd condition to her will laced with an old family feud and superstition. What did it matter to Dana that the two families shared a history of violence over a hundred and thirty years ago? And how could her grandmother be so callous?

Finally, standing on unsteady legs, she picked up the wadded letter. Dana leaned her back against the wall and slid down hard to the floor. Head in hands, hot tears of disappointment rolled down her cheeks as the cruelty of it all came crashing down on her shoulders.

She'd not only lost the grandmother she thought she knew, but she'd also just lost the chance to embrace passion from a man she was beginning to trust.

*****

His lips pressing against hers, gently covering her mouth. His mouth, warm and soft, sending a pleasant swirling sensation in the pit of her stomach. His lips rising from hers as he opens his eyes. His sweet adoration sending her pulse racing double-time. The kiss leaves her weak, but Rome's smile is devastating...

Dana woke up like a shot, gasping for air as she gently touched her fingers to her lips, mixed feelings of delight and horror surging through her.

Rome?

This was not her typical dream brought on by a sexual need. This was sweet and romantic—almost—loving. Was Rome her dream lover? Or was this dream brought on, somehow, by the disturbing letter sent to her from the grave?

Had she found the one man who could release her inhibitions then have him cruelly snatched away before she had a taste of sensual pleasure?

Was it worth the risk?

Everything she knew, everything that meant something to her could be ripped from away. "It's so unfair." She fell into bed and softly cried herself to sleep.

*****

"Hey, Kimberly, can you taking care of Mr. and Mrs. Gomez this morning?"

"Sure, Mr. DeMitri. Their wedding proofs came out gorgeous. The new Mrs. Gomez will love 'em."

Rome's assistant, Kimberly, a pretty Chinese-American photography student working her internship from USC, loved photograph as much as he did. "Thanks. I've got an errand to run. It shouldn't take long."

"No problem."

Rome gathered Dana's purse and headed to her shop.

He was anticipating a romantic dinner with her this evening. "Yeah, If only I don't scare her off with my magnetic charm and wit." So far, he'd frightened her naiveté and inexperience with his frankness. But damn it, anything else, in his mind, steered toward deceptiveness. And he'd already had his fill of deceiving her. He wanted her, to protect her, make love to her. Would Dana still want him, knowing he could never fully give everything of himself—never able to love her?

*****

"My God, Dana, you look like death warmed over!"

Dana tried to avoid looking up at Cynthia's face when she opened the shop door the next morning. "I didn't sleep well."

She dropped her purple backpack against the counter and said, "Hey, let me see. Oh, you've been crying, haven't you?"

Dana shrugged her shoulders. "I just miss my grandma is all." Well, it was partly true.

"I'm sorry. Have you tried the cucumber thing for the swelling?"

"No."

"What about a cold compress or a dish towel and some ice."

"Is it that bad?"

"Not if you want to look like a prize fighter."

"Ugh—"

"I'm kidding. I'm kidding. It just looks sore." Cynthia reached out to touch Dana's puffy dark circles around her eyes.

Dana winced. "Aaaa. Okay, okay. I'll go upstairs and get some ice. In the mean time, you can start stocking the art books at the front counter. I'll be right back."

Dana struggled to maintain an air of calm as she went up to her apartment. Her heartache showed no signs of relenting, but she refused to let her grief get in the way of her success. She was going to open her store on time and didn't have time for personal distraction. Nor would she let her lust for a man she hardly knew give her grandmother's lawyer the means to take away the one thing that meant something to her. Besides, she'd gone without a man for this long, hadn't she? She'd just continue to be the sensible Dana that her grandmother knew her to be.

With ironclad determination, she grabbed a few ice cubes from the fridge and wrapped them in paper towels before going back down.

After reading the shocking letter last night, she had decisions to make and some a little research to do.

"Cynthia, I need to make an urgent errand and I may be gone for a couple of hours. You okay on your own for awhile?"

"Are you kidding? You've left me with enough work to do for ten people."

"Then stop looking so happy about it." She placed the cold towels to her face.

"Yeah, I love my job!" Cynthia laughed.

Dana shook her head as she headed out the door.

*****

When he walked into *The Enchanted Frame* Rome found someone there, but she wasn't Dana. The woman was pricing a stack of antiqued silver photo frames. She was dressed strangely, wearing all dark green. From her tight sleeveless sweater, to her slim ankle-length skirt—right down to her nail polish and makeup.

"Excuse me?"

She looked at him a little startled. "Sorry... you nearly scared the pants off me. The stores not open yet, sir. You'll have to come back next week for the grand opening."

"Actually, I'm here to see Dana. Is she around?"

"No. You just missed her. Said she had some business downtown." She smiled as her eyes gave him the once-over. "You look familiar. You a friend, or something?"

He smiled right back. "You could say that. She left her purse at my place last night." He held it up as proof, swinging it back and forth from his index finger.

"Oh, you must be the musician." Her grin widened.

"Among other things."

"So, her purse was at your place, huh? Well, no wonder she hit me up for cash for morning coffee." She surprised him with a quick wink.

"Yeah, well... can I just leave it here?"

"Sure. She likes to keep it in the locked cabinet in the back," she said as she walked behind the counter and took out something from a drawer. "Here's the key. The cabinet's a little old. You have to kind of wedge it to get it open."

"Thanks." He took the key. "I'm Rome, by the way," he said as he extended his hand.

"Cynthia. Nice to meet yoo...ou, you're the photo man from next door."

"Guilty, as charged."

"Mmm, the plot thickness. Tryin' to make the moves on the landlady, huh? Don't worry, your secret safe with me." She winked and waved her green-tipped fingers across her lips in faux silence.

"Thanks a lot," Rome laughed.

"But she's a good girl, Mr. Photo Man. So play nice. Okay?"

Rome gave Cynthia a mock salute and went to the stockroom to find the old cabinet.

Dana had turned even the back room into a cozy little nook, complete with two over-stuffed chairs, a matching loveseat, and a round wooden table painted with the same design as her logo. Not his style, but it suited Dana—it was, well, charming, actually. Rome shook his head and smiled. Only Dana would think to brighten a stockroom.

In the far back corner was the old cabinet. Yep, it had seen better days, and she'd painted it, too. With an antiqued white finish and painted ivy leaves wrapped around the legs, up to the cupboard hutch and around the top edge, it added to the enchantment of the shop—and its owner.

Rome knelt down pushed the key home and turned the lock, but the door wouldn't budge. He pulled again and managed to knock off the paperwork piled on the middle ledge. Then he gave it some brute force. *Ah, shit!* Not only did the door opened but the handle came off as well, leaving a jagged edge of wood sticking out where the handle should be.

Well, he'd play handyman later.

He placed Dana's purse out of plain sight behind some boxes when something fell from the top shelf.

"*Ow!* What the hel..." It hit him square on the head—hard. He stopped in mid-curse when a tablet, about the size of an eleven by fourteen enlargement, fell open.

"Well, look at that. Cynthia sure can draw some wild pictures." The drawing was of a couple making love. Well, actually, they were in a wild passionate embrace—a naked passionate embrace. He peeked around the corner to make sure Cynthia didn't catch him with her sexy pictures when he noted the discrete signature around the curve of the man's buttocks.

"*Holy Christ.*" The drawing was signed D.S. Baker.

Rome looked closer at the male figure, the neck arched, his face contorted at the moment of release, and the woman had her head turned up, gazing into her lover's eyes... *Dana?* And the man...he looked so much like Rome—it was damn eerie—almost disturbing how close she came to duplicating his face. *And the rest of his parts, too.*

She'd skillfully portrayed a glowing passion in both lovers' faces, mirroring Rome's own need for the artist. Dana's desires more vividly presented but no less fervent. He thumbed through a few more pages. Several more sketches were completed within the last few weeks. Most were of a single figure—the man alone with his face shadowed, dating well before Rome knew her.

"So, she needed a face for her fantasy man, huh?" Rome smiled. He was more than willing to supply her with fantasy material. Fantasy—hell, forget fantasy. With this new evidence of her secret earnings, he now a tool to coax her—unfurl her fiery passion with a gentle push. They'd both slide over the precipice of pleasure—together. *Tonight!*

Chapter Ten

"I WANT TO CONTEST MY GRANDMOTHER'S WILL."

Dana sat far back in the tan vinyl side chair, on the opposite side of her attorney's faux cherry wood desk.

Jack Hartman was an attractive man with a warm, friendly smile, of average height and intelligent green eyes. She imagined he was sharp in the courtroom as well.

A man her grandmother would have approved of for a husband.

Too bad she wasn't interested.

He leaned against the front of his desk facing her, pensive. With one ankle casually crossed over the other, he stood standing a little too close, invading her space. Dana wished he'd sit behind his desk so she could relax.

"You can, of course, Dana. But you may not want to."

"Why not?"

"Your grandmother included a 'no contest' clause when she drew up her will."

"But what does that mean, exactly?"

"Here. Read for yourself." Jack reached for a folder from his uncluttered desk and handed it to her. "Second page, fourth paragraph down."

Dana read it. Twice.

"So, there's no way I can challenge it?" She looked passed him, staring blankly at the paneled wall where a reproduction of a George Wright's Fox Hunt painting hung above his desk.

"Sure you can." He leaded toward her, placing his hand on her shoulder. "Just keep in mind that successful contests are rare."

"But in your opinion, Jack—do you think I should?" Dana could smell Binaca on his breath and his riotous aftershave assaulted her sinuses. She closed her eyes and tried to hold her breath.

"Dana." He waited until she opened her eyes and look at him. "Is there a serious issue with this family? Do you or your family owe them money?"

She laughed half-heartedly. *If only...* "No, nothing like that. The problem is one of the DeMitri sons, the oldest, is leasing a store-front and an apartment in my building." Well, that was partly true.

"Oh, I see." He leaned back again, then and placed his chin on his steepled his fingers. "And you're wondering if this could be considered 'an association with the family.' I understand." He rocked his fingers back and forth.

"Technically, I'd say yes. However, in my opinion, the letter implies an association of a *personal* nature. If someone were to argue against you, though, it could be interpreted either way. Moreover, it could be disputed also. To err on the side of caution, Dana, I'd advise you to break the lease and have him move out as soon as possible."

Dana felt the lump in her throat grow three-fold as her attorney spelled out exactly what she had feared.

"There is a complication. I don't hold his lease, Jack. It was sublet by the previous owners of the business, which is why I didn't even know about him living there until we actually met."

"Well, it's an indirect connection. That's fortunate. No one could easily make the connection to you."

"But why would anyone bother? The only other name mentioned here is the attorneys office."

"Unfortunately, the only one who *cannot* contest would be you. Did you have any aunts or uncles?"

"No."

"Good. The less family the better in this case. Anyone not named in the will who believes they were unfairly excluded may challenge it."

"It says here that an executor should be appointed," she said as she skimmed the document carefully, hoping for a something she might have overlooked. "Was there?"

"Yes. Unfortunately, your grandmother appointed her attorney."

"Patricia is the executor to her will? That's odd."

"Why?"

"Well, Patricia and my grandma used to butt heads. In fact, I wondered why she bothered to keep Patricia as her attorney."

"That actually might work in your favor, Dana. If we can prove to the court that the testator was persuaded or intimidated by her attorney, then you might have a case to contest."

"Really?"

"Or, if we can prove your grandmother was physically or mentally impaired at the time the will was drawn up—"

She laughed. "That's not likely. Her physical health was poor, but her mind was still sharp."

"It may be worth checking out. Is that what you want to do?" His sincerity was reassuring despite her initial unease.

Dana looked at her hands. They were balled into tight fists, her knuckles white. Was it worth the risk?

She'd never risked anything in her life. Never once did she do anything that her grandma thought questionable, always depended on Dana to be the sensible one. She was tired of being the boring, sensible Dana everyone depended on. Her grandma wasn't here now to tell her she was being silly and irresponsible, was she?

Dana smoothed her hair back from her face and took a cleansing breath. "Jack, can you at least look into it. And if I decide to pull back..."

"You wouldn't be risking anything unless we actually petition the court."

She swallowed hard and lifted her chin. "Do it. I want to contest it," she said meeting his gaze with a newfound strength.

"Is the income from one tenant worth the risk?" Jack reached down and placed his hand on hers.

"It's not just the tenant, Jack. It's much more than that." Suddenly feeling a bit more uncomfortable, Dana slipped her hand from under his.

She didn't want to live forever under her grandmother's thumb, while looking over her shoulder, wondering if someone was watching—waiting for her to slip up.

"There's one more thing you should know."

Biting her lip, Dana waited for the other shoe to drop.

"Ms. Wilson stands to receive everything should you lose your inheritance."

Dana's mouth dropped open. Her confidence quickly deflated like a needle to a balloon. *Geez, Louise.* This was worse than she thought. Her inheritance wouldn't go to some charity. It would go directly to Patricia?

When she didn't respond, he continued.

"Watch your back, Dana. This incentive is enough for even the most ethical attorney to hire a look-out."

Resentment replaced shock, toward Patricia Wilson, toward her grandmother. Hurt by the betrayal of her grandma. Angry with the deception of Patricia.

"Thanks for your help, Jack."

"Dana, listen. I know this must be a shock to you. If you need someone to talk to...somebody to confide in..."

"Thank you, I will," she interrupted.

"Have dinner with me, Dana."

Her stomach twisted as he took both her hands to help her up, trapping her between the chair and his body. She had to get out before he tried to kiss her.

"That's really sweet, Jack. But I'm just not interested. I'm sorry." She pushed passed him and walked out before she felt guilty for turning him down.

*****

Later that afternoon, Dana took a satisfying breath of accomplishment after she'd managed to clear most of the stock from a new shipment of art supplies, clearing them from her gilded table.

She held her sketchpad, leafing through the pages while the meeting with Jack was still weighting heavy on her mind.

Dana dropped the pad onto the table and quickly closing it when she heard the newly installed door-chime ring.

Darn—no time to hide it. She'd be devastated if anyone ever found it.

Putting her forlorn thoughts from the afternoon aside, she walked to the front and saw him.

"Rome? You're...um, a little early." She fiddled with the buttons at the front of her dress. How could she have forgotten about dinner tonight?

Rome gave her a lazy grin. "I missed you."

His eyes and that sexy smile always made her heart quicken. As the shop door closed behind him, the heat of the warm spring evening rushed in. *Was the air conditioner still working?*

"That's really sweet, Rome, but I still have a ton of stock to put away." She needed distance from him, but he followed her as she walked to the back table.

"All right then, I'll help you finish," he said as he walked past her to the remaining boxes of brushes and pencils still stacked on the table.

"Mmmm, what is *this?*" His enthusiasm made her head jerk up.

Oh God! "No Rome, please don't." She tried to remove it from his hands but she only managed to put herself between the table and his big body. He lifted it above his head, the pad well out of her reach. Keeping her wedged hard against the table, he slowly leafed through it—every page. Heat flooded her face. All her erotic thoughts, thoughts of him—were within those pages.

After several agonizing minutes, he finally said, "I think *this one* is my favorite."

His voice was rough but quiet. She glanced down and saw he'd chosen the picture of a man and a woman in a lover's lotus position, facing each other, with arms and legs entwined.

Dana gazed down at the woman—mouth open as if to allow a moan to escape while the male figure held her hips and back, ideally positioned to kiss and caress her freely. "It's a very erotic, yet romantic pose. Don't you think?" His tone was light and pleasing.

She closed her eyes while she heard him flip through the pages again. Only this time she found the pad opened to an empty sheet. She looked up at him, puzzled.

"Here," he said, handing her a pencil.

She automatically took the pencil not really understanding what he wanted. He turned her to face the table.

"Draw for me, Dana," he said it so seductively, she felt her back melting against him. His warm breath against her neck sent tingling sensations all over her body. He wasn't touching her, but had her pinned against the table with his arms on either side, palms firmly placed on the table.

Suddenly, she wanted to do anything for him as long as his body stayed close to hers. He smelled so good. Every spicy male scent of him hypnotized her as it rushed through her lungs and sending heat between her legs. She couldn't believe she was actually doing this—with Rome watching. Dana never tried to draw without a fresh visual image of her dreams before. "I don't know if I can do this."

He nuzzled her ear with the tip of his nose. "Sure you can," he whispered. His voice husky and warm against her neck, making her skin tingle.

She placed the pencil to paper and started to draw.

"Yes, that's it," he said as she began drawing the figure of a nude woman sitting on a table, her feet propped at the edge. "Yes," Rome whispered. She bit down hard on her lower lip. "Now, describe it to me. Tell me," he whispered softly in her ear, "She's open and vulnerable, isn't she?" His tongue traced the inside of her ear. "Is she pleasuring herself, Dana?"

"No," her voice was shaky. "Her lover... she's waiting for him..." She felt her mouth go dry. "Her lover is here." She quickly drew a dark-haired man with a perfect profile and determined eyes. "He's here to...um...," she cleared her throat, "... to pleasure her." Dana nearly jumped out of her skin as Rome traced her erect nipples over the fabric of her dress.

"What's he doing now? Tell me," he said while unbuttoning her dress, letting the bodice fall open and to the side.

He contoured his lower body against hers as he cupped her lace-covered breasts with his palms. She felt his erection harden against her bottom.

"Rome, please stop—right now—" She let out a tiny gasp as he lightly kneaded her with his hands. She stopped protesting when he began pinching lightly at her nipples with his thumb and forefingers. She had to say something, anything to make him stop, "Cynthia could walk in any second... Oh! What are...?" she really needed him to stop—right now.

He started nibbling behind her left ear, before he bit at her earlobe and suckled gently.

"No, please." She wasn't sure what she was pleading for.

"All right. I'll stop." Still wedged against her bottom, shifting himself back and forth as his erection thickened, he released his hold on her breasts. "What's he doing to her now?" he asked.

"He's, umm...pleasuring her with his... mouth." Her words came out jerky and breathless as he raised the skirt of her dress up her thighs. *Oh, Lord.* He was tracing the lace of her panties at her inner thigh.

"Does she like it? Or is she repulsed?"

"She...likes it," she managed. "He's nearly brought her to..." She took a gasp of breath as he continued to play at the edge of the laced fabric between her thighs. Dana tried to concentrate as she drew the man's hands on the woman's inner thighs, spreading her wider.

"Rome!" She abruptly dropped her pencil as his fingers gently pushed aside the lace-trimmed panties. His caresses explored and parted her, searching.

"Damn," he whispered to himself as he ripped the seam of her panties and tore them from her body. "I can't get enough of you."

His brutish actions excited more than frightened her. Her breath quickened. Rome quickly returned, continuing the exquisite assault while one large roughened finger pressed into her. She cried out. Her inner muscles contracted around his finger as he stroked in and out gently. The fire within her grew rapidly, intensifying with every swift movement of his hand.

"God, you're tight. Am I hurting you, sweetheart?"

"Yes. No. A little... Oh, Rome, please..."

He removed his finger, now wet from her arousal and moved upward, stroking gently until he found her center and gently pinched at her clitoris. Massaging lightly back and forth. A startled moan escape her throat, as the pleasure began building, deepening. She arched her back, trying to adjust herself against him—hoping to end the torment.

"Shh, not yet."

She groaned, disappointed as he removed his hand.

"It's okay." He kissed her neck as he turned her to face him. "I want to see you."

Panting, she looked at him in fascination as he unbuttoned his shirt, pulled it from his shoulders, then let it flutter to the floor. She only had a moment to view his lean and powerful body before he unzipped his pants and nudged them down past his hips with his thumbs. She stared down at his erection, mesmerized as it sprang forward like an invitation. Instinctively, she wrapped her hand around him, feeling his length gently. His penis felt like smooth hardened heat in her palm.

"Mmmm, don't start that," he said smiling at her.

"Fair's fair," she replied looking at him with half-closed eyelids.

He returned her brazen behavior by pushing her dress down and over her hips as he lifted her bottom up onto the table. The only garment remaining was her laced bra.

He quickly removed it.

His month opened slightly. "You are the most precious thing I've ever seen." His eyes were bright with arousal, looking up from her flushed face and breasts, down to the blonde curls at the joining of her thighs.

She'd never felt sexy or desirable before. But his declaration made her feel cherished. Her heart felt alive, while her head said, "he can never be mine."

Tears sparkled in her eyes. "Oh, Rome," she sobbed as she wrapped her arms and legs around him. He replied by reaching between their bodies and placing his erection at her entrance. She stilled, afraid of the pain she remembered from her first and only time. But as he pressed forward, sinking into her, deeper and deeper, filling her, she only felt pleasure and heat.

He briefly placed his cheek on her shoulder as he filled her to the hilt. His chin felt rough against her skin.

He kissed her then. Softly at first, his lips telling her what she feared to hear out loud.

"You feel so good. Warm. Tight." Remaining inside her, unmoving, his kisses grew hungry—ravaging her mouth as she felt him grow larger from within.

"I can feel you inside me," she said. "Please..." She wriggled against him, waiting. But he still wouldn't budge.

He withdrew from her, moaning as he pulled back from her body then pressed back in slowly. Again and again. Slow and sweet. Each time driving deeper than the last. Every thrust pleasing her senses and tugging at her heart. He quickened his pace, harder and faster as his body pumped wildly into her. She held on tight, biting into his shoulder as she felt her orgasm build, contracting her intimate muscles hard around him. Rome sucked in his breath.

"Now! I need to see you *now*. Oh God," he clenched his teeth, "I can't hold... *open your eyes for me, Dana!*"

Answering his demand, she opened her eyes watching as he reached between their bodies stretching her outer lips, rapidly massaging her with his thumb. She watched him as he watched her, both riding the spiraling pleasure that enveloped them. He stroked her faster and faster with the same rhythm of his hips as he thrust harder with each stroke. It was too intense to hold back.

Throwing back her head, she allowed the convulsions to start. She clenched hard inside, gripping around him. "Yes," she screamed as her eyelids drifted shut.

"No, Dana. Open your eyes..." He was panting hard against her face. "Let me see!"

She did keep them open this time. Watching him as his body bucked against hers—his own climax taking over as they rode the whirlwind together.

As her mind returned to reality, she realized, watching each other climax this way was more intimate than anything she could've imagined. She cried softly against his neck, knowing they hade no future together, and listened while his breathing returned to normal.

"I'm in trouble," she whispered, more to herself then him.

He chuckled as he fell against her. He wrapped his arms around her, holding her close.

"No you're not, sweetheart." He stroked her hair back from her face. "I slipped on a condom when you weren't looking. You're safe with me." When she didn't respond he looked back at her with a sweet smile, thumbing the tears off her cheeks, replacing them with soft kisses.

She shivered slightly as the hum of the air conditioner returned. She wanted to laugh, too.

He'd misunderstood what she meant. "The only time I wasn't looking was before you got here."

He raised both eyebrows at her.

"You didn't."

Nodding he said, "I slipped one on before I got here."

"But—I didn't feel it when..." she felt her cheeks burn as she turn away from him.

"I told you I'd missed you. I've been rock-solid since the other night you melted right in my hand."

She shivered again. This time it wasn't from the ventilation.

"Dana, sweetheart, you're getting cold," he said as he held her close. Her trembling limbs still clinging tightly to him, absorbing the warmth from his body. "We should get dressed," he said, groaning as he withdrew from her.

He removed and disposed of the condom and hiked up his pants before he picked up her clothes and helped her dress. Soothing the worry from her forehead, he smooth her bangs back and kiss her. "Someday soon, I want to photograph you. Just like this... with your cheeks glowing from lovemaking."

Rome glanced down at the floor and laugh slightly, picking up her useless panties then stuffed them into his pants pocket.

"Thank God I locked the front door," his eyes twinkled. "No telling who might've walked in."

"You planned this!" Dana shoved at him hard. She started walking away from him on shaky legs, still struggling with her dress, feeling foolish. She'd been ambushed. Tricked. This was no spontaneous seduction.

He followed her.

"Would you have stopped me if you'd known?"

She shrugged. Would she?

He was fully dressed now, reaching for the sketch. "Can I keep this? Maybe I'll frame it."

Her eyes went wide. Was he kidding?

If he was, she just couldn't see the humor in it.

In the aftermath of the most fulfilling moment of her life, he wanted to play—tease. She could feel only devastated. Because her could never be hers.

"Rome, I think you should leave now."

Chapter Eleven

"ROME, LET ME GO!"

"I'm not letting you run out on me this time." Refusing to let go of her until he'd totally and thoroughly made love to her, Rome scooped Dana up tightly in his arms and carried her out the back door.

"Where are you taking me? I'm not going with you to your bedroom, Rome."

"Yes. You are," he said, pleased with himself. "I'm not letting you go until you're so worn out from my loving, you won't be able to leave."

She seemed to stiffen slightly at his challenge. Then he felt her go limp, slipping purposely from his arms and her legs hit the ground running.

"Oh no you don't," he laughed when grabbed her around the waist and flung her over his right shoulder.

"Hey, put me down." She tried to shuffle and kick her legs until he gave her butt a nice hard smack.

He liked the feel of his hand on her bottom and left it there—letting his fingers flex into her soft flesh.

"Stop that." He smiled at the laughter in her tone.

He continued his gentle assault until he reached the top of the stairs to his apartment. Swinging her around so she was closest to the door, he handed her his keys. "Open my door, would you?"

She giggled as she fumbled with them hanging upside down over his shoulder. "I don't believe I'm doing this, Rome, the blood is rushing to my head."

He smirked. "Mine too." *Among other places.*

After she dropped his keys twice she finally managed to get his door open.

"You can let me down now."

"Not until I have you securely in my bed—naked."

She gave an exasperated scream.

It was dark inside his apartment with a hint of moonlight streaming through his Venetian blinds in the living room. Without letting her lose, Rome walked to his hallway closet.

"Here, take these. And this too." He stopped and spun around looking for his auto lighter.

"What is it?"

"Just wait. Ah, here it is. Now for some fun!"

"You're scaring me."

He heard shakiness in her voice. He was going have to do this slowly so as not to frighten her.

"Hey, it's okay. You'll like this."

"What's in the bag?" He heard the plastic bag crinkle.

When he made it to the bedroom without tripping or smashing his shins, Rome sat her at the end of his California king bed. The Venetian blinds were cranked open, allowing the glow of the streetlights to stream softly across her face. *Damn. Where was his camera when he needed it?* He brushed his lips against hers and said, "Close your eyes."

He could sense her hesitation.

"It's okay. I promise. Now close your eyes." He brushed his palm lightly over her eyelids to make sure they were closed. "Promise you won't open them until I tell you."

"Okay," she sighed.

Rome went to work. Retrieving the bag, he dumped the contents onto the dark navy comforter. Inside were eight scented candles of various sizes and colors. Most were earth tones of sandy beiges and light greens, scented in vanilla and cinnamon. Earthy with a hidden bit of spice. Just like Dana.

He placed the candles strategically around the room. Then clicking on the auto lighter, he lit each one until the room glowed in a cloak of yellow warmth. The aroma of spicy vanilla filled the air.

"Mmmm, something smells nice. Can I open them now?"

"Just one more minute, sweetheart." He lighted the last one and placed it near a mirror at the headboard, illuminating the room with a soft radiance.

Rome knelt at her feet and took her hands before he said, "Open your eyes."

As her lashes flew open, he noticed they held a gleam—a natural radiance that no makeup could improve. She scanned the room, and her eyes brightened as her mouth dropped open in wonder.

"I hope you approve."

"It's beautiful, Rome."

He saw an unreadable emotion flicker in her face.

"Hey. Look at me, Dana." Her cupped her chin and brought her face to meet his. "You're not thinking of running again, are you?" He offered her a one-sided grin.

"No. I just keep wondering," she whispered.

"Wondering what?"

There was a long silence before she responded. The anxious look in her face worried him.

"Why—?"

"Why what, sweetheart?" he asked as he gently kissed his way down her face and down the curve of her neck.

"Why you're being so..." her voice caught, "so wonderful, because there's nothing really special about," she took in a shaky breath, "No one has ever made me feel... Why me, Rome?"

"Shhh. I'm not going to answer that question. In fact, I think by tomorrow morning, you can answer that question yourself."

"Most men don't usually notice me, Rome," she said flatly. "But you... you make me feel good about myself." She reached out and touched his cheek. "You make me feel special...wanted."

Rome stopped what he was doing, and shut his eyes—wanting to kick himself. The guilt was closing in on his heart. If circumstances had been different, he might have been one of *those* men. Would he have given her a second look had it not been for his father's will?

He couldn't, wouldn't think in those terms. He wanted Dana. But she deserved to be desired for who she was. Not for some bizarre family obligation. He should tell her the truth, but Rome knew it would shatter her fragile self-confidence. He needed to convince her what a desirable woman she was. Help release her passionate side hidden just beneath the inhibited veneer.

He kissed her then—long, soft and reassuring. Coaxing her response as he drank in her sweetness. Her lips parted, answering his tender demand. His tongue dove deeply at her shy invitation, devouring her softness as he gently explored. "Mmmm, you taste sweet," he said.

Dana wrapped her small hands around his neck and returned his kiss, tantalizing his senses. He had to have more of her, all of her—again and again. He would probably never have his fill of this sweet fairy disguised as a woman.

"Dana... I want to see you. All of you," he whispered as he moved back from her swollen lips.

"What do you want me to do? I'm afraid I'm not very good at this."

He stood and pulled a chair out from the corner of the room and turned it backward, placing it near the foot of the bed. Facing her, he straddled the chair.

"Stand up," he said. His voice a smooth and gentle command. Seducing her with words.

She silently obeyed.

"Undress for me, Dana."

"What? No, I can't!"

"Yes, you can. Do it—very slowly so you won't get nervous. I want to see every part of you. Enjoy each part of your body as you reveal it to me."

She stood a moment wide eyes looking at him.

"I've already seen most of you, sweetheart. You have nothing to be ashamed of." He reached out to take her hand, caressing her fingers. They trembled against his palm.

"You can close your eyes if it's easier."

"Okay. But I told you, I don't think I'm very good at this."

"Let me be the judge."

Rome noticed her nipples peak against the fabric of her dress as she inhaled deeply and closed her eyes.

"I know this is a little uncomfortable for you. But trust me. Okay?"

She answered by letting both straps to her dress fall as she slipped each front button free, slowly, until she reached the last one below her waist. He could glimpse the lace bra as it peeked out from the gap.

"Mmm, that's it. Nice and slow."

"Like this?" she asked, keeping her eyes firmly shut. He watched as she let the top of her dress slide down her arms, still held at her hips.

His fingers ached to fondle and caress her lace-clad breasts. But instead, caressed her with his eyes as she discovered for herself what a sensual creature she was. "God, you excite me, Dana. More than you know."

She giggled softly.

"I love watching you," he said reassuringly, crossing his arms over the back of the chair.

He watched her let the dress float down past her hips and fall to her feet, leaving her dressed only in a thin layer of lace at her breasts. "I don't know what happened to my panties," she said, then unclasped her bra, removed it and threw it over her head.

"Don't worry. I've got them for safe keeping," Rome said as he patted his back pocket.

Surprising him, Dana opened her eyes and let out a triumphant laugh. "I did it!"

*****

She should have felt exposed. Instead, Dana felt decadent standing naked in front of Rome still fully clothed. For the first time in her life she felt cherished.

Her body was still reeling from his lovemaking. But it was now humming—almost vibrating with need all over again. He did that to her. Just a look from him made her body strangely hot. She felt the wetness between her legs, intensified by the lack of fabric to shield her.

"You look good enough to eat. Now, come to me," he said as he stood and reach for her.

She went without hesitation. Trusting him. Rome took charge of her body with quiet reassurance and his eagerness excited her. He wanted her, and it made her feel powerful. She found herself so easily caught up in his enthusiasm she forgot to be shy and embarrassed. Instead, she felt desirable and purely sensual.

"Can I help you with yours, now?" she asked as she attempted to undo the few hooked buttons on his black denim shirt.

"No. You'll get your chance. Tonight is just for you. I'm afraid once we're both naked, I'll lose all control."

"Is that bad?" she asked.

"Not usually," he chuckled as he ran his finger down her nose.

The simple gesture made her skin tingle.

"But I want to make you so completely sated you'll never run away again."

She smiled, but Dana knew her face was flushed. Rome spoke so frankly, so easily about his desires she found it difficult to keep up.

In one forward motion, she was in his arms. He reclaimed her mouth as he crushed her to him before he eased her down on the bed.

"Turn over."

"Huh?"

"Turn over. And stay toward the edge."

"Okay." *Trust, remember to trust.*

Dana gasped slightly when she felt a cold line drawn down the middle of her back.

"What are you...?"

"Relax. It's just body lotion. Lie back down, sweetheart. Let me take care of you tonight."

With generous sweeping strokes, she felt his hands fan out in strong circles at the small of her back. As she lay in his bed on her belly, he massaged her like an instrument. Becoming attuned to her body's responses. Dana surrendered completely to his whim while her body, in turn, communicated with sinuous motions.

He unselfishly pleasured her with a lover's gentle touch, relieving all her anxieties. With strong kneading strokes, Rome's gentle pressure circled her bottom and down the backs of her thighs. Exploring her body as she became accustomed to his touch, making her feel pampered and secure as the aroma of the candles and flickering lights cocooned her within the sultry air of intimacy.

Trust.

Her body was melting under his gentle massage as he worked his ways down her calves and to the sensitive balls of her feet.

"Ahh, that's the spot," she laughed. All those hours on her feet today were disappearing between Rome's fingers.

"Good thing you have two. I can work the other when I'm done with this one," he said as he worked his thumbs in small circles around the bottom of each foot. "You know the foot is one of many erogenous zones of a woman's body."

"Mmm... really? After this I believe it."

Her feet were putty in his hands as he moved back up her thighs, kneading the tender flesh just above her knees then between, avoiding the place where she wanted him most. Her bottom rose instinctively, waiting for him to explore deeper. But he ignored her plea, moving along the sides of her ribs, lightly grazing her breasts with his fingertips.

Lightly kissing and licking at the nape of her neck he said, "Roll back over, now."

She was powerless to resist anything he asked. Her body felt like chocolate on a hot day.

Rome handed her the tube of lotion. "Here, pour some of this in my hands."

After she squeezed a generous amount into his palms, he rubbed his hands together briskly to warm the lotion before laying his hands on and around her breasts and stomach. Soothing and arousing.

"Rome, please..."

"Soon..." he said as his hands dipped down at her hips, gently massaging her pubic mound and back up to her breasts. Pinching them between slick fingers, then encircling and kneading them until she felt her nipples turn rock hard under his hands. She wasn't sure she could take much more until she felt him slide one hand down between her legs, parting her.

"Ooh..."

"Tell, me what you want, sweetheart. Anything."

Unable to speak, she watched through half-closed lids as he slid his body down the bed and knelt between her thighs.

"What are you...oh, God..." She nearly leaped out of her skin when his lips and tongue dipped between her sensitive folds.

He lifted her knees up and propped her feet on the edge of the bed, leaving her open and revealed. Reminiscent of the drawing she had made for him.

His tongue danced around her hooded clitoris. "You taste good," he said as he continued taste and tease.

Her body throbbed from his mouth's intimate massage as he circled and probed. Searching. Finding all her hidden desires as his mouth caressed her—licking deliciously up and down her swollen sex as the heat built inside her.

"Please, I want you inside me."

He left her then, and Dana heard the whoosh of fabric as Rome tore off his shirt and removed his jeans. She watched, fascinated, as he unwrapped the foil packet and rolled on a condom.

"I want to do that sometime," she said.

"Next time, I promise."

He lay beside her, their skin touching. It felt glorious. The prolonged anticipation was almost unbearable. She drew his face to hers. Their lips met with a smoldering heat as he forced her lips open with the thrust of his tongue. She could taste her own husky heat from his lips, then felt him nudge her knees apart as he settle between them.

He fondled and caressed one breast as he eased the tip of his erection into her with the other. Just a tease—not quite entering her.

She pushed her hips forward. He shifted away. Teasing her with his penis.

"Patience, Dana. I want this time to go slowly."

"Rome, you're driving me crazy," she said as she grabbed his butt and thrust her hips forward causing him to enter her fully. "Mmm...yes, that's better."

"You little witch," he groaned as he nipped at her neck.

He gathered her hard against him and grasped her bottom, holding her steady as he rammed hard and fast against her—into her, nudging at her cervix with each stroke of his shaft.

She crossed her ankles around his back, letting him take the lead. "I love the way you feel inside me," she said, shocked at her bold admission yet feeling safe within his embrace.

"Oh, Dana...I love the way you feel, how you contract around me when I'm inside you."

She knew he was holding back his own release as his beautiful face strained, waiting for her. A hot ache began to grow inside her. More then just pleasure building at her core.

Her fingers dug deep into his shoulders as her body vibrated with renewed desire. He sensed the change in her body as the contractions took over. She felt him move faster and faster and watched with pleasurable fascination as his skin glowed with sweat and his face contorted as he let out his groan of release.

Dana had a sudden feeling of indefinable rightness. She pushed the thought away—afraid of what it might mean. This was more than just a sensual experience. Something more was forming between them.

As their breathing returned to normal, Rome rolled over taking her with him until she was on top of his chest.

"Thank you," he said.

Confused, she asked, "For what?"

"For trusting me."

And she did.

But could she trust herself not to fall in love?

Chapter Twelve

"DANA?"

Rome woke with a start. He'd slept fitfully, holding her close all night just in case she decided to bolt while he slept.

He loved the way she felt in his arms, letting her go only once during the night to blow out the candles. The sensation of melting into her—looking into her warm hazel eyes, brightened from his pleasuring. The way her nipples became erect from his touch—running his fingers through the softness between her legs. Oh, and how their bodies fit together so perfectly when they made love.

"Good morning," he heard her say as she walked into the bedroom holding a breakfast tray. She looked so small and adorable, wearing his denim shirt. He smiled wide with approval.

"I couldn't sleep with all the noise outside. So, I got up and made us coffee and toast. I hope you don't mind."

"The noise?" He'd slept like the dead.

Rome heard the ruckus below his bedroom window—slow, steady chants of angry female voices screaming obscenities about *Volupté* and child pornography.

Shit. The protestors were back.

"Ah, no of course I don't mind," he said as he walked naked to the window and glanced down at the street level. "Well, at least there aren't as many this time. Our cookie sheet waving bakery lady is heading the pack," he said, more to himself. "Goddamn nuisance. I photograph families for chrissake!"

Rome glanced back over his shoulder and saw Dana holding out his mug of coffee.

She seemed uneasy, either from his nakedness or his irritable tone. He wasn't sure which.

Rome took the mug from her hand and set it on the nightstand. With the harsh morning light streaming through the windows there was no longer the protective cover of the night to hide behind, so he had to assume it was the former rather than the latter. A bond was beginning to form between them and he wouldn't have her shying away simply because he was comfortable with his own body.

"Hey. Look at me," he said, holding her face in his hands, lifting her gaze to his as he smoothed the hair back from her forehead. "I want you to feel comfortable with me. Looking at me. *All* of me, Dana. Just like I love looking at every part— every inch of you." She looked up and gave him a shy smile then bit at her lower lip. The cute blush in her cheeks was back, and he brushed his lips gently over hers. "I don't want you feeling embarrassed with me," he said more forcefully than he'd intended.

Rome realized she still needed time to become accustom to him and shouldn't feel hurt by her sudden inability to look at him. But damn it, he wanted her to be at ease with him *now*.

He unbuttoned the shirt Dana was wearing and pushed it off her shoulders, leaving her naked.

"I don't want to be," she said, shrugging her shoulders.

"Good," he said, trying to soften his tone as he lead her to his bed. "Now, come here and let me look at you in the day light."

Rome sat at the end of the disheveled bed as Dana stood gloriously naked between his knees. "Am I ever going to get you to go to dinner with me? We missed dinner last night." His hands roamed intimately as he spoke, exploring her body all over again.

"Maybe," she said. He watched her eyes and felt her uneven breath against his cheek while he lightly traced the hollows of her back. Dana lean forward to lay her head on his shoulder when Rome felt her stiffen.

"What is it?" Rome asked. She was staring at his right thigh.

"Where did you get that?"

"The scar?"

She nodded.

"It's a long story," he said as his mouth playfully capturing one pink nipple letting his tongue fondle and tease. Trying to distract her. He wasn't ready to discuss his past. Not yet. "Maybe I'll tell you all about it... when you finally let me take you to dinner." He continued caressing her breasts with his lips and tongue. "But for now I just want to touch you."

"I love it when you touch me," she whispered against his ear.

"And I want to find which parts you like me to touch best."

"All of them..." she moaned seductively. "I want you touching all of them."

Laughing, they fell together onto the bed. "Then you won't mind if I kiss you here," he teased as he tried to kiss her armpit.

"Hey—"

"...Or here..." he continued, nipping at her ribs sending her into a fit of giggles.

"Stop... ahh..."

As she wriggled from him teasing, he wedged himself between her legs and stared down into her face.

"Has anyone ever told you how beautiful you look in the morning?" he asked.

She stopped laughing and looked thoughtfully at him.

"You're the only one."

"Who was he?" His voice was harsh.

She went rigid beneath him. "Who?"

"The fool who left you fearful of intimacy?" He covered her cheek with his palm. "The reason you run when I feel us growing closer?"

"It was a long time ago, Rome. I'd rather not talk about it." Her voice sounded so small and it tore at his insides.

"I won't force you to discuss it, sweetheart, but if what he did makes you reluctant about us, *when* it happened doesn't matter, does it?"

She looked at him with glittering eyes, and felt the need to hold her close. His hands played with the recesses of her back in slow soothing motions.

"His name was David."

Rome remained silent, waiting for her to continue.

"We only had one date. We were both sixteen...virgins, curious." She sighed against his neck as his hand reached the curve of her bottom. "I was upset at Grandma about something. I don't really remember what. Probably my clothes. She was always strict about what I wore, so I felt sort of rebellious that night."

"What happen?"

"David borrowed his dad's car. We ate dinner at a drive-through then drove out to Turnbill Canyon Road. You know, the winding street with that creepy tree. He said the ghost of a man who hung himself on the tree appeared every night at midnight. So we parked and waited.

"He was cute and I thought he liked me, so I didn't mind when he started kissing me. It was nice at first, until he started to tear at my clothes. I was a little scared, but I just thought this was how it was done.

"It happened so quickly. One minute we were kissing, the next I was naked from the waist down and he was on top of me. It was the first time I ever *saw* a man...he was so...big..."

Rome felt her body shake and he wanted to castrate the bastard.

"...he tore inside me and I screamed...but he wouldn't stop and...God it hurt, and I thought he'd never stop. When he ripped me open I... bled all over the back seat of his father's new Cadillac." Warm tears fell from her face onto Rome's shoulder as she continued. "He said his dad was going to kill him and that it was my fault the upholstery was ruined. Later, he told his friends my...umm...vagina was a frigid ice box and his penis nearly froze off from the chill." She laughed a little, "I wish it had." Dana lifted her head and looked in his eyes, "I never told anyone about this before."

He brushed his lips across her eyelids, "I'm glad you told me, sweetheart."

Dana jerked her shoulder. "I've never really dated much since then. Never really wanted to...until I met you." Dana stared at him with such longing. Rome felt his insides stir at her admission. She kissed him then, lingering, savoring, as if to wash away the ugly memory. Replacing it with new ones, and he wanted to weep with her, for her.

He felt her smile as she kissed him. Rome kissed her back as he circled his hips, teasing them both from the contact.

The guy was an asshole. "You didn't deserve what happen, Dana. He didn't deserve you. You're a bright and passionate woman." She sighed deeply, her breasts pressed against his chest. "God, you make me hard just by breathing, but I'd never force you to do anything you didn't want to do."

"I know that." She wriggled under him caused the head of his shaft to nudge at her entrance and he groaned from the contact.

She giggled then sighed when he pressed in just a little further, and the noise from the outside was forgotten. Her sigh was the sweetest sound he'd ever heard. He pulled back out and slid his now rock-hard penis up and down her folds, teasing her clitoris with its tip in achingly slow motions.

"Rome, you're going to make me late for work."

"So?"

"So... I have a store to get ready for opening. Cynthia and Rick will be waiting for me..."

"It's still early...mmm, you so feel good. Too bad I don't have a condom handy—"

"Hey, Rome, those damn women are back. Oops—sorry."

"Aaaah!"

Rome heard Tony storm through his bedroom door as Dana screeched and ducked under the sheets.

"Christ, Tony. Don't you knock?" Rome yelled, pulling the comforter around Dana.

"Sorry, man," he said, still standing there like a jackass in the doorway.

"Do you mind?" Rome growled.

"Huh...Oh yeah. Sure. Is that *Dana* you have trapped under there, I hope?" Craning his neck as if that would help him see her better. "Hi, Dana."

Rome wanted to laugh when he heard a muffled "hi" from beneath the covers as Dana's hand peek out from under the covers to wave at his nosy brother.

"Get out!" Rome commanded.

"I'm leaving. I'm leaving... See ya, Dana."

She groaned.

"It's okay, sweetheart. He's gone."

"Oh God! I'm so embarrassed. How did he know it was me?"

"Probably because you were with me at the lounge the other night," he lied. "And you took me home, remember?"

She nodded.

His mouth swooped down to capture one quick kiss before he swatted her bottom out of bed. "Come on—you have a store to open and I have an obnoxious brother to get rid of. But tonight I'm taking you to dinner—like it or not," punctuating his demand by tapping his finger to her cute nose.

She kept his shirt to wear back to her place. He just pulled on a pair of jogging shorts before scooting her out the back door while Tony perused his DVD collection.

Once he'd gotten her safely and discreetly home, he returned to face his brother's optimistic face and stupid grin.

"Nice goin' Ace. You could've scared her off permanently," Rome said as he combed his fingers through his messy bed-hair.

"Hey, I just came by to give you some good news. But after what I just saw... it looks like you don't need it. Good work, by the way."

"Uh, shut up, man." Rome said, slightly embarrassed. "So, what have you got?"

"Well, I've got a reliable source in place."

"Uh huh," Rome replied, more than a little uncomfortable his brother was having Dana watched. "Go on."

Pulling a sheet of paper out from the back pocket of his well-pleated khakis, Tony cleared his throat and read from a list. "Dana Sarah Baker. Born in 1978, both parents died when she was a kid. Raised by her grandmother, Greta Baker. She worked for The Huntington Library and Museum before her grandmother died. Loves art museums and art in general. Her favorite artist is Peter Paul Rubens—Hey, isn't he the artist known for painting all those dead naked guys?"

Rome sighed. "Yeah. But he also painted *The Rape of the Daughters of Leucippus*." The sarcasm was lost on his brother.

Tony shrugged. "Humm, I was always partial to that one in art history class. Anyway, she likes gourmet coffee and is known to do just about anything for chocolate chip cookies. Her favorite color is light blue and—"

"Stop! Don't tell me anymore. I think I can manage on my own from here."

*****

Dana was getting nervous. She was careless last night. Being with Rome was risky and she was suspicious of everyone. Anybody passing by the display window might be watching her.

"Agh... I think Mrs. Hilson mixed up decaf for regular again. This stuff is awful!"

Cynthia drew Dana from her thoughts.

She looked down and realized she'd been painting gray roses with purple stems on the wooden stool she was working on. "Oh, great," she mumbled. She had to pay more attention to her work or she'd never sell any of her creations. "Why don't you go tell her before she has more unhappy customers." The woman was probably too busy waving her utensils in the air to worry about her customers anyway.

"I think the only customers she'll get today are us and those wacky soccer moms screaming in front of Mr. Photo Man's place. Cookie?" Cynthia asked, as if having protestors on their sidewalk was a nature occurrence.

"Do you have to ask?" But then this was L.A. Everyone became used to everything around here.

"Right." Cynthia set aside the poster book she was ordering from and ran out the door, leaving Dana alone with her thoughts.

Her dependable employee was turning into a friend, didn't want to blow it by suspecting even Cynthia of spying.

Rick, her new framer, was busy setting up the framing equipment. She glanced toward him and found him looking at her, then just as quickly glancing away. *Could he be...?* "I'm becoming paranoid." For all she knew, even the protestors could be reporting to Patricia Wilson.

Rome. She wouldn't give him up. Not now, knowing the pleasures of his seductive and irresistible touch.

She was falling fast. It was freighting and thrilling beyond anything she'd ever experienced.

In spite of her busy schedule, thoughts of him constantly intruded into her day. She was painting delicate little roses up the legs of a wooden stool, but her body still tingled in remembrance of his touch. He was gentle and patient. His touch was like an addictive drug— first a taste, then the addiction. And she wanted all of him. Body and soul. She knew it wasn't possible, but his sensuousness threatened everything that meant something to her. Her shop. Her home. She couldn't give those up those things either.

She wanted it all.

Maybe the smoldering passion he'd awaken was just temporary. No, she refused to believe that and she certainly couldn't continue to hide behind closed doors. Rome's determined nature would make sure she didn't. Even knowing all the possible consequences. Even after a full night of lying in his arms. And she still wanted him even now. "I can't let him go. Not yet." *Maybe never.*

And he wanted to take her out—in public. On a regular date. She couldn't keep dodging his invitation to dinner.

Then she remembered something, "The scar on his thigh—"

Dana rushed to the stock room where she stashed her sketchpad. Out of habit, she'd always kept it close.

Rick was still making frame samples in the frame room and thankfully couldn't see her.

Flipping through several pages, she finally found it. The drawing she'd made the night after her grandmother's funeral. Face covered by shadows. His beautiful chest corded with muscle and sprinkled with dark hair. *And the scar on his right thigh...*

"No—it can't be."

She shut the sketchpad with a snap and put it away when she heard Rick shuffle close by.

She had a life altering decision to make. Stop seeing Rome, continue to hide, or have some fun and some fantastic sex with the only man that ever made her feel special.

Perhaps her heart had already made the decision long ago.

Dana's thoughts drifted, remembering her grandmother and the bracelet with the missing charm. She now understood how Sarah Baker must have felt for her own Romano.

"Man, I need to start working out," she heard Cynthia say as she walked in armed with coffee and cookies.

"Huh." Dana went to help Cynthia with the goodies. Maybe things would make more sense after a dose a cookies and coffee.

"I keep seeing too many beautiful blonde women around town with perfect bodies and I'm beginning to get a complex."

"Oh, stop it, Cynthia. You look great. Besides most of the 'perfect' women in L.A.

have to pay through the nose for a surgeon to get those bodies."

"Like you should talk," her friend laughed, "I don't see you going to a surgeon. Look, there's another one."

Dana glanced outside and saw a beautiful blonde with her hair slicked back in a ponytail wearing dark glasses and tight jog pants. "I see what you mean." The woman looked vaguely familiar.

"Geez, I should just kill myself and spare the agony," she teased.

"Oh, I don't know. I think I'd be too uncomfortable with all the male attention having a body like that," Dana said half-heartedly.

"Yeah, you've got all the male attention you need with Mr. Photo Man."

"What do you mean?"

"Oh, come on, Dana. Fess up. The musician next door is strumming your cords—admit it."

"Cynthia!"

"What? Like no one would notice? That man has the major hots for you. And you do for him."

Cynthia was way too perceptive. But she needed someone to confide in. Someone who knew the robes.

"Cynthia, do you do much dating?"

"Not lately. Why?"

"I'm not sure how to ask this so I'll go right out say it."

"Okay, shoot."

"Umm, how long did it take you to...you know... get used to looking at the male body?"

"What?" Cynthia laughed.

"And what, exactly am I suppose to *do* in bed besides... letting him *do* everything?"

"Dana, you shock me," Cynthia said in a mocking gasped as she glanced around to see if anyone was listening. "You want to talk about sex? You know it's my favorite subject," she whispered.

"I'm not joking. I really need help here. I need to know some secrets to drive a guy crazy."

"Well, let me think," she said as she tapped her fingernail against her pierced lip ring. "I once inserted an Alka-Seltzer inside me and had sex with my boyfriend while it fizzed and fizzled. Talk about stimulating! He was at my beck and call for a month."

"That's not exactly what I was hoping for," Dana grimaced. "What about before that? Was there ever a time when you weren't so comfortable with yourself or with your boyfriends?"

"Humm, I'm not sure I can think that far back."

"Please."

"Okay. But if I tell you this, promise you'll buy my coffee for a week."

"Deal."

"All right. About five years ago, I was majorly paranoid about my body or making the wrong move with my boyfriend. I thought if I made the wrong move or acted too forward he'd think I was a slut and break up with me."

"So, what did you do?"

"He got so tired of doing all the work, he asked why I'd never touched him. I think he was actually insulted that I hadn't."

"I guess I could see his point."

"Yeah, well I figured if he couldn't see me or touch me while I was touching him I'd be okay. So, I borrowed a pair of my uncle's hand-cuffs, he's a police officer for the LAPD, and stole one of my mom's silk scarves."

"You didn't?"

"Yep. I cuffed him to the bed and blind folded him."

"Did it work?"

"Oh, yeah! Best sex we ever had while we were together, which didn't last long after that night."

"What happen?"

"Well, I kind of forgot the key to the handcuffs," she snorted. "When I went to get it from my uncle's belt, he'd already left. So I had to ask my brother to cut my boyfriend loose with a hack saw while my poor baby lay there naked and helpless. He was so pissed off, he never forgave me for that—so, we broke up."

Dana couldn't help it. Giggles bubbled up from her gut, then Cynthia chimed in. Laughing hysterically—they couldn't stop. When they finally got themselves under control, Rick came up behind them.

Had he overheard?

"I've all these samples finished. Where do you want me to hang 'em?"

They both looked at each other, then started another round of laughter.

Rick looked at them like they'd lost their minds.

Chapter Thirteen

DANA WANTED TO PLEASE HIM TONIGHT.

Can I do this without making a fool of myself?

She'd convinced Rome to bring his car around the back to pick her up and asked for a place to dine outside of L.A. County. Thankfully he'd agreed. If they ate downtown, the chances of someone recognizing her were too great.

Checking herself in the dresser mirror one last time, Dana hoped her trip to The Beverly Center Mall was worth the cost and the effort. She felt daring in a modestly low-cut, royal blue dress that fell a few inches above her knee. It felt slinky and sensuous against her bare legs. She was unaccustomed to wearing three-inch sandals, but Cynthia said guys went wild for them.

"I can do this." Resolved to taking a chance on her newfound confidence, she stuffed a few needed items in her purse and walked downstairs to Rome, waiting patiently for her.

Her stomach fluttered when he got out of the car and came around to open the passenger side door for her. Dana drank in his incredible form while he stood there. He looked sinfully handsome in charcoal slacks and a black silk shirt. His smile was wide as his lips parted in a breath-taking display of straight, white teeth.

"Hi." The warmth of his smile echoed in his voice.

"Hi, yourself," she said confidently returning his smile and took the hand he offered. Tonight she wanted no shadows across her heart.

"Damn! You look good enough to eat," he said, as he looked her over seductively, solidifying her courage and determination.

"Thanks. So do you," she replied, acutely aware of his tall, handsome physique and the spicy scent of his cologne. He towered over her by nearly a foot, but somehow, she felt safer with him then with anyone else in the world. And her heart sang as her head maintained the warning signal. *This is only temporary.* Crushing the thought away, she stood on tiptoe to touch her lips to his. He bent to meet her halfway with a soft, tender kiss, reveling in the sweetness of his mouth.

"Mmm, and you smell great too," he said. "Now, get in before I decide to tear your close off right here."

She smiled and silently obeyed. *No shadows tonight.*

They drove for several miles without speaking. But the smoldering gazes and seductive smiles left no question what was on each other's minds.

As Rome merged on the 405 Freeway, he reached out and caught her hand in his, lacing their fingers together. His hand felt firm and strong—protective, gently squeezing her left hand until they arrived at their destination.

When he parked the silver Jaguar in the Irvine Park Place parking garage, he made no effort to retrieve his hand. Lazily, he brought her hand to his mouth for a moment, brushing his lips across it.

"If I wasn't so hungry I might be tempted to do something really shocking right now," he said, reluctantly giving Dana her hand back. "In fact, I'm afraid if I kiss you here, we won't leave this parking garage until morning."

"Then I better get out of the car. I'm starved."

"Wait. I'll get that for you," he said taking his car keys and sliding out of his seat to open her car door.

"Such a gentleman."

"Just to throw you off track. I don't plan on being gentlemanly later," he teased and wiggled is eyebrows at her.

"I'm counting on it."

Though the restaurant was busy with patrons, they were immediately seated in a secluded corner of the elegant dining room.

Rome ordered for both of them since Dana had no idea what she wanted. She was too nervous to choose anyway. It wasn't until the waiter left before Rome spoke.

"So, what does a pretty lady like you do before she decides to open up a frame shop?"

Dana's normal reaction was to say, "I'm not pretty." But tonight with Rome, she felt beautiful. So, she smiled and accepted the compliment. "I used to work at The Huntington Library, in the acquisitions department. That's where I learned about framing."

"Sounds fascinating. How did you land that position?" He leaning closer, looking genuinely interested. Most guys would shrug if she mentioned her job, then talk about their latest promotion.

"My grandma was a docent there for years. When one of the framers retired, she put in the good word for me. I was there for a few years until she died. Then I got my building and my store. And you know the rest."

"Have you always been an artist?"

"I've been drawing and sketching since I was a child, if that's what you mean."

"And how long have you been...?"

"Drawing pictures of couples making love?" she offered.

"Yeah," he laughed.

"Only since I met you," she smiled. "Actually, the two drawings you saw were the only ones."

"They looked like us," he replied as he placed a warm hand on her bare thigh. She saw his eyes dilate as he looked intently at her.

Time to put her plans in motion, she thought. "I guess I draw what I know," she teased, placing her own hand on his leg.

"Yeah, but I have to confess something."

"What?" She pulled her hand back.

"I found your drawings the day I brought your purse back. No, I didn't exactly find them—your sketchpad sort of *fell* on me."

"What?" she laughed. "And now you're wondering about the dates on the drawings?"

He nodded "Yeah, and why the man looks an awful lot like me." Rome gave her such a sexy-as-sin look, she almost forgot the question.

Dana looked down at her shacking hands in her lap. How much should she tell him? *What* should she tell him? How could she explain to him what she refused to believe herself?

"Rome, I..."

"Excuse me miss, sir, your salads are ready."

"Thank you." Rome said to the waiter. He studied his water glass a moment before turning back to face her, letting her direct the conversation.

He was definitely a patient man. A quality she truly loved about him.

Love?

Dana took a deep breath. "I've had these dreams, these visions for a long time—since my parents died, I think. I can't really remember exactly. But these visions of a figure...

of a..."

"A man?" he offered.

"Yes. He appears in my dreams. At first, I didn't even know I was recreating him in my drawings. I hardly remembered the dreams back then. I discovered some old sketchpads when I moved recently. It was full of drawings—drawings I don't even remember doing. After that, the dreams became much more vivid and I was able to remember everything when I woke up." She shrugged, feeling her face heat up. "Now, I keep my pad and pencil by my bed. I've never really known who he was or if he was even real." She looked up at Rome's handsome face, "Until I saw you that night in the lounge and—" Dana felt her confidence fall backward remembering that night.

Rome placed his finger under her chin, forcing to look at him. "—and I messed things up." She opened her mouth to protest, he added, "No, it wasn't you who screwed thing up that night. I'd just gotten some bad news and wasn't exactly myself. So, let's put that night behind us, Okay?"

She nodded. He'd more than made up for it last night.

"So, now, you keep your pad and pencil by the bed and...?"

"...I met you. Now, I have a face to match the body." At least that was partly true.

He gave her a wicked smile and kiss the inside of her wrist. "I'm happy to give the artist inspiration for her creativity."

Dana's stomach rumbled audibly.

Rome chuckled. "We'd better eat."

They were both famished and didn't talk again until every scrap of lettuce was gone from their plates. Dana was relieved Rome didn't ask more about the drawings. But she had questions of her own.

"Rome, tell me about you—all I know is that your father founded a racy magazine."

Dana reached over and traced her finger along the top of his thigh. "Why don't you start by telling me how you got this nasty scar on your leg."

"My brother, Tony, was a rebellious teenager. If things didn't go his way, he acted out physically, sometimes violently." Rome stopped and took a drink from his water glass.

"You fought, didn't you?" she asked.

He nodded. This was obviously a difficult subject for him.

"Was it over your father?"

"No. This time it was a woman...a girl actually."

"Oh." That wasn't what she expected. "Were you in love with her?" *Please say no.*

"No. Tony was," he said flatly. "We were on Dad's yacht for some family get-together when Tony started an argument with me. He accused me of things that weren't true... and a few things that were. I accused him of lying and we got physical—I'll spare you the details." He sighed. "Anyway, long-story-short, we both fell overboard while the boat was in motion. Tony was never a skilled swimmer and got sucked under. I was trying to bring him back to the surface when I got sucked under, too. Next thing I knew, the boat was above our heads and I..."

Dana covered her shock with her hand over her mouth. "Oh, God. No!"

"Yeah. I was able to get my brother pushed away in time. But the propeller nicked me in the leg. I nearly drown.

"A hundred stitches and six months of physical therapy later, I was good as new."

Dana doubted it was that simple. "I'm sorry. How did Tony take it? He must have been tormented with guilt."

"Tony is Tony. He takes most things in stride. I think his rebellious side ending that day, though. Soon after that he hooked up with Dad at the magazine. I think it was his way of avoiding me."

"Or, maybe it was his way of redeeming himself. Even if it was with your dad."

"Yeah. Maybe."

Change the subject. "So how did you get into photography? Was it you father? Your family must have known a lot of talented photographers."

"No, it actually wasn't my dad. It was my college professor. He introduced me to my true passion for ancient ruins. Traveling the world requires a lot of photo documentation. Photography was sort of a by-product."

"You mean like the Mayan pyramid photographs I saw in your studio?"

He nodded.

"Sounds fascinating. I've never really been anywhere," Dana sighed, "I wanted to travel when I was little. But with grandma so ill it wasn't possible. I guess I'm kind of a home body now."

"It's never too late," he said holding her hand, tracing her lifeline lightly, sending erotic shock waves through her. He must have noticed because he looked into her eyes and brought her hand to his mouth then traced her palm with his tongue.

Dana closed her eyes, loving in the sensation.

"I love traveling, looking for exotic places and ancient architecture," he said still nipping and licking at her palm. "Photographing remote areas of the world few people ever see. At first, it was just an excuse to get away from Dad. But after awhile, I was addicted."

Dana watched Rome's animated face as he spoke of his travels and felt envious of his adventurous spirit. She shook her head, "I don't think I've even been out of California. With the world at odds with each other, I'm terrified to leave home." She shivered as he continued to kiss his way up her arm.

"Well, I'll have to take you to Italy one day. Visit The Colosseum. Or The Parthenon in Greece," he said as his lips works their way to her earlobe. "It's an artists dream. You'd love it."

Only in my dreams, she thought.

Dana heard their waiter clear his throat and she tugged her hand back.

Rome gave her that naughty grin and she felt her face warm. *Darn it!* She was supposed to be a seductress tonight, not the shrinking violet.

"Your dinner," the waiter said. "Please let me know if you need anything else," he said and quickly disappeared.

Dana breathed in the aroma of filet mignon and fresh steamed asparagus garnished with strawberries and melon. Choosing a strawberry, from her plate, Dana delicately picked it up and offered it to Rome. He watched her as he bit into the ripe fruit from her fingers, letting it drip down her thumb. Rome licked the dripping juice up, sucking lightly at her fingers as he polished off the ripe fruit. Dana wasted no time on her plan. Using her available hand under the table, she caressed his thigh, lightly tracing circles around and around and up to his hip. She felt his leg muscles contract from her touch. She picked up a piece of asparagus and he eagerly accepted it from her fingers while she crept her hand dangerously close to his crotch.

"Mmm, I'm beginning to get a taste for green vegetables," he groaned as Dana traced a line around the bulge of in trousers.

She was feeling very wicked, and actually enjoying every minute. "Darn, I'm out of veggies. What I'm I going to feed you now?"

He wiggled his eyebrows at her before she realized what she was implying.

"Here, it's my turn," he said as he took a piece of melon from his plate and fed it to her. Sweet juice dripped down her chin and he licked it off tracing his tongue up to her mouth, plunging between her lips.

Dana groaned deep in her throat when she felt his fingers crawl up her inner thigh.

"Ooops, I must have forgotten something..." she giggled when he looked up her wide-eyed.

"Mmm, no panties. You're going to kill me, woman."

She was disappointed he didn't take full advantage. He merely traced her hairline until she was soaking wet with anticipation.

"Bad girl, look what you did."

He drew her hand to the tent in his pants. She continued to giggle as she pulled at his zipper and ran her hand over the fabric of his shorts, up and down his ridged shaft. "Lord,

I'm glad these table clothes are long, otherwise our waiter might get a shock," he said, gritting teeth as his eyelids grew heavy.

"And I never had this much fun eating fruit and veggies," she said, reaching below his shorts to tug him free.

He pulled back. "Uhh...let's finish our meal—*fast*."

"Oh, you're no fun," she laughed but finished eating while Rome allowed his erection to subside—somewhat.

Their waiter took the empty plates and returned with a dessert tray. "Care for cheesecake or crème brulee?"

"Just the check, please." He glanced at her, "We're in a hurry."

"Of, course, sir."

Rome left cash on the table and nearly lifted her up off her toes when they ran out the door.

He had her in his arms the moment the car doors were closed. "Damn, I was about ready...to come...all over the table cloth back there," he said between heated kisses.

"Mmm, well that was the idea," she said. "Take me home and make love to me, Rome."

"You don't have to ask me twice." He nearly burned the rubber off his tires when he turned out of the parking lot and onto the freeway toward home.

*****

Rome drove his Jag to the front of his studio to find Tony's BMW parked in his spot. The lights to his apartment were blazing.

"Oh, great. Tony's here."

"We can go to my place," Dana offered.

"No. I better find out what he wants. Come up with me?"

"Umm..."

"If you're worried about this morning—don't be. You've got nothing to be ashamed of. Although I can't speak for Tony."

"All right."

"The protestors are gone. I wonder what he did to pull that one off?"

"Maybe they just got tired," Dana offered.

Rome could hear the noise from his place as they took the stairs. "More likely, my brother charmed the pants off one of them—literally."

"Is he throwing a party?" she asked, shrinking behind him.

Rome wasn't going to let her get away. "He knows if he so much as brings a girl up here, I'll kick the living crap out of him."

"You sound just like an older brother." He heard the nervousness in her laughed, and squeezed her hand for reassurance.

Rome didn't bother with his apartment keys because the door was already wide open. The TV was blaring, folk music was coming from his bedroom, and people were in his kitchen. "Tony, I thought..."

"*Romano*! You're here."

"Mom? What are you...?"

"*Bonjour*, Romano. *Comment allez-vous?*"

"Hey, Philippe. Long time, no see," Rome said a little shell-shocked as his mom embraced him and kissed his cheek.

"There's my boy, handsome as ever," Claire said.

"Mom, you look beautiful."

"It's those Parisian spas," she said cheerfully. "They make even a sick woman glow."

"Where's Tony?" Rome asked.

"Oh, I think he had a hot date. We're just borrowing his car," Claire winked.

"Did you happen to notice anyone camped out at my studio door?" Rome asked.

"You mean the women?" Claire asked, taking a bite of a chocolate-filled bagel. "Sure, we did. One of them was an art enthusiast. She recognized my charming husband and was so thrilled to meet him, Philippe offered them all free admission to his next showing." She smiled brightly at Philippe. "A nice grandmotherly shop owner offered us free bagels, then they all packed up and left."

"Wow." Rome stared at his step-dad with his mouth.

"Hey, bro."

"Jules? My God, you're here!" Rome grabbed his youngest brother in a bear hug as they both gave each other a strong slap on the back. "How's London treating you?"

"It's great. Those British chicks dig me," Jules said with a smile just like their mother's.

"Julian stop," Claire said then faced Rome. "He's in the top two percent of his class," she said proudly. "My baby boy is going to be a famous scientist one day."

"Uh, Mom..."

"Hey great. I always knew you where a wisenheimer," Rome said, but just as proud of his youngest brother's achievements. "So, what are you doing? I'd didn't expect to see you for at least another couple of weeks," Rome exclaimed.

"Oh, heard you're getting married...had to be here to witness that."

Rome flinched, remembering Dana behind him.

"Mom, Philippe, I want you to meet someone very special," Rome announced. "Dana, sweetheart. Come meet— Dana?"

"Umm, it looks like she flew the coop, bro," Jules laughed.

Ah shit.

Chapter Fourteen

ROME WAS GETTING MARRIED.

Dana was hyperventilating by the time she reached her apartment.

Married?

She would not cry. She had to remember, this was just a temporary affair between two consenting adults. That was it. This was definitely for the best. He'd go on with his life—she with hers, and she'd be safe from speculation and fear of getting caught and losing everything.

Yes, definitely for the best.

But why did it hurt so much?

Was it really a betrayal if you didn't tell a lover after a night of hot steamy sex "Oh, bye the way I'm getting married?"

She wasn't an expert by any means, but she'd doubt it.

A crash sounded from down stairs.

"Must be some party," she thought.

But then she heard it again.

"My shop—"

Throwing off her high-heeled sandals, Dana ran barefoot downstairs and opened the shop's back door.

When she entered, the security lights were off and the darkened-silence gave her the chills. The slam of the shop's front door startled her as a dark figure ran out and up the street into the night.

Without thinking, Dana ran after him.

"Oooww," she screeched as she stepped into a several sharp object with her bare feet. How could she be so stupid? Panic and shock was seeping into her veins, crying as the pain shot through her.

"No!"

The store reeked of spilt turpentine and broken linseed oil jars.

Feeling violated and freighted, Dana managed to hobble to the main light switch as tears of pain streamed down her cheeks. Thankfully, the lights flicked on like normal. The shop looked all right too, except for a few crushed bottles and squashed paint tubes—until she saw it.

The frame room was in complete chaos. Most of the damage lay in a heap of broken pieces. In fact, every decorative picture hanging from floor to ceiling just this morning, now ripped and torn open with glass spewed everywhere.

Then she remembered her sketchpad.

"*My drawings!*" She sighed with relief when she found them still safely tucked inside the old creaky cabinet.

She went for the back wall-phone but the line was dead.

"Oh, God."

Bleeding from the lacerations in her feet, Dana limped to the front counter, searching until she found the phone stuffed under several boxes of overstock paint. "Thank God."

Dana dialed 911 for the police, then dialed Rome's apartment. She should talk to him, let him know the cops would be here—but that's all.

"Hello?"

"Rome?"

"Um, No...this is his brother, Julian. Rome went to get my dad some good ol' American beer. He should be back soon."

"Ahh..." Her voice shook. *What to say?*

"You want to leave him a message?" Julian asked.

"Sure. Just... just tell him not to worry. The police will be here soon. But...it's nothing to be concerned about." She hung up in case he asked questions she wasn't prepared to answer.

She tried hopping to the first aid kit but gave up after slipping twice on her own blood. "Oh, forget it." Maybe the cops have some band-aids.

Minutes before the police arrived, Dana started shaking from the cold. She hadn't realized how chilly it was tonight.

*****

Rome loved his family, but they had piss-poor timing. After the erotic dinner with

Dana, his only goal for the rest of the evening was to get sweaty and naked with her—not play host to his continent-hopping clan, though he was relieved to see his mom.

He was turning on Larchmont Boulevard when his cell phone hummed. *What now, bean dip?*

"Yeah?"

"Rome? It's Jules."

"Did Mom inspect my fridge again?" he laughed. His mother always critiqued his cupboard contents and usually found them lacking. He got a kick out of it. When he was away at college he'd fill his kitchen with nothing but cookies, potato chips, and soda when she came for visits just to tease her.

"No. Listen, I don't want to alarm you, but..."

"What's wrong?"

"Well, a woman called. She didn't give me her name but she sounded a little upset," Julian said.

"What did she say, Jules?" Rome asked, spacing his words out carefully with a thread of warning in his tone.

"She said the police were on their way over but not to worry. I'm not sure what she meant. She hung up before I could get a phone number."

"Dana!" Rome shouted.

"What?"

"It's Dana. Julian, do me a favor. I'm still five minutes away. Go next door to the frame shop, take Philippe with you. Make sure Dana's okay. I'll be there as soon as I can."

"Yeah... okay, man. No problem."

"Take care of her until I get there. If anything happens to her..."

"Yeah, I got it, man." Rome heard him say before he disconnected the phone as he zipped through L.A. traffic.

Rome nearly rammed into a parked police vehicle down the alley when he arrived. Blinded by the flashing lights, he stumbled his way out of the car and sprinted through the open back door to Dana's shop.

The smell of paint thinner nearly knocked him over.

"Dana?"

"We're over here, Rome." He heard his brother say over the chattering police radio and several people talking at once.

"Is she okay?" he asked as he found her crouched on the floor behind the counter.

"I'm fine, Rome," Dana said. She was giving a statement to the woman police officer who was handing her a blanket.

"What the hell happen here?" Rome asked his brother while Dana continued to talk to the officers.

"Seems she walked in on a burglar," he told Rome.

"Dana, sweetheart? Are you... your feet are bleeding!"

"I'm fine, Rome. I just stepped in some broken glass." Her voice sounded distance.

"She's bleeding pretty badly," Julian said softly.

"Hey, can I get a medic over here?" Rome demanded.

"Rome, they've already got someone coming." Julian grabbed Rome by the arm.

"I'm fine!" Dana croaked. He noticed the blanket again. She seemed so small and fragile sitting there alone on the floor. A strong wave of protectiveness for her swept through him like the Santa Ana winds.

"No, you're not fine. You're shivering and it's seventy degrees outside." He scolded. "Plus, you may need stitches and probably a tetanus shot." He knelt beside her on the floor and placed her in his lap, blanket and all. She tried pushing at him but he wasn't budging. "You're staying right here until they clean up your wounds. Then I'm taking you to the hospital."

Dana stopped arguing and settled against his chest, absorbing the heat from his body as the shock wore off. He felt his legs and back start to sweat from the heat of both of their bodies but he wasn't letting her go until the shuttering in her body dissipated.

Rome held her there until the cops left, then carefully carried her to his car. Once safely buckled in and wrapped tightly in the blanket, Rome drove her to Cedars Sinai Trauma Center.

Thankfully, the damage wasn't too severe. After two hours in urgent care, they'd removed the glass shards from her feet, and stitched up her big toe and a few in each heel.

Rome filled her pain medication at the hospital pharmacy before he took her home.

He put her into bed with a hot cup of tea his mother made. Disturbingly quite, Dana obediently sipping up the last of the tea then silently crawled under her covers and stared at the ceiling.

Gently brushing her hair off her forehead, Rome sat beside her whispering everything was all right, until her eyes drifted shut.

Satisfied she was okay, he went down stairs and found his mom sweeping up the glass while Philippe and Julian tossed broken frame pieces in the Dumpster out back.

"Hey, thanks you guys," Rome said a bit awkwardly. "Mom, you shouldn't be overdoing it."

"Oh, horsepucky. I'm fine, honey."

He wasn't going to argue. "This isn't exactly how I envisioned you meeting her."

"Nonsense, Rome," his mom said. "Be grateful we were here when you needed us." She touched his cheek.

"We need to find out how the bastard got in."

"Don't worry, *le fils*," Philippe said. "Let the police do their job. And we'll take care o' *zis*." He put his hand on Rome's shoulder, "You take care of your *l'amour*."

"Hon, it could have been a lot worse," Claire said.

He placed his hand on hers, "Yeah, I know. Thanks."

"Go back to her, Rome. She'll need you more than us tonight." Claire smiled then went back to sweeping.

Rome went to his place and grabbed a few things before returning to a sleeping Dana. Setting his stuff beside the bed, Rome removed his clothes, then crawled in beside her and pulled her close. She signed in her sleep and curled into him.

"Don't leave me," she pleaded.

"I'm not going anywhere. I'll stay for as long as you needed me, sweetheart."

"Mmm..." was all she said before her breathing pattern became steady again and he knew she was asleep.

Too restless to sleep himself and too hot to stay under the covers, Rome climbed out of bed and took his guitar out of its case.

Playing always soothed his nerves when life wore on him. He played a smooth, melodic song, strumming soft and low in an almost hypnotic rhythm. If Dana woke, he hoped the music would sooth her spirits.

He must have played for nearly an hour when he noticed her sleep became restless. Her mouth opened and she moaned as if in pain—nearly suffocating and kicking at the blankets. He dropped his guitar and knelt beside her when her breathing came in short, quick pants. She was trying to say something.

"Nnnn...ooo..."

Rome took her hand and tried to coax her out of the nightmare, brushing the beads of perspiration from her forehead and feeling helpless.

"Rome!" she screamed as she jerked up. Her eyes open staring straight at the wall, disoriented and trying to catch her breath.

"Shh, I'm here, Dana," he said softly.

She clung to him tightly, weeping softly into his shoulder. He rocked as if she were a child for what seemed that hours, but perhaps were only minutes passed. Her sobs bore straight to his heart, wishing he could chase away her shadows. He wanted to kill the bastard who put them there.

Once he heard her breathing return to normal, he tried to get her to talk. "Tell me about your dream, sweetheart."

She shook her head. "I can't."

"All right. We'll let it go for now. Feeling any better?"

She pushed at him, removing herself from his embrace.

"You shouldn't be here, Rome," she said.

He could see her tears glistening down her face from the soft glow of the streetlights streaming through the curtains. She turned away as she spoke.

"It's okay. They know I'm here. My family can manage on their own for the night," he assured her. "Philippe and Jules are keeping watch tonight. Everything is going to be fine."

She looked at him them with wide-eyes. "You told them you were here? Oh God, what they must think!"

"They don't mind, really."

"I know your family must be very open minded, but what about your *fiancée*?" Her frown turned into a sneer as she looked at him, another silent tear fell.

"Dana." He reached for her.

She jerked away. "Please, don't."

"It's not what you think," he sighed.

"I heard your brother say you were getting married. That usually includes a fiancée." Her eyes narrowed as she looked at him accusingly. What could he say?

"Dana, you're the first woman I've seen steadily for a long time." He shrugged, looking straight into her tear-filled eyes. "My brothers and I... we, umm... we've had this long-standing joke between the three of us—who would marry first?" he said with a choked laugh. "When one of us had a steady girlfriend, we'd say 'so, when's the wedding?'" She didn't look convinced. "Look sweetheart, Tony told my family about you—about us."

"So, you're not getting married?" she asked with so much hope in her voice he wanted to shout victory.

"Not today," he teased, smiling at her as the sides of her mouth tipped.

She threw arms tight around his neck.

"I'm so relieved. I thought your family might accuse me of corrupting you or something."

"Hon... ahh, I'm glad but I...can't breathe."

She let go of his neck so abruptly they both fell over and landed hard on the floor.

"Oww."

"I'm sorry, did I crush you?" he asked.

"No, my feet just hurt," she relied.

"You need to take a pain pill. I'll get you some water."

He came back with a glass and the medication. After she swallowed it, he took the glass from her, setting it aside, he held her face in his hands. "About what happened tonight."

"Look I know it was forward of me and if you didn't...mmm..."

He smothered whatever ridiculous thing she was going to say by pressing his lips against hers, gently devouring her softness. Then he pulled back and placed a kiss on her forehead.

"I loved everything we were doing at the restaurant. I plan on trying that again. But I was talking about the break-in."

"Oh."

"I don't want you working alone in the shop. At least, until the cops catch this guy."

"Rome, I have a business to run."

"Just for a while. Promise me."

She rolled her eyes. "I'll make sure Cynthia or Rick is with me while I'm working."

"You shouldn't even be walking while your stitches are healing. I don't suppose I can talk you into staying in bed all week."

She wrinkled her nose at him.

"That's what I thought. We'll talk about it tomorrow."

Rome noticed Dana was still wearing the dress she had on at dinner. Lifting her arms, he peeled it up and over her head, leaving her clad only in a lacy-blue bra, then crawled back to bed.

"You're still not wearing any panties," he teased as he unhooked her bra leaving them both naked.

"Rome, will you hold me? Just hold me tonight?"

He'd give anything to making love to her tonight. But her trust in him was growing stronger, despite her believing Julian's stupid remark about the marriage.

"Anything you want, sweetheart. I'll hold you all night if that's what you want."

They did sleep, for a while.

When Rome awoke several hours later, he found her watching him.

Silently, he slipped on a condom, then carefully rolled her onto her back and slowly entered her, rocking, loving her gently. Cautiously.

She instinctively responded, lifting her hips to join him, welcoming him with an unbearable tenderness. He whispered lovingly into her ear, stroking her hips and lifting her closer to him. Placing feather-light kisses over her eyes, her face, her mouth. He felt the warmth of her breath against his cheek in long, surrendering moans as her inner muscles squeezed around him creating an intense hardening in his erection unlike anything he'd ever experienced. He continued to slide into her silky-slick folds while holding her excruciatingly close until they both climaxed.

The pleasure was pure and explosive.

She fell asleep then, his body still locked with hers. He heard her whisper 'I love you' in her sleep. It gave him a feeling of indefinable rightness. As if suddenly, his life fell into place for the first time.

In a flash of insight, Rome knew his pursuit for marrying Dana had altered significantly.

He couldn't keep up the deception any longer.

Chapter Fifteen

ROME WAS ASLEEP—IN HER BED.

It was still too surreal to believe.

He looked so beautiful, so peaceful.

Dana couldn't rest while her feet throbbed and itched against the bounded wrappings around her feet. She got out of bed and threw on an oversized T-shirt, then took more pain medication.

Sitting back on the edge of the bed, she couldn't keep from studying the man lying supine in her bed. His face was turned toward her with a serine expression, so unlike the passion-filled features she'd come to know.

He'd tossed aside the sheets during the night, now lying naked and filling the bed. His chest rising and falling in a restful rhythm, his penis, though flaccid, still impressive and powerful nestled against the bulge of his testicles and dark curly hair between his legs. She'd never looked so closely at a man before and found the experience heady and arousing. His presence caused a sensuous stirring previously unknown to her. As if her sexual awaking was laying dormant—just waiting for him. Waiting to be discovered and nurtured, eagerly unfolding from his touch.

She snagged one of her paper pads by the nightstand and sat cross-legged in a chair by the bed to study him, memorizing every line of his nose, the generous curves of his full soft lips. Lips so soft, had it not been for the beard stubble, they'd look almost feminine. The shadow of his bread gave him a sensuous and manly appearance. Sexy. His dark hair fell in thick shiny tendrils across his forehead, unruly from sleep. Her fingers ached to lace through the tousled mass but feared she'd disrupt his peaceful slumber before she finished her study of him.

He possessed a firm strength, even in sleep, that drew her, but there was something else. Something new about him—a contentment to his face she'd never noticed. Was it there before? Perhaps it was the same expression reflected in her own face. Despite the events of last night, Dana suddenly felt as if she could do anything as long as Rome was with her.

She noticed how his long sturdy legs and massive shoulders overwhelmed her small double bed mattress as it bowing from his weight. Smiling, she thought she needed a bigger bed, then dismissed the idea.

This was just temporary. She had to stop thinking of them as a couple. It would only lead to heartache.

Maybe it was already too late. She was falling...deep.

Instead of worrying about her heart, Dana busied herself with her artistic assessment.

It was simpler and easier to justify her long, steady gazes as she looked at him with an artist's eye. Her hand drew smooth lines across her paper, his broad shoulders and his muscular arms, his chest. In sleep, Rome held a certain grace and virility that could tempt even a sainted woman. It was no wonder the triplet blondes found him fascinating to watch. Even Dana couldn't keep her eyes from returning to his sex and wished she had the courage to show her appreciation for his body while he was awake.

She continued to sketch his manly organ, when it began to harden before her eyes... His flaccid penis was growing as and she watched him, mesmerized by the changes.

"Like what you see?" he teased as he stretched his body, his feet dangling off the end of the mattress. "Why aren't you naked and in bed?"

She glanced at him to find him watching her through heavy lidded eyes.

"I didn't wake you did I?" She shut her paper pad.

"No, I just noticed you weren't in bed." A sleep-filled, sexy grin spread across his face and she felt her bones melt. "Perusing my... attributes?"

"Well..." she cleared her throat, "with an artist eye, of course."

"I'm disappointed," he said in a mock pout. "I was hoping you found me so devastating you'd decided to tie me to your bed and keep me as your love slave."

"Thought about it," she teased. Looking away thoughtfully for a moment, she asked, "Rome, I... this is a tough thing for me to ask, but..."

"Anything. You know that."

She looked at her hands in her lap. "I've...never really looked—I mean *really* looked at a male body before." She looked at him briefly to gauge his response. "I'd like to. Would you teach me? Show me how to please you?"

"Mmm, yeah, I'd like that. But only on one condition."

"What?" She chewed at her lower lip.

"We'll need a few... things first."

"Things?"

"Yeah," he said scanning the room. "Do you have any scarves or neck ties somewhere?"

"Umm, maybe." *Scarves?* "You'll have to look for yourself, though. My feet are out of commission right now."

"Sure, just tell me where."

Rome slid from bed as graceful as a cat, so incredibly comfortable with his naked body. So casual, she thought, as if they'd been together for years. Dana only wished she was as comfortable with her own body.

"Ah ha... black silk! These will do."

"My panties! Rome?"

"I just need one more...here's one. Humm, a *pink* scarf. Well, it will have to do, I guess."

He stalked back to the bed eyeing her reaction to his nakedness. It made her all the more uncomfortable.

"Don't worry," he winked. "After this, you'll be begging for me to strip every time we're together."

She simply sighed.

"Here, take these..." he said as he sprawled back to the center of the bed, placing pillows behind his head.

Dana took her panties and scarf from his out stretched hand. "Okay, now what?"

"First, you need to take off that shirt. We need to be skin to skin for this."

"This is going to be really tough for me with you watching," she said shyly.

"Exactly. Now take one of these and blindfold me." He smiled at her at her questioning look. "It's okay."

"Blindfold you with my panties?" she wrinkled her nose. "Are you sure?" *She* wasn't sure.

"This way you can look all you want and not feel self-conscious."

She smiled wide as her face flushed with excitement. "Really? I like that idea. Here, lean forward." Tying the black panties together then around his eyes, she said, "No peeking."

"I promise."

"What about..." she smiled to herself, "Never mind," she said feeling naughty and loving it. Dana guided Rome's hands to her brass headboard and tied them together with the pink scarf.

Love slave, indeed, she thought. She giggled a little when he tried to tug at his wrists. "Tell me what to do."

"Just touch me—everywhere."

Dana straddled his hips and gazed down at the feast before her. Like the first time she ate ice cream at Baskin Robbins. All those flavors to choose from. Her mouth watered as her eyes wandered loving each part of him.

"Mmm, where to start?"

"Anywhere you want. I'm at your mercy."

Feeling deliciously powerful, she leaned over him, bringing her fingertips to his face and neck. His firm sensual mouth, so perfect for kissing. She pulled his bottom lip between her teeth and sucked it gently into her mouth, tracing it with her tongue.

"I've wanted to do that since the first time you kissed me," she whispered. A growl emerged from his chest and she felt that vibration zing through her like warm electric currents.

Feeling mischievous with her seductive self-assurance, Dana smiled to herself when his hips buck slightly. She moved to his right ear, tracing her tongue around the rim, her warm breath blowing softly against it and her confidence spiraled upward. He was holding back—and it thrilled her.

Oh, how in heaven was she supposed to keep her heart at a distance when this beautiful man lying before her fulfilled her every fantasy? She wanted to weep and to revel in the joy of him, all at the same time.

Grinning, Dana sat up to tease at his flesh with the tips of her fingers, trailing them around the corded muscles of his broad chest and ribs, trying to learn him by heart. His body captivated her just as Rome, the photographer, fascinated her.

Leaning down again, she flick her tongue around each dark, manly nipples. Rome's chest expanded as he sucked in his breath, sending her spirits soaring in the wonder of this man. She tugged one brown nipple into her month, gauging his response as she licking and suckling before moving to the other again. His erection pulsed against her bottom and she felt incredibly aroused knowing she was the cause.

"You're killing me," he groaned, and she let out a giggle while snaking her mouth and tongue down the center of his chest then to his rock-hard abdomen, teasing his flesh with her hair as it trailed above her head on his belly.

"Lord, woman, you don't need my help. You're driving me nuts."

"Is that a good thing?"

"Oh, yeah. Come closer," he hissed through clenched teeth. "I *need* to kiss your breasts while you drive me insane."

She liked that idea. Swishing her chest back and forth, allowing her nipples to tease his skin, she sat with her back arched and drew his head to her left breast. Rome took one ripe nipple between his lips, licking in circular motions, moistening her breast. Explosive currents of pleasure raced through her. She pulled back one nipple and brought the other for equal attention. She was in control.

"Mmm, I love how your skin tastes," he said. "Do you like it when I kiss you here, Dana?"

"You're making my body tingle all over," she said, breathless. Releasing her breast from his mouth, she straddled him, watching in wonder as his penis sprang forward. She could feel the warmth of his hips between her inner thighs as she massaged his belly and ribs, trailing butterfly kisses along his navel, reaching dangerously close to his erection—now throbbing from her indirect attention.

Working up the courage to touch him there, Dana laced her fingers through the course hair nestled around his penis and testicles, gently scraping her nails at the roots, traced her thumbs in tiny circles at the soft flesh of his inner thighs. Rome's hips rocked forward, trying to coax her closer to his sensitive member.

"Touch me, Dana," he pleaded.

She did. Her small hands took him, holding him, encircling the base with enraptured curiosity, learning with an artist's eye and touching with the stroke of a curious lover. She loved the softness of the skin and the steel hardness beneath.

Slowly, seductively, her hand slid upward, finally arriving at the head of his erection, smooth and shiny, she rubbed it as if it were a succulent fruit. Round, ripe and beautiful. There was nothing else to compare to the male anatomy, she thought, and grinned when Rome breathed in harsh, uneven rhythms from each stroke of her hand. With a ripple of feminine fascination, she skimmed the pads of her thumbs slowly down to his testicles. Cupping them gently. Kneading them. Weighing them in one palm while thumbing small firm circles at his perineum with the other. Loving how he felt in her hands, not only because of the softness, warm to the touch, but because of the pleasure coursing through him as he groaned through clenched teeth. It was like magic—watching him.

"Am I doing this right?"

"A little harder, sweetheart. Mmm, that's it!"

She gripped him tight with both hands, amazed as his hips pulsed against her, allowing him to set the rhythm. With daring confidence, Dana bent her head and flicked her tongue across the head, liking the salty taste of him and the musky scent of his sex. She licked at him again and again before lightly sucking on the top, increasing her own arousal as his body stiffened in response.

"Oh, God... stop, stop! Right now!"

Dana tensed. "Did I do something wrong?"

"No, you were doing everything right. A little too right. But I want to try something else. Take the blindfold off me."

Timidly she asked, "Can I leave your hands tied?"

"Sure," he chuckled.

"Good," she said, still in control.

"I've created a sex monster," he grinned while she removed the blindfold from eyes. "Now, you wear the blindfold."

"Rome!" she protested, then tied it around her eyes and felt silly wearing her own underwear on her head. "Okay. Now what?" she asked as she spread her hands across his chest for balance.

*****

For a moment, Rome thought he was going explode with Dana's innocent exploration of his body. Her delicate fingers felt like magic against his skin. Sex had never felt this fine before—and they hadn't really had sex yet! He wasn't sure if he was going to make it through without coming all over himself. He had to concentrate on Dana, teach her. Show her how to make love to a man. But that was becoming so damn difficult when all his body wanted to do was nail her to the mattress.

He had to stop and change tactics before his tutelage came to a screeching halt.

Rome desperately wanted to touch her, but his restraints prevented him. Though he could easily release himself any time he wished, he remembered his promise to Dana. He had to let her do this on her own.

"Please, tell me what to do," she asked.

Rome watched her feel her way around his pectorals and abdomen, as if memorizing the texture, and every ridge, every dip in his torso.

"I want you to talk to me... tell me what you feel," he said, still trying to control his own desire as he watched, surprised at how weak and powerful she made him feel just by simply touching him. "What do I feel like to you, Dana? How do you feel when you touch me?"

"Ahhmm... I feel heat."

"Good. What else? Just throw out the words as you feel them, forget sentences or poetry. Just words, feelings."

"Beauty. Perfection, soft yet hard, dreams and fantasy melding together. Sweat, bone, muscle, strength. Confidence, generosity, inspiration."

"What inspires you?"

"Your strong yet soft, sexy voice. It excites me. I can feel it vibrate inside me when you speak."

God, she was a treasure. "Don't stop."

"Sensual, erotic...and I love how you sigh and moan when I touch you. It makes me feel strong. Like I can do anything."

"You can, Dana. Anything," he whispered, encouraging her to reach beyond her comfort zone and unleash the passion he knew was hiding deep inside.

"And I love how you smell when you're aroused." He watched as she drew in a deep breath. "I could inhale your scent all night. And I love how you hold my hand when we're in the car, how you hold me all night. And how you stroke my hair. I've fantasized about you for a long time, wondering what it would be like to make love with you."

"And now?" Her honesty hit him hard in the chest.

"It's everything and more... more than what my dreams ever were. You're more then any of my fantasies and... and I can't believe I'm telling you this," she confessed, shaking her head. "I should be embarrassed but I'm not. Not now. Not with you."

"Don't ever be ashamed when we're together. Now, tell me what you want to do most?"

"I want to kiss you here." She said as she grasped his penis between her palms. It throbbed at her belly as she sat astride him, feeling him, stroking.

"Why don't you?"

"If not sure how. I'm afraid I'll do it wrong or you'll think I'm a hussy if I do it right."

He laughed at her innocent declaration. "There isn't anything you could do wrong, sweetheart, except ignore me there."

"Really? Then you'll let me know if you want me to do something different."

"Absolutely."

She drove at him like an eagle to its prey. Her enthusiasm warmed him as much as it aroused him. She made him feel like a god. His mind wanted to step back and find the guilt still hiding deep down. But he released his guilt last night when he decided to release himself from his father's demands.

Tony would be royally pissed, but he'd get over it. Nothing was worth losing this innocent woman's trust.

"How am I doing?" she asked as her pink tongue darted out from her mouth and circled the crest of his shaft in feather-like flicks. Then wrapped her lips around the head tasting him like a candy sucker while her hands caresses and squeezed.

"Ahh...I think I've died and gone to heaven..." he whispered. He was imploding inside himself before he needed to and he wanted her closer to him. "You know what I would love?"

"What?!"

"I would love to feel myself between your beautiful breasts." He waited for her look of surprise, but it never came.

"Like this?"

Oh, her enthusiasm!

"Mmm, oh yeah. Take off the blindfold, sweetheart. I want you to look at me. At us. Are you okay with that?"

"I'll try," she whispered. Then she continued to rub him between your breasts, but she seemed pensive. "Close your eyes and don't think. Just do."

"No, I want to see, too."

Rome picked up the pace as his hips jerk involuntarily between her chest. "I think we should stop before..."

"No! Let me watch you."

He let her, finding he couldn't deny her anything. Suddenly he released his own hands from the loose restraints then squeezed her breasts together around his cock as it swelled. The sensation intensified into a burning heat of dizzying euphoria.

"God, you feel wonderful!"

"I think I like watching." He could feel her tongue reach down with sly little licks as he pulsed between her breasts, her nipples pointing at him, driving him over the edge. His breathing intensified as his pelvis thrust wildly. His body went rigid as the intense pleasure increase. He felt his stomach contract and his thighs tense. Then she did something completely unexpected—she mounted him like a goddess atop wild animal, then thrust his erection into her body in one smooth quick motion as her head threw back in elation and he thought he would die on the spot.

She screamed with release and his cock grew unbelievably large and he grasped her hips, bucking into her faster and faster until his back arched up one last time before he spent himself into her. Then gently falling back down from the clouds.

"That... was incredible, what did you... do, Dana?" He could barely catch his breath. "I wasn't wearing anything," he said holding her back from him to look into her flushed face.

"It's okay, Rome." She lifted her head up from his heaving chest. "It's the wrong time of the month."

"Still, we shouldn't have done that without protection." He brought her head back to his chest, stroking her hair and tracing her spine. Needing to feel her close. To believe she was for real. That she was his. "I'm just worried about you. You would tell me, wouldn't you?

If...?"

He felt her nod her head as she yawned. "Yes, I wouldn't keep something like that from you."

"Good," briefly brushing his lips to hers. "Now, let's get you and your wounded feet into the tub."

"Rome?"

"Yeah?"

"Can we do that again?"

"God, woman," he chuckled. "You're going to kill me."

Chapter Sixteen

"WHAT HAVE YOU FIND OUT?" Patricia stared ominously at her nieces, annoyed as they stared back with their mother's azure blue eyes. Annoyed even more that one sheltered girl like Dana Baker could cause her so much irritation and inconvenience. Patricia Wilson wanted back what was rightfully hers.

"Nothing."

"She has what Greta Baker stole from me. I want it back!"

"Don't worry. It's only a matter of time before Ms. Baker gives in to the DeMitri charm."

"I can't to rely on Miss Priss Baker's hormones alone. We need to know the location. I need to know where it's hidden." She tried to disguise her annoyance from the girls. "With the building still under Baker ownership, finding it will be a challenge." She sucked in her breath. "We'd have it already if your brother hadn't bungled the burglary to her apartment."

"Yeah, he had some dumbass idea it was hidden behind a frame. I think he got the idea from a movie or something." They all laughed—except Patricia. Her livelihood was at stake and her idiot nephew could stew in prison for all the good he did.

"One of the sons lives in the apartment right next to hers. Isn't that enough proof?" one of them asked.

"No. She has to be with him in a more 'friendly' capacity or my proof means dick."

"If he's half the man his brother is, she's already been flat on her back—several times," one of them commented with a smirk. They all let out a knowing giggle.

"Then it's up to the three of you to prove it."

"We'll get it," one of them said with enthusiasm.

"This just doesn't feel right," the other said, "What if Greta's granddaughter doesn't even know about it?"

"Of course she knows!" Patricia snapped. "Greta would've made sure of it." Patricia looked at each of her beautiful girls, basking in the knowledge of her power to exploit their gratitude into blind obedience. "Look, one of you will have to get close to Dana Baker. Gain her trust. Befriend her and take a good look around her building."

"For what, exactly?"

"A journal. A document, a lock-box key, a safe deposit key. Something to give me a clue to where Greta hid my property. Unless Ms. Baker decides to start a social life, we'll need to find it by other means."

"I think I can do that," one of them said, eyeballing her sisters for back up.

"Fine. Just get me what I need. And just remember who raised you after your mother was killed." That old threat always seemed to work with them.

"No problem, Aunt Patty."

God, she detested it when they called her Patty.

Patricia nodded. Confident she could count on their intelligence to get what she needed.

"If she owns the whole damn building, this is gonna time some time."

"Then get going," she sighed. "And go post bail for your brother, for chrissakes, before some butch decides to hot-stick it to him, then do what you have to. Just don't be stupid enough to get caught."

"How do we bring back the proof, wear a spy camera in our bra?" one of them laughed.

"Oh, like you haven't done that before," the other said.

"Ladies—just go get your brother. I've got clients to see," Patricia sighed, and thought vamping wasn't what it used to be.

*****

Dana sat behind her counter in a satisfied daze as she heard the locksmith repairing her back door were the burglar gained entrance the night before.

She and Rome made love twice that morning before he placed her in the tub with her bandaged feet dangling over the edge, and bathed her like a child.

For someone who valued independence, she thoroughly enjoyed his *thorough* attention to her cleanliness. It was soothing to have someone wash her for a change. Smiling, she wondered what happened to the sensible, level-headed woman she used to be.

Rome had interviews and research scheduled for his trip to Central America that was *coming way too soon* and he wouldn't be back for the rest of the day.

Philippe and Julian camped out in her shop last night since her back door lock was broken. And by the time she and Rome came down stairs, Philippe had already left. Julian left soon after to shower and change.

Thanks to Rome's family, a new alarm system was scheduled for installment later in the afternoon. They'd been generous about everything and she was exceedingly grateful.

The locksmith's power tools hummed a tumultuous rhythm matching the disorderly commotion swimming through her brain. The more she dwelled on her morning with Rome, the harder it was to fill out the insurance forms her claims agent left earlier. When her agent and the appraiser made an agreement on her financial loss, she finally had time for reflection. And again she wondered what on earth a burglar could be looking for. She didn't have anything of real value except the building itself. No expensive paintings or high-end equipment.

It was really odd. Even her agent looked at her strangely, as if she had something to do with the break-in. The only viable explanation he could write on her claims evaluation was vandalism. And for the first time in her life, she felt a vague and shadowy fear. Because vandals only vandalized with a willful and malicious intent to destroy property. It also could frighten and intimidate.

Had it not been for Rome and his family, that's exactly how she'd feel. But somehow, she felt safe instead.

But who? Who would want to cause her harm? Unless they were really looking for something. Maybe something of her grandmother's hidden away in the shop someplace. But what, and why?

God, it was as if she was frozen in an odd limbo, an alternate universe where all decisions and actions were impossible simply because someone wanted something from her that she didn't have to give. Which left her with what?

Her shop. Her feelings for Rome. New friends.

Dana was sure she should be doing some serious soul-searching right now, but she was tired of struggling. Tired of trying to fit the pieces of the puzzle together when she wasn't sure if there was a puzzle. Maybe, she was just tired from the roller coaster ride from last night. The more she thought about her feelings for Rome, the more uneasy she felt about her grandmother, the letter, and the thought of being watched. And there was the possibility her grandmother was hiding something. Something that someone wanted badly enough to tear her shop apart.

Rick arrived after Julian left for Rome's place. Dana quickly put him to work to repair the broken frames. Some were actually repairable. Most weren't. He was acting strange again this morning. But he always acted a little odd around her. According to Cynthia, he was just shy. But he made Dana uneasy, and she wondered for the hundredth time today if he had something to do with the break-in. No, that was ridiculous. He framed all the pictures. Why would he rip them apart?

Geez, Louise. She was tempted to just fire him. But he was too darned skilled. She'd hate to let go of such a talented framer.

As her suspicions of Rick grew, Dana became more and more suspicious of anyone. Everyone. People looking through her shop window. Even the geeky tourists with their cameras and cheesy Hollywood T-shirts.

Dana sighed contentedly. This morning, she refused to care. After the mind-blowing sex from the last two days, she didn't want to think at all. Her nights with Rome were enough for her normally sensible brain to go haywire.

Rick walked toward her.

"Well? What do you think, can we salvage anything?" Dana asked.

He shook his head and looked at the floor. "All the pictures were torn to shreds. Some of the frames I can repair, but we don't have any pictures left once the frames are fixed." She heard the weariness in his voice and she warmed slightly toward him.

"Rick, I know you worked hard on these pictures, but right now we have to work with what's left. Just do what you can for now. We'll come up something."

He nodded still looking at his feet, then glanced over at hers, "Your feet are bandaged."

"Yeah. I know."

"Huh," and he went back to work.

"I hope *I* can come up with something," Dana mumbled, then smiled to herself for the first time that day. Then she went back at her insurance forms.

She was feeling pretty good, all things considered. Too good, in fact.

It's got to be the drugs.

It's probably why she really let go of her inhibitions last night. Not that she'd take even a second back. Rome had been so loving and so patient with her. Even if they hadn't made love, it would have still been one of the most erotic moments of her life. A moment in time she would cherish, even if their relationship couldn't last.

Dana felt that familiar twist around her heart. She was walking a very thin line. A line that was becoming tightly woven around her heartstrings. It was a fragile line that could easily break if she made a single misstep, and resented keeping Rome a secret. Not that she had many people to tell. But what if Patricia might be out there—somewhere—watching her? It was wearing her down.

Or was it the smell of chemicals and turpentine that still permeated the air?

Philippe thoughtfully placed oscillating fans around the doorways and windows to release some of the smell. But it would take several days of airing out before the shop smelled normal again. Maybe she'd send Cynthia out for scented candles and incense, she thought when she saw Julian arrive with company.

"Hi. We're here about the job, er, jobs." His irresistible grin, so much like his brother's.

Dana stared at all the familiar faces, dumbfounded.

"Come on in," Julian directed. He looked at her first before admitting them, "If that's okay with you, Dana?" Julian asked.

"Umm... yeah." she nodded from behind the counter, still sitting in the chair Rome had brought down for her.

"Hi, Dana."

"Victoria. Right?"

"Nice to see you again," she said smiling with perfect bleached-white teeth.

Dana knew it had to be Victoria because she hadn't met her two sisters yet. The woman was beautiful even make-up free in plain jeans and a T-shirt. Dana felt that familiar feeling of blending into the walls in comparison.

"How did you know...?"

"Oh, Rome mentioned it to Tony and Tony called us..." said Echo looking sleepy and rumpled as he staggered in and propped himself up onto the counter.

"Well, I can't tell you how happy I am to see all of you again...considering. I'm sort of... stationary for now."

"You know my brother," Julian said. "Rome's recruited us to make sure you don't lift a finger."

Dana was once again surprised, there seemed to be no limits to Rome's generosity and protective nature. Yet here they where, all eager to help.

"I'm sorry to hear about what happen," Echo said as he place his hand gently on her shoulder and looked at her bandaged feet, then he glanced around at the mess that was left after Rome's family cleared up the breakage. "We're here to set things right, Dana. And I'd do anything for my cousin," he smiled at her, "and that includes helping out his lady."

Dana balked. Was there anyone from his family that didn't know? She stiffened. The more people who knew about her affair, the harder it was to hide. "Don't you guys have jobs?" Dana asked skeptically. "Not that I'm complaining."

Echo looked at the ceiling, scratching his beard stubble and Victoria smiled and said, "I'm self-employed. This bozo called in sick. So Tony dragged him out of his drunken bed."

"Hey, I'm not drunk!" exclaimed Echo, "I just have a headache. Besides, I can make up time tonight."

"Echo's a *Jeet Kune Do* expert," Victoria said with admiration.

Dana saw Echo's face flush. "I don't want you guys to get into trouble or put you out for my sake," she said.

"It's no biggy—really," Echo said, "I teach at night and work at the sound studio when they need me."

Rick remained silent, watching from the frame room.

"So when's the big day?" It was Victoria's other sister. Dana wasn't sure which one.

"The big day?"

Dana must have been staring because the woman blushed slightly and said, "I'm sorry, Victoria isn't the best at decorum. I'm Grace, her younger sister."

"Yeah, if you call a whopping ten minutes younger," Victoria said in mock annoyance. "Elizabeth had a photo shoot for some lingerie website, so she couldn't come."

"Oh," Dana said. "I'm grateful for any help. The opening's this Friday."

"That doesn't leave us a lot of time," Julian said. "And you have to stay put," he laughed.

She should be angry with Rome for being so heavy-handed, but it was so sweet of him to find her impromptu help. She silently wished he were here. But then looked at all the eyes and ears that might witness them together and quickly changed her mind.

"Hello, I'm looking for a Dana Baker."

"Hey, there cutie," Victoria said to the FTD guy carrying an armload of baby daises and tiny pink rose buds. "I'm not Dana, but I can be if you want me too."

Dana watched as the poor guy flushed profusely.

"I'm Dana! Those for me?" She reached for the clipboard to sign her name. Attached to the bouquet in place of a bow was a pair of bright pink fluffy slippers.

"Gee, I wonder who these could be from," she heard Victoria teased.

"I don't know. There's no card," Dana noticed.

"No offense, Dana. My brother is a generous guy," Julian said, "but I don't think Rome would think to buy a woman slippers."

"Oh," she said disappointed. "Maybe the card fell off." Panicked, she thought, *What if Patricia planted a micro vid-cam in the flowers? Oh, God! I'm losing it.*

"What's going on? Dana, what the hell happened here last night?" It was Cynthia carrying her usual coffee and bag of chocolate-filled bagels.

"Good morning, I hope you brought enough for our new recruits," Dana said, avoiding her question.

"Geez, this place smells like crap! What happened?"

"We had a brake-in. Nothing's missing. Just a lot of broken stuff."

"The pictures! All our hard work," she said as she dropped her breakfast on the counter and looked the place over.

Echo picked up the bag and started eating from it.

"Shit, I'll kill the asshole that did this," Cynthia said as she looked back at Dana and saw her bandages.

Dana simply raised her eyebrows innocently as she watched Cynthia ears turn red.

"I'll stuff his balls down his throat," she mumbled and went to work. "Oh, and it's nice to meet everybody. I hope you all ate your Wheaties this morning. If not, I recommend Mrs. Hilson's chocolate-filled bagels... like the ones your friend... just polished off," Cynthia said staring at Echo as he licked his fingers and shrugged.

Julian and Echo offered to buy coffee for everybody while Cynthia and Dana started a game plan.

"I'm officially making you my store manager," Dana said.

"Really? Me? Does this mean I get a raise?" Cynthia asked.

"Unfortunately I can't afford to give you one until after we open. Plus, I'm not completely myself. I'm still under the influence of Vicodin. I might increase your salary to what you actually deserve," she teased.

Cynthia shocked her and gave her a hug. "I'm so sorry you got hurt last night, I wish you'd called me."

"There really wasn't time. Plus, Rome's family hasn't let me out of their sight. They've been great."

"You know..." Cynthia said, "...that man has a major bone for you. What's he like— you know, in bed?" she whispered.

"Oh, stop it. And he does not have a..." she blushed, then smiled and said, "I'll never tell."

"Oh, please. Anyone with one eye and half a brain could tell you've got Mr. Photo Man wrapped around your panty line."

"I'm not even going..."

"Umm, there's a delivery here, Dana."

"Can you sign for it please, Rick?" Dana asked.

"Yeah, okay," he said, seeming more nervous then normal with new people around.

"I better go help him. He's great at framing. He's useless for anything else," Cynthia said as she followed Rick out the back.

"Mmm, just the way I like 'em," Victoria said.

"I'm sorry?" Dana asked.

"You know, cute, quiet, and talented," she said.

Dana looked at her.

"What, you don't think he's cute?"

"It's not that," Dana thought for a moment. "He makes me nervous. Like he's watching me. I can't put my finger on it."

"You want me to watch him for ya?" she asked as she wiggled her perfectly plucked brows.

"I'm not sure if you're kidding or not, but yeah. I need someone to keep on eye on him."

"I know how to handle men, honey." Then she walked to the frame room with a little more swing in her hips then normal.

Dana sighed, and thought about Rome again.

"Dana."

Dana turned to find Claire coming through the front.

"Hi, Claire. Thanks for being here last night."

"That's what family's for. Is there anything I can help with?"

"Gosh, no. I've got more than enough volunteers today," she laughed. "But you can sit and keep me company while everyone else is doing my job."

"Sure. We can girl-talk."

"What's Philippe doing today?"

"Oh, he's gone off to Los Angeles County Museum of Art to get the hall ready for his showing next week," she sighed. "He's got a one-track mind when it comes to his art. I feel like it's his mistress and I'm the doting wifey waiting at home."

"But you admire him for it," Dana noticed.

"Yeah, it's what I found so sexy about him when we first met." She looked nostalgic for a moment. "Back then, Alberto, Rome's father, was on his usual foire of boob-collecting and I was feeling sorry for myself. So, I went to an art show somewhere in Hollywood. I can't even remember the place. But I remember Philippe. He was so handsome and charming. When our eyes met, I knew. I knew this man—this brilliant artist was my sole mate. My marriage to Rome's father was failing at the time."

"Really? That must have been a little frightening," Dana said, listening intently.

"No, I was too self-absorbed to be thinking 'oh my God, I think my life is about to change' but that's exactly how it happened. He came up to me that night and said he'd recognized me. He said I had a 'beautiful form' and begged me to model for his next series of sculptures. And the rest is history," she sighed. "I don't think Rome ever forgave me for leaving," she sighed. "When I left, he stayed behind. But he did get Barbara in the bargain."

"Barbara?"

"His step-mother. There wasn't another woman on the planet he loved more. "He still drives her car," she said smiling sadly.

"The silver Jaguar was his step-mom's?"

Claire nodded. "That's probably why he's in love with you too. You favor her in a lot of ways."

Change the subject—fast. "Had you met him before?"

"Who, Philippe?"

"Yes. You said he remembered you."

"Oh, God no. A face like that I would have remembered. No, he remembered me from Alberto's first Volupté issue, early seventies, I think."

"Was there a feature on the family? Is that how he recognized you?"

"Gosh no, honey," Claire laughed. "I was *Volupté's* first centerfold babe."

"Oh!"

"Umm, Dana?"

It was Rick—again. Dana could usually tell it was him by the odd way he shuffled his feet when he walked.

"What's up?" she asked when he dropped several boxes of stock on the counter.

"Well, when we framed those pictures that got messed up?"

"Yes." *Why can't he just get to the point?*

"Well, here's the thing. Most of the posters Cynthia ordered were already framed. And now there aren't any others to replace them."

"Well, what about the one's we salvaged from the break-in? Can't we re-use those?"

"The thing is, there's maybe only three or four that survived the break-in."

"Oh dear," Claire said looking at her sympathetically. "I hope your insurance will cover the damage."

"It will. Unfortunately, not in time for the store to open."

"Can't we just order more pictures?" Rick asked.

Though that was the obvious choice, Dana had maxed out her credit with the vendor when she placed her order. If she wanted to place another order, she'd have to max out her personal credit card.

"There isn't time, Rick."

"Humm, an art store with bear walls could be problematic," Claire commented. "But Dana, aren't you an artist? Don't you have artwork of your own to use until you re-stock?"

"Not unless we want to hang my hand-painted stools and cabinets from the ceiling, that's about all I have of my own stuff."

"Actually, that might be sort of cool," Cynthia said as she walked up to the counter, "having some of your stools hanging down, you know, like how they hang baskets and pots from the ceiling at *Crate and Barrel?* It would defiantly look artsy."

"Yes, but I don't think I have enough of those either. Plus, that still leaves me with blank seafoam green walls."

"Hey, I know. Let's get some art students from the university to loan us their artwork, you know, like on consignment?" Cynthia suggested.

"That's sounds doable..." Dana shrugged as she took a box cutter from the counter drawer and started opening the boxes of paint supplies that were just delivered. She wasn't convinced of Cynthia's idea either.

"Yes, but you might end up with pieces that aren't exactly appropriate. It might come off as amateurish," Claire commented.

"You've been in the art world longer than any of us, Claire," Dana said. "What would you suggest?"

Dana's feet were starting hurt.

"Mmm, give me some time to think. I'm sure I can..."

"What the heck is this!?" Dana exclaimed. "Cynthia!"

"What did I do know?"

"I just opened up a box of pencils and found these," Dana said holding out a box to Cynthia.

"Oh, these?" Cynthia said as she slid the contents out of the box and observed them carefully.

"Hmm, very creative," Claire said.

"Creative? Claire—these are pencils with penis heads for erasers!"

"What was that about penis heads?" Victoria asked enthusiastically, walking in on the conversation. They attracted Grace's attention, too.

"And there should be a couple of boxes of pencils with boobs in there too. I couldn't leave the guys empty handed," Cynthia said.

Dana snorted. She definitely needed another pain pill.

Claire laughed and said, "I'll be your first customer. Sell me the whole box. I think they're clever."

"Tiny little dick heads," Victoria laughed. "I'll take a whole box to go."

"Wait until you see the naughty pink erasers."

Dana groaned.

"What's wrong with that?"

"Cynthia, this is an art store. Not *Frederick's of Hollywood.* Where would we even display something like this?"

"They're just pencils," Cynthia replied. "This is an art store, and artists need creative tools to create art. We could place them in the glass case here under the register counter. I'll display them discretely with a 'for her only' and 'for him only.' Trust me, in this town, you won't be able to keep in stock."

Victoria took a box then head to the frame room.

Several minutes later, Dana saw Rick approach. "What now, Rick?" She was starting to feel edgy. She definitely needed a pain pill.

"Did you ask Victoria to help me in back?" he asked.

"Yeah, why?"

"She's rearranging all my equipment and decorating it all girly-like."

He'd just said more words in one breathe then she'd ever heard him say. "Is that bad, Rick?" Dana wanted to laugh. "Just let her. You can change it back later."

"All right." Dana shook her head. He sounded so dejected. Dana still wondered if it was an act to get girls to feel sorry for him, like guys who took people's dogs for a walk to get women's attention.

What a motley crew this was turning into. She had a store manager that wanted to sell naughty art supplies, a former pen-up girl, two knock-out blondes for stock girls, a singer who constantly sang Stevie Ray Vaughan's *Pride and Joy* to himself and ate their breakfast, and a framer who was afraid of girls. Then there was herself—an artist who didn't paint. Her furniture and erotic sketches not withstanding.

"Claire, do you think you could help me up to my apartment? I need to take my medication."

"Oh, sure, honey."

Dana looked at Rome's mom and saw where he got his beauty. Claire had the same shiny brown hair and distinctive nose. Although their eyes were different, there was an unmistakable family resemblance. Dana could easily see Claire as an airbrushed babe with a staple in her navel. Even now, Claire had poise and grace that made her stand out among other women.

"What? Do I have lipstick on my teeth?" she asked when she noticed Dana staring.

"Huh? Oh! No. I was just noticing that Rome doesn't have your light-green eyes."

"No, he's got his father irresistible brown ones and my sweet disposition—poor thing," she laughed. "Here, let's get you upstairs."

"Damn imbeciles!"

"Ah, Philippe. You're back," Claire said mildly as she helped Dana stand up from her chair.

"Fools—they have no respect for true art," he shouted.

"*N'agac,ent*, my darling," Claire crooned. "Let me get our invalid up stairs and you can tell me all about."

"Harrumph."

She winked at Dana. "Artists are such grumpy people," she whispered.

"I heard *zat*, kitten."

She made kissy noises at him and Dana noticed his face relaxed and envied what the couple had together.

As they hobbled up the stairs, Dana had a wild idea.

She quickly took her pain pill then asked Claire to have a seat before she lost her nerve.

"I'm guessing you want to asked about my son," Claire said.

"Well, yeah... but not right now. I have an idea I need to talk to someone about."

"Sure, hon."

Dana reluctantly pulled out her drawings and handed them to Claire. Ordinarily, she'd never in a million years show these to anyone voluntarily.

Must be the drugs.

"Tell me what you think," Dana said closing her eyes a moment for strength, "and please, be honest."

She handed Claire the less graphic drawings and held her breath.

"Oh, Lord. These are...really something. Beautiful, actually."

"They're drawings of your son," she blurted. "Well, the idea of him anyway." Dana briefly explained the history of her dreams, the drawings, and Rome... but not the sex part. "I was thinking... what if I used portions of these, maybe a sexy, manly leg, an enlargement—or mural-sized part of his chest, maybe a discrete drawing of his cute butt..." she looked at Claire, and blushed, remembering she was talking to the man's mother, but found Claire nearly mesmerized by each piece. "If it sounds like a stupid idea, please say so. But I'm kind of desperate for filling wall space right now."

"These are really wonderful. Has he seen them?"

"Yes, he, aah... encouraged me to draw some of them actually..." she cleared her throat.

Claire gave her a knowing smiling.

"But do you think Rome would mind having his body parts scattered on my shop walls? I know how sensitive he is about his father's magazine. I know this is art, but I'm just not sure."

"Well, if you keep each piece abstract yet still recognizable as the human male form, I think it would be a fantastic idea."

"Really?" Dana watched as Claire looked them over again and smiled. She must have recognize her son's features in them.

"You know... the women in this town, and a lot of men for that matter, will go gaga for these. It's just a matter of marketing."

"Well, I'm not real good at that. Plus, I've run out of funds. I can't afford any more advertising."

"Then you're in luck. Philippe is a genius at promotion. I'm sure if we show him these, he'd be glad to help."

"Just don't tell him about what we talked about. In fact, I don't want anyone to know they're mine."

"Are you certain? Because these are really good."

"I'm sure."

"All right. We'll just tell everyone they're on consignment."

"Thanks," Dana said as she let out a long breath.

"So, who's going to be the mystery artist?" Claire asked. "We'll need a name."

"T.S. Miles," Dana said. *This was insane.*

Claire raised her brows.

"My mother."

Claire gave her the thumbs up.

It was definitely the drugs.

Chapter Seventeen

ROME LEFT FINKLEMAN'S OFFICE feeling guilt-free and light hearted. Although he wasn't looking forward to telling Tony, Rome knew his brother would get over it. Hell, he'd probably start his own magazine and make it twice what *Volupté* was.

Rome's inheritance would have made his traveling costs easier to bear, but he had more important things to consider, now.

Dana.

The image of her sweet oval face and luscious body burned in his brain and he felt a ridiculous grin spread across his face. A familiar heat zinged through him, remembering her small frame imprisoning him in her heat as she straddled him.

Rome pinched the bridge of his nose and sighed. He had to come clean today. He wanted to tell her everything, now that the deal was off—no ulterior motives were hanging over his head.

His cell phone rang, shifting his lustful thought aside.

"This is Rome."

"Hi, Rome. It's Kimberly. Your Beverly Hills office called and they've got a, umm, situation."

"What's going on? Did Roger call in sick again?" His manager at his Beverly Hills studio had a nervous stomach and sometimes backed out when important clients scheduled a photo shoot.

"No, he's actually in Maui for the Henderson wedding."

"Oh, right. It's this week. Well, Wendy's there, isn't she?"

"She's actually the one who called," Kimberly said. "It seems Cher is getting married again and her photographer got busted for drugs. He's in jail, so she's in a bind and needs somebody ASAP."

"Cher? As in Sonny?" Rome asked.

"Yep."

"I'll be damned."

"So anyway, I guess the wedding is in Santa Fe, New Mexico, and Wendy can't get a babysitter for the three day drip."

"Three days? Jesus. Must be some wedding. Who's she marring, Prince Charles?"

"Very funny. I think he's some Canadian actor. Young, cute, sexy, you know the type," she laughed. "Anyway, Wendy's panicked. What should I tell her?"

"Call her back and tell her I'll be there within the hour. I've got family at my place," *and Dana to check on.* "I'll need to make some arrangements. Also, find out where exactly in Santa Fe this place is and get me a couple of plane tickets and hotel reservations. Oh, and tell Wendy I'll get a baby sitter for her."

"You got it, boss."

"Thanks, Kim." He hung up cursing. Although he could use some major funding after dumping his inheritance, he hated leaving Dana for too long.

When he arrived at her shop, it looked like grand central. Cynthia was on a ladder hanging who-knows-what from the ceiling, Grace was on her hands and knees with her ass in the air painting a banner that said GRAND OPENING FIRST 100 GUESTS-FREE GIFT, Echo was stacking paint jars while singing *I wanna be your teddy bear*, and amazingly, his mother was pricing paint brushes. *Will wonders never cease?*

"Hi, Mom."

She looked and smiled at him. "Hi, sweetie."

"Anything interesting happen while I was out?"

"Julian left with his father to the LACMA to re-negotiate for a another hall."

"What happened to the other one?" Rome asked.

"It seems the museum felt a collection of a newly discovered Russian paintings by one of the czar's children took priority over a modern sculptor. So, they gave Philippe the boot."

"Oh, boy. I'm glad I wasn't here to see it."

"Yeah, it was bloody," she sighed, then went back to her paintbrushes.

Rome shook his head and walked to the back. Rick was showing Victoria how to use the mat cutting machine, "Hey, guys. Where's Dana?" Rome asked.

"Oh, hey, Rome. She's upstairs," Victoria said. "She went to take a pain pill a while ago. I've haven't seen her since."

"Thanks." He ran up her apartment stairs two at a time, whistling to himself. Her door was cracked open, so he knocked lightly and walked in.

"You know, Claire, I'm not so sure about this. Don't you think Rome will recognize his own bu... *Rome!*" Dana shouted with a nervous laugh. "I... thought you were your mom." Her color flushed to an adorable fuchsia.

"Thanks a lot." She was sitting on her living room floor, crouched down over several newspapers, with paintbrushes and paint tubes cluttered everywhere—a quilted blanket covering or protecting a large canvas. "What am I supposed to recognize?"

"Nothing."

"Uh huh."

"It's a... surprise," she said with a tight smile.

"Well, I like surprises..." he said grabbing her by the waist, hauling her up on her toes, and kissing her senseless. "Mmm, I missed you today," he said as he inhaled the scent of her hair.

"We've been so busy here," she said, breathless. "Did anyone see you coming in?"

"Yeah, I came through your shop first. Why?" he asked as he set her back down.

"Oh, umm. Never mind." She settled herself on the floor again and hugged her knees to her chest.

He watched the play of emotions on her face while she traced an invisible pattern on the quilt before she looked up at him.

"How'd the research go?" she asked. He had fibbed a little and said he had to do research today.

"Fine."

"That's nice." She seemed distracted.

"Listen, Dana. There's something I need to tell you."

Her eyes snapped to his. "What?" Her brows creased with worry. She clamped her jaw tight and stared up at him.

"I... aaa," he ran his hands through his hair. *Damn.* "I've just landed an important three-day photo gig in Santa Fe," *I can't tell her—God, I'm a chicken shit.* "I'll be leaving tonight."

"Santa Fe, New Mexico?"

"Yeah. But I thought we could grab some dinner before I go. I'd like to spend some time together before I leave. That is, if you think you can pull yourself away for an hour or two."

"No. I'd better stay here." A perplexing look spread over her face as she kept her eyes cast down on the quilt. *Withdrawl.*

"I'm sure Mom can hold down the fort while you're gone."

"It's not that." She looked at him with an odd expression and felt an unwelcome tension build in his chest.

"What is it? Your not still embarrassed about this morning, are you?" *Please say no.* After the best sex he'd ever had, the last thing he wanted to hear was regret for what they shared.

"Embarrassed? Oh, Rome. This morning was wonderful," she said with less enthusiasm then he'd hoped. "I'm just not feeling well. The medication makes me sleepy."

"Okay. Well, I'll bring something back. We'll eat in." He searched her face for sudden apprehension.

"Thanks, Rome. But...I'm not really hungry."

"All right then. I'll bring something back later. I'm sure you'll be hungry then."

She nodded.

He kissed her then and saw her look away as he pulled back. Something was definitely eating at her. He knew her feet were still hurting, so he didn't press.

"Okay, then. Chinese or Mexican?"

She sighed and gave him a resigned shrug then looked down at her hands. Her lower lip trembled as she returned his gaze.

"Something *is* wrong." He crouched down and brought her chin up with his hand, forcing her to look at him. "What is it, sweetheart? Have I done something? Are you upset about Santa Fe?"

She gnawed on her lip. "Dinner here sounds good, actually. I think I *am* hungry," she said, changing the subject.

Panic rioted through him. "Are you afraid that jerk will come back and break-in again while I'm gone?" He gritted his teeth at the thought of that asshole touching her, breaking into her apartment while he was away.

She shrugged again. "A little of both, I guess."

"You could come with me. We could stay a day longer. Visit the Chaco Canyon ruins..."

 "No, Rome." She shook her head. "Even if I wasn't feeling very well, I'm under time pressure. Plus, I don't think it would be a good idea."

"Why? It'd be fun," he said, trying to lighten the mood. "You could masquerade as my assistant," he winked.

"I just don't think it would look right." Her voice sounded strained and tired. "Everyone would know I wasn't your assistant the second I pick up a piece of equipment. I don't know the first thing about operating a camera."

"What's the big deal? Just point and shoot." Unwelcome tension was building in his gut.

Rome watched as she twitched her mouth and rub at her bandaged feet.

"But that's not it. Is it?" he asked, trying to draw a response from her.

As she looked up at him, strange and disquieting thoughts began to race through his head. Rome saw the spunk and inner fire was missing from her eyes. He couldn't deny the evidence any longer.

"You *are* ashamed...?" he asked. Realization slapped him hard in the face, "...of us... of what we did?" He felt a heaviness centered in his chest.

"No," she whispered, her voice faint.

"You're afraid people will see us together. Is that it?" he said as the thought froze solid in his brain. Since he was a kid, the undeniable facts of his family's history clung to his back like a sack of volcanic rocks with a pain once hot and fiery on the surface, now a deeply rooted ache mixed with tormented memories that twanged with renewed hurt.

"It's not like that!"

"Being seen, out in the open with one of those *DeMitri boys* whose father sold naked pictures of women...," his voice dripping with sarcasm. "...right next to the *L.A. Times* and *Good Housekeeping.*"

"Stop it," she said, covering her ears.

Anger pooled in his veins. Why did he think she'd be different? "After all we've shared, it still comes down to this," he hissed as he stood and spread his arms out wide. "My family's reputation might tarnish your image. Scare away sales..."

"It's not what you think," she cried.

"You know, this is all starting to make sense," he said more to himself. "Meeting you out of town for dinner, parking around back, hiding at the back of the club." Rome ran both hands up and down his face. "Jesus, you're worse than those nutty soccer-mom protestors. At least they're honest. I know they hate my guts. You don't mind fucking me. You just don't want be seen with me."

"That's not true. You don't understand. I just can't..."

"Can't what?"

He waited. Challenging her to admit the truth. Her silence told him what he needed to know. Would he ever be able to live down the stigma of being Alberto DeMitri's son?

He never expected this of her. Dana, of all people.

Tension surrounded his heart like ice as he reeled with hurt and confusion. His brows drew together in an angry frown, and when she lifted her eyes to his, and saw a flicker of pain.

"Dana. Either you tell me *exactly* what's wrong or I'm walking out," he said, in a moment of panic before he realized the weight of his ultimatum. "I want... no, I *need* a normal, healthy relationship. Just two people who care about each other and don't give a rat's ass what others might think," he said as he watched, warily, while she chewed on her lower lip and stole a look at him. "Who cares if people know we're sleeping together, for chrissake, or having an intimate dinner together. You're with me. Not my father. Not my father's reputation. And not that fucking magazine."

He felt a moment of guilt and tenderness when he saw the raw hurt glittering in those beautiful tawny eyes. He pushed away the gamut of conflicting emotions as the silence between them screamed volumes.

As she looked up at him, it took every ounce of willpower not to pull her into his arms and comfort her.

"I can't. I'm sorry," she whispered.

"Then I guess that's it," he said trying to keep the pain from his voice. "I'm going to Santa Fe. When I get back, you let me know what you decide."

She stared at him with a glazed look of despair and hating himself for it.

"Good bye, Dana." An acute sense of loss stabbed at him.

"Rome...wait," he heard her cry. But he'd already closed the door.

Chapter Eighteen

TIED TO THE BED, UNAFRAID. Naked, on her belly with her legs roped to opposite posts, her hands bound together and attached to the headboard with a rose-red cloth.

She feels the soft caress of silk against her back and between her legs. Smooth strokes across her shoulder blades and down her ribs. The touch of the cloth, so light, it merely heightened her senses. She could smell his scent, feel his heat. Though he's crouched at her side still fully clothed, she feels the intimacy between them.

The room is dark, but turning slightly she can see him, silhouetted against the streetlights through the window. She watches as his arm moves slowly in circular motions, directing the fabric across and down her body until it centers between the cleft of her bottom. With her legs spread wide, she has no protection against his gentle assault as he parts the lips between her thighs with the delicate touch of silk.

She hears a hoarse moan and realizes it's her own as he strokes. Her lips parting further of their own accord. She's helpless to stop it. As the heat pools intensely, her bottom arches upward to match each delicate stroke, wishing he'd replace the silk with his fingers and tongue.

Suddenly, the stroking stops. No! she wants to scream, but her voice caught in her throat, then he starts over again at the top of her shoulders and neck faster and faster as if he were giving her a mock whipping. Harder and faster the silk comes down on her flesh and she begs and pleads for him to move lower.

She turns to look at him, plead with him to join with her. To release her from the yearning and the heat as the passion and desire whirls from her head, her chest and nipples.

Feeling the mattress against her skin, need throbbing from her core—aching for release. She looks into his glistening eyes and begs him without speaking. He shakes his head, signaling he's not willing to give her what she wants most.

Ring, ring, ring.

She cries out in frustration as she looks over her shoulder to find him now hovering above her, covered in black from head to waist—a faceless shadow.

Ring, ring, ring.

His cock, large and violent-red, pulsing and threatening as the smell of turpentine and paint thinner drifts through the room and into her lungs. She screams as his arm swings up. No longer holding silk, but black leather strips attached to a short stick.

Ring, ring, ring.

Screaming inside her head. No! This man is not her lover. He's an impostor, here to cause her harm. Positioning himself between her spread thighs as the strips of leather taunt her. She writhes against her restraints causing numbness in her hands as she tugs harder. His engorged member probes at her entrance before he brings the whip over her, down hard, stinging against her bottom as he thrust deep into her...

"No...!"

Dana screamed herself awake as the phone by her bed persistently rang until she reached over to pick it up. Her sketchpad fell with a *thunk* to the floor.

"Hel..." She tried to clear her groggy voice as she stared shocked at the sexually graphic sketch that now lay on the floor near her new pink fluffy slippers.

She tried her voice again. "Hello?"

"Dana, thank goodness you're all right."

"Jack?" she said somewhat relieved. "I tried to call you but your secretary said you were out of town."

"Yeah, I was. I called you back as soon as I got your message. But a woman answered. She said you were sleeping."

"Oh, that must have been Claire," she said.

"Did you get the flowers I sent?" he asked.

"You sent them?" she asked.

"Yeah. Didn't you get the card?"

"Uh, no. It must have fallen off. But how did you know?"

"Well, when I called you back, they told me what happened," he said, with more sympathy in his voice then she wanted to hear at the moment.

"That was sweet of you, Jack. Thank you. I love the slippers." She was still staring dumbfounded at the drawing.

"I found some information for you," he said.

Dana's throat ached with defeat. "I'm not sure it matters anymore," she said more to herself then to Jack.

"Convinced your tenant to move out then?"

"Not exactly."

"Well, for what its worth. I found a piece of information that might swing in your favor," he said with triumph in his tone.

"Okay."

"Apparently, Greta Baker and Patricia Wilson had a joint venture of kind before Patricia went to law school. They parted ways when Patricia thought Greta was siphoning money out of the accounts."

"What?" Dana grasped the phone so hard she thought it might break in two. "They had a business together?"

"Not a business, exactly. More like a joint investment. Now, before you jump to any conclusion, Patricia sued Greta but the case never went to court."

"Patricia dropped the case?" Dana asked.

"I'm not sure, really. There's nothing to indicate what happened. However, if we can prove that Patricia extorted the conditions in your grandmother's will, I might be able to convince the probate judge to throw out the contest clause."

"That's good news, Jack," she replied in a low voice. She hoped the news didn't come too late.

"You don't sound relieved. Believe me, Dana. I think we can beat this."

"Thanks, Jack," she said. "And thanks again for the gift."

"No problem, kid. Take care."

Dana hung up and jumped out of bed to retrieve the drawing. "Ow...darn it!" she yelled, forgetting about her stitches. She slipped her feet into the cushiony pads of her new slippers, then hid the pad of paper between the mattress and the box springs.

As she shuffled herself into the kitchen to make coffee, Dana noticed the morning sun streaming through the window above the kitchen sink. The dark cloud that hung over her heart since Rome left yesterday started to drift a little. She missed him terribly. She wondered if he thought of her too.

Or maybe he's with another woman.

She shook the thought and made toast while she ate an orange and watched the coffee drip slowly into the pot. The aroma of morning coffee never failed to cheer her spirits.

Rome had to take staff with him, right? So, in the literal sense, he probably did take a woman. She shook her head. "I'm being paranoid."

Careful not to open her stitches, she walked to the living room where she'd left her artwork last night. She'd hid them from Rome. She wasn't prepared to explain them yet. Once he saw the finished product, she was certain he'd approve—hopefully. "Soon you'll be decorating my shop walls." She smiled with a renewed sense of pride.

She'd chosen a variety of canvas sizes and mediums to create interest for each section of her supply aisles. A large drawing of Rome's perfect muscular chest in pencil and charcoal to go above the pencil and pastel aisle. A square-shaped, monotone painting of the rich outline of his broad back in reds and browns to decorate the wall above the paint aisle. And several small sketches of hands in various elegant gestures for frame-and-mat samples. Her personal favorite was a large rectangular painting in blue hues of Rome turning his head, looking over his shoulder with only his sharp, confident chin, the strong muscle of his jaw, and massive left shoulder in view.

They weren't finished, just the rough drafts were laid out. She needed to work fast.

Dana realized, as she wandered around her apartment, that her feet weren't as painful today. Hopefully, she wouldn't have to take any more medication. It made her feel woozy and foggy-brained.

She finished some smaller sketches to hang on the dividing support column by the frame room while she finished her breakfast, then showered and changed.

She carried her finished pieces down to the shop to see if there were any signs of humanity this early, Dana heard an odd noise coming from the stock room. It sounded like an injured animal. She tiptoed softly, avoiding the swoosh of her new fluffy slippers, not wanting to frighten it. When she approached the stock room, she saw Rick leaning against the wall. His jeans at his ankles and Victoria on her knees with her large breasts exposed—her lips wrapped against Rick's penis.

Dana threw her hand across her mouth before the gasped escaped her throat. She heard that odd moan again. It was coming from Rick. Throwing his head back as his face contorted while his hips gyrated against Victoria's mouth.

Geez, Louise, Victoria really does know how to handle men, Dana thought, then tried to back up quietly.

One of her slippers fell off of her bandaged foot and she lost her footing. A loud crash sounded as Dana fell against a display of art books and calligraphy pens. She held the screech lodged in her throat.

"What the hell was that?" she heard Victoria say.

"Oh, God... who cares? Don't stop!" Rick replied. Dana could hear the lust filled pattern of his breathing. "It's probably just a cat."

Dana back up against the wall in the frame room and closed her eyes, waiting for her heart to stop pounding. She still had her palm against her lips as she breathed deeply through her nose. She had to wait now before she could go back up quietly to her apartment without the two of them seeing her.

Had they stayed here all night? Dana should have felt disgusted or even outraged that her framer and sort-of employee were fraternizing on her property. Maybe even a little upset. But she was feeling light-hearted this morning after her call from Jack. After her love making with Rome, she couldn't fault Rick and Victoria for a little "freestanding" fun. That's what she thought it was called. She'd read that in the *Volupté* magazine Cynthia gave her.

"First, tell me another one of your deepest, darkest secret," she heard Victoria demand in a deep, seductive tone. "It turns me on."

"Oh, yes," Rick moaned.

What was this, sexual coercion? Rick won't stand a chance.

"I'll let you touch me if you whisper your naughty secrets to me."

Dana still had her eyes closed tight. She *did not* want to hear this. But unless she wanted to embarrass them and herself, she had to stay put.

"I don't have any more secr...oooh, God yes!"

"I saw you watching Dana yesterday. Do you find her sexy? Hmm, is that why you watch her?" she heard Victoria ask. "Do you imagine her doing this to you. Mmm, you're sooo big."

Oh, dear! Was Victoria doing this for her?

"I never...I just..."

"Then why do you watch her, big boy?"

Dana fisted her hands tightly to keep from grinding her teeth.

"A favor...for a friend," he said.

Huh? Now he had Dana's attention.

"Would I like your friend? Mmm, maybe we could have a threesome. Is your friend as sexy and hot as you?" Victoria asked him.

"I can't say...I swore...!"

"Didn't your mama tell you never to swear in front of a lady, Ricky?" Victoria laughed.

I knew it! The little turd. He had to be talking about Patricia Wilson. Who else would send a spy to watch her? *Darn it!* He was too good a framer to just fire him.

Dana heard another muffled groan from Rick and decided it was now or never to bolt back up stairs.

This time, she left her slippers behind.

*****

"He's a virgin."

Dana looked up as Cynthia and Victoria approached the counter where she was finishing a few more small drawing of Rome's hands. "Who is?" Dana frowned, still trying to forget the Victoria-and-Rick exhibition this morning.

And she missed Rome.

"Rick. That's why he's so nervous around girls," Victoria said with a wide grin on her face. "Can you imagine, he's twenty-six and never had sex before."

"Easily," Dana mumbled.

"Isn't that sweet!" Victoria exclaimed.

"Yeah, I guess. If you like the inexperienced type," Dana said wondering when Victoria was going to get to the good stuff and tell her why he was *really* working here.

"I wouldn't say inexperienced," Cynthia said as she plopped down onto the counter the last of the Walter Foster *How-To-Draw* books to be priced and stocked. "He's not completely naïve, and pretty girls always make him nervous."

"Humm, Rick," said Victoria with a dreamy look in her eye.

"So, when did he tell you this?" Dana asked, hoping it would lead into something more interesting other then Rick's sex life, or lack there of.

"This morning," Victoria said cheerfully.

"I've always known," Cynthia mumbled. "He's a friend of my brother's."

"We both got here around six to get an early start. He was feeling quite chatty."

No kidding.

"Geez, I can't believe it," Cynthia snorted. "That guy needs to move out of his mother's house."

Victoria laughed through her nose at that.

"Did he tell you anything else interesting?" Dana sighed.

"Yes, he did," she smirked, "but that's private."

"What could be more private then telling someone you're a virgin?" Dana asked innocently.

"With Rick? I don't think you want to know," Cynthia said walking away with a wrinkle in her nose.

"He told me I give great head," Victoria said quietly, then walked back to the frame room.

Dana just stared at her.

The shop phone rang from underneath the books still lying on the counter. Dana had to dig to find it.

"Hello," Dana said pleasantly.

"Hi." It was Rome.

"Hi."

"I miss you." She heard him sigh heavily. Dana smiled, thinking he was probably rubbing at his neck like he always did when he was thinking.

"I miss you, too," she whispered. "I'm really sorry about last night."

"Me too," he said.

"No, you've got nothing to be sorry about. You were right." She sighed into the phone. "I'm just not used to all of this. Used to us." Dana wished she could see his face. "How's the wedding? Meet anyone interesting"

"Lavish. Hectic. And no, no one interesting."

"Really?" she laughed.

"Yeah."

Neither spoke for a moment and Dana closed her eyes and remembered the dark chocolaty color of his eyes, and the scent of his skin.

"Your feet, sweetheart. How are you feeling?"

"Better. They don't hurt as much."

"Good...I, good."

"Rome?"

"Yeah?"

"Will you take me to the movies?"

She heard him laugh on the other end and thought it was the most beautiful sound she'd ever heard.

"Is that a yes?" she asked.

"Yes. What kind of movies do you hate?"

"Huh? Aren't you supposed to ask what kind I like?"

"No. Because if I take you to a movie you like, you'll be more interested in the movie instead of making out with me."

She laughed hysterically. She couldn't help it.

"That's not the reaction I was hoping for," he said.

"Jackie Chan. I hate Jackie Chan movies," she said finally.

"Jackie Chan it is," he said. "I should be home before your big day," he said. Then Dana heard mumbling on the other end, "...hey, Wendy, use the other one. It's in my bag...I'll be right there..."

Dana closed her eyes and wondered who this Wendy person was.

"Sorry, sweetheart. I have to go."

"Duty calls. I understand."

"I can't wait to get you naked," he whispered.

"Rome..."

"Humm?"

"I have a confession to make."

"What is it, beautiful?"

"Your naked body is hanging all over my shop walls."

Chapter Nineteen

"NO, NO, NO. I REFUSE!"

"But, Philippe, darling, there are other places to show your work. The LACMA isn't the only prestigious place in Los Angeles. What about the Museum Of Contemporary Art?" Claire asked him.

Dana had over heard this conversation for the third time today. They both played their parts well, just as Claire said they did. The moody artist and the doting spouse.

When she heard the back door open and close, she assumed Philippe went out to smoke a cigar. "Is he okay?" Dana asked Claire.

"He'll be fine. He found a chip in one of his 'ladies' that wasn't there when the sculptures were packed. He's ready to sue the packaging company, the airlines, the museum." Claire signed. "I think it's he's way of dealing with fear."

When she didn't elaborate, Dana asked, "What about the Library?"

"Huh?"

"Would The Huntington Library be an acceptable place for your husband to show his work?"

"It's a little on the conservative side..." Claire said placing her finger to her lips while she thought on it. "Does the museum admit modern artists?"

"I can ask. I still have contacts."

"I'll give you my first born if you can pull this off," Claire joked, winking at Dana, "and you'll have the undying admiration of my husband."

"Let me call first," she said as she dialed the number from memory. Dana looked at Claire and crossed her fingers as she waited for an answer. She got an answering machine.

"Leo? Hi, it's Dana. Listen, I have a favor to ask. A friend of mine wondered if The Library would be inclined to have a one-man showing. I'm sure you've heard of him. His name is Philippe Roche, the French sculptor? Anyway, give me a call when you get in." She gave Claire an apologetic smile. "Sorry, he's probably giving a tour at the moment."

Claire nodded.

The phone rang immediately after she hung up. "That was fast," Dana laughed. "Hello?"

"Hi, Dana?"

"Yes. Who is this?"

"This is Tony. Rome's brother."

"Oh, how are you?"

"I've been better, thanks. Listen, Dana...I was wondering if you'd meet me for lunch," Tony asked.

"Excuse me?"

"I need to talk to you...about Rome," he said. Dana thought she detected some hesitation in his voice.

"Rome? What is it, is he all right?" she asked suddenly panicked.

"He's...fine. It's nothing like that." His tone was sarcastic. "Can you meet me at Callendar's in an hour?"

Dana rubbed at her temples and thought of a million reasons why she shouldn't have lunch with Rome's brother. But then, he *was* Rome's brother and she didn't want to be rude either. "Ahh... listen, Tony... I'm not sure I can leave. I'm kind of busy. Can't we do this another time?"

"Look, Dana. I don't know what you said to him, but he's been acting... irrationally. Since he met you, he hasn't been himself."

"I don't know what you're talking about."

"Come on—you must have said something." He exhaled loudly. "Look, all I'm asking is for you to meet me. I wouldn't ask except... it's important."

She gave an exaggerated sigh. Rome's brother had a knack for theatrics. And it was starting to scare her. "Maybe we should wait until Rome gets back..."

"No! No, he'd be pissed if he knew about this."

Dana said nothing.

"Are you still there?"

"Yes. I'm here."

"Will you meet me, then?" he asked.

"Uh, I'll think about it. If I'm not there in an hour, don't wait to eat."

"Good. If your not there by half past the hour, I'll know you've changed your..."

She hung up.

One hour and twenty-five minutes later, Dana walked into the restaurant looking for Tony. She'd changed into a twilight-blue colored pantsuit thinking it might strengthen her courage to face Rome's brother, but with her bandaged feet, she had to wear her white Reeboks without the laces. Although her feet no longer hurt, the look was less than professional.

She found him sitting in a booth next to the front window wearing a sharp navy suit and a crisp white dress shirt with a tie made into a perfectly formed Windsor knot. His dark blonde hair was slicked back in a ponytail that trailed between his well-formed shoulder blades.

He was reading the editorial page of *The Wall Street Journal*. Well, he was *trying* to read it anyway. Dana imagined it was difficult to read with a beautiful woman on his lap while she played with his ear.

"Mmm, honey, you smell good enough to eat," she heard him say as Dana approached with apprehension.

The woman giggled, "That's because I smell like apple pie, silly. A whole pie fell down the front of my apron this morning."

"Mmm, I love pie..." Tony said as he nibbled on the woman's neck like she was his lunch.

"Am I interrupting?" Dana asked tentatively.

"Hi," Tony said smiling as he raised his head from the woman's neck when she reached the table. "I'm glad you could make it." It was amazing, he'd said it so casually, as if she hadn't just disturbed his afternoon nooky fest.

"I almost didn't. Look, Tony.... I feel really uncomfortable meeting you like this. I feel like I'm going behind Rome's back."

Tony folded the paper up as the woman removed herself from Tony's lap and said, "I better get back to work. Do you both know what you want to order?"

Open mouthed, Dana looked up at the woman astonished.

"I think Ms. Baker will need a minute, Cindy."

"Okay. I'll be back."

Dana continued to stare while Cindy the waitress swayed her butt as she walked to the kitchen.

"You were groping our waitress?"

He shrugged as he set his paper on the table. "I come here often," then said, "You know, these commentators don't know dick about the real world."

If he wanted to change the subject she was a master at it. "We all live in different worlds. Maybe the writer just has a different perspective then you," she said smiling.

"On an average day, I'd agree with you."

"And today isn't average?" she asked.

"Not by a long shot."

Well, she'd have to agree. "What did you need to see me about?"

"Let's eat first. I'm so hungry I could eat a..."

"Waitress?" Dana said, smirking behind her menu. She peeked over her menu and he winked at her.

"Maybe two...I'm *really* hungry."

She returned her eyes to the menu when Cindy the waitress came back for their orders. "So, have you decided, honey?"

"Um, yes. The chicken Caesar, please."

"I'll have the usual, sweet cheeks."

"You got it, handsome."

Dana just shook her head.

"What?" he asked in fane innocence.

"You're nothing like your brother, you know that?"

"Thank God," he laughed.

Not knowing how to respond, she remained silent, content to look out the window to people—watch until lunch arrived.

Her cell phone played an electronic version of Mozart's *Symphony Number 40*, breaking the uncomfortable silence. She looked apologetically at Tony before answering. "This is Dana. Oh, hi Leo. You got my message? Uh huh..." Dana looked casually out the window leading toward Wilshire Boulevard, watching the lunch crowd pass as she listened to Leo. It was better then watching the odd twinkle in Tony's eyes. "Oh, I see. You're sure? No, no understand. The Library has a reputation to maintain. Yeah, I miss you too." She hung up and returned her attention to her lunch mate. He'd gained another admirer while she was on the phone.

"So, baby, I've got family visiting. I promise to call you next week." He told the woman as she pouted her silicone-plumped lips at him. She kissed him hard on the mouth and walked away less than happy.

"Another admirer?"

"Yep. I'm a charming guy."

"Hmm, and modest too."

Tony gave her a one-sided grin then sipped at his water.

"So, what do you do when you're not charming the ladies, Tony?" She had to admit there was something to be said for a man that looked like a well-dressed pirate.

"I live and breathe to be in the presence of beautiful women," he said. The humorous glimmer never left his eyes. She imagined that was also part of his appeal.

"Do you choose the models in your magazine based on breast size, or how well she pleases the boss during the interview process?"

"Neither, actually. The camera chooses them." He smiled. "If one or two prefers the added bonus of my attention..." He shrugged his perfectly formed shoulder, then took a bite of his chicken pomadora.

"Uh huh. Do you hand out spot bonuses too?"

"Only during the holiday season." He gave her a smile not unlike one Rome would send her and it gave her pause.

Dana hadn't realized until then how much Tony looked so much like his older brother. They had the same chocolate brown eyes that Tony seemed to use to full advantage, and the same masculine build. Only the hair was different.

He raised his brows at her when he found her looking him over. Before the awkwardness of the moment took over she asked, "Tony, did your mother have blonde hair?"

"Yeah. Why?"

"I just realized you and Rome could be twins expect for the hair. I can't believe you two have different moms."

"Yeah, everyone says that...except Rome is much too serious. I, on the other hand, don't even take myself too seriously. Life's too short."

"I agree." *Too bad she had trouble with that herself.* She took another bite of her salad before asking, "Are you going to tell me why I'm here? Or should I guess?"

He took a breath to respond when she heard a shrill of excited women approach their table.

Geez, Louise. Getting a moment alone with this guy was as impossible as a bargain sale at Neiman Marcus. As the three girls twittered away talking over each other and competed for Tony's undivided attention, Dana took the time to finish her lunch and people-watch. Someone or something on the street caught her eye.

Who or what was that? In a flush of panic, Dana grabbed her purse and started up from the table. *Was Patricia still having her watched?* "Um...I'm sorry...I have to go..." she jogged across the row of booths toward the restaurant's back entrance.

"Hey, Dana wait! I'll come..." was all she heard him say as she pushed through the heavy oak and etched-glass doors of the restaurant. Not watching where she was going, Dana fished for her car keys and she walked through the parking lot.

Someone with a body as hard as freeway barricade rammed into her, knocking her solidly to the ground. A man wearing a black-hooded sweatshirt jacket and dark sunglasses slid her purse from her arm and ran off with it.

"Hey, you jerk!" She got back on her feet and sprinted after him... and her purse. Running across the street and into the La Brea Tar Pits parkway. Dana's feet started to throb and she stumbled, falling to her knees. Tears of pain filled her eyes from the sting. When she looked up, someone ran passed her, catching up with the purse thief.

Through her labored breathing, she wanted to laugh when she realized it was Tony. His fist met the thief's face as he relieved him of Dana's purse. She smiled through the burning pain of her torn up knees and throbbing feet recalling a similar display from Rome at the lounge. They were definitely brothers.

The Tar Pit's Security witnessed the scene and apprehended the man from Tony's grasp as he walk to her aid.

"You okay?" He extended a hand to help her up, her purse safely tucked under his arm.

"That depends on your definition of 'okay'. I think the jerk stole my purse *and* my wits," she said trying not to be girly and let the tears of fear and pain fall passed her lower lids. "Ow, my knees."

"Here, let me help you." Tony hoisted her up off her feet. She was starting to feel dizzy.

His compassion and chivalry reminded her so much of Rome, she found herself crying despite her efforts to hold it in.

"Hey, it's okay. They caught the guy. It's all right." He gave her a brotherly one-armed embrace.

Unable to speak without gasping, she just nodded and wiped her hand across her drippy nose. He gave her a bear hug, locking her arms at her chest and said, "We never did get to have that talk," Tony said, wiping the hair from her forehead. The gesture was so familiar, she thought, *He really is Rome's brother*. Their manners were alike—when it came to a crisis, anyway.

"Come on. Let's go someplace where we can talk without interruption."

She nodded as he led her back across the street and to his red BMW in the parking structure adjacent to the restaurant.

He opened her door first, pushing the seat forward to grab a tissue box from the back before he put the seat back in place for her. He waited until she had her seat belt buckled, handed her the tissue box and her purse, then closed her door.

"Thanks," she said through her stuffy nose and blew hard into a tissue before he opened his own door and slid behind the wheel.

Dana closed her eyes while her heart rate settled to a normal pace as Tony drove through downtown, not minding where they were going as long as she wouldn't be accosted.

She opened her eyes as they were entering the parking structure of a familiar high-rise with dark walls and large tinted windows.

"Where are we?"

"*Volupté* Headquarters. You asked what I do when I'm not charming women. Well, this is where I live...literally. My penthouse is on the top floor."

"Oh, my." She barely got a good look at the outside before they where underground in the reserved parking area.

Tony parked his car in his designated parking place and helped her out of the car.

"What are we *really* doing here?" she asked.

"I found something the other day I think you should see."

"Okay. But I need to get back to my shop soon or else Cynthia might send out the FBI looking for me."

"No problem. This won't take long. Plus, we need to get you cleaned up."

Tony led her through the parking structure to the elevator lobby. It was carpeted in a plush golden color with warm white walls and soft glowing light fixtures.

The interior of the elevator was covered wall-to-wall in mirrors including the button panel. Tony pushed level PH and they ascended without stopping between floors.

When they reached the top floor, Tony had to use his card key to enter. The elevator doors opened into a short entryway that led into his living room.

"Geez, this place is huge and—*bright*," Dana said while Tony walked to the bathroom. The décor was overwhelming. Where the elevator lobby was warm, this place... "Looks like this place was decorated by Andy Warhol on Prozac," she said to herself. There were bold colors everywhere. Not a single pastel to be found in the place. "Looks like a color war exploded in here."

He laughed as he came out of the bathroom and handed her some rubbing alcohol and band-aids for her knees. "Yeah, Claire had it decorated when she was still married to Dad. I think she did it to piss him off. But he liked it. So it stayed this way."

"Thanks," she said, taking the alcohol from his hands as she continued to look around at the odd surroundings. "You mean, you grew up here?"

"Oh, heck no. Mom hated this place. She insisted Rome and me live in a real home. So Dad bought us a house off Third Street. He just used this place to work when he had deadlines or whatever... so now it's mine, for the time being," he mumbled as he looked at her strangely.

What did that mean? "Are you ever going to tell me why our meeting was so urgent?"

Tony rubbed at the back of his neck and stared at the floor looking uncomfortable. "Dana, listen about Rome...he... we are..." he sighed. "Come in here. I want you to see this."

"Okay," she said, puzzled by his apprehension.

She followed him down a dimly lit hallway cluttered with pictures, photographs and paintings. One large canvas propped up against the wall caught her attention. It looked like the image of a very young Claire. She looked about twenty years old in the painting. Her beautiful face brightly painted into nine squares, each in groups of three with slightly different hues. "Hey, you do own an Andy Warhol!" She picked it up to examine it.

"Yeah. Claire asked if she could have it back. I had to dig through all of Dad's shit to find it."

She placed it carefully back down and followed him to the room at the end of the hall. She found him digging through some large framed photos in the closet. The room looked like an old unused office. Well, she assumed it was an office. It was the only room so far that wasn't exploding with color.

"Ah, here it is." Tony pulled out a flat neatly wrapped package about sixteen by twenty inches large. He propped it on the old oak desk by the window and pull open the dusty drapes to let the afternoon light filtered in.

"What is it?" she asked, anxious to know what was so important.

"Just wait," he said as he tore open the brown wrapping, revealing an old and aging photograph.

"Ohmygod—" she looked at it and blinked. Then blinked again. The black and white photograph, probably taken decades ago, was of a nude woman, reclining on a voluminous chaise longue with a hint of a smile on her lips, looking shyly away from the cameraman's watchful lens. "It looks...it looks like my grandmother," she said in a suffocating whisper, staring at the picture in astonishment as her lung refused to work.

"No, Dana. It looks like you."

Chapter Twenty

TONY TENDED DANA'S SCRAPED KNEES, handed her a bottle of water then insisted she take a Tylenol. Satisfied she was comfortable on the neon-green leather couch, he left to wrap up Claire's painting and the photo of Greta Baker.

He insisted she keep the nude photo of her grandmother, although Dana wasn't sure how she felt about the picture. She wasn't sure she wanted it in her apartment, but graciously thanked him for the gift. She also took the Andy Warhol for Claire. She'd re-frame it for her as a thank you gift.

Tony dropped her off at the restaurant parking structure and helped her load the photo and the painting from his handsome BMW sedan into the hatchback of her sensible Honda, then she drove home.

Dana parked in the alley behind her building and saw Rome's Jaguar parked along the back wall. Her insides lurched when she spotted him walking out of his back door, drinking in the sight of him wearing snug faded black jeans and a gray polo shirt. She'd never seen a more welcoming sight.

Her feelings for Rome were intensifying, far beyond a point of simple casual lovers. It should have frightened her, but she felt too content to worry about tomorrows and maybes. She had to live her life now.

He hadn't noticed her lazily observing him.

"Here Oscar, where are ya, pal?" He held out a plate making kissy noises as he knelt down and set it on the ground. A large black and white cat, as big as a house, bolted over the wall, running at light-speed to the dish. It made her heart swell watching Rome feed the scraggly fuzz ball. Rome patted the its head, murmuring to it as she approached.

"Hi," she said. "I didn't know you had a cat."

"I don't," he said, stroking the animal while it dug into the plate of tuna. "He adopted the building. He's kind of the studio mascot. Hey, come here," he said still knelt low to the ground as he grabbed her around the waist and kissed her belly. "Mmm, how I missed you." He turned his head into her stomach as he squeezed her.

Dana giggled, feeling giddy at the sight of him, and held his head at her stomach, bent down to kiss his hair. "I missed you, too."

"So, tomorrow's the big day, huh?"

Was it tomorrow? "Yeah, I guess it is," she said feeling blissful despite the rocky afternoon. "I think your mom wants to play hostess for the opening."

"You'd better let her or we'll never have a moment's peace."

"Oh, I intend to. She's wonderful with people." Especially with Philippe, she thought. "When did you get back?"

"About ten minutes ago. I just brought my luggage upstairs and found Philippe in a typical agitated fury and Mom calming him down, so I came down for some quite time."

"Yeah, he's been at it *all day*," she laughed.

Rome stood up then and bent to give her one long hard kiss, squeezing so tight she could barely breathe but too happy to complain. He held her there for a long moment then said, "I brought back a wedding favor for you at the bride's insistence." He kiss here again before he released her then walked to his car, opened the car door and reached inside the glove compartment, pulling out a tiny box. "Here. Open it." He placed the gift into her palm.

"I can't believe it. A gift from Cher," she said as she unhooked the top of the delicately embossed box. Inside was a cluster of small red candies held tightly together with black lace. "What are they?"

"Take 'em out," he said smiling.

Rome took the box from her as she pulled at the lace. It unraveled in her hand and revealed—"A black laced thong?" she asked, then laughed until her eyes watered and some of the candy fell off her hand. "Only Cher would give hot cinnamon candies in black panties! I love it..."

"I thought you might," he said, with a twinkle in his eye and she knew he was remembering the night she blindfolded him with her own black panties. Taking the box back from him, she carefully placed the gift back inside.

"Thank you."

"You're welcome," Rome murmured as he trailed his finger down her cheek.

"Oh, I've got something that might cheer your mom up. Help me get this stuff out of my car, would you?"

"What is it?"

"Just wait."

"What the hell happened to your knees?" His harsh tone surprised her.

"I had lunch with your brother." *Gee, like that explained everything*.

"Jules skinned your knees?"

"No. I mean, I had lunch with Tony."

"What? Tony took you to lunch?"

"Yeah. Why? Is that bad?" she asked, a little confused at his angered tone.

"Did he say anything? Did he tell you anything?" He looked at her like she'd just killed the family pet.

"Not really. I think he wanted to..." she thought he did anyway, but after the purse-thief incident, she sort of forgot to ask what it was. "...he said he had to talk to me and it was urgent. But then I was knocked down by the purse thief ..." she was babbling as if she were guilty of something, "...and then I chased him and fell and skinned my knees..."

"You okay?" He briskly grabbed her by the shoulders. "Were you hurt? Where was Tony?"

"Well, he hit the guy in the face and got my purse back...and then we went to his place... and I lost track of time and..."

"His place? And why the hell did he want to talk to you?"

She jerked from his grip, "Because my knees were hurting and I needed some band-aids... and he wanted to show me something. What's the big deal?" Why was she being defensive? She had nothing to hide. And why was he so upset? Was he worried about the theft, or about lunch with his brother?

She was starting to get a headache.

"So, he didn't talk about me? About... us?" His voice softened.

"No. He wanted to," she shrugged, "Then he changed his mind, I guess. Why?" she frowned, "What's wrong?"

"Nothing. Never mind," he mumbled as he walked to her car. "Come on. Let's get your things." He turned to face her. "But Dana, promise me, when we get up stairs you'll tell me everything...and I mean everything," he said, "Okay?"

"Fine." She shrugged, still confused and angry, more at herself then him for feeling like she needed to explain her actions. She had nothing to be defensive about.

*****

When Dana said she'd had lunch with Tony, he'd panicked. Rome was certain Tony found out he'd signed the waiver, releasing Rome from his inheritance. He hadn't confronted

Tony yet—he wanted to tell Dana first. He needed to come clean before Tony said something stupid that she might take the wrong way. But then he got called away, forced to wait to tell her.

"Darn it!" he heard her yell as she dug through her purse.

"What's wrong?" he asked.

"Oh... I can't find my keys."

"Well, you must have them, you drove yourself home."

"No, I keep my car keys separate from my apartment keys for when I take it to the car wash," she said as she dumped the contents of her purse onto the driver's seat. "They must have fallen out when that jerk snatched my purse."

"You sure you don't have 'em?" he said sternly, looking over her shoulder.

She groaned in response, scattering her lipstick, sunglasses, and who-knows-what else women carry in their purse as they fell to the floorboard.

"Get your locks replaced, Dana. Immediately."

"I will—but I have to get into my apartment first."

"You don't have a spare?"

He heard her let out a whoosh of breath. "Yeah. I gave Cynthia all my duplicate keys when I made her store manager."

"You'll have to wait, then. I just saw her leave about five minutes ago."

"Oh, she's probably gone to lunch. *Darn it!* I really need to change out of these torn pants."

"Well, come up to my place, then," he said as he pulled the wrapped pieces from her car. "Mom could use the support."   "Okay."

"Dana, I mean it about those locks," he said again. He didn't want to be worrying that some creep was walking around with Dana's apartment keys.

"I will, I promise."

They entered Rome's apartment as Philippe and Jules were in the middle of an argument. They both stopped talking when Rome and Dana walked in.

"What's going on?" Rome asked.

"Oh, the usual, honey," Claire said. "Don't worry about it. It's nothing that an empty gallery hall for Philippe and a private place for Jules won't cure." She sounded exhausted.

"Jules. You should've said something, man. Here," Rome reached into his pocket and pulled out a set of keys and tossed them to his brother. "You can stay at my condo."

"Hey, thanks," Julian said. "I'm not going to find walking cheese or lumpy milk in the fridge, am I?" he asked, wrinkling his nose up at Rome.

"No. I still have the place cleaned once a week. And, I never really eat there much anyway. And Phillip, I'm sure there's a solution to your gallery problem." Philippe looked at him with tired eyes. "What if we open up my studio for your showing?"

Philippe just stared at him.

Dana arched your brows at him. "You have a condo?"

Ah, hell. He wasn't ready for this conversation yet.

"Thanks, Romano." Philippe said, but I'm sorry to say, your studio is *trop petit* for the number of guests I expect."

"Oh, well..."

"What if we used my store too?" Dana interrupted. "Maybe even have a showing—sort of an evening block party or a moon-light sidewalk festival showcasing your art work."

"What about your friend, Dana...at the Library," Rome heard Claire whisper to Dana.

"I'm sorry, Claire. I spoke to Leo. He said the Library is familiar with Philippe's work. They think his work is too..."

"Erotic?" Claire asked.

Dana gave her an apologetic look and nodded discreetly.

Claire put her hand on Dana's arm. "I understand. Not everybody appreciates the human form like we do, Dana," she said, winking at her then looked directly at Rome with a conspirator's smirk.

What was this about? Lord, knowing his mother, it could be anything.

"I have to confess, I'm not familiar with your husband's work. Does he have any pieces here?"

"No. The crates are too large. Rome's place couldn't fit Phillips's work plus us," she laughed. "We've got them stored in a secured storage facility in the Wilshire district. But he's still not sleeping well over it."

Rome shook his head.

Dana nodded in understanding.

"I think Dana brought something for you, Mom," Rome said.

"Oh, yes...I almost forgot."

"Here, let me get it," Rome offered.

"Tony asked that I bring this to you, Claire."

"Oh! My Warhol," she screamed while ripping the brown wrapping from the large canvas. "I thought I'd never see this again. Lord, I was so young then."

Rome watched the changes of expression on his mother's face. He put his arm around her. A gesture he hadn't felt like doing in a long time. She looked up lovingly at him, her eyes glittering. "I was pregnant with you when this portrait was done." She sighed deeply, then said, "I always thought my marriage to Alberto was a mistake... until I looked at you for the first time, Romano."

He hugged her then and looked over her shoulder to find Dana watching the exchange between mother and son with a sad smile. What brought on the sudden sadness, he wondered. Family maybe? But this would soon be her family, too. He'd make sure of that.

He cared about Dana more then he'd ever cared about any woman. And the feeling didn't frighten him or make him want to high-tail it like it had countless times in the past. He smiled back at her, then kissed his mom's cheek and released her to allow her to swoon over her recovered treasure.

"I think you're much prettier now then you were then, Claire," Dana said, as the two women in his life study the nine squares of boldly colored portraits.

Claire laughed, "Marry her, Rome...fast before you change your mind."

"*Mother*..." Rome warned in a harsh whisper.

Rome's eyes shot to Dana's face but she was still looking at the painting and laughing as if Claire was teasing.

"What's the other package, Dana?" Claire asked.

"Umm... I'm not sure I want to show that to anyone."

"Oh, come now. How bad can it be?" Claire said she grabbed for the package.

"No! Wait..."

It was too late. His mom already had the paper off before Dana made another step.

"Oh my..." Claire said. "You know, I actually remember this photo."

"What is it?" Rome asked, now too curious to know what had Dana flustered and his mother reminiscing. "Holy shit." He whispered. "Dana, it's...you."

"No it's Greta Baker," Claire announced, causing them both to stare at her.

"You knew my grandmother?" Dana asked, with a catch in her voice.

"Oh, no, honey. I just remember the picture. I was mad as hell at your father, Rome, for not getting rid of it. I was intensely jealous, and very insecure about our age differences Having a naked picture of his ex-fiancée in our home wasn't very reassuring."

Rome looked at Dana's blank face, and thought she might go into shock.

"Dana, sweetheart...are you okay?" Rome asked, coming up behind her and stroking her arms in his hands.

"In fact, Rome," Claire continued, "I'd forgotten about the picture until you called me and asked about Alberto's family history."

Dana still hadn't moved.

"Then, that obscure comment his drunken father had said all those years ago started to make sense."

"Mom, let's talk about this later." He gave her a warning look. He needed to talk to Dana alone. To make her understand before she jumped to the wrong conclusion about his motives for wanting her—especially since she was gaining confidence in herself. And with him. This newfound trust was still too fragile.

"No, Rome let her finish." Her voice sounded so weak, Rome just wanted to hold her—protect her. Even if he had to protect her from himself.

"...so after we talked, all pieces started coming together..."

"What pieces?" Dana asked.

"Mom, you said he was a stupid old drunk. Why would anything he said have any relevance to Dana's grandma? Why would you believe him, anyway?"

"Because he may have been right. The curse, the suicide, the journal your father left you... I understand now why Alberto insisted you marry a Baker woman—"

"Mother."

"...and why you were so evasive when I asked when you were getting married."

Dana moved out of his reached and looked at him with an unreadable expression. "Your father insisted you marry me?"

Damn it to hell. Rome rubbed his temples and closed his eyes briefly, hoping for divine intervention.

"Rome?"

"Sort of."

"Sort of? Or what... he'd disinherit you?"

Rome looked away from her face.

"You're kidding, right?"

"Well, it's more complicated than that," he said, rubbing at the back of his neck. "Tony would be disinherited, too."

"I see. Were you ever going to tell me this?"

"Oh, dear. Did I let the cat out of the bag?" Claire asked wringing her hands. "Did you even ask her if she wanted to marry you, Rome?"

"Mom, would you excuse us?"

"I'll just go check on Philippe," he heard her say as she scurried out of his living room.

"So, were you ever going to ask me?" Her eyes were bright with anger. Anger at him. Anger he deserved.

"Yes."

"So, all along... your interest in me, it was because of your father."

"In the beginning it was."

"Why?"

"My father had some hair-brained idea that our family was cursed with three generations of failed marriages. He believed marriage to a Baker would break the curse."

She nodded, staring blankly at the portrait of her grandmother. "And marrying me, you'd break the family curse and you'd get your father's money." It wasn't a question.

God, she was so stiff. So fragile. He felt her emotional wall starting to build. He had to make her understand before she closed him off completely.

"Dana..." He reached out for her.

"Please, don't touch me."

"Dana, in the beginning it was just to save Tony from losing his job, but after..."

"After what? The sex? Or after you decided I was a desperate case. That I needed a real man to coax me out of my sexual shell? Well, congratulations you accomplished your goal. Too bad you couldn't keep it under wraps until *after* the wedding... so you and your brother could collect, then what...? You'd ignore me? Divorce me?" She swiped at her angry tears. "Make me a kept woman while you go out to the lounge and scam for other women who actually *are* beautiful and adventurous? Tell them a sad story about how you had to marry a plain and boring Baker woman who doesn't know anything about satisfying a man in bed. Score with sympathy? *Is that it?"*

"Stop it, Dana. You know that's not true!"

"Don't I? How long did you plan on keeping up this charade, Rome? Until the sex got boring? Or until your time ran out?"

More angry tears roll down her cheek and wished like hell she'd just slap him or hit him. Her self-deprecation was back. And listening to her tearful accusation was more painful than a punch to the gut.

"No," he said, shaking his head and tried reaching for her again. "Dana, sweetheart, just give me five minutes to explain."

"There's no more to explain, Rome. Your mom is right. This is all starting to make sense." She picked up the photo and with shaky hands tried to replace the torn wrapping. She turned to him again, opened her mouth to say something. Only a sob escaped, then darted for the door, tripping on the carpet on her way out.

"Dana, please listen..."

"There's nothing left to say. But I'm sure there's plenty of women at the lounge willing to listen while warming your sheets," she spat before closing the door firmly but gently behind her. Taking his heart with him.

Chapter Twenty-One

DANA HEARD A NOISE COMING FROM the front room. It wasn't an obvious sound, just a thump against the dining room hutch and a click of the latch.

Her head throbbed and her eyes hurt from crying herself to sleep. She'd promised herself not weep for something that was never real. But her heart wasn't listening to her head.

She heard the thump again. It was so faint, it could have been a tree branch brushing against the outside wall. But there was no wind and the trees along the street had recently been trimmed.

Swoosh. Swoosh. Thump.

Her nerves tensed.

She slipped quietly from bed and grabbed the baseball bat from the closet. With her heart in her throat, she realized she'd forgotten to call a locksmith to have her locks replaced. Her mind worked overtime imagining her stolen apartment keys in the thief's hands. Inside her home. She shook as the fearful images built in her mind. The blood rushed through her ears until she could hear nothing else. Peeking out of the bedroom to the kitchen, the time on the microwave blinked 12:00 AM. A power outage? She turned to read the time on her alarm clock. It had a battery back up. It was 4:30 AM. She'd been asleep for three hours. Three hours for someone to turn off her alarm system down stairs. Easily sneak into her apartment. *With her key.* Icy fear twisted inside her as she came to an abrupt stop, her heart jumping in her chest.

Silently padding toward the living room, she heard a creak on the floor behind her.

Dana turned on the ball of her right foot when a sharp pain hit her in the ribs. Confusion and pain had her body falling to the hardwood floor. Her breath cut off as a chill of black silence enveloped the room.

Just breathe, she thought as her eyes refused to focus. Her pulse beat erratically as her breath came in shallow, quick gulps.

She heard a rush of footsteps toward her front door then a close of the latch. But the spots in her eyes prevented her from seeing as she fell into a comfortable numbing blackness.

"Dana?"

A voice. If the voice would just stop.

"Dana? Can you hear me, Dana?"

"No... don't... I can't..." she croaked. *It hurt. Her body hurt.*

Someone was shaking her. *Stop it.*

"Dana, wake up!"

"What?" She sat up and groaned. "Oh, God. My chest! It hurts... What happened?" She looked up and found her attorney leaning down to offer her a hand up. "Jack? What... are you doing here? What time...?" It was difficult to breathe. Dana could barely put two words together.

"It's about seven," he said. "I knocked, but when you didn't answer, I noticed your door was open." The compassion in his voice made her want to cry all over again. "I found you on the floor, unconscious. Can you stand?"

"Umm... I think so. Jack, why are you here?" she asked again.

"I had some information, some documentation you should have to move forward with contest of the will."

"Oh." She nodded and it hurt. She stayed seated on the floor holding her head in one hand and her left ribs in the other.

"I thought it would be easier if I just stopped by to drop them off. Lucky for you I did. You may have a concussion if you fell and hit your head."

"No..." she shook her head, recalling the intruder, "...my ribs... my chest...something hit me. What happened?"

"You tell me. What do you remember last?"

"I can't... I heard a noise and then I... oh, God." She placed her palm against her temple trying to remember the chain of events.

"You've got a nasty bruise on your forehead, Dana. Let me get you some ice," he said, as he helped her to the couch. She lay down and closed her eyes while listening to him move around in her kitchen. "Can I get you a couple of aspirin, or something," she heard him yell as he walked to the other room. The sound vibrated painfully in her head.

"I have some Tylenol in the cabinet above the sink," she said. It came out as a whisper but it still hurt to talk. She wished she could remember why she was on the floor.

Jack came back with a glass of water and some pain relievers. "Here, let's get you into bed."

"No, I have to get downstairs... get ready to open my store."

"I don't think that's going happen. You need stay down," he said, as her helped her up. "You should report this to the police, Dana."

She felt too weak from the crying, from the heartache and the lack of sleep, not to mention her aching ribs and the lump on her head. She had no will to resist.

"Do you need anything else before I leave for the office? A cup of tea, maybe."

"Jack, I really need to get my staff together... plans for the day," she slurred slightly.

"Tell you what, let me get everyone together. Map out your plans and I'll pass it on. How does that sound?"

"Well, all right... until my headache goes away."

"Good. Now, whom do you need me to contact? Do you want one of your employees to call the police for you?"

She nodded, only because she was still incapable of making a simple decision.

Two and half hours and three cups of tea later, Jack had contacted everyone.

Rick and Echo had helped her down stairs while Cynthia and Victoria threw insulting innuendos at each other.

She kept herself busy—kept her mind off Rome. *And how he'd made her feel special.* Her throat tightened knowing it was all a lie.

By mid-morning, Cynthia and Victoria had called a temporary truce and were pulling together to get things going for the ten o'clock opening.

Echo was adamant about driving Dana to the doctor.

"I'm coming with you," Claire insisted. Dana found it a comfort to have her along.

After a diagnosis of a minor lump on the head and a bruised rib, Dana also had her stitches removed from her feet. She could at least tie her shoelaces now. Her doctor recommended she stay in the hospital for twenty-four hour observation, but she refused to be away from the shop for that long. They couldn't keep her against her will, so the nurse wrapped her chest up like a mummy around her middle, then Claire and Echo took her home. Dana was anxious to get her doors open to the public.

There was a commotion out front when Echo pulled over to the curb

"What's going on?" she asked as Echo looked passed her out the passenger window.

"Looks like the cops are here," he relied.

Echo got out of the car quickly to help Dana out and carefully held her at the waist as if she were going to break.

"What's going on?" Dana asked again when they walked in on a flurry of raised and confused voices.

"These police officers won't stop harassing us!" Cynthia yelled.

"Are you Dana Baker?" one officer asked.

"Yes."

"I'm afraid you'll have to vacate the premises."

"What?"

"You're to leave the premises immediately."

"By whose authority?"

One of the officers handed her a document signed by Patricia Wilson. Dana hadn't been very careful hiding her relationship with Rome lately, but it wasn't blatant—unless Patricia *did* have had someone watching her. *But who?*

"You!" she said accusingly at Rick. "It was you. You've been spying on me, you little worm," she said pointing her finger into his chest.

Rick raised his hands up while backing away from her. "I... he said it was only... he told me to just give him inside info. That's all. I swear."

"He? I'm talking about Patricia Wilson."

"Who's Patricia Wilson?" he asked.

"You don't know her?"

"Never heard of her in my life. Honest."

"Them who?"

"Tony."

"Rome's brother?" she asked.

Rick nodded.

"Look, lady if you have an issue with this, you'll have to take it up with the court."

"Can I at least get my personal belongings?"

He nodded. "You've got five minutes."

"I'm sorry everyone," Dana said biting the inside of her mouth to keep from sobbing.

"But Dana, your store? The opening?" Cynthia asked and Dana noticed the tears in her eyes.

She hugged her friend and told her it was just a temporary setback.

Dana wanted to believe it too.

After packing a suitcase and a few personal things, including all her sketchpads, Dana left her dream shop behind.

"Echo, can you drive me to The Wilson Attorney office? I probably shouldn't drive with my ribs still throbbing."

"Are you sure you don't want to wait for Rome to take you?"

"No. I need to leave now."

"Sure. I've got all afternoon free."

Echo was being a sweetie helping her out to the car. He was so much like his cousin, it made her want to cry all over again.

"Dana, honey," Claire said, "you shouldn't go half-cocked with this Wilson woman. Especially if you're not feeling well."

"I have to find out, Claire. I need to know what she knows. About me. About Rome."

"Okay. But where will you go after that? Do you have a place to stay?"

She didn't answer.

"That's what I thought. Look, hon, I know you and my son aren't speaking right now, but I wish you'd still think of me as a friend. Someone you can confide in."

Astonished at Claire's words, Dana a felt a single tear fall. "Thank you." It was all she could manage to say.

"Come on. I've got somewhere you can go."

*****

Rome couldn't sleep last night.

Couldn't think.

Couldn't breath.

Shit, he was feeling like the jerk Dana believed him to be. He'd gone to the twenty-four hour gym last night and ran on the treadmill for two hours. When his workout clothes started to get chalky white stains from his own dried sweat, and his bum leg started aching, he'd thought it was time to leave.

He'd been sitting at the front desk since seven in the morning, trying to balance the books, but only managed to stare into space. He'd had a light schedule today and let Kimberly have the day off to study for an exam.

Why couldn't he just tell her? Tell her she meant more to him then just a stupid family obligation. More than a promise to his cocky brother.

More than the stars and the moon. *Damn!* He was starting to sound like a sappy greeting card for crissake. She was driving him insane. Just thinking about her face, her neck, her skin. Her legs wrapped around his waist... and he had a raging hard-on. Worse, he couldn't do anything about it. Not now anyway. Dana had a store to open today. She wouldn't have time for a lovesick pleading, or even a roll in the sheets.

So, he left his cold sheets empty last night and slept a measly two hours in his recliner.

Besides, she needed time to think things through. He was sure once she thought about it, she'd know he wasn't just after her to score his father's money. Wouldn't she?

Lord, be hope to God she would. He needed her more than he cared to admit. Needed her there every morning, beside him in his bed. Not just to warm his sheet... although that too was nice. No, he wanted her—all of her.

"Rome?"

Rome stirred from his self-induced trance by the silky voice of one the sexy sisters... "Victoria, right?"

"Rome," she sounded breathless. "Dana's in trouble..."

*****

Echo sang along to some Inde-rock band on the radio while they drove through the ceaseless traffic of the L.A. streets. He dropped Dana and Claire off somewhere Downtown. Dana wasn't paying much attention, so wrapped up in her own thoughts, until Echo opened her car door.

"Where are we?" she asked.

"This is Rom..." Claire nudged him before he could answer.

"It's the family condo. We use it when we're in town."

Dana allowed them to lead her inside. Once Claire was satisfied Dana was comfortable in one of the bedrooms, she let Echo leave them.

"I've got your things here, Dana. Is there anything you need right away?"

"No. I'm fine, thanks." She hoped Claire would leave her in peace. She needed time to erase the pain in her heart. Just having Claire around reminded her too much of Rome. "You don't have to stay and baby-sit me, Claire."

"Nonsense. You should stay put. Besides, if I go back, I'll have to put up with a cranky husband. I'd rather stay and talk. If you don't mind the company?"

Dana sighed. The woman was being so kind, she didn't want to kick her out. "No, I don't mind."

"Can I get you anything?"

"I need my medication. Can you get it for me? It's in my bag."

"Sure." Claire retrieved Dana's meager belongings she brought along and felt a stab at her heart thinking about all she'd lost. *No.* She shouldn't think about that right now. She had to think about recovering... and confronting Patricia.

"Here you go... oh what's this? Oh, Dana, are these your concept drawings for the store?" Claire asked.

Dana felt her skin flush when she realized Claire found her most private sketches in her bag. There was no sense in hiding any longer since she'd used parts of them to cover her store walls.

The store she no longer owned.

She closed her eyes tightly, trying desperately to breathe normally with her sore ribs, and waited for the inevitable questions. And waited. She peeked out of one eye. Claire was sitting cross-legged on the floor by the bed examining one picture in particular—hard.

"What is it?" Dana asked, her when she didn't respond as Dana expected.

Claire frowned for a moment, then looked up at Dana. "Where did you get this?"

Dana's mouth opened slightly at the older woman's question. Claire had already seen most of her other drawings. Did she think someone else drew these? "I drew it," Dana said matter-of-factly.

"That's not possible."

Dana felt a little insulted. "I may not be as talented as Philippe but..."

"No. You don't understand. You could not have drawn this *one*, at least not from scratch."

"But I did... several months ago, in fact," Dana said with more emphasis this time. She started to feel defensive about her work. "It's the only thing I *can* draw. I've tried other things but nothing as passionately or as realistic as these drawings."

Claire stared at her as if she were looking at a ghost.

"Claire, you're scaring me. What-is-it?"

"I've seen this before."

"You mean you've seen my sketchbooks before. I showed them to you, remember?"

"No, I've never seen it in pencil before. I've seen this painting before."

"No, I can't work with paints very well... unless it's on furniture," Dana laughed half-heartedly.

"Are you up for a short drive?" Claire asked as if she didn't hear her.

"Uh..."

"No, course you aren't. Never mind."

Before Dana could respond, Claire walked into the living room to make a call. She couldn't hear what was being said but it was obvious an argument was ensuing. Not wanting to be involved in a family squabble, Dana shut her eyes and tried to relax. She had plenty of problems of her own.

And what on earth was Claire talking about? Another painting? Had someone found her drawings and made a copy... in another medium? It was inconceivable, really. Until she'd met Rome, Dana had carefully guarded her secret for fear of her grandmother finding them.

She heard Claire's footsteps as her sandaled feet clomped on the carpeted floor. "Victoria's on her way to stay with you while I'm out."

"I don't need someone to watch me, Claire. I'm fine. Really."

"All the same. I'd feel better if someone stays with you."

She nodded, felling a little foggy from the dull pain. "How did you find Victoria?"

"I called Tony and asked for her cell number. Look, I've called a cab..."

Dana laughed.

"I'm glad I could make you smile despite this mess."

"No, it's just... well, no one in L.A. takes a cab. It's so New York." *Geez, what a stupid remark.* She was getting dingy. She had good reason to be. At this rate, she was lucky she wasn't going completely insane.

Claire glared at her.

"Okay. I'll be good. When's she coming?"

"Hi, I'm here!" she heard from the door.

"That was fast," Claire remarked.

"We were just around the corner," Victoria said, sounding rather glum.

"We?" Dana asked.

"Dana."

It was Rome. He very cautiously approached the bed.

Claire corralled Victoria out of the room and out the front door before Dana could mutter "get lost."

"What are you doing here, Rome?"

"Why didn't you call me immediately? God, I broke out in a cold sweat when I found out," he shouted. "I blame myself. I should have insisted you get those damn locks replaced last night," he pinched the bridge of his nose as he paced at the end of the bed. "And evicted...Dana...why didn't you say something? Why didn't you tell me?"

"I didn't call... because I was out cold, for one. And I didn't say anything because... I didn't want to see you..."

"You don't mean that."

She didn't answer. She couldn't stand to even look at him. Not now. Not when the hurt was still fresh like an open wound soaked in seawater. Cool and stinging across her flesh.

"Did you at least call the cops?" he asked.

She hadn't. But the cops did showed up...to kick her out. What should she do about it now?

"Why are you here?" she asked again.

"I was worried. I thought you needed me."

She had to fight to keep her heart from melting from his words.

"Because... I live here. And because, sweetheart, you're lying in *my* bed. Right where you should be."

Chapter Twenty-Two

IN HIS BED?

Before Dana understood his meaning, Rome grabbed her bare ankles and dragged her to the end of the king-size bed. Panic rioted inside her brain. "What are you doing?"

"Proving that you're wrong." His voice, rough and harsh as it spun threads of desire and dread into her soul.

She could feel her body tingling where his hot hands held her ankles. Like a magic pill, his presence took away the ache in her ribs and the pounding in her head to a point where all her thoughts, feelings and sensations were centered on him.

To her astonishment and fear, he had become her center. She'd allowed him to enter her heart as easily as a hot knife through butter. Now, she felt raw and exposed as if she'd torn open her chest and allowed him to burrow into her heart's core, leaving an empty shell after she walked away. Walked away from the deceit and the lies... and the delicious way he made her body feel alive.

She wanted to weep. She wanted to scream at the unfairness of life. She wanted to hurt him they way he'd hurt her. But Dana knew she couldn't. She loved him. She loved him even when she didn't want to love him. It was too painful. Losing Rome, she realized, was more painful then losing her shop. Though her shop was her dream for the future, nothing could compare to these past weeks of ecstasy within Rome's arms.

She felt Rome jerk her shorts and panties off in one skillful motion, jolting her from the tormented thoughts.

Before she had time to scream or kick or protest, he pressed her knees apart with his large hot hands and dove his head between her thighs.

A moan, deep and jarring erupted from her throat. A sound she'd never heard from her own throat. *No!* She tried to say. But "no" what? No, don't stop? No, you can't do this?

But he was. He was doing what no other man had ever done nor would ever do. Rome could bring her to a height of pleasure and pain and ache within seconds. Something she'd never thought possible. Never in all her years of living or the years to come, would she feel this free, this is wonderful. Then she knew. She knew why she wanted to scream.

"No!" she wept. "No..." *Oh, God* his tongue felt so good. So warm. She felt her insides expand and contract as his lips, his tongue circled her labia then sucked hard at her clitoris. She felt the wetness from her body and the heat of his mouth merge into one as her hips involuntarily buck to match his motions. And then his tongue thrust inside her, mimicking the motion of lovemaking. His mouth loving and punishing at the same time. Proving to her, just as he'd said—*that she was wrong.* That this is what she was meant for. *He* was what she was meant for.

His persistent thrusts continued. The scent of her own sex surrounded them, making her more aware of how exposed she was. Of how she'd allowed him to possess her, enslave her, so easily with her own desires that she felt ashamed. Ashamed that she was so easily swayed. So easily controlled. "No," she said again. This time in a whisper of defeat. Sobs bubbling up inside her as the pleasure intensified to an unbearable level, shattering her senses.

His tongue then gentled, centering on her clitoris as he released her knees and parted her outer lips with his thumbs. The sensations pulsing deep from between her center, down to her toes and back up into her heart.

She felt the tears of joy and sadness fall from the corners of her eyes and onto the sheets. The gentleness of his tongue was her undoing.

He suckled and caressed, again and again. Each motion sending shock waves throughout her body. The sensation suddenly too intense. Building too fast.

He sensed her impatience, and increased his speed. Circling her core faster and faster as her hips continued to rock and buck to meet his mouth.

"Oh, God..." she screamed. *"Yes!"* Grasping his head hard against her.

"Mmmm..." she felt him hum against her body as the convulsions of her orgasm took over. She held her breath and her heart fluttered wildly against her chest as the strong climax spun its magic around her, raising her out of her own body before slamming it right back, bringing her forcibility down hard onto the sheets.

Her labored breathing the only sound in the room. Rome's intimate kiss became tender and gentle while her muscle contractions continued even as her climax had stopped.

As her breathing returned to normal, Dana fought herself. Her mind and her heart at odds. She had to leave... now.

*****

He couldn't believe Dana ran from him—again.

After, what he knew was a mind-numbing orgasm, Dana ran out on him.

Even with her injuries, she'd actually grabbed her bag and left.

He should have insisted she stay. *Shit*, he should have strapped her to the bed. At least he'd know she was safe. But no, he'd let her walk out.

Rome could still taste the sweetness of her sex on his lips. Couldn't she see how well they fit together? How her body fit perfectly to his? Just the way her body responded to him should have proven that to her.

What else could he have done? He should have stripped her naked and hidden her clothes so she couldn't leave him.

He should have continued loving her. Should've given her more mind-blowing climaxes so there'd be no room in that beautiful mind of hers for anything but his loving.

But that was just it—she didn't *really* know how he felt. How could she? He'd never expressed anything beyond the physical satisfaction of their relationship. How was she to know it wasn't just great sex? And it *was* great. There was no denying that. But there was so much more to their relationship than just lust. He should've been up front with her from the beginning. Told her about the ridiculous marriage thing right away.

He felt like an ass. Now, convincing her she was beautiful and sexy and a joy to be with would be an up-hill climb. Making her believe he cared for her more than anyone else on the planet—that was going to be the toughest part of all. But he was up for the challenge. If it meant getting her back, he would do it.

He was in love with her.

The realization hit him full-force. He loved her. So, why couldn't he just tell her?

Because he was being a stupid shithead jerk. That's why. He rubbed at his weary eyes, trying to clear his foggy brain. He should run after her. No, he needed to give her time to cool off. She was royally pissed and he couldn't blame her. He'd treated her like a lover... not like someone he was *in love with*. That was the difference.

He'd rush back home. Tell her. Beg her to forgive him. Pride no longer had meaning when your heart ran out the door leaving a hole in his chest the size of California State.

Home.

When had the shabby apartment become home? He'd always considered his condo home. Strange, he hadn't been back here to the condo since he'd met her. And it felt damn good to have her here in his bed. Even if he was punishing her with long drawn-out orgasms. Actually, he'd punished himself. His body still ached from touching her.

And he had to get her back—fast!

*****

When Dana reached the sidewalk from Rome's condo, Victoria was waiting in her car. "Victoria? Have you been waiting all this time?"

"Nah. I had Echo take me home so I could pick up my car," she replied. "Hop in."

Dana eyed the Metro bus that whizzed by and considered her options. She really wasn't prepared to talk about her problems with anyone. But taxis were expensive in L.A. and the buses were unreliable. "Okay. Why not?" Dana said, more cheerfully than he felt. She climbed in and Victoria drove forward without asking where she wanted to go. She wouldn't have an answer for her anyway. Dana wasn't sure were she should go. She needed a place to stay. She needed to confront Patricia Wilson.

She needed Rome. The Rome she *thought* she knew.

She refused to cry again. She had to move on. It was great while it lasted. Wasn't it? She was able to give herself freely, experience pleasure without fear. Without pain—physical pain. She'd broken free of her inhibitions that had trapped her like a cage all these years.

Her heart was another matter. What if she was able to experience these feelings only with him?

Her mind went back to her dreams, her drawings and her perfect man. Rome *was* her perfect man. Even if his face was unknown to her in the past, she knew with her entire being that Rome was the man in her dreams. Not just a faceless and vague image, but the actual man she was meant for. He had to be.

Why did he have to crush everything between them by lying to her?

"Dana?"

Victoria's voice jarred Dana's thoughts from the haze in her mind. Her voice sounded weary. She looked up at her friend with concern. "What is it?"

Victoria sighed heavily before continuing. "I need to tell you something. And you may not want to speak to me after I tell you this, so promise you won't jump out of the car at the next red light."

She gave a half-hearted laugh, "I'm sure it can't be *that* bad, can it?"

Victoria just eyeballed her before returning her gaze on the street ahead.

Dana waited for her to continue.

"You mentioned before that you thought Rick was spying on you."

"Yes. He even fessed up to it."

"But he wasn't doing it for who you think he was."

"Huh?"

"Rick wasn't spying on you... *I was.*"

Dana blinked at her, staring at her until she explained everything. It didn't making any sense.

"Grace, Elizabeth... me... We were all sent to spy on you. To watch and see if you broke your probate agreement," she looked at Dana through the corner of her eye. "That's why my sisters and I...well," she laughed uncomfortably. "We decided to pose for Tony, for his magazine—get to know him, get to know his brother... and you." She shrugged. "Catch you in a compromising position."

"Spying on me...for who? And why?" Her voice was shaky.

"My Aunt."

"I don't understand. Who's your aunt?"

"Patricia Wilson."

Dana felt the bile rise in her.

"I don't remember our mom. She died when the three of us were just babies. Our aunt took care of us. Our older brother, too. There was no one else.

"I know she resented it, sometimes resented us... but she still supported us, put us through college..." Dana watched her take a deep breath. "Growing up, we knew something was going on, something bad. As kids, I guess you just sense things like that. We just didn't know what, exactly," she shrugged. "We still don't. But my sisters and I felt we owed her a boat-load of gratitude for raising us... at least until now."

"Why?" Dana felt as if a heavy weight was pressing into her chest, making breathing impossible. Why was this happening?

"Because, I don't like what she trying to do. I may not know what her motives are, but I know I don't like her means-to-an-end."

"Are you saying you blindly did her a favor by spying on me and you don't even know why?"

"Pretty much."

Dana settled back into her seat and stared out at the street. "Turn right."

"What?"

"I said, turn right—at the next street."

"Where are we going?"

"We're going to visit Aunty Patty."

*****

Rome arrived back home and found everyone, including Tony, waiting there. They were all talking at once. "What's going on?"

Everyone instantly shut up and turned around to stare at him.

"What?" Jesus, all he wanted to do was take a shower, then go to Dana. He didn't need his eccentric family bugging him right now.

Tony, Julian, and Philippe continued to stare as if he'd grown antlers. His mom was more subtle. She smiled as she broke from the group to put her arm around him to urge him over.

"You fuckin' won't believe this, bro," Tony blurted as Rome walked to the dining room table where everyone's attention shifted. "Remember all those crappy old photos, pictures, and paintings Dad used to hide from us when we were kids? You know the ones with the old photos of naked ladies n' shit?"

"Yeah. And we always managed to find them anyway. So what?" he said, as he looked at the image they were so mesmerized by. "Holy hell. Where did *that* come from?"

Claire sympathetically looked up at him with. "Honey, I'm sorry. I hope this doesn't embarrass you. But..."

He looked at his mother's nervous express and waited.

"I saw Dana's drawings..."

"Shit!"

"That's not the half of it," Jules said. "Mom, tell him the rest."

"Well," she sighed. "When I saw one drawing in paticular, I'd thought she'd copied it from somewhere else." She shrugged. "I didn't recognize it as you at first because of the shadowed face. But it was disturbingly familiar. When Dana said it was from her own imagination, I suddenly remembered why it was so familiar."

"She dug through Dad's old closet where I found the picture of Greta Baker," Tony said. "And there it was... It looks just like you, man. Well, the parts we can see anyway," he laughed.

"Screw you, Tony!"

"Rome, stop it," Claire scolded.

"Sorry, Mom. This is just a little freaky. Is there a date on it or an artist signature?" he asked.

Philippe picked it up carefully examined the edges and the back. Touching the corners and brushing his hand across the canvas for indentations or other markings. The painting had darkened over time. It was particularly dark across the face of the image. Any small details, like a name or a date was difficult to see. "*Oui.* It looks like... ummm, eighteen-eighty *somezing.* Ah, here. On *ze* back," he said pointing to the wooden canvas bar on the bottom that read PROPERTY OF S BAKER.

This whole crazy situation was all starting to make sense. The puzzle pieces of his family, his ancestors... the journal, his father's will... the stupid curse. Dana. "Hang on a minute," Rome said as he ran to his bedroom and found Sarah Baker's journal on his nightstand, then came back to the fascinated faces of his family. "Mom, take a look at this," he said, as he handed the leather-bound journal to her.

She took it from his hand, looking at him quizzingly and opened it up. The yellowed newspaper clipping fell to the floor. She bent to pick it up, then put it back in to the folds of the paper and read aloud the inscription. "Journal of Sarah Baker?"

"Dad left that for me. At first I thought it was some kind of a joke. But now, it's all starting to make sense. The painting. Dana's dreams."

Tony snorted. "Are you saying you two are the reincarnation of...Ah, man, it's too bizarre to even say."

"No!" he shook his head as he ran his hand through his scalp. "No, I'm not saying that at all. I'm suggesting that Dad orchestrated all of this. The will, the marriage. All of it." Rome ticked each one off his fingers, "He knew about the journal. He knew about my resemblance to his great grandfather. Hell, he even had an affair with Dana's grandma. The only missing pieces are Dana's dreams."

"But honey, does it really matter how it happen? Or why?"

Rome looked at his mother through his red haze of renewed anger at his father.

She hugged him. "What really matters is that you love her. And I'm pretty sure she loves you, too."

He looked over her shoulder at the three men, all displaying looks of confusion.

He hugged his mom back. "Yes. Yes I do," he said. Now letting the idea easily roll around in his head. The thoughts and feelings more easily said aloud. "But she's still pretty upset with me."

"If she truly loves you, honey, she'll come around. But you may have to grovel a little first," she laughed. "We women need to know we have you men in a sling before we'll give in," she said as she winked at her husband. Rome was astonished to see Philippe's cheeks color. Would he still respond to Dana like that after years of marriage?

Marriage. Funny it didn't frighten the shit out of him anymore. He would give her some breathing room. Not much... maybe a day? Twelve hours?

In the mean time, he had to get his groveling gear on. What did a man wear when he had to get on both knees and beg for his woman to forgive him?

"White," Claire said as if reading his mind. "Wear all white. That way the evidence of your pleading stays on your pants knees."

He hugged her again. "White it is."

Chapter Twenty-Three

DANA WAITED WITH VICTORIA in Patricia's office lobby, listening to a hushed argument emanating from the closed office door.

She hadn't spoken another word to Victoria since they arrived. Her courage and determination forming like a rock in her mind. She had to get to the truth. She had to know what her grandmother and Patricia were involved in. Had to know her family's link with Rome's. She had to know before she grimly set about building a new life for herself.

Achy and exhausted, Rome's words returned to haunt her over and over. *I'll prove you're wrong.* A flash of her future looked like an endless tunnel of tedious days, lonely nights, and a renewed sense of how alone she was.

Patricia's office door swung open, and Dana forced an iron control over her emotions. She had to get through this without any emotional outbursts.

She looked up expecting to find Patricia's censured face. Instead— "Jack?" Dana said, when she stood up and saw her attorney stepping out of Patricia's office.

"Dana?" he said in startled tone. He gave her a tight smile as he approached. "How are you feeling? Better, I hope."

"Yeah, thanks. Umm, what are you doing here?" She realized how intruding her question sounded. He was an attorney. And attorneys conversed, even argued with each other. It was idiotic to make assumptions.

"I..." he gave her an apologetic look.

"I called him," Victoria interjected.

They both turned and looked at her.

"She did," Jack nodded, placing a comforting hand on Dana's arm.

"I called him after the police escorted us out the building. I knew you weren't in the best frame of mind and thought you might need... help."

"Oh." She was moved by her friend's thoughtfulness. "Thanks, but I think I need to handle this on my own."

"Dana, I'd advise against it," Jack said.

"Jack," she said, as she placed her hand on his, "I appreciate that, really. But I think I have some old business to settle here."

He took a deep breath as he looked at her then said, "All right. I'll wait for you out front."

"Jack..."

"Please, Dana."

"Okay." She turned to Victoria. "Thanks for the lift."

"Are you sure you're okay?"

Dana wasn't sure what that meant anymore. Was she okay? Everything that ever meant anything to her was hanging in the balance, her body was beat, her emotions were in shambles, and she had no place to live. "I'm fine," she answered finally, then walked through the office door.

She found Patricia hastily writing a note when she looked up. The older woman's eyes, clear and cool as ice water. Dana imagined it was a look most women attorneys practiced. But when it was centered on her, it had Dana feel tremulous.

"So, I assume you're here to contest Greta's will," she said, without reflection.

"No, actually, I'm not."

Patricia's brow rose slightly. It was the only hint of emotion on her face. The woman stood up and walked to an elegant oak file cabinet and retrieved a file from the top drawer. Patricia opened it and quickly tossed it on the desk to Dana. "I assume this is you in the picture."

Dana stared down at the black and white photo, too startled to offer any objection or confirmation to the attorney's accusation. It was a clear picture of Dana, in a tight embrace... with Rome's brother, Tony. She hesitated, torn by conflicting emotions of anger and uncertainty. "It is me, but I didn't..."

"I thought so. However, I didn't think you'd admit to it so quickly," her voice was stern with no vestige of sympathy in its hardness. "You surprise me, Dana. I thought Greta's instructions were quit clear. But then you *are* Greta's granddaughter... I should have expected you to be contrary."

"What were you holding against my grandmother?" Dana asked with as reasonable a voice as she could manage.

"I don't know what you're talking about."

"She never mentioned any unusual clauses in her will before she died, and she certainly never mentioned her connection to the DeMitris. She would have said something to me."

Patricia merely stared at her ominously as she continued. But Dana was beyond the point of intimidation. She had nothing left to loose. Although her spirit was in chaos, she had to know the truth.

"She may not have mentioned her connections to *that* family, my dear, but connected they are, indeed," she replied. Her voice condescending with cool authority.

Dana crossed her arms tightly around her chest and waited for her to continue. She wasn't leaving until she heard the whole of it.

"Greta and Alberto DeMitri were carrying on together for *years*. I have no clue how Greta's family felt about it, but Alberto's father actually encouraged the behavior. *The old fool.* Alberto got his rocks off on taking pictures of him and Greta while they were..." she wave her hand assuming Dana understood were she was going with this. "Anyway, he eventually got bored with Greta and moved on to screw anything in a skirt under the age of twenty. Dirty minded bastard always preferred the young ones," she muttered. "One day, Greta walked in on him with two other women. I'm sure you can imagine her shocked surprise. Distraught over Alberto's betrayal, she tried to set their 'love' photos on fire...right there in his bed. Of course by then, his two whores had grabbed their clothes, screaming. But before they could reach the door, Greta pulled out a gun from her purse." She stopped for a moment and walked to the window overlooking Wilshire Boulevard. "I'm sure you know of his founding the magazine," she said abruptly.

Dana nodded, confused by this new information about the woman she'd known all her life.

"Well," she laughed without a humorous tone, "He'd threatened to publish the photos in the magazine if she ever breathed a word to the press about his preference for under-aged girls. Stupid, considering she held a gun to his balls. She was so enraged, Greta pulled the trigger.

"She missed.

"Instead, she hit one of the young women... killed her instantly."

Dana merely stared, wavering as she tried to comprehend what Patricia was saying.

"The woman was my sister."

"Oh, God." Dana placed a hand to mouth and felt the blood drain from her face. "You were the other woman."

Patricia nodded. "I witnessed *everything*."

"So you... blackmailed her."

"More or less. I was very young and stupid and not a quick thinker. But Alberto, Greta and I formed an odd...alliance. Bonding the three of us together for the rest of our lives. We swore never to reveal the circumstances of my sister's death so long as we agreed to make it look like a suicide. Greta got her photos back, I got fifty grand to keep my mouth shut, and Alberto went on screwing and photographing young women."

Dana shook her head in denial. "I don't believe you," she whispered. Her voice shakier than she'd like. "Your sister—why didn't you call the police? Why didn't anyone report the shooting?"

Patricia waved her hand as if the incident were a simple traffic ticket instead of a tragic life-changing event. "There was no love lost between us. She was a slut and she reveled in hooking up with wealthy men. She was pretty enough. Men fell over themselves for my sister. I knew she was trying to get pregnant for the third time. Alberto was her latest target. Thought I'd help her out this time. Maybe blackmail him for money."

The older woman's voice was so cold and exact, it gave Dana the chills. "After he married that cutesy-doll, Claire, Alberto signed over *that* building to Greta, it was a piece of junk back then, and gave me another fifty grand. Hush money, he called it. After all, what was money and property when you never wanted your lady love to know the truth." She gave a lady-like snort. "That marriage lasted less than two years."

Dana was horrified by the woman's callousness. She spoke of her own sister's death as if it was information from an article in a newspaper. Detached and unsympathetic. It sickened her to think her grandmother could associate with such a person, let alone live a lie of murder and conspiracy. Her stomach churned. Dana thought she was going to be sick.

"Why?" her voice cracked. "Why do you want it now? My building, I mean."

"I intend to level it. Sell off the lot in pieces. Maybe build luxury apartments on it. It's prime property now. Who would have thought?" she mumbled the last words as if thinking aloud.

"So you had me watched... to get my property?"

"Of course," she said coolly. "I wanted Greta to pay and I want her lover to pay. And so will you."

"For your sister's life?" Dana asked. Still wondering where she fit into all this. "None of this makes any sense."

Patricia shook her head as she looked passed Dana listlessly. "I wanted them to pay for taking away my youth," she sneered through her perfect white teeth. "Why should you be allowed to live off the fruits of my dead sister? To be allowed to carry on with one of that bastard's sons."

"I don't understand." Dana calculated how many steps it was to the door to make an escape from this mad woman.

"When they killed my sister, I was left to take care of the triplets and their brother—illegitimate brats." Dana heard the bitterness spill over into the attorney's voice. "Oh, I grew fond of them over time, of course. But Alberto's hush money didn't last long. What was left put me through law school and I gave each of the children a college fund so they wouldn't end up like their mother... screwing rich men so she could live in wealth."

Dana kept her hands tightly locked together to keep them from shaking. Would Patricia allow her to leave the office alive after this revelation? "Why tell me this? Why now? What makes you think I won't go to police myself? Or contest the will—tell the court you inflicted undue stress and coercion on a client to sign a document again her will."

"Because, the moment you contest, you'll forfeit your inheritance, including the building. You'd still end up with nothing."

"Then I've got nothing to lose."

"Except Greta's good name and reputation while I run it through the dirt. But coercion? Maybe. It was easy to convince Greta to the terms, leaving me a loophole to squeeze more out of her. She easily believed it would never come to this. Her sweet innocent granddaughter would never fool around with anyone, let alone a DeMitri bastard," she laughed without mirth, "What a joke."

Dana squelched the pain the woman's words caused. "But what does this have to do with my grandmother's Great-aunt Sarah?" Dana asked, still tormented by confused emotions spinning like a whirlwind in her mind.

"Who?"

"Sarah Baker. Grandma's letter said our family hadn't spoken to the DeMitris since the murder of her Great-aunt Sarah."

"My poor ignorant girl, I'm sure Greta fabricated that story to justify the clause in her will."

Before Dana could respond, Patricia's secretary pounded on the door, interrupting any rebuttal she had to offer.

Patricia sprang up from her high-back leather chair and briskly opened the door. *"What is it, Ellen!"*

"I'm so sorry to disturb you, ma'am." The woman was practically wringing her hands. "But, well, your client, Mrs. Peters, she's threatened to put Mr. Peters champion collie to sleep if he doesn't agree to her divorce terms. He's really upset."

"Stupid, bitch..." she muttered as walked out the door leaving Dana to herself.

She bolted from her chair and ran out of the office and into the stairway, not wanting to take a chance waiting by the elevator. She had to get out before Patricia decided she wasn't worth keeping around, now that she knew everything.

Everything? Was her dear grandma, the woman who cared for her, read to her, kissed her scraped knees and, made her cookies... could she be a murderer? As her feet worked automatically down the stairs, six flights, down, down, she felt her life spinning uncontrollably. Down, down, left foot, right... if she could just make it down the stairs and onto the street. A tumble of confused thoughts and feelings assailed her. Imagining her grandma, holding a gun to her head, as she tries to reach Rome's comforting embrace, unable to reach him. Fearing for his life. Fearing for her own life, wondering if Patricia would now send a hired killer after her. Wondering if the bugler in her apartment was sent to murder her. Down, down... She felt drained, hollow and lifeless. As if her whole life had been a lie. All the while, Rome's name lingered there, around the edges of her mind. Down, down...

She needed to get these confused thoughts and emotions in order. She needed time to reorient herself. Think rationally. Figure out what she was going to do. Where she was going to go.

Three more steps, two more steps...

"Dana, *my God*. Are you okay?" It was Jack, waiting for her just as he'd promised. "You look like you're ready to faint. You're so pale."

"I'm fine," she said, more tersely than she meant to.

"How long has it been since you've eaten?"

When? She couldn't remember what day it was, let alone if she'd eaten all day. "Umm..."

He gently nudged her out the door to his car. "Come on. Let's get some food into you before you collapse."

"Fine." Dana felt as empty as her voice sounded. Even to her own ears. The thought of food made her want to throw up. But decisions were always easier when the baser needs were satisfied. She should eat. There. A logical thought—good. An improvement to the emotional chaos. "Fine," she said again as Jack buckled her seatbelt for her like a child, then went around to the driver side and climbed in, then headed east on Wilshire.

East was good.

Chapter Twenty-Four

"OKAY, GOOD. NOW, TOM, CAN you put your arm around your fiancée? No, a little tighter around the waist. And Tina, tilt your head at little to the right. Great. Perfect. And one...two... three..." *Click.* "Very nice," Rome said, adjusting the Bronica camera while it processed a temporary Polaroid for the couple to look at. He angled the 62 millimeter for another shot of the adoring couple's engagement photos. He'd worked non-stop since his family left his apartment.

Since Dana ran out on him.

Maybe he'd work out for a couple hours at the gym tonight. Work off the intense sexual energy. He felt a twinge of pain and regret squeeze at his heart as he thought of her. It wasn't just sexual energy he was suffering from, and he knew it.

He was crazy in love.

She'd reached his vulnerabilities with maddening speed. Surrounded him with her intoxicating sweetness, leaving his heart powerless to resist. He admired her on so many levels, it was difficult to know when the exact moment happened, when he knew he had to make her his. He admired her driving intelligence. Her enthusiasm for her shop. Her eagerness to learn and take charge with their lovemaking—something more than a purely sensual experience, something so intense it pulled him to her, upsetting his balance with Dana at the center. Like a beacon, guiding his heart to the light after years in darkness. It was no mystery why his reaction to her, his feelings toward her were so swift, so violently intense. He'd walk through glass on his knees and beg if that's what it took to make her see how they were completely and total destined to be together. Fated for each other.

His body ached to touch her again. To feel her softness against the contrast of his firm chest, the contours of her body molding to his own. These thoughts of Dana were unrelenting.

The disturbing irony about the painting and his mirror likeness to his ancestor left an eerie feeling of incompleteness. As if he was meant to find the key to a mystery and set things to right. But what *things*? What was the key that linked the puzzle pieces together? How did Dana fit into this? And her dreams... was her subconscious foreseeing these past few events? Or was she recalling dreams carried through her family DNA? Could a memory be past down like blue eyes and dark hair?

When his family finally stopped harassing him about the painting of his Great-great grandfather, Tony went back to work, and everyone else left to help Philippe. Rome came down to work, keeping himself from walking over to Dana's and beg on his hands and knees. If he just gave her a little more time...time to miss him, time to cool off, she'd welcome him back with open arm. "Yeah, right." He needed to stop tormenting himself. He'd made an error of judgment. He hade to move forward. Right the wrong he'd inflicted on Dana, then ask her to be his, always.

"What was that, sir?" Kimberly asked him.

"Nothing. Just thinking," he said, masking the inner turmoil in his mind with deceptive calmness. "Can you grab the gold reflector panel, Kim? I want to get a close-up this time." Rome noticed his assistant wasn't very responsive today. "Kimberly?"

"Uh? Oh! Sorry, I'll get it."

Once Kimberly propped the panel at an angle that reflected golden light toward the couple, Rome instructed them to embrace. "Okay, now look into each others eyes. A little closer, hold it, hold it..." The couple kissed. "I said 'hold it' you two." They kept kissing. Rome cleared his throat. Kimberly looked like she was ready to burst into tears.

Rome ran his hands over his face. It had been a long day. His clients threw their arms tightly around each other for a very passionate kiss. "Umm, I think we can give them a minute, Kimberly," he said. He could tell she was holding back from crying.

She ran from the room and into the reception area. Rome followed her, more concerned with his assistant than finishing the shoot. Kimberly threw her face into her hands and convulsed with sobs. "Kim, what's wrong? Are you sick?" Rome asked as compassionately as his impatience could allow. It was running thin after his afternoon with Dana, and then the episode with his family.

"He left..." she sobbed. "He... left me."

"Who? What are you talking about?"

"John," she cried. "He said I was boring and predictable. That another minute with me and his dick would die of loneliness," she gasped, trying to breathe through the exhaustive tears.

"Hey, come here," Rome said, as he tried to comfort his assistant. Embracing her, he patted at her back while she wiped her nose on his shirt. *God, he didn't need this.*

"Kim, it's obvious this asshole did you a favor."

"Uh?"

"What if you married this guy—then found out he was a jerk. You'd be in for bigger problems then just a broken heart."

She nodded and sniffled. "You're right, Mr. DeMitri. It just hurts."

Lord, didn't he know it? He understood all too well how heartache could mess with your mind and cause many sleepless nights. He held her away from him to look at her bowed head. "Why don't you go home, Kim? I can finish up here by myself."

"No. No, I need to work. I'll just think about things if I go home."

Rome handed her the tissue box from the desk. "Okay then. Let's see if we can get these two out of the lip-lock. I hope we don't walk in on them tearing at each others clothes." He winked at her at she cracked a tearful smile. "That's better. Now get back in there and earn your salary," he said in mock demand.

"Yes, sir. Ready for duty."

*****

"I can't believe it took near-exhaustion to get you to have dinner with me, Dana," Jack laughed as he ate heartily at his mushroom burger and fries. Dana could barely swallow a few spoonfuls of soup. Just the smell of food in the diner made her gag.

"I sorry. I'm not very good company right now." She was so tired. Her head ached and she tried to smile at him, grateful he was here for her. But her mouth wasn't cooperating.

"No problem. I understand." His voice was soothing yet oddly disconcerting. Dana felt a little uncomfortable knowing Jack was attracted to her. She was never very comfortable around men.

Except Rome.

The day's events weighed heavily like a stampede of wild bulls running over her chest, preventing her from breathing in enough air. She felt as if she were living in a nightmare, unable to wake up. Slowly, her confusion over Patricia's account of her grandmother's youth evaporated, replaced by an anger she'd never felt before.

She had to read that letter again.

The one her grandmother left. Find some hidden meaning, something, some clue, maybe the bracelet? Anything. A fragment or a hint her grandma may have left to the mystery surrounding her family. Some secret to tie the pieces neatly together. Otherwise, she'd never be able to forgive and move on with her life.

Sarah Baker. She had to be the key to all of this. Somehow, there must be a connection to this insanity and her great-great aunt. But, what?

"I need to get back into my apartment," she blurted. "Right now." Her voice sounded harsh even to her own ears. "I don't care how, but I need to get back in there."

"Dana, you should rest," Jack answered calmly. "You're not yourself." He sighed, knowing she wasn't going to relent. "All right, let's go." He stood and threw a couple bills on the table, then helped her out of the booth.

Jack parked his beige Mercedes coupe at the nearest empty spot to Dana's shop. They'd walked by a few shops, passing Rome's studio before reaching *The Enchanted Frame*.

Dana glanced at the front window to Rome's studio and saw a couple embracing as she passed by. Dana caught herself looking again uneasily over her shoulder, confirming her disbelief. Rome holding a woman tightly in his arms. *Another woman.*

With a sudden and violent pang of realization, Dana's fears were culminating into this one moment of confirmation. Dana was a fool to believe time could change who she was. She'd been the fool—for the second time in her life. Not the result of pain inflicted by an ignorant boy. This pain was soul-deep, embedded in her heart as it was slowly, completely splitting in two. Everything she'd ever suspected, believed about her inadequacies, her short comings, were confirmed by this one act of betrayal by the one man whose body spoke volumes of love, but his mouth never spoke the words.

"Dana?" With his gentle hand on her forearm, Jack led her back to the car. "We should park in the alley. What you're doing isn't exactly legal."

She obediently followed him.

When he turned into the alley and pulled up along side the door to the backroom entrance, Dana was out the car door before Jack had the car in park. "Dana, wait."

But she was already out of earshot.

Finding a nice chunk of loose concrete from the street, Dana held it firmly in her hand and climbed onto an abandoned crate by the wall, then banged forcefully against the shop's small bathroom window with the concrete, cracking thick frosted glass until she'd managed to break clear through. The shards fell with a crash to the toilet below. "Jack, give me a lift up?"

"As your attorney, I'm obligated to advise against this."

"So noted, counselor," she said. "Now, can you help me here. Please?"

"Okay. Just get what you need and get out."

"All right." He gave her a leg up as she levered herself through the small window. Her bruised ribs ached as she fell to the bathroom floor.

"You okay, Dana?"

"I'mm... ahh," she had to catch her breath, "Yes." A warning voice in her head told her to act fast. But her legs stood frozen in place. What if she couldn't find the clues she needed? What if there was nothing to explain this?

Her legs moved forward as if controlled by an unknown force. Moving of their own accord, slowly through the store. Taking in everything, the smell of paint, the new carpet. The hastily painted pictures of Rome's hands and arms and neck, enlarged on canvas, hanging everywhere. On the walls, the support columns, in the display window. And the furniture she'd lovingly painted that once belonged to her grandma. The old cabinet... her beautiful table... the table where her and Rome first made love...

Dana was assailed by bitterness and grief as she looked around at her dreams now shattered.

Before her bitterness turned to tears, she took the steps to her apartment as quickly as her weary legs allowed. Having very little to eat, she was running on pure adrenaline.

The letter. She had to get the letter. She had to leave while she still had some fragment of self-preservation left.

The apartment still looked the same as when she left it. Before, it held a promise of hopes and dreams. But now, it just seemed lifeless and stale.

She found the letter and the pouch that held the bracelet. They were in the nightstand drawer, right where Dana had left them. It seemed like a lifetime ago when she'd last saw them.

Were they a lie? Did her grandmother make up this story about her aunt's death to cover up a murder? And the bracelet? Was it a gift from her lover? Or just a cheap piece of costume jewelry purchased at the Renaissance Fair? She could easily have it appraised, she supposed. But the seeds of doubt were there, and she had to know. Dana knew she'd never be able to have one restful night of sleep until she knew for sure. She had to. It was her only tether to hold on to. The only driving force keeping her from curling up in a corner—letting insanity take over.

The next several minutes were a blur. Like waking up from a dream and not remembering anything but the odd feeling something significant was about to happen.

Dana went to her closet and took out the wooden baseball bat. Grasping it tightly in her left hand and the letter and pouch in her right, she descended the stairs to the shop.

Setting the letter and pouch down on the overstuffed chair, near the back wall, she went back to the table, her grandmother's table, the table her and Rome made love.

With one arm, she swept everything off the table, allowing them to crash to the newly tiled floor.

She thought she heard Jack from outside, but the blood rushing through her ears made his voice seems muffled and distant.

With an Indian war cry, she swung the bat over her head and hit table hard—square in the center. The hit wasn't hard enough or loud enough to satisfy the rage forging through her. She swung again. Her teeth tightly clenched as she cried out in furry. This time the bat made a dent in the painted wood.

She swung and hit—again and again and again. Then swinging her weapon at the legs, breaking one off, then the other. The table, now an odd V shape, lying at an angle like a lifeless tree branch after a storm.

She whacked at it from the side and down the center again.

Whack. Whack. Whack.

She was sick with the struggle ragging within her... sick with her grandmother's manipulations. Sick with heartache and Rome's lies. Breathless with rage. Numb with shock and anguish.

Whack. Whack. Whack.

Her breath burned in her throat as her own anger and hurt no longer controlled. Her heart hammered at her ribcage, gnawing at her bruises, but her body was beyond feeling pain. Bereft and desolate, her fury and anguish peaked, shattering the last threads of her self-control.

Visions of Rome holding other women. Lots of other women—in bed with other women. Repeating the same sweet words to them as he'd spoken to her. Damn him for awakening her body only to arouse old fears and uncertainties she believed were buried forever. She was suddenly an awkward teenager again, filled with humiliation and regret. The same nauseating, sinking despair. The swell of pain beyond tears.

Whack. Whack. Whack.

She'd managed to break through the base of the wood, now in splinters at her feet. It still wasn't enough.

Whack. Whack. Whack.

She continued her assault, smashing the bat into the tiled floor. She heard a faint voice from behind her, off in the distance. She ignored it. Pounding at the floor, now broken tiles mixed with painted wood pieces.

Whack. Whack. Whack.

She pounded at the wood base of the old floor. Cracking sounds of rusted nails breaking through aged wood.

"Dana?"

Whack. Whack. Whack.

"Dana! Stop it!"

She felt strong arms clamp down around her shaking arms, forcing her adrenaline-filled body to stop.

"Stop it, Dana." The male voice carried a unique force that pulled her out from her trace of fury. "What the hell are you doing?"

It was Rome. He'd gripped her so tight she was forced to drop the bat from her hand. It hit the floor with a loud *clank*. Alarm rippled along her spine as she stared down at the damaged she'd caused. Stunned and sickened, the shock of defeat against Rome's granite-hard hold left her immobile. "Don't touch me... don't touch me." Her voice sounded weak and hollow even to herself.

"Dana, calm down. You're shaking and you're in shock, calm down. Shhh, calm down. That's it," he said with quiet emphasis, trying to reach her. "Jesus. What a mess."

With her energy now drained, it took every effort to look at him. Her body, now boneless as she buried her burning face against his shoulder. The fabric of his shirt felt warm and comforting against her cheek.

Unable to control the spasmodic trembling, she yielded to the strength of his grip. "What's wrong? What happened?" The last traces of resistance vanished as one long compulsive sob retched from her lungs. "Hey, its okay. You're okay, sweetheart," he said comforting, willing her to relax with his voice. "Shh, it will be okay." He stroked her hair as the tremors subsided.

There was a long brittle silence in the air as Dana forced her body to relax again against his hold. *Lord, he felt so good.* Like being wrapped in a warm blanket on a cold night. She missed this terribly.

But the relief was short lived. She felt an abrupt tension in his posture as he held her. Puzzled she looked up at him. Rome was looking passed her, toward the damaged floorboard. "My God," he whispered.

"What is it?" she asked, as he abruptly released her.

He didn't answer.

She watched Rome kneel down by the hole in the floor where the floorboard was broken clear through. He tugged at the remaining pieces stubbornly hanging from a rusty bent nail.

"Look, there's something here," he said, tugging at the loose wood. "Ow," he shook his hand sharply, when a splinter wedged into his skin. "Do you have a pair of gloves or something?" he asked as he sucked on the tip of his finger.

"Yeah." She grabbed Rick's leather gloves from the frame room and handed them to him.

Her knees still weak and shaky, but her pounding headache and adrenaline rush suddenly forgotten as she watched a hole in the floor appeared.

"Look. This wood is newer than the rest of the floor," Rome noticed.

"Earthquake damage?"

"Maybe." With one last tug of the broken floorboard, a hole, measuring two feet square, revealed a shabby rust colored cloth. A corner of the cloth was shredded clear through, exposing a glint of gold. "Maybe not."

"*Ohmygod*? What is... how long has it been down there?"

"Well, if this cloth is any indication... a very long time." He gingerly retrieved the object from the hole and held it with both hands, weighing its mass. It was less than ten inches square. "It's heavy," he commented as he pealed away the shredded remains of what was once a plush velvet pouch.

Like the one holding the mysterious bracelet, Dana thought. Only this one was much larger.

"Look at that!" His tone, eager and excited as he held the object in his right palm.

"*Oh, its beautiful!* Is it a jewelry box?" Dana asked.

Under the tattered fabric was an ornate octagon-shaped brass box with an intricate design so delicate, the brass nearly looked like gold lace. It hade a delicate handle on the lid, two golden balls connected by a thinly curved U-shaped design.

"No, I think it's an old Victorian lock-box," Rome said. "See the ornate key hole and latch? My mom used to have one. But the latch on hers was broken so she kept it for a sewing kit."

"It's gorgeous."

He turned the box on is side and back. The bottom and right side was slightly pitted and incrusted with a thin greenish layer of patina usually associated with aged metals. Rome shook it gently. "There's something in here. Too bad the key wasn't in the hole with it."

"Are you sure it's not?" she asked.

Rome felt around the hole with his gloves hand. "Doesn't look like it. Can't we just break it open?"

"It would a crime to break something so beautiful. The box itself is probably worth a fortune."

"A locksmith, maybe?"

"Wait a minute. I wonder..."

"Dana...?"

She walked to the stock room and brought back the pouch carrying the bracelet from her grandmother. She opened the gold-threaded synch, then turning it upside down, letting the piece fall into her palm and showed it to him. "This is an heirloom my grandma left me. It belonged to her Aunt Sarah." Dana let the velvet pouch fall to the tiled floor as she carefully examined each charm attached to its chain. "Look. It has a key charm!"

"It's a charm, Dana. It's too small."

"Try it anyway."

Rome took the bracelet from her palm, holding it from the key charm as the others tinkled and pinged against each other. He placed the key to the keyhole. "It's not it."

"Darn it! Now what?"

"Is there anything else in the bag?" he asked.

"No," she sighed as she picked the pouch back up. "Just the bracelet... wait a second." She felt along the seam of the pouch. "I think there's something stitched into the fabric."

"Here, let me see," Rome handed her the lock-box and took the pouch from her. He felt around and back against the seam. "I think your right. We need a knife to tear the thing open."

"I have razor blades in the frame room," she said, eagerly walking to the back, still holding her treasure in her hands.

"That should do," he said, following her. He took the blade she offered and carefully tore at the hem of the fabric. A small bronze skeleton key fell out on onto the framing table.

They both looked at each other and smiled in earnest.

"Let's say we open this puppy up."

Dana nodded at him, unable to speak as Rome inserted the old key into an equally old lock and turned.

"Damn, it's stuck. Maybe this isn't the right key."

"It has to be!" she cried. "Try again."

He did, with a little more force. He grunted once, then a *tink* sounded and the lock popped open.

Dana held her breath as he lifted the lid. A whiff of smelly, dusty mold and corrosion assaulted her nasal passages.

They both looked down at what looked like a brown paper pouch. "What is it?" she asked.

Rome shook his head and lifted it out of the box, blowing off the dust and soot. Underneath were several more, "I think they're old photographs," he said as he turned the pouch over. "It has something written on it." Written in boldly scripted letters, it said one word: INSURANCE.

"What does it mean?"

"I'm not sure." Rome opened the paper pouch and pulled out several aging photos. "Pictures of my father..."

"...And Patricia...all of these are. And what's that there?" she asked.

He pulled out another envelope. "A property lean."

"No these, look." She pulled out three waded up rolls of paper. "Old bearer bonds. My God, Rome, there must be several hundred thousand dollars worth!"

"Holy, hell," he whispered. "If they're still collecting interest, they could be worth ten times that."

"Do you think they're still good?"

"As long as we still have a Federal Reserve, I don't see why not. Ask your lawyer, he'd know," Rome commented.

"An excellent idea, lover boy."

A sound of soft-soled shoes lightly shuffling on the debris had their heads whipping around to the sound of Jack's patronizing voice—and a gun pointed at Rome's chest.

Chapter Twenty-Five

"WHO THE *HELL* ARE YOU?"

"The man holding a gun at your chest, asshole!"

"*Jack*! For godsake, what are you doing?" Dana pleaded.

"Dana? Who the hell is this guy?" Rome whispered.

"My attorney."

"Your attorney?" He turned to Jack, "What, did she not pay her fee on time?" Rome mocked humorlessly.

"Go ahead, laugh it up. Because you won't be laughing when I shoot your dick off, pretty boy."

"Why are you doing this? I thought you wanted to help me?" she asked while struggling with the fact that everyone she'd ever trusted had deceived her—even her attorney.

"Help you? Yeah, well, turns out, you helped me instead, honey. I've been looking for that fuckin' thing for years," he said, as he stabbed his left finger at the box, still holding the gun in his right. "I'd have preferred to fuck you for it. Pump you for info first, babe," he said bluntly, then shrugged. "But it was apparent you were oblivious to its existence."

Dana saw Rome advance forward toward Jack—and the gun. She moved to block him. She couldn't let Jack kill him for defending her honor.

Jack raked his eyes across Dana. "Thought you were too good to have dinner with me," Jack continued. She almost felt sorry for him, but his look chilled her. "Had we been lovers, Dana, this would've been so much easier, more pleasurable, ending less painfully. We could've found the money together. Partners. In *and* out of bed." He let out an exaggerated sigh. "I was so disappointed you'd chosen this filthy DeMitri spawn for your sex toy. But alas, you've done all the work for me. Breaking-and-entering is such a nasty business. I wasn't looking forward to doing it again. Your alarm system is a bitch to disconnect." His voice flooded with sickening triumph. "I'll thank you for it—later." He licked his lips as his mouth spread into a thin-lipped smiled as his eyes turned cold and calculating. "Hand it over, babe, before I kill your boyfriend."

"Jack, I don't understand. Why?" Jack's face showed a perverse pleasure in her distress.

"Because he knew his aunt and your grandmother hid the box somewhere in this building," Rome replied. He was trying to nudge her away from the line of fire, moving himself as the target.

Dana gave Rome a confused look, then stared at her attorney.

"Very good, photo man. I see your brain works as well as your—"

"You're Patricia's nephew?" Dana interjected.

"You sound surprised. But then, you always were naïve, too trusting."

"You can't have this, Jack. I won't let you," her voice was wavering. "You won't get away with this."

"Dana," Rome said calmly. "Give him the box, sweetheart. It's not worth it." He was still trying to signal her. Her mind still whirling, Jack, the man responsible for everything happening to her. Everything, including her bruised ribs and losing her shop.

"But he broke into my home! Stole my piece of mind... let me believe... Oh, God..." everything she told her attorney, she'd been telling a thief and a madman. "My purse? My keys?"

Jack reached into his jacket pocket, still keeping his eye on Rome, retrieved her keys and threw them on the framing counter. "Yes, much easier than picking a lock. Causes less suspicion, too." He rubbed at his thin jaw. "Should have killed your brother while I had a chance. Fucker nearly broke my jaw." His eyes went cold again. "Now, give me the box!"

"Is this why Patricia had me followed? Why you're stalking me? For this?" she said as fear and panic whirled inside her head.

"My aunt has nothing to do with this. I found out about the money years ago. It wasn't until the old lady died when I realized were she'd hidden it all those years ago."

"But I thought Patricia wanted the building back out of revenge for her sister's death." Dana felt Rome lightly tug at her elbow.

"Revenge?" Jack laughed and shook his head, "Aunt Patty killed our mother out of *jealousy*. Not revenge," he said ominously.

"But I thought..."

"My mother and Patricia were both having an affair with that DeMitri scumbag. Then he decided to marry Greta Baker, keeping my mother as a mistress, then dumped poor old Patricia." He snorted. "When she found them in bed together, she shot my mother. She would have killed him too had his fiancée not walked in on the whole thing."

Her grandma wasn't a murderer.

A screeching howl sounded as something came up behind Jack, distracting him for a fraction of a second. Rome didn't hesitant. He dodged at Jack's right arm.

Dana saw a black streak dart across the tiled floor. Jack's finger move tight against the trigger.

"No!"

A single shot was fired in a deafening roar, rocking the walls and rattling the glass cases. She threw herself at Rome's hulky mass, not thinking of her own safety, trying to protect him—narrowly shoving him out of harms way.

They both landed on top of Jack, the gun went flying out of his hand, across the room and under the counter.

"What was that?" she asked.

"Oscar," Rome grunted.

The cat?

"Get the fuck off me!" Jack snarled between his teeth.

Dana felt Rome go limp under her. Blood from his jeans seeped out. "Rome? Rome!" She leaped off his limp body and he moaned and rolled over on his back. "Your leg." His *bad* leg. She looked at Jack. "We have to get him to a doctor."

"Not so fast." Jack found his gun and pointed it at her head.

"You can't just let him bleed to death!"

"Can't I? Here," he threw her some rags and a bolt of hanging wire.

Since it was all she had to stop the bleeding, she took it while Jack stuffed the dusty bond notes into his jacket pocket, leaving the photos and the box aside.

Rome groaned in pain as she wrapped his wound with the rags. The blood still oozed through the fabric of his jeans. "It's not enough, Jack. I need more cloth."

"Make due."

"Look," she shouted, "I've had a shitty day today, okay? Most of which is your doing, Jack. Now take the damn bonds and get me more rags before he bleeds to death." Dana was shocked at her own uncontrolled outburst.

"You've got some mouth on you, woman."

She didn't have time to react before he cold cocked her in the temple with the butt of his gun. Piercing pain shot through her head and neck as she tried to gulp in air. Her body pulsed with white-hot pain while she tried desperately to remain conscious... for Rome. He needed her. He needed... no, the pain...

*****

Rome woke with an intense pain throughout his body. *Where the hell was he?* His first thought was he'd fallen asleep at his desk. His leg felt numb, and his body felt weak. Was he coming down with the flu? He tried to move, causing a knife-stabbing throb from his knee to his hip.

His vision was fuzzy, and he couldn't get enough oxygen in his lungs to even moan from the agony of his leg. *He shouldn't have worked out so hard last night.*

He heard voices in the distance. "You idiot. You really screwed up, big brother."

"Shut up, Liz! What would you have me do? Wait for Miss Priss to just hand it over freely? I don't think so. No one is that stupid."

With startling awareness, Rome remembered where he was before he even opened his eyes. He tried to open one eye a fraction, to make sure Dana was all right. He didn't want Jack to know he was conscious. He needed the element of surprise, assuming he had the strength to even stand.

Where was Dana?

"Well, don't let your dick talk your head into some other boneheaded plan. I know you wanted her to yourself," Rome heard Elizabeth said.

"I got the money, didn't I? So shut the fuck up!" Jack tone was becoming more erratic and impatient with his sister.

"What about the deed? Was it in there? This whole thing won't mean diddly do-do without the deed."

He didn't answer.

A deed. Was there a land deed in the box? Rome couldn't remember. Making a simple coherent thought proved difficult.

"Aunt Patty is right. You *are* a worthless shit."

Rome heard a cracking sound of flesh again flesh. He'd assumed the "worthless shit" just assaulted his own sister.

"That's it. Go ahead hit me again. Makes you feel like a man? Huh? Hitting women?" Elizabeth said the contempt. "I hope you rot in prison, you stupid fool." He heard footsteps as the back door slam shut.

With his eyes cracked open he realized he was slumped on the floor in Dana's stock room. Rome felt for his hands. As he expected, they were tied behind his back.

Thankfully, Jack hadn't tied his legs. If only he could stand. In his pain-induced fog, Rome knew he'd lost a lot of blood.

He tested the bindings for leverage. There wasn't any. But they were rags—not rope. *Good, easily torn.*

A muffled cry sounded from the overstuff loveseat on the opposite side of the room.

Dana! He was instantly alert. His pain forgotten. She cried again. Rome angled his head and saw Jack bent over Dana's supine body, tying her hands to the column above her head. Her mouth gagged. Jack tore open Dana's shirt with the razor they'd left in the frame room. Rome saw frightened tears streak her sweet face as she tugged at her restraints. Her shirt open, revealing her bound ribs and soft white breasts quivering as Jack's mouth slammed down hard on one nipple, pinching violently at the other. Dana twisted side-to-side, desperate to escape, whimpering in pain.

Anger of volcanic proportions flooded Rome's head. He shoved his body against the old cabinet. It teetered, and Rome thought it might actually topple on him. Jack was oblivious to Rome, as he removed his hand from her breast and ripped at Dana's shorts— kneading at her bottom with his now free hand.

With fierce determination, Rome found the broken handle from the cabinet door and wedged his biddings under it, sawing back and forth, ripping at the threads, one at a time. *Not nearly fast enough.*

"Mmm, I've wanted you for so long," Rome heard Jack say and felt bile rise in his throat when he saw the bulge in Jack's pants, rubbing himself against Dana's near-naked body. Her gag came loose and she bit her attacker hard on the shoulder.

"You little bitch!" he yelped as he backhanded her cheek. She cried out and Rome's heart was pounding so loud in his ears he hardly noticed he'd ripped the cloth almost free.

"Jack, please stop! Don't do this. I'll give you the money. You can have what ever you want," she pleaded as Jack reach for his zipper. Rome ripped the remaining threads of his binding and lurched at Jack like a madman.

But Jack was too fast and Rome, too weak. A simple punch to the gut had Rome falling back before he could raise his arm in defense. "Since lover boy is awake now, he can watch while I fuck his woman."

Rome yelled "no" but his lips and throat wouldn't move. His body felt like lead weight, holding him down when Dana needed him the most. He was failing her all over again. He had to stop Jack from hurting her, even if it cost him life. He had to protest her from this crazed eccentric who claimed to be versed in the law. A madman who held Dana's life in his hands. *He'd rather die a thousand times before be let this prick touch Dana,* he thought as he fell silently back into unconsciousness.

*****

God, no... not again, was all she could think. *I won't allow this to happen again. I've got to help Rome.*

There was an eagerness in Jack's eyes as he ripped at her clothes. Dana's stomach clench. She'd always thought Jack was an attractive, if somewhat average looking man. But now as she looked at her attorney, former attorney, Dana realized there was an aloof coldness behind the bright, easy smile and softly controlled voice. A voice she thought was pleasant. A voice that would now forever haunt her, just as her high school date had all those years ago. She tried to keep her fragile control in check as she thought desperately for a way of escape before he killed them both. She had to find a way to suppress Jack's anger. She stilled, letting his hands and mouth roam freely, trying not to flinch.

"Your tits taste so good. I knew they would, Dana." His voice repulsed her. "You're so pretty. I knew we were meant for each other the first day you walked into my office." Jack's admiration might have flattered her in the past, now it sickened her.

His touch gentled as his expression darkened with lust instead of violence. This odd surge of affection frightened her. She suppressed her anger and disgust under the appearance of indifference, at least until she could decide what to do. Perhaps make him believe she desired him as well. Trust her enough to release her restraints. *Or release Rome.*

If he raped her, at least there'd be no surprises this time. She wasn't an innocent. She was naked and vulnerable, yes, but not helplessly ignorant to men. Men who used sex and violence as a weapon against women. She wasn't going to let Jack steal her self-confidence even if he violated her body. And she rather he rape her than have him take his anger out on Rome. *Please let him be all right.*

Her nerves tensed and skin burned like acid as Jack's mouth sucked sloppily at her breast. She withheld a cry as his fingers worked painfully at her other nipple. Panic welled in her throat when his head lifted from her chest and he tore her shorts and underwear from her body. He hesitated while looking over her naked form, unable to keep his raw emotions in check. She hated how vulnerable she was, tied, and unable to hold him off. She tugged again at the cloth wrapped tight at her wrists.

"We're both going to really enjoy this, Dana. Won't we," he said, tauntingly with a strange and detached inevitability in his tone as his fly rubbed mercilessly between her legs—legs now held firmly in his grip.

And then it hit her.

She had to make him believe, convince him that she wanted him just as much. Give him what he desired, just enough to let his guard down. Just enough time to escape.

"You're right, Jack," she chose her words carefully, as to not provoke his anger. She moved her hips sensuously as every fiber in her being wanted to revolt. She hoped her thin smile was convincing. "It will be good between us," she choked on her own words. "I've always wanted you, Jack. I just didn't think I was pretty enough to attract a real man like you."

His brows shot up as he gave her a nasty half-smile.

"Kiss me, Jack. Show me how a real man can kiss."

She saw uncertainty creep into his expression as he hesitated, measuring her for moment before he slammed his mouth hard on hers, plunging his tongue into her mouth. It was sour and unrelenting.

"You like that, don't you, babe." He said the words tentatively as if testing the idea. Testing her.

"You know it," she said, trying to sound sensual instead of frightened. "Let me put my hands on you, Jack. Untie me, I need to touch you. Please, Jack, now," she pleaded.

"Oh, yeah..." blinded by his own lust, he released her.

But she needed him to trust her, so she hesitated making her move and kissed him back. Wrapping her arms around his neck, pulling him down as she levered her knees between his legs. She had to keep Rome's safety at the center of her mind, to keep Jack from making her gag. She was more afraid for Rome than for herself. Especially if Jack still wanted her. But she wouldn't kid herself that he'd wanted her more than he wanted the money and the deed.

"I want you naked too, Jack," Dana said, hoping he wouldn't notice how her hands shook.

"First, say you want me to put my cock in you." She hesitated. "He tugged painfully at her hair and she yelped. *"Say it!"*

"Put your cock in me, Jack," she whispered. A faint thread of hysteria was in her voice.

Jack must have sensed her panic as he narrowing look of speculation.

Out of the corner of her left eye, Dana saw Rome stir. Then as quick as a cat, Rome shot his fist at Jack's head, jerking from the blow. Dana knew she wouldn't get a second chance to strike, then rammed her knee squarely into Jack's testicles. When he jerked forward, he released her hair and she instantly shoved her elbow into his eye socket, forcing his weight backward.

Dana leaped from the loveseat and lunged for the bat, left haplessly on the floor, slamming it down hard onto Jack's collarbone.

Curses and screams fell from his mouth.

"You filthy bastard," she screamed as she swung the bat at his thighs and back. *"You disgust me!"* She threw the words at him like stones. Words she'd never utter out loud in her life. "I can't believe I trusted you." She was crying now. Letting the tears of fury cloud her vision. She didn't care if she killed or maimed. She continued to lash out until she fell to her knees and sobbed. She felt Rome's gentle hand on her shoulder. Relief flooded her, throwing herself against him. Holding his weakened body tightly against her own—he was alive.

"He's unconscious, sweetheart. Let go of the bat," he said gently. "Dana, you'll have to listen to me. I can't do this without you," she could tell how the loss of blood had weakened him. "Dana, we have to tie him up until the police get here. Okay?"

She nodded. Unable to speak through the sobs that racked her body, her energies spent. She shivered from the draft in the room, but too exhausted to cover her own naked body, holding Rome in her arms.

"It's over, sweetheart. Shh, it's over."

Chapter Twenty-Six

"HOLY SHIT! WHAT THE HELL happen?" Tony's voice rang out from the doorway. "It looks like Hiroshima in here."

"Tony, man, am I glad to see you." Rome could have kissed his brother. "Tie that son-of-a-bitch up..." Rome said through harsh breaths, waving a heavy hand toward Jack's limp figure, "...before he comes to. And call the police..." he said, conscious of Dana's emotional state rather than her state of undress—as long as she was safe. He felt her shiver against him. "...and hand me your jacket, will you?"

Her eyes looked up at Tony as he removed his navy jacket and placed it carefully over her shoulders. "My God, Rome. You're bleeding everywhere," Tony exclaimed.

"The bastard shot my bum leg. Must've gone clean through." He still held Dana's stiff body tight, not willing to let her go even to check his own wounds. "Just a flesh wound, bro," he added, when Tony's face started to turn green.

"And Dana? Did he...?"

Rome shook his head. "No. She out smarted the bastard." God, he was so proud of her. His innocent seductress turned into femme fatale right before his eyes. So incredibly brave in the face of danger. When he saw her kissing the asshole back, his first reaction was astonished fury. After he placed his ego in check, he realized Dana was luring him in. He couldn't believe the fucker actually released her. He wanted Dana to want him so badly— wanted to believe it, Jack was easily tricked. Rome almost felt sorry for him. *Almost.*

Tony hog-tying Jack's wrists and ankles together with his silk tie, "I hope you appreciate this is a hundred dollar silk tie, jerk off," he told a groaning Jack, then took out his cell phone from his belt case. "Get her covered, Rome. Your mother and Jules were out parking the rental truck... Yes, I need an ambulance Asap," Tony spoke into his cell phone giving the woman on the other end their location. "There's been a shooting... and an attempted rape... Yeah, I'll hold." Tony let out a deep breath and rubbed his forehead. Rome wanted to laughed. Tony was started to act just like him. "I can't believe 9-1-1 just put me on hold."

"Eeeh!"

All three of them turned, startled by Claire's screech as she stared down at Jack, tied up on floor... and the blood.

She fell in a dead faint.

"Well. I guess she won't be riding in the ambulance."

"Tony, you've got a sick sense of humor." Although breathless and in pain, and probably permanently damage, Rome just felt damned lucky to be alive.

He looked down at the woman in his arms. Her naked back warm against the skin of his arm, her soft breath against his neck, and he knew he'd never loved anyone as much as he loved Dana Baker.

Damn lucky.

*****

"Okay, Ms. Baker." The head nurse handed her a clipboard. "Just sign this release form and you're free to go."

Go? Go where? Dana signed the form, collected the few things Claire thoughtfully brought the night before, then sat on the bed, possibly feeling worse than when the medics brought her in the night before.

She was treated for extreme exhaustion and minor dehydration and suspected Rome's mother had something to do with the hospital staff keeping her over night.

Dear Claire, Dana thought. She was the mother Dana never had. How her mother might have been had she lived.

"Hey, sunshine."

"Cynthia!" Her friend was pushing in a wheelchair. Typical Cynthia was adorned in a snug-fitting burned orange jumpsuit with a sash tied around her head, hanging down her back like an Indian headdress. "I'm so glad to see you."

"Oh, girlfriend. I was scared shitless when they said you'd been kidnapped. I feel like it's all my fault, too."

"Why? You didn't do anything."

"I insisted Victoria call her brother." She looked out the dusty window of hospital room. "When the cops kicked us out of the store, I panicked and thought your attorney should be notified, you know, in case he could help us. Maybe I did it for selfish reason." She shrugged.

"You're not a selfish person, Cynthia. Under the same circumstances, I probably would've done the same thing."

"God, if only I'd known... Victoria should've known... he's her brother for godsakes." She sighed. "I just wanted my job back. I hope you don't hate me."

Dana took her friends hand. "I don't hate you. And I'm sorry about the job. Unless the Library takes me back, I'm out of a job, too."

"Are you okay? I mean *really* okay... that slime didn't touch you? Because if he touched you, so help me I'll bust his balls. I don't care if the bastard's in jail with a broken collarbone... I'll still kick his ass."

Dana laughed. She'd missed Cynthia. "Yeah, I'm okay."

"Well, I've brought your chariot, m'lady." She wheeled the chair to the bed where Dana was sitting. "Jump on. I'll push you outta this joint."

"Did I really break Jack's collarbone?"

"Oh, yeah. I think ol' Jackie boy will think twice before he tries to assault another woman." She smiled. "You kick ass, girl."

"Thanks." She was silent while Cynthia wheeled her through the hospital hallway. "How's Rome?"

"You should ask him yourself." She punched the button for the elevator. "I'll take you to his room if you want."

"No. No... I'll go by myself."

"Okay." They got in the elevator, went down one floor before the doors opened again. "He's the third door on the left."

"Thanks, Cynthia."

"Sure thing. I'll wait for you in the lobby."

Dana hated the wheelchair. It made her feel like a fraud. She left it by the elevator and walked the rest of the way to Rome's room. Hanging by the doorway, she thought of what to say to him. *Thanks for nearly getting killed because of me? Oh, by the way, I saw you with another woman, good-bye?* A stab of guilt surfaced in her mind.

With a deep cleansing breath, she walked in and saw him—lying in bed. His hulky form asleep, his dark hair a sharp contrast to the stark white pillow beneath his head. His strong forearm limp against the neatly folded sheet, an IV needle taped inside his elbow. His beautiful body, scarred because of her. He looked so weak, and her spirits sank even lower. Couldn't bear the sight of him without breaking down.

Silently, she turned on her heal to leave, but his voice drifted from the bed in a hushed whisper. "Hi, beautiful."

"Hi." She turned and smiled, walking to his side and took the hand he offered. It felt strong in hers despite his weakened state. "I thought you were sleeping."

"Nah, they've got me on this pain-drip thing... makes me groggy." He shut his eyes.

Dana thought he'd nodded out again. She swallowed the sob that rose in her throat when she felt him shudder as he drew in a sharp breath.

"Sorry, I can't keep my eyes open." He tugged on her hand. "Come here," he said pulling her closer and gently kissed her, lazily tracing his finger up the tender skin inside her wrist and up her forearm. The simple touch warmed her, that familiar tingle travel up her arm and down her legs. *Damn him.* How was he capable of seducing her so easily?

"Ow," she flinched when he touched the bruise on her wrist. She tried to tug her hand away. He gripped it tighter.

"Let me see."

Dana held out her wrists, both covered in welts and purple marks. As he held her wrists, his soft expression changed, as if he'd been struck in the face. Turning them back and forth. Dana tried to hide her shame and misery as he probed and assessed her injured hands.

He sighed heavily, "I'll kill the bastard," his voice filled with anguish. He wouldn't kill him for his own injuries—but for hers.

She felt guilty and defeated. She loved Rome. She always would. But Jack had sliced open a newly healed wound. How desperately she wanted to cling to Rome, needed him to comfort her. But her mind was congested with old fears and doubts, struggling with uncertainty, aroused when she saw Rome holding another woman.

"Dana, I need to say something. Tell you something." He released her wrists.

"What?"

"Please, sit down."

"Okay." Her body trembled, nervous of what he had to say—what he might *not* say.

"When that gun was pointed at my head, I realized something..."

"Rome..."

"Please, sweetheart, let me finish. I realized that it didn't matter what my father thought or what my brother needed." He reached for her hands again. "For once, I wanted to take something that *I* wanted. Not because of family obligation, or because my business would profit from it. I wanted something for myself."

"What was that?" *God, no.*

"You, Dana. I want you." His dark, intense eyes looked into hers. "Marry me."

"Rome, please. I..." she tried to stand up. He wouldn't release her.

"Not because of the money or Dad's stupid will. But just...because."

"Just because?" she asked, flatly.

He nodded.

"No other reason?"

"Because I want you. Because we fit well together," he laughed uncomfortably, "...and God, knows we're great in the sack. I think we could make each other happy."

Her spirits were sinking fast. "No other reason than that, then?"

"What other reasons could there be?"

"What if I don't want to get married?" She had to sheath her inner feelings before the tears threatening to fall.

"All right. We'll live together then." She watched as his face closed, as if wall had just erected, shielding his heart from hers.

She shook her head. "I can't."

"Why?" His voice sounded chilled and uneasy.

She couldn't falter. She had to be strong for her own preservation. She'd never be the woman waiting at home while her husband was fooling around with his assistants and receptionists. "I saw you, Rome. I saw you with her."

"Saw what? With who?"

"I thought I could trust you," a single determined tear fell down her cheek. "And without trust we have nothing. I thought we had something special. But when I saw you with her, in your studio, your assistant, the one with long dark hair... I knew everything had been a lie. All the attention, the seduction. Telling me I was beautiful... it was all to get the money wasn't it? Your father's money. You'd marry the plain girl... she's so desperate for attention, she'd marry anyone who asked... then have your pick of gorgeous women while away on business. It made perfect sense." She paused to catch a quick breath, her fears stronger than ever. "But I will never be second best in a marriage. Never. And I'll never marry a man who doesn't love me." She jerked her hands free, his silence solidifying what she'd believed all along.

"You don't mean that." His voice, carefully neutral.

"You don't love me, Rome," she said quietly, "You just think I'm an answer to your problem." Anxious to escape the torment of his presence. "Goodbye, Rome." She backed up and retreated from the room. Toward the open elevator door and jumped in. Ignoring his voice booming down the hall as he called out to her.

"Dana... please, Dana, wait..." Disturbed by the pain filled tone as he cried out to her, she punched the button to the lobby and the doors closed.

When Dana entered the lobby, Cynthia stood up from her chair to go to her. Victoria was there with Rick. His arm wrapped protectively around her.

Julian and Echo were like tattered bookends on opposite side of the immaculate lobby sofas, asleep. Dana just gave Victoria a burning glare.

"Dana, I swear, I had no idea he was planning any of this," Victoria pleaded. Dana noticed the distinct black and blue mark across one of Victoria's normally perfect eyes. "You have to believe me."

Dana just looked at her and frowned. She sounded sincere, but Dana was too heart sick to think. Then she noticed the telltale bandaged knuckles on Cynthia's right hand and felt a smile tug at her lips. Cynthia's cheeks darkened as she glanced at Victoria, then back at Dana. "It's true, Dana. She didn't know about Jack. Him and Elizabeth had planned everything. Even Patricia didn't know. They were planning on framing their aunt for the money and some land in City of Industry somewhere. But Elizabeth had no idea about the kidnapping or Jack's resorting to violence to get it."

"Those pictures you found, Dana," Victoria urged, "They weren't just some nudy pictures of women. They're evidence your grandmother kept hidden."

"Evidence against Patricia," Dana offered.

"Yes, they were. Dana..." Victoria said, cautiously, "Aunt Patty killed herself last night." Dana heard the catch in Victoria's voice and suddenly felt her grudge begin to melt.

"I'm so sorry, Victoria. But I can't handle this right now. Cynthia, can you please take me back to the apartment. I need to get my car."

"Are you okay to drive?" Cynthia's concern was her undoing. She broke down in tears, falling slowly to the lobby sofa.

"God, Cynthia," she whimpered, "I was so scared. He nearly raped me. Tried to cut me. I couldn't go through with it. Not again. Not like last time. I wouldn't let him. And I nearly got Rome killed." Her misery was like a steel weight hanging from her shoulders. "He wanted the money. He *just* wanted the money. I should have just..."

"He wanted *you*, Dana." She felt the sofa dip as Victoria sat beside her. "I knew he had a crush on you. It was partly why I agreed to help you with your shop. I thought I could get you two together. I thought it was an innocent attraction. Grace and I were relieved he was showing some interest in a woman. He never had before. He was always so, I don't know... solitary, I guess." She placed her hand on Dana's shoulder. "That was before I knew you were already in love with Rome. When I told him, he became enraged. Said he'd steal you away—no matter what it took. But I had no idea he'd become obsessed. Even Elizabeth didn't know about his plans. When they arrested her last night, she agreed to testify against him if she received immunity. Dana, we'll make sure he never gets out of prison. I don't care if he's my brother."

Dana looked up at her friend's eyes and nodded. Turning to Cynthia, she said, "Please, I have to get out of here."

"What about your store? Your stuff? They can't expect you to just leave everything," Cynthia insisted.

"I need time to think." She needed time to erase the pain. Time away from everything that she'd carelessly let slip through her fingers. Everything that reminded her she'd never love another person as much as she loved Rome.

*****

He was his father's son. And he was a horse's ass. Rome shouldn't have asked her, shouldn't have suggested they get married. Not if he wasn't willing to go the distance.

He loved her. He knew he did. And he was certain she loved him back. But would he fall into the DeMitri curse just as his father did? His grandfather? Maybe it was better for Dana that she turned away. Saving herself the heartache later in life. Later, when his hormones might rules his life. Later, when much younger women could make him feel like a man—just like his father.

But Rome didn't want younger women. He didn't want any other woman. He only wanted Dana.

No other woman could reach him like she did. Understand him with frightening clarity. Damn, she even knew him before they met. The drawings, the paintings, the dreams… Was she, on some unconscious level, reaching out to him—months before? Years? Maybe his soul wasn't ready to listen. But his heart was.

He'd seduced her body, but she'd seduced his spirit, his soul, now burning with fire from his heart as well as his body. His life before Dana seemed like an endless line of gray. Shuffling through his life, nearly colorblind. She showed him, through her dreamy innocence and passionate determination an intimacy of like minds, a hot melding of colors reds, purples, blues, a renewed vibrancy of color to his life. *From black and white to Technicolor*, he thought. He couldn't go back to his old life. Not without her in it.

Why had he never taken her picture? Because he was afraid. Afraid he'd see his father's image in himself. His father's image reflected back through her eyes—her love for him, pure and naked. Vividly revealed and unhidden. Dana's love for him was there in her eyes—and he'd squelched it. She'd welcomed him into her body, overcome her fears of her past, and he'd failed her. Not by betraying her. But by letting her believe her own fears—his silence only confirming them when he should have adamantly denied it.

Hers contrasted is own feelings, still buried beneath the hurt of a little boy abandoned by his mother. Ignored by his womanizing father. It was his head he was battling now. His head kept telling him *you are your father's son—you are destined for failed relationships. Don't fight the inevitable.*

Every woman in his life, every woman he'd loved had left him. His mother,

Barbara... Dana... The harder he fought, the more he became his father. If he and Dana made a go of it, would he eventually push her away? Seek other women's company? Create an emotional rift between them? Distrust? Hell, she already didn't trust him. Rome knew Dana was talking about Kimberly. He was comforting a friend in need. He had nothing to be defensive about. Had his reflexes been normal, he'd have defended himself.

Maybe it was better this way, but he didn't care about being right. He didn't care that his body ached and that his leg might never be the same. Rome felt like his heart was being ripped from his chest, an unbearable pain greater than having his thigh sliced like a vegamatic from a boat propeller. More than lying on the floor in a puddle of his own blood from a gunshot wound.

So why did he let her leave without saying *I love you.* "Because I'm a horse's ass."

"You need to lay off the morphine drip, pal. You're talkin' to yourself."

"Hey, Jules. What's up?"

"Oh, I'm on my way back to school. Since the wedding was a false alarm, and Mom's doctors have her illness under control, I figured I'd better hit the books."

Rome snorted, "Don't want to keep those Oxford babes waiting, kid."

Jules gripped his brother's outstretched hand—secret handshake style, "You got it. But you know, Rome, being a ladies man isn't what it used to be."

"*Really.* How's that?"

"Well, let's just say, if you found the right one, don't dick around. Grab her and don't let go."

"Christ, now I've got both my little brothers giving me love advice when neither of you have ever had a relationship last longer than a nad yank."

Rome saw something like loneliness flash across his younger brother's eyes. "Hey, I've dated. Look, I'm just saying it would be nice to have someone... ya know to talk to, I mean *really* talk to once in a while."

"You have to get to know a woman first, Jules."

"Exactly."

"Try telling that to Tony. He seems to think he can know a woman just by knowing how intelligent her boobs are." *Geez, he did need to lay off the meds—he was feeling philosophical.*

"I happen to like intelligent tits."

"Hello, to you too, Tony. Don't you knock?"

He gave Rome a wide grin. "Not when I'm the topic of discussion."

"You look like you're up to no good, Tony. What's going on?"

"You know, Rome you outta be more grateful. I did save your butt yesterday. Which by-the-way, I never did tell you why I was there in the first place."

"Spit it out before you choke on the canary."

Jules smirked, sat down, casually crossed an ankle at his knee, and watched the display.

Tony cleared his throat. "I came by to give you the news."

"You're going to make me pry it out, aren't you?"

Tony shrugged out of his perfectly tailored black double-breasted jacket, took out a sheet of paper, then draping the jacket across the bed. "Finkle-*berry* died two days ago."

"What!"

"Yep. The old geezer died in his sleep. Apparently, before he could process your waiver to the probate judge, which by the way, she threw out the marriage clause. Claimed it was archaic and patriarchic, so she tossed it out."

Rome remained silent.

"Do you know what this means, man? We're free and clear."

"Congratulations, Tony. I guess this means you've secured your position with the company."

"Rome, this means you don't have to get married. It means you can be the globetrotting traveler, taking pictures of ancient dead people's architecture or what ever the hell you want."

Whatever he wanted. What he wanted was to have Dana with him while he traveled the world. He wanted her to want him. Hell, he'd never travel and stay here in L.A. for the rest of his life if that made her happy.

Her shop. That's what made her happy.

"Rome did you heard what I said? You're financially independent. You can do what ever you want."

"Jules."

"Yeah, Rome."

"I think you might want to postpone your trip for a little while longer, Man."

"What are you planning, Rome?" Tony asked.

"I'm planning on getting out of this damn bed for one. Then I need to make a trip to the Wilson Attorney's office."

They both looked at him like he'd lost his mind.

"With my leg out of commission for while, I'm going to need both of you to help me out here."

"With what?" they asked in unison.

"I'm not peeling your mother off the floor again, Rome. So don't go getting yourself shot. I'm getting a bad back."

"Tony... shut up," Jules retorted. "What do you need, Rome?"

"First, I need some clothes," Rome said, as he ripped the IV from his arm, and gingerly climbed out of bed, groaning slightly when the room started rotating. "And tell the damn operator of this merry-go-round to stop the ride and let me off. My head is spinning."

Tony grasped at his brother's arms before he fell flat on his face. "Yeah, but first you should cover your ass before the nurse sees you out of bed."

"And it's such a cute ass, too, bro."

"To hell with you both. I'm leaving on my own," he said, took two steps and crumpled to the floor in a heap at his brother's feet.

"Shall we leave him here, Jules?"

"Nah, his lady just dump him today. We'll spare him the humiliation for once," Jules said. "Besides, it's not everyday you become independently wealthy."

"Yeah, but I think the only thing that'll make Rome happy is getting Dana back."

"Yeah, poor chump."

With that, they both heaved an unconscious Rome back on the hospital bed. Then left the room.

Rome's buttocks still hanging out of his bedclothes.

Chapter Twenty-Seven

August 10

"DANA, YOU NEED TO EAT. You're loosing too much weight." Leo placed a plate of melon and cheddar cheese in front of her, and she wanted to gag.

"Thanks, Leo. I'll try." Her ribs had healed, no longer hurting when she breathed, but more pronounced then her dear friend thought healthy. She'd poured her heart and soul into her furniture painting—turning garage-sale furniture into works of art, but not much else. In her work, she found mindless solidity that helped camouflage the loss and the heartache.

Her nights were an endless torment, starting with the cold sheets against the heated memories of Rome's body, punctuated by dreams that continued to taunt her. Night after night, Rome was there, just beyond her reach. Not inviting and comforting as before, but cold and distant—chilled by distrust and betrayal. Caution and insecurity kept her from calling out to him, reaching for him. The dreams were eerily silent, stirring an even greater unease in her mind before the gray of dawn flickered through the bright white vertical blinds, covering the length of the guest bedroom window.

It was a beautiful Saturday morning. The wind blew the normally L.A. smog away the night before, but she was content to stay indoors and finish a set of nightstands. Blue skies and fluffy clouds were the theme of the day for her painting inspired by the weather, her art pieces simply reflected her mood. Yesterday, the squirrels cackling outside her window inspiring a set of bar stools with brown legs and green seats with nature's critters crawling up and around the legs.

A woman from San Marino already had her eye on them.

Leo and his life-partner insisted Dana stay with them until she got back on her feet.

Their place was a plush apartment near The Grove Shopping Center. Everything was within walking distance, making life bearable since she'd sold her car to pay for basic living expenses. So, she walked to her part-time job at the Starbucks Coffee House in Farmer's Market on Third Street.

Every penny she had, all her life savings had gone into *The Enchanted Frame.* With the help of Leo's connections, she'd been able to supplement her income with the sale of her painted furniture.

Dana was often surprised at the price she could get for her work. Soon, she'd be able to afford her own place again. Attain the independence she craved so much.

She'd re-read the letter from her grandma several times after everything had settled, and decided to wear the charm bracelet—for luck. Somehow, it made her feel closer to her grandma, even if she just carried it in her pocket. It still made little sense though, the letter, the charm, all the heartache and lost lives. Even after everything she learned from Patricia. But she did have the lock-box and the photos inside. Unlike Patricia's account of the night of her sister's death, the photos were not of her grandmother and Alberto DeMitri, but of Patricia and Alberto in various states of lovemaking. Although the photos were very mild by today's standards, Dana imagined her grandmother kept them in case she felt the need to use them against Patricia. Just chose not to, or never needed to. Creating a scandal thirty years ago could have ruined a career or tarnished a woman's reputation. Especially in Patricia's chosen field of law.

As for the bond notes, Dana couldn't allow herself to benefit from death or blackmail, so the notes stayed in the box, along with the photos. The land deed inside one of the envelopes—Patricia Wilson's name was listed as the sole owner. Dana thought it was only right that Victoria and her sisters have the deed back.

As it turned out, the vacant lot was located in a richly populated industrial area. When the time came, the sisters agreed to auction off the lot and divide up the proceeds.

The phone rang and she heard Leo answer. "Yeah, she's here, hold on... Dana it's for you, hon."

"Thanks, Leo." She took the cordless phone from him and walked out to the patio overlooking Third Street.

"Are you watching the news?"

"Cynthia?"

"Dana—turned on channel seven. You won't believe it!"

"Okay, okay." She walked back through the sliding glass doors. "Leo, turn on channel seven. Cynthia says to hurry."

Leo grabbed the remote to his high-definition TV and the screen crackled on. *...in* *the City of Industry, police have uncovered the skeletal remains of a woman on an abandoned lot. Approximate age and identity are unknown at this time...*

"Hey, look... it's Grace and Victoria!"

"Yeah, there... in the background."

"My God, Cynthia... do you know what this means?"

"It means Patricia's untimely suicide wasn't so untimely. Seems she not only killed her sister all those years ago, but covered it up too."

"I feel terrible for them, Cyn. Imagine finding out your mother was murdered by her own sister."

"Yeah, too bad the police can't prosecute. All the guilty parties are now dead."

"Maybe now they can put their mother to rest." Dana hoped so. Despite everything, Dana couldn't hold a grudge again Victoria. Her devotion to her aunt, Dana realized, showed an uncommon strength in character, and couldn't blame her friend for her loyalty to family. It wasn't Victoria's fault that Patricia was deceiving everyone all these years. "So, how's *The Monkey Shop*? I hope they pay you what you're worth."

"It's okay. I like they people, but I gotta tell ya, the minute you get your shop back, I'll be outta there faster than a teenage boy can..."

"Yeah, I get it!"

"Hey, did you hear about Rick and Victoria?" Cynthia's voice kicked up a notch.

"No, what happen?"

"There're getting married!"

"You're joking," Dana laughed.

"Nope. Next month. She says there honeymooning in the Old Mission Peninsula or something."

"What the heck is in the Peninsula?"

"Cherry orchards of all things. Victoria says she's got a thing for cherries. Whatever the hell that means."

"I'm happy for her." Dana laughed at the inside joke.

"Rome's leaving town."

Dana stopped laughing. "When?"

"Soon, I think. He's going to South America."

"The pyramids," Dana said, sadly. "Thanks, Cyn, for the update."

"Sure. We still on for lunch tomorrow?"

"Yeah...I'll see ya then." She was barely paying attention when Cynthia hung up as her thoughts weighed heavy on her mind.

Rome was leaving. To travel—to explore. It's what he'd wanted all along. And she was a homebody. Dana had accepted that.

She was also coming to terms with the secret her grandmother kept—the murder evidence she'd hidden all those years. At least now, her parting letter made more sense. But it didn't put Dana's mind at ease, and there was still the mystery of the charm bracelet and Aunt Sarah.

The pieces still didn't fit. Had her grandma fabricated a story about the bracelet to hide the truth?

Perhaps the answers died along with her.

Too many secrets. A lot of lies. And one murder. Her mind was reeling with questions. No wonder Rome's father thought he was cursed. He'd been haunted all these years by the murder of his mistress.

She heard Leo click off the TV as he came up behind her, touching her on the shoulder. "You okay, hon?"

"I'm fine, Leo. Just tired."

"You workin' this afternoon?"

"Yeah. In fact, I better go." She looked up at the clock. "Geez, Louise, I'm gonna be late."

*****

With Sarah's journal in hand and his walking cane in the other, Rome tried to talk himself out of this. He'd thought of mailing it to her—she'd refused his phone calls. Sent back letters unopened, and ran into the nearest ladies room if she spotted him. However, Dana *did* keep the box of chocolate chip cookies he'd sent for her birthday. Rome smiled, remembering.

Today, she may just punch him in the gut and tell him to quit stalking her. *But mailing it was the chicken shit way out*, he thought. He had to face her. Convince her to listen.

He smiled to himself and walked through the door.

The coffee shop door chimed as he entered. The pungent aroma of fresh espresso overwhelmed his senses. It was a busy place on Saturday afternoon. Too many people coming in after sending too much money at the mall and employees behind the counter yelling out lattes and cappuccino orders. But he didn't see her.

Rome turned to leave when he spotted that cute behind sticking out from a display unit in the corner. She was stocking the bottom self with bags of coffee beans. *Perfect.*

He cautiously walked up behind her. Her hair was pulled up, covered by a green scarf and she wore a green apron with the ties wrapped around her waist several times. She looked thin and her shoulders lacked that confident edge he'd loved so much.

"Hello, beautiful."

Dana stopped in mid-motion, but didn't turn around to face him.

"I've brought you something."

"Go away, Rome. I'm working." He noticed her voice quiver. At least he wasn't the only one with shaky nerves.

"I wouldn't have to bother you at work if you'd return my calls."

"I don't want... I can't talk to you," she whispered.

"If you won't talk, will you at least listen?" he pleaded, when she shook her head. She still wouldn't stand up—still wouldn't look up at him. "Although I find the view from here delectable, if you don't stand up and look at me, I may be forced to do something drastic and stupid." He bent to touch her shoulder, loving the feel of her, even through the thin fabric of her navy cotton blouse. "So save my fragile ego from embarrassment and just listen—please."

She cocked her head slightly. "Like what?" she asked, rising on her knees pushing several strands of hair from her forehead.

"Oh, I don't know. Jump on a table and sing Barry Manalow ballads—badly—at the top of my lungs." And in his present physical condition that would be a real challenge. But he didn't need to point that out.

"These people take their coffee very seriously, Rome. They might have you arrested."

"It would be worth it if you'd just look at me—hear me out?"

She still wouldn't look him in the eye, and it pained him deeply.

"Where's your supervisor...?" He looked around for someone behind the counter. "Excuse me?" He limped a few steps to the crowded counter.

"Rome, don't embarrass me."

"Excuse me. Who's in charge here?"

"That's me. Is there a problem?" The supervisor was a tall, heavy-set guy, in his late twenties. He had an honest face and a belly that dwarfed his standard-size apron.

Dana was trying to hide behind the display unit. Rome took her hand and pulled her to his side.

"I need to borrow your employee for ten minutes. You see, I'm desperately in love with her, but I'm a jackass, too scared to tell her. So, do you mind...?"

"Rome?" Dana scolded. "Don't do this."

The supervisor's face broke out in a wide grin and nodded his approval. Rome had the attention of the caffeine-deprived mob waiting in line.

"Go for it, dude!" someone yelled from across the room.

His free arm around her shoulders, Rome corralled her to an empty table littered with coffee cups and an empty scone bag. "Sit."

"Okay. I'm sitting."

He watched her shoulders slump as she scanned the place and their unwanted audience, and then plunked down in the chair like a scolded child. Her eyes cast down at her hands in her lap.

Rome groaned softly as he sank down on both knees at her feet, gripping his fist tightly at his cane for balance before letting it drop to the floor. Taking both her hands in his, he dipped his head until his eyes found hers. He was distressed to find she had purple half-moons under her eyes, and her cheeks were more pronounced from weight loss. But she was still his beautiful little fairy.

"Dana, sweetheart." He touched her cheek and she looked up, her eyes now bright with unshed tears. "I love you, and I *am* a jackass for not telling you before. I was just... terrified I'd be just like my father. Always hurting the women who loved him—pushing them away. I didn't... I couldn't do that to you. So, I made myself believe that I needed you to fulfill my father's dying wish... to help Tony... the magazine—" Rome felt his own eyes burn. He shrugged. "But the truth is... I was just afraid."

"Of what?"

"That you'd see me for who I really am—leave me when you didn't like what you saw."

"I love what I see, Rome. It's just... we're too different. It wouldn't work between us. We each want different things. Things that you can't compromise away, or find a middle ground." She looked into his eyes, "Sooner or later, you'd come to resent me. I'd be holding you back."

"No, never."

"Really, Rome? How can you be so certain? After your dad died, you told me you didn't want to end up like him. A lifetime of regrets. I don't want to be the reason you have regrets."

Rome felt his own face wet from angry tears. How could she believe he would do that? "What about us? What we have together? Doesn't that mean something to you?"

"I love you, Rome. But I can't be the wife you deserve." Her own tears shiny brightly against her soft skin as the afternoon sun streamed through the window. "You want to travel and climb ancient pyramids, take pictures of celebrities while they say their vows hanging from the cliffs of El Capitan. I just want to stay home and... paint furniture."

Unable to say anything more, Rome handed her the journal. "Here, take this. It belonged to my great-great grandfather. I think you should keep it."

"But..."

"Shh," he placed his finger to her lips. "Don't say anything. Just take it home. Read it." He brushed his lips across her forehead. "I'm a patient man, Dana. I love you and I'm not giving up on us."

The crowded coffee shop was silent as he took his cane, trying not to curse from the burning pain in his thigh, and stood up.

He turned, looked into her sparkling eyes one last time, then quietly left.

*****

April 1, 1892
From the Diary of Sarah Baker

Dear Diary,

> *I have lost all hope.*
>
> *Today my beloved is to marry the woman of his family's choice.*
>
> *Why cannot Father understand. I thought he would be pleased with my choice for a husband. I am beyond exhaustion and I can no longer weep from my loss. My tears have long dried, leaving a hollow in my heart. Once my happiest blessing, the fatherless child growing inside me has become my curse.*
>
> *My attempts to convince Father that I must marry the youngest son of his closest friend has painfully failed, leaving me no choice save one.*
>
> *May God forgive me...*

Dana set the diary down and rubbed her face in her hands. Thankfully, her roommates were at a party tonight. She had time to think things through... and read Sarah's journal. Every page. Including the newspaper clipping lovingly preserved within the journal's protective leather cover.

And Sarah's final entry.

Another family mystery solved, she thought, and hopefully, the final mystery to a long line of secrets and carefully concealed lies. Sarah was never murdered as the press had alluded. Instead, she'd killed herself and her unborn baby. She'd ended her life tragically for love—and because she'd run out of choices. Dana imagined a woman of Sarah's time had few choices to begin with. And an unmarried pregnant woman had none.

Was Sarah's Romano like her own Rome?

How much was Dana herself like Sarah?

She got up from the sofa and went to her room. There, in her makeshift closet was the alluring photo of her grandma, Sarah's painting of her beloved, Rome's great-great grandfather...and Dana's own drawings. She carefully lined them up one-by-one against the wall, each one representing a generation of love and tragedy.

Somehow, seeing them together like this... it was as if a light switch suddenly flicked on in her brain.

All had come full circle.

She stared at the picture of Sarah's Romano and smiled wistfully, his profile and jaw line, same well-built shoulders and strong arms so much like her Rome—arms that comforted, arms that held her firmly against him while they made love. She touch the canvas, traced the lines where the paint left streaks.

"What were you thinking, when you painted this, Sarah?" Did Sarah have the same erotic dreams? The same nightmares?

Dana often wondered if she resembled Sarah. She never saw a painting or a photograph of her, although her grandma once told her the Baker women closely resembled one another. The youthful image of Greta Baker was a prime example. They had the same straight blonde hair, lithe petite bodies and light brown eyes.

She glanced back at her own creations—a truly beautiful man, she thought. *Even her own versions of Rome couldn't compare to the real thing*.

That's when she saw it.

The scar. The scar on Rome's thigh. It was the same. Romano had the same scare! Exactly the same. It wasn't possible...was it?

At first, Dana had an ephemeral thought—what if some part of Sarah's memories were linked to her own. Sort of a genetic remnant passed down through each generation. Sarah reaching out to Dana from the grave—telling her to follow her heart—reach for the moon when it was within her grasp.

But now...?

No—she'd had it backward.

It was *Romano*...reaching for Sarah through Dana... asking, needing forgiveness— a second chance, through his own flesh and blood.

Through Rome.

Choices.

Perhaps Sarah had no choices, but Dana, on the other hand... did. Dana had free will.

"Choices..." She shook her head.

There was no other choice. Perhaps there never was. Was her fate—her legacy— sealed on that first night her dream man appeared in the dark recesses of her sleep-filled mind?

If Dana had to roam the world to have him, to make Rome happy, she'd do it, if it meant following her heart.

Live life. Don't waste it as Aunt Sarah once did. But the nagging fears left an indelible mark on her brain.

It was hard to ignore.

Chapter Twenty-Eight

"DAMN IT!"

The blender exploded. Iced cappuccino spewed everywhere— her face, her apron, and all down her denim dress. Customers blurted insults as the line to the register went out the door.

"Miss, can I get some service here?"

"Where's the cashier?"

It was Sunday, and Dana wished she'd never gotten out of bed this morning. One of the girls from work called in sick and Dana came in to cover for her. Unfortunately, the toilet in her bathroom overflowed and she had to search the building for a plunger. Her boss wasn't pleased when she showed up a half hour late. All the worse, Dana had to cancel her lunch date with Cynthia. She'd missed her friend, and was looking forward to an afternoon of girl talk.

And she couldn't find Rome. After her discovery last night, she desperately needed to see him, to talk to him. But he wasn't around and no one seemed to know where he was. She was worried he'd left the country before she had a chance to see him, say all the things she should've said from the beginning. That she loved him with everything she was. That she'd follow him to South America and back if it made him happy. That she wanted to make wild crazy love with him, under the stars, just the two of them, alone in the universe.

"Dana, the phone, it's for you," her supervisor eyeballed her as he passing the phone. "I don't want to remind you about personal phone calls, Dana," he whispered.

"Sorry. I'll be quick." She cradled the phone on her shoulder as she toweled off the sticky mess. "Hello?"

"Dana, thank God, I found you!"

"What's wrong, Leo. I can't be on the phone long."

"I've got an emergency here at the Library."

"It's Sunday, Leo. You don't work on Sunday."

"I know, we had a... an urgent issue come up here. Listen, I have a huge favor to ask."

"This better be good, Leo. I'm kinda in a bind." She grabbed a towel and tried to wipe some of the cappuccino from her face, taking off most of her make-up.

"There's a package at the apartment. I need you to bring it to me as soon as possible."

"I don't have a car, Leo, remember... and I can't afford a taxi all the way out to San Marino."

"I'll leave cash with the grounds parking attendant. I'll tell him you're coming and have it there when you arrive."

She let out an exaggerated sigh.

"I left the package on the sofa at home. Please, Dana I wouldn't ask if it wasn't important."

"You owe me big time, Leo."

"Thanks, kid. I'll make it up. Kiss, kiss."

She groaned as she hung up.

*****

"Well, Oscar, I hope our lady shows up." The fat fur ball willingly received the petting and attention as he mewed and looked up at Rome from the comfortable spot on his lap. Oscar's yellow feline eyes blinked up pitifully. "You've already eaten pal, we have another mission to accomplish."

Rome sat, anxiously stroking Oscar's fur on a park bench in the middle of The Camellia Garden, one of several gardens within The Huntington Library grounds. He felt surrounded by the plethora of mythological statues and flowering shrubs, complete with some sort of Italian baroque fountain.

"A little garish, don't you think buddy," Rome said to his fuzzy companion. He brought the butterball with him in case he needed back up.

Oscar made a human-like groan and hopped off Rome's lap and ran down the expanse of the lawn that encircled the shady gardens.

"Leo! Where are you?" Rome heard Dana's angry shouts from across the opposite side of the North Vista. "This package better be worth it, *pal*... You just got me fired!"

He continued to watch and listen to Dana's quick, calculated steps—feeling slightly guilty for her upset. *Slightly*. He smiled to himself, watching her. She looked as adorable as a bedraggled kitten with her hair disheveled, more and mascara on her eyelids than her lashes, and her button-down dress had more buttonholes than buttons.

And he couldn't love her more.

She didn't see him until she was nearly two feet in front of the bench were he sat. "Leo's not here, sweetheart. I am."

"Ahh, Rome! Geez, Louise, you scared... what do you mean he's not here? He just called me and said it was urgent."

"It was. *It is.*" He didn't dare touch her while she was agitated. "I asked him to call you. I wasn't sure you'd see me."

"Oh," she said softly. "Oooh!" she said again, as she took in the bed of red and white flower pedals at her feet, the lighted candles, and the adorned dining table filled with fruits and cheese. Rome cautiously took her hand—now that the wind was out of her sails. "I've... Where've you been, Rome? I wanted... I needed to..."

"You wanted what?" he grinned.

She smiled shyly at him. "Never mind." Her beautiful eyes brightened before she knit her brows, frowning at him. "I'm a mess, Rome. If I'd known—," she said quickly running her fingers through her hair. "Oh, God, my makeup!" She cried then, large shining tears rolling from her lower lashes, causing even more make-up streaks down her face.

"You look beautiful." He lightly kissed each knuckle on her right hand, rubbing it softly against his lips. "Sorry you couldn't find me. I've been *unavailable* for a couple of days," he said, keeping his meaning vague.

"How are you, Rome...your leg?"

He loved how her cheeks quickly went from angry red to adorable pink. "Healing." He picked up his cane from the grass beside the bench. "I'll be carrying this thing around for a while, but I get around."

He saw the look of guilt cloud her eyes.

"Stop it, Dana. It wasn't your fault."

"I know... I just can't help reliving it, trying to replay it in my mind..."

Rome spread his knees from his seat on the bench and pulled her between them, holding her gently around the waist as she stood, placing his cheek against her breasts. "There's nothing more you could've done, sweetheart. He intended to kill us. You saved us both, with a little help from our furry friend, Oscar the grouch." It felt wonderful to have her in his arms again. "Mmm, you smell like sweet coffee candy." Rome wanted to hold her like this, revel in the feel of her, for as long as she'd let him. He felt her let out a nervous chuckle before she finally relaxed against him, curling her shoulders and head against him, wrapping her arms tightly around his big body.

"I had a fight with the iced coffee blender. The blender won."

He laughed, his heart felt lighter than it had in weeks. "I hope this is the right place," he said, lifting his head and gesturing toward the natural beauty encircling the European-like garden. "I had no idea The Library had so many gardens."

He felt her stiffen. "I heard you're leaving soon."

Rome gazed up at her. "Who says I'm leaving?"

"Cynthia told me. So, you're all pack and ready for South America?"

He nodded. *Just ask me to stay*, he thought. "I have something for you," skirting her question, "If I can find my assistant. Oscar! C'mon bud." A jingling sounded from behind a camellia bush. The cat crawled out, and stretched lazily before he walked to the bench. "Up here, Oscar. Give our lady her present."

A tiny package, wrapped in plain brown paper and a burgundy ribbon was attached to Oscar's new collar. Rome carefully removed it and placed it in his palm, then held the gift to Dana. "Here. This is for you."

She hesitated for a moment, before taking it from his outstretched hand. It was sweet how her hands twitch as she tore at the paper.

Inside was a burgundy velvet box with a gold-plated lock and hinge. Dana popped the lock open and flipped the hinge up.

"It's a gold charm!" She looked carefully at it. "Rome, you found the twelfth charm. How...?" she asked, retrieving something from her pocket.

"I didn't." The charm was a lifelike depiction of a newborn baby with its tiny arms stretched out—reaching. Rome knew the charm was meant for Sarah.

"Look, Rome, this was once Sarah's charm bracelet. It had twelve hooks on the chain. But see—only eleven charms. Romano must have known. He must have had this last charm made, knowing his beloved was carrying his child. He'd meant to give this to her—*he intended to marry her all along*." Her enthusiasm was strangely and wonderfully arousing, and he smiled wide, happy his gift gave her so much pleasure.

"It was in a box my father left me," he said. "It was with Sarah's journal. I wasn't even sure it was hers. I'd hoped..." She kissed him then—hard. Oscar was still perched on Rome's lap. Rome broke the kiss. "Hey, get lost, buddy."

Oscar grumbled, jump off his lap, and went back behind the bushes.

Rome longed to continue, to kiss her until her lips were swollen and her body was aching for him. But that would have to wait.

An envelope fell from his jacket, casually draped over the bench. He bent to retrieve it. "Oow." His injury prevented him from reaching for it. "Dana, sweetheart, can you reach that," he sucked through his teeth as the stab of pain subsided. "I'm okay, I'm okay." He gestured for her to go ahead when she gave him a worried expression.

"What's this?" she questioned.

"Have a look."

The envelope was newly sealed with Dana's name typed neatly on the front. She gave him a speculatively look as she tore it opened.

Inside was a sheet of paper, a legal document with two signatures at the bottom—Greta Baker and Dana Baker.

"Look familiar?" he asked.

It was the original deed to her building.

Dana placed her palm against her mouth to hold in a sob. In one forward motion, she locked her arms around his neck. Arms trembled as she buried her face against his shoulder.

"You have your beautiful shop back, sweetheart," he whispered into her hair, drawing comforting circles on her back with his palm.

"Oh, Rome..." she cried softly, bringing her head up to look into his eyes, "I don't know what to say. I'll pay you back. I promise."

Rome smiled, brushing her disheveled hair away from her sweet face. "I'm counting on it. We can negotiate your payment later."

She smiled tentatively as she hiked her skirt up just enough to straddle his lap.

"I love that look in your eyes," he said.

"What look?" she asked innocently while she held him.

"The 'make crazy love to me now' look."

"Is *that* the look I gave you?" she teased. "How do you know it isn't just the 'I'm really grateful' look?" she said, pulling back from him, gazing lovingly in his eyes.

"Marry me, Dana." His playful tone became serious.

She looked away, hesitating, biting at her lower lip.

"I'll stay close to home." Emotion filled his voice. "Be content with family photography and running my studios locally. I'll have my staff do the off-site trips—" He brushed his hand across her cheek. "So I can stay home with my beautiful, loving wife."

"You'd be giving up your dream, Rome. I can't ask you to do that for me. I know how much your photography means to you. And what about your dream to travelling the world? You'd give it all up, just to be with me?"

"It would be worth it—if I could wake up to your sweet face—make you coffee every morning—before you get grouchy," they laughed, hers through tears. "If it's what I have to do to keep you—if it makes you happy, Dana, I'd never leave the city again."

A mischievous grin overtook her features as she tilted her head to his and kissed him with a hunger that matched his own. Urgent and exploring. Devouring, yet soft at the same time. Her small hands took his face, holding it gently as she traced and explored the recesses of his mouth.

"Say you'll marry me."

"No-o-o-o."

Her refusal faded into a moan as his mouth spread kisses over her face and neck. As his hands moved over her body, he murmured, "Please, marry me?"

Rome swept her up weightlessly from his lap and trapped her down against the seat of the bench, gathering her in his arms as he held her snugly against his body, looking hard into her desire-filled eyes.

"I'm still thinking—" she held her arms out to him, beckoning him to her.

"Then I'll make you forget about thinking." His head dipped and his mouth closed over the crest of her breasts. She arched into him with pleasure.

As though his words released her, she flung herself against him, burying her hands in his hair, kissing with an eager determination. He knew she wanted to steer this one when she rose up to straddle him again.

And he let her—this time.

Her dress crept up onto her thighs as she moved closer to him.

Slowly, he moved his hands upward, skimming the sides of her legs. He could sense the arousal building inside her as he gazed into her eyes—sharing in the intense physical awareness.

Rome felt an aroused shutter run through him as he sucked through his teeth. Her closeness sent a giddy pleasure down his spine, and his groin stirred at the contact of her bottom against his growing erection.

This new eagerness in her excited him, more then he could've imagined. It was intoxicating. And if he didn't get her out of her dress soon, he thought he'd explode.

Slowing, he unfastened the remaining buttons of her denim dress, exposing the dainty peach lace surrounding her soft breasts. "I need to touch you," he pleaded with her as she raised a modest hand to her chest.

"I want you, Rome. Now."

"Then take me," he smiled.

"But what about the grounds keepers? We're in the middle of the Library grounds—"

"They've all been given the day off." He gave her a smug smile. "Are you aware that I'm a wealthy man now—thanks to my old man and his deceased attorney. Money tends to motivate people faster than free-beer-night at *The Lava Lounge*."

"You got the money?" she asked.

He nodded as he traced his fingers lazily down the soft cleft of her breasts.

"But I thought you had to be married or something?"

He shrugged to make light of this sore subject. "Judge threw it out in probate. Tony's already out celebrating with several of his favorite ladies. I've never seen him so elated. He took his entire staff to lunch at Benihana's after he heard the news."

"I'm happy for both of you." She gave him a lustful look when she felt his fingers skimming around the edge of her panties.

He kissed her then, his hands roaming freely over any inch of flesh exposed. "I love touching you... your skin is so soft." He kissed the hollows of her throat and felt her pulse beat rapidly against his lips. His beautiful fairy princess.

By seducing her, she'd unwittingly seduced his soul. She was gentle and serene, more delicate and radiant than ever. She had unlocked his heart with her sweet and giving nature. He felt as if could do anything, as long as she was with him.

He felt his head spin, watching her now. She looked like a wild beauty, with wisps of her hair falling freely around her face like golden mist. "I need to see you—every part of you, before I burst," he said, tugging at the capped sleeves of her dress, letting them fall down her arms. His breath caught at the sight her waiting breasts, her nipples barely visible against the peach fabric of her bra.

He groaned as she surged her breasts forward, peeling the lace cups from her body, presenting herself to him, making him feel like a god and a servant all at the same time.

"My God, Dana, you'll give me a heart attack." His hands lifted her breasts as he swooped down to devour one dusty pink nipple with his mouth, beading the other with his fingers, until it was rock hard.

Her hips undulated against the growing bulge in his pants. "I love it when you touch me, Rome." Her head fell back as she cupped her breasts to his face, pressing them closer together, allowing him to fondle and taste them freely with his mouth. "More, I need more." He loved how her voice simmered with unchecked passion.

"Are you still thinking?"

"Yes. Oh, yes..." Her voice a broken whisper, she reached between their bodies and carefully unzipped his pants, freeing his throbbing penis from his trousers. Her bright face smiled with eagerness when she saw his response.

He grabbed at her hand. "You still haven't answered my question," he said, his voice, thick and unsteady from arousal. But he wasn't letting her off the hook. "Are you going to marry me?"

"I need to be sure we're compatible," she teased, fondling him playfully with soft, silky strokes. She had no idea how sensuous her voice sounded to him, pushing him closer to the edge of insanity. But he had his own plans of seductions.

"Oh, I think we're compatible." Rome removed her dress, letting it fall to the lush grass at his feet. His leg ached from her weight, as little as it was, but an ache in his leg was tolerable. He would be ruthless in his quest to have her—as his wife. A cry of relief and excitement broke from her lips when he traced his fingers between her thighs. "In fact," he laughed. "I know first hand we're compatible." Her peach colored panties, his only barrier to touching heaven. "Marry me."

"Rome, please..."

"Say it. Tell me you'll be my wife."

He let his finger graze under the edge of her panties, feeling the softness of her hair and the moist flesh of her labia. "Can you feel me here, touching you? Do you like it when I touch you here, sweetheart?" He stroked and circled, searching until he found her clitoris, swollen and eagerly waiting for his touch.

"Oh, yes...your finger feels delicious."

"I love how you melt into my hand," he whispered against her slender neck, lightly nibbling as he continued to probe, using two fingers in search of her wet entrance. His own arousal bucked against his belly between them. "Tell me, sweetheart."

"Please, Rome, now!"

"Not yet, sweetheart. I want you up, were I can taste you. That's it." He peeled away her panties as she stood on the bench, leaving her decadently naked in the middle of the garden. Natural and perfect. "You're so beautiful," he said, as he dipped his head to her pubic mound and drew in the musky scent of her, smoothing his nose and mouth across the silky curls hiding the center of her arousal. He felt her tug at his hair, guiding him closer to her center. He gave her inner folds one soft, quick lick of his tongue. "Say you'll marry me, Dana."

"Rome, please...now."

"Marry me." His tongue again flicked between the outer folds of her sex. Merely taunting. Teasing. "Say you'll be my wife," he begged, as he parted her with his thumbs, blowing softly against her hooded clitoris. He blew again, and it swelled forward—reaching for him.

"Say 'yes', Dana. Say it!"

Rome heard Dana's small cry of protest. He answered, circling the swollen bud, not quite reaching, intending to torment rather than pleasure. But he tormented himself as well, unwilling to wait another second to taste her. His tongue dove inside her, reaching between her inner muscles, so incredibly wet from his torment. She tasted like heaven. He could never get enough of pleasuring her sweet body.

"More, please. I need you inside me, now. Please," she begged when she could stand it no longer.

"Not until you say yes."

She pulled her body from his reach, she grasped the collar of his shirt with both hands and yanked hard—buttons flying. Her eyes blazed with pleasure and wonderment. It pleased him to know the sight of him gave her pleasure as well. "You're so perfect, Rome. I love touching you." Breathless, she stroked her hands across his chest. "You're my dream come true."

"I'm all yours, sweetheart, if you want me. Just say it." Dana's arousal faded slightly, her expression pensive. And it worried him. "You're thinking again." He took her hands, encouraging them to explore to her heart's content. She kissed his face, his neck, his chest with sensuous timidity. Her courage and passionate nature suppressed by the light of day and expanse of the outdoors.

Her hands explored his erection while writhing her hips against it, touching her own pleasure points with his as she stroked him lovingly, until he couldn't stand another second. "Hold...hold it. Ahh. On your knees, Dana, I need to get into my pocket." Still wearing his pants, he heaved his hips up from his good leg, taking both of them up enough for him to grab a condom from his pocket, and allow his drawers to fall at his ankles. "Here." He handed her the package, allowing her to touch him and place the protection on his aching member.

She had it in place with lightening speed, because before he had time for any more teasing, she'd sheathed herself over him, taking him in to the hilt. "Oh, you feel so good." He thought he'd come right then, but she stopped, tilting her pelvis against him as she rose up again.

"Am I hurting you?" she asked, worried about hurting his injured leg.

"Yes. But it's not my leg that hurts, sweetheart." Rome wrapped his hands around her rounded hips and guided her back down against him, then took her hands and placed them on the back of the bench behind him, angling her, allowing deeper penetration while hitting her clitoris against his straining belly. He'd never felt anything like it in his life.

As her body accepted him inside, again and again, as the friction of their skin was building with slick heat and desire, he thought his heart would burst with the joy of this woman, his Dana. "I love you, Dana. God, how I love you..." he yelled out his release the moment he felt her inner muscle quivering against him. "Marry me. Damn it... say you want me!"

"Yes! Yes, I want you. I want you!" she screamed, as the birds in the tree overhead flew away in fear. As the last of their climax faded, she fell hard against his chest, holding him there tightly against her moist breasts. Her warm panting tingled against his neck.

His leg hurt like hell. But damn, if he didn't care. His was holding a dream in his arms, and he wasn't ready to wake up.

Dana turn her face to his ear and whispered, "I can't move. Am I hurting you?"

"No." He lied. "I love being inside you like this. You excite me even when I'm completely spent," he laughed. "Please tell me you'll go on the pill before we get married. I can't take the torture anymore."

"Are you sure this is what you want, Rome?"

"I've never been more sure." He felt his penis pulse inside her again. She bit at her lip. "Stop that. You're thinking again," he said, astonished that she'd even ask at a time like this. "You're turning me on right now, and I've just spent myself. That's never happened before."

She smiled shyly at him. "I can feel you getter hard inside me."

"Than don't *ever* question how you make me feel. Okay?"

She nodded, even as she was swaying again him. "Rome, is there really something in the package Leo had me bring?"

He laughed against her neck as he nuzzled its softness. "Open it if you're so curious."

She shifted on his lap to take it, giving him a skeptical look as she tore at the paper. "My drawing! You framed my drawing..." her cheeks brightened and her body melted against him.

"...from the first night I make love to you," he whispered, trailing kisses along the curve of her shoulder.

"I love you, so much, Rome." She set the picture down and held him tightly. "I would love to share my life with you." Tears filled her eyes as she smiled at him. "Yes, I will marry you, Romano DeMitri."

"*Finally,*" he groaned, holding her against him, his arms firm around her waist as he bucked inside her body. His flesh met hers in a hot velvety smoothness that no other experience in his life could compare. And no words could describe.

His last thought before his mind-shattering orgasm was of his ancestor, Romano and his lady Sarah, if they'd found love beyond death. Because he knew, with everything he was, that he'd find Dana, wherever she was, even in the next lifetime.

Epilogue

The Los Angeles Times

Sunday, September 16

Title: SOTHEBY'S - EAT YOUR HEART OUT

GREENRICH MALL HELD A CHARITY AUCTION during an evening block party complete with jazz band, Checkered Blues, dancing, an extraordinary four and half million dollars in proceeds. All donated to The Los Angeles Women's Foundation and Rape Prevention Center. Rumor has it that the charity function was funded with a recently discovered treasure of unclaimed bearer bonds that matured more than thirty years ago.

An unprecedented turnout at the Greenrich Boulevard last night, the street was packed with collectors, art dealers, museum representatives, and just plain art enthusiasts. The highest selling item was a newly recovered Andy Warhol silkscreen titled *Nine of Claire* that sold for a bargain price of three and a quarter million. The highest bidder, though absent from the festivities, was rumored to be a very sexy singer just recently married. The original owner of the painting was none other than ex-Volupté Magazine cover model, Claire DeMitri Roche, and the mother of said singer's photographer.

Other big ticket items were several erotic sculptures donated by the artist, a French sculptor known for his volatile temper as much as his art, Philippe Roche.

Dana Baker DeMitri, the auction's coordinator and owner of the elegant art shop, *The Enchanted Frame*, sold several pieces of her own artfully re-painted antiques.

When this reporter tried to interview Dana and her new husband, Romano, the heir of the *Volupté* fortune, the couple apparently had left the function early to catch a plane to

Boston for their honeymoon.

The brother of the groom, CEO to Volupté Magazine, was spotted dancing the night away with three lovely ladies before leaving the scene in a monster truck limo.

Ladies—he's gorgeous. And still single...

About the Author

Bonnie Louise Williams lives in Los Angeles County, California. She's been a huge fan of romance novels since reading her first romance, *Knight in Shining Armor*, by Jude Deveraux, and was hooked forever.

She's a member of the National Romance Writers of America and the local RWA Orange County, California Chapter. She holds a degree in fine arts, as well as a Bachelors Degree in business. Currently, she works in the accounting field while developing her career in writing.

Her current titles include *Sketch Me Naked, Tempt Me, and Tease Me, and* an online romantic comedy series *The Lonely Guys*.

She is currently working on her fourth erotic novel *Hot Fusion*—a futuristic erotic romance.

Bonnie also has a non-fiction title—*How to Write That Sexy Romance In 2 Weeks or Less*—a writing workshop for anyone who has ever wanted to turn there sexy day dreams into stories.

Find out more about the author by visiting her website at

http://www.bonnielouisewilliams.com.com